COURSE CORRECTION

DOUGLAS MORRISON

COURSE CORRECTION

DOUGLAS MORRISON

Stonehouse Publishing
www.stonehousepublishing.ca
Alberta, Canada

Stonehouse Publishing Inc is an independent publishing house, incorporated in 2014.

Cover design and layout by Janet King
Printed in Canada

National Library of Canada Cataloguing in Publication Data
Morrison, Doug
Course Correction
Novel
ISBN: 978-0-9866494-0-0 (paperback)
First Edition

CHAPTER 1

Travel Plans

Michael stared in disbelief as the man shoved the flight attendant aside. He didn't notice the food trays fly across the cabin, scattering their contents over the passengers in the first row. His eyes were locked on the cockpit door the man had just leapt through, slamming it shut in one smooth motion.

'This can't be happening,' he thought. They were just a planeload of ordinary people, what use could they be to anyone? If something like this was going to happen, shouldn't there be some kind of warning? The flight had begun in such a...well...a normal way.

* * *

Michael Barrett smiled to himself as the engines of the Boeing 747 were advanced to full throttle. Though muted by distance, and the thick glass of the viewing windows, the roar was still something he could feel as well as hear, and those sensations never failed to thrill him. As he watched, the mammoth machine gained speed, slowly at first, but then noticeably faster until the nose wheel lifted from the pavement and the aircraft rose majestically into the air. He meant to watch it until it disappeared from view, but before that could happen a massive Airbus began rolling on the same runway and his eyes were drawn to it as its engines roared to full throttle and it too began its gravity-defying takeoff roll. He promised himself that he would get his pilot's licence when he got home from this trip.

He had always found airports exciting places to be, even when he wasn't going anywhere. It was more than just the bustle of activity and the sight of the airliners disappearing into the skies on their journeys to all points of the globe. Even though the jet age had started well before he was born he still thought it somewhat amazing that starting from almost anywhere, you could be in an exotic location on the other side of the world in a matter of hours. But today was even more thrilling than usual because he was going somewhere himself, and for the first time in his life his destination was outside North America. The flights that had brought him to this point in his travels had left him more tired and jet-lagged than he'd ever been before, but there had simply been too much to watch since disembarking from the last flight to even think about napping.

Through the floor-to-ceiling windows in the departure lounge he could take in much of the activity of the Frankfurt airport. Everywhere he looked airliners adorned in exotic livery were moving back and forth across the ramps and taxiways. Some were travelling under their own power while others were being towed to and from their gates. Somehow, while all this was going on, a constant stream of trucks and buses wove back and forth among them without seeming to disrupt the constant flow of the aircraft that they existed to serve.

The pre-boarding announcement for the flight from Frankfurt to Athens came over the speakers as he sat estimating the number of passengers in the lounge. Those passengers travelling with small children, and those needing extra help boarding, began making their way through the gate and onto the plane through the jetway. Since nothing else had been announced he relaxed a bit, now fairly certain that his seat was secure and that he'd soon be joining them onboard. In the meantime he shifted his attention to the sky.

The sun was still obscured by the layer of cloud he'd descended through a few hours earlier, but even at that early hour the late-July morning had been unbearably hot. Not that he'd felt much of it, just a brief, oppressive, muggy heat as he'd walked up the jetway and into the terminal building. Once inside the shelter of the terminal the air conditioning kept the worst of the heat, if not the humidity, at bay. He was trying to convince himself that the clouds were a bit thinner now. Maybe as the day wore on the sun would appear. He hoped it would be bright and sunny in Athens.

"You are from Canada?" A heavily-accented voice broke his train of thought.

"Excuse Me?" He turned to face the direction from which the voice had come. A friendly-looking middle-aged man and his wife were smiling at him from across the aisle.

The man pointed to Michael's passport and repeated his question. "You are from Canada?"

"Oh, uh, yeah, I'm Canadian." Michael glanced down at his passport, as if to make sure that he was answering the question correctly. "May I ask where you're from?"

"We are from Greece," the man replied with a nod toward his wife. "We are just returning from Canada. Our son lives there. You have been to Greece before? You have family there?"

"No." Michael could not help but smile back. It was nice to see friendly faces this far from home, after so many hours of travel. "Actually, I've just always wanted to see your country." He laughed self-consciously, almost embarrassed to speak his thoughts. "When I was in school one of my teachers taught us Greek history, you know, all the mythology? Well, that and the real history." He thought back to those Social Studies classes, the movies that he had been shown and all the pictures and maps. They had captured his imagination and given him the desire to someday see the country for himself. "I've just always wanted to see Greece, it looks so beautiful, and it has so much history. My country is too new to have such a rich past."

The man smiled proudly and nodded in agreement. "Greece is the most beautiful country in the world! But Canada is very nice too." He sounded sincere as he tacked on his comment about Michael's native land.

Just then the gate attendant announced that the seats in the rear of the aircraft were ready for boarding. The man said something to his wife that Michael did not understand, and the couple rose to their feet. "They have called our seats, we must board now. But when we arrive in Greece we must talk again. I will tell you about some things that most tourists miss seeing."

"Thank you," he replied with genuine gratitude as the couple shuffled off to join the growing line. He checked his own seat assignment on the boarding pass and settled back to rest for a few more minutes until his seat was called. It was his fourth flight in less than eighteen hours and as exciting as it was he was beginning to feel worn down.

Another block of seats was announced before his row was finally called. He merged into the line of passengers which moved steadily toward the gate attendant but much too slowly for his liking. When he finally made it to the front of the line he flashed his passport picture and handed the attendant his boarding pass. The computer beeped as the boarding pass was swiped across the scanner, and a green light announced that he had permission to pass through and join yet another lineup in the Jetway.

Once aboard the plane he squeezed past a few passengers partially blocking the aisles as they wrestled oversized bags into the luggage bins and made his way to his assigned aisle seat. He had really been hoping for a window seat for this final leg of the journey. It seemed very unfair to him that he'd been looking forward to this trip for so many years only to have to settle for an aisle seat for his arrival in Athens, but all of the window seats had been claimed by the time he'd arrived in Frankfurt to check in.

Before sitting down he looked at the over-wing exits, then forward up the aisle to the main entry. It was about the same distance to each, but with fewer seats in first class the front door was likely the best to head for in an emergency. With that crucial decision made he stowed his bag and plopped into his seat. As he fastened the seatbelt he felt his impatience growing, mentally trying to urge the crew and passengers to hurry up and get the trip underway. This is really it, he thought, he could feel his excitement growing once more, he was really on his way to Greece! The ancient buildings, the rugged coastline, and the brilliant blue waters of the Mediterranean Sea were all waiting for him, just a little over three hours flying time away. One more flight and he would set foot in the country he had dreamed of visiting for so long.

But the closer the time for departure came the more the other passengers seemed to be purposely slowing things down. One family, speaking heavily accented English, was causing a scene because they were not all seated together. The harried flight attendant was trying to get everyone settled so they could get ready for departure and was trying, without any apparent success, to convince them to wait until they were in the air to sort things out. Behind him a businessman was trying to convince another attendant that he was special enough that he should be allowed one more piece of carry-on luggage than the airline normally allowed. No mere economy class passenger was he! Why, his frequent flying alone kept the airline in business. Michael sighed deeply, silently willing them all to pick up on his impatience, sit down, and just fasten their seatbelts already! Even as his impatience simmered he admitted to himself that it was partially from being over-tired. He took a deep breath and tried to relax. He knew from previous flights that even after everyone was seated they still couldn't depart until the pilots were ready and they'd received their clearances.

He stretched out as best he could in the seat, wishing he could recline it, but that would only earn him a stern, but friendly, reminder from a flight attendant that he could not do that right now. He liked to claim he was five feet nine inches tall, and likely was if he wore the right shoes. Normally being a bit shorter than most of the people he knew bothered him, but not on a crowded airplane. It was a bit of an advantage here since it gave him a little more room to stretch and twist.

The plane seemed to be fairly full, almost every seat was now occupied, and he was just beginning to think that perhaps everyone was onboard and they could get going when the PA system crackled to life. "Ladies and gentlemen we are just waiting for a few more passengers from connecting flights. Once they are aboard we will make our final preparations for departure."

He gave an inward sigh and glared at the door, willing the late arrivals to hurry up. The words were barely out of the attendant's mouth when a harried looking couple rushed aboard. They looked both relieved to have made the connection, and embarrassed for having made everyone wait. Everyone stared at them as they made their way down the aisle. They smiled weakly at the man that had to stand up to let them into their seats. Surely that must be everyone, Michael thought, but no effort to close the doors was made by the crew. There must be more to come, he realized with another sigh. It was starting to feel like he'd never get to Greece.

He noticed two of the attendants glancing at their watches. One of them picked up the phone to call the flight deck. It encouraged

Michael to see that the crew was also getting impatient to get going. Just as she began speaking into the phone, a lone man walked through the door. He looked quite calm in contrast to the previous couple, there was no look of apology or embarrassment on his face at all as he surveyed the cabin, as if he were trying to select a seat rather than just finding the one assigned to him. The attendant hung up the phone, looked at his boarding card as he held it out, and pointed to the aisle seat across from Michael. The man nodded as if he'd known where he was to sit all along. He sauntered down the aisle, stowing his bag before working his large frame casually into the seat as if he had arrived hours earlier than required.

"Boarding complete," came the clipped announcement over the PA system, and the door was closed and locked.

A muted thud from beneath the cabin announced that the baggage doors were now closed, and a few minutes later the plane pushed back from the gate. As the engines spooled up and the flight attendants took their places for the safety demonstration, Michael tried very hard to pay attention, mostly because he felt he should. After so many flights in such a short time he could almost recite it for them. Except this time it was repeated three times. Once in German, again in English, and finally in what must have been Greek. That caught his attention. It brought a fresh surge of excitement to realize that he was so close to his destination that they were speaking the language.

He wondered, briefly, how hard it would be to learn Greek. The alphabet sure was different, but as the plane trundled out towards the runway he felt his eyes growing heavy and he almost dozed off sitting upright in the seat. Even the sudden roar of the engines as the pilot brought them to full power could not force him to open his eyes. The sudden acceleration pushed him back into his seat, and as the aircraft rotated for the take-off he drifted into a much needed, and long overdue, sleep.

* * *

As the Airbus poked through the clouds and into the sunlight, a cell phone rang in the pocket of a man standing in a lavish office a thousand or so miles to the east. The office was situated on the top floor of a large, luxurious home that fit in well with the immediate neighbourhood, but stood in rather stark contrast to the rest of the country. "Hello? This is Danic."

Danic nodded as the caller spoke, not stopping to think that the motion of his head could not be seen by the man on the other end of the phone. "I think you'd better tell him yourself," he said, cutting off the flow of words. His boss had his own cell phone, but no one he knew, not even the man's own family, had the number. Surely there were people that knew it, it was rumoured that a girlfriend or two had it, but part of his job was to run interference against the routine incoming calls. He took a few steps towards the ornate desk and handed the phone to the short, heavy-set man whose salt and pepper hair made him appear older than he actually was. The greying hair was a hazard of his job. The weight was a silent consequence of his over-indulgence, which was one of the perks of his position.

"It's Vasili," the man said to his boss, identifying the caller which elicited an impatient motioning for the phone. He was still learning which calls to block and which to let through but the impatience of his boss told him he'd made the right decision this time. No thank you or acknowledgement was given as the man took the phone. At times he felt like just another piece of office equipment.

"Yuri Stepanovich?" the caller asked.

"Yes, Vasili."

"Sasha called. He and his men have boarded the plane."

"And what of our friend?" There was more than a hint of impatience in the question, as he felt he should not have had to ask in the first place.

"He is onboard as well. Everything is ready." I wouldn't have called you if he wasn't, Vasili thought to himself, though he didn't dare speak the words.

"Good. Call me when you have more news." With that he pushed the button to end the call and tossed the phone back towards the man who had answered it. Danic panicked and grabbed for the phone, managing not to fumble or drop it. He wasn't so much afraid of what would happen to the phone if it hit the floor, as what would happen to him. He had been warned by his predecessor to be ready for anything when he'd taken the job. Yuri Stepanovich was a difficult man to work for; it was hard to please him and almost impossible to know when you'd succeeded in doing so, but fail badly enough and it might not be just your job that was in jeopardy.

*　*　*

Michael's sleep must have been very light, as much as he'd needed it, because he was roused from his nap by the sound of a chime from the PA system. He saw that the seatbelt light had been switched off, and fumbled for the button that would allow his seat to recline, and leaned back to get more comfortable. He reclined it as far as possible which was not anywhere near enough. The Airbus was still climbing and after making himself as comfortable as possible he opened one eye to look at his watch. Try as he might he could not figure out what time it was back home, or how many hours it had been since he'd had any real sleep. Since he didn't have a window seat, and it was sometime in the very early hours of the morning as far as his body was concerned, it seemed like a good idea to try to get back to sleep. The flight to Athens was scheduled to last a little over three hours and he figured if he could get some sleep now he might have the energy to see a bit of the city after checking into his hotel. True, he'd miss the opportunity to eat yet another over-heated airline meal, but at the moment the need for sleep was much stronger than the need for food.

But sleep refused to come as easily as he'd hoped. Despite as much tossing and twisting as the seat would allow he could not find a position comfortable enough. With a sigh of resignation he slouched down into the seat, stretched out as much as possible, and reached for the inflight magazine. Attempting to shake the cobwebs out of his head he thumbed through it looking for an interesting article. Hours ago, as he'd prepared to board the first flight, the thought of the travel alone had been exhilarating, but now he just wished that the flight would end. He would clear passport control and customs, claim his baggage, and find the shuttle to his hotel. Maybe eating the airline meal was a good idea, he decided. If he didn't have to eat in Athens it would mean more time to see the sights.

He stretched upright and craned his neck, trying to look past the couple seated between him and the window, but all he could see was a solid cloud layer thousands of feet below. He was still holding out hope that the skies would be clear and sunny at his destination. They always were in the travel brochures. He turned his attention back to the inflight magazine but found it was only good for about ten minutes before he'd seen everything that even remotely interested him. Unfastening his seatbelt he stood up and opened the overhead bin to retrieve an Athens city map out of his carry-on bag. Settling back into his seat he unfolded and was studying the well-worn map when the drink cart made its way up the aisle. Since he was only a few rows behind the first class section he was quickly served a Coke and a coffee. If he couldn't sleep he'd make full use of the caffeine.

With his drinks and the map spread out on the folding table he hunched over the map and began planning yet another walking tour. By the time he'd once more dug into his carry-on to retrieve a couple of travel guides to cross-reference with his map, the flight attendants were loading up the carts in the rear galley in preparation for the meal service.

A passing shadow caused him to look up as a rather unpleasant-looking man in a rumpled suit came striding up the aisle ahead of the economy class meal cart and walked right into first class. He was quickly intercepted by a flight attendant. Though he couldn't make out all the words it was obvious from the man's gestures that he wanted to use the first class lavatory. The attendant was politely, but firmly, letting him know that it was for first class passengers only. That was not an answer he was willing to accept. He was no longer asking, but rather demanding, to use the lavatory. His voice had risen enough that Michael could now make out his words, which came out with a Russian-sounding accent.

"Sir, please take your seat or use the toilet in the back of the plane," the flight attendant said, matching his volume and tone. The passenger was a good foot taller than she was, but she didn't let that intimidate her, standing her ground firmly.

The man's voice continued to rise and he could now be heard several rows back. "Is busy!" He shouted, pointing angrily at the aft lavatory. "And food is in way!" He added with another angry gesture towards the meal cart, as if somehow it was all her fault that it was blocking the aisle just when he needed to use the toilet.

"Sir, this is for first class passengers only." She repeated for at least the fourth time, regaining some of her composure and trying to calm him down. "If you'll just step into your seat we can push the cart past you and let you by."

But the man refused to be placated, his voice becoming angrier with each fresh outburst. Neither of them was willing to give in. There was a growing buzz among the passengers and some appeared to be getting ready to step in to assist the flight attendant when suddenly the man stopped talking. His attention was distracted by something in front of him. Michael's full attention had been on the argument but now he followed the man's gaze past the petite flight attendant. Another attendant was just hanging up the phone on the bulkhead between the cabin and the cockpit. She must have been talking to the pilots because she picked up two meal trays and stood expectantly by the door to the cockpit. A moment later the door was opened from the inside.

Suddenly, so quickly that it caught everyone off-guard, the man grabbed the attendant by her shoulders and shoved his way past her. She let out a startled shriek and tried to fight back, shocked into action as the argument turned physical with no warning.

Michael, and a number of other nearby passengers, added their own cries of protest and began yelling at the man in a variety of languages. A few tried to jump to her assistance only to find they were securely strapped into their seats. Before they could release their buckles the man had spun her around and shoved her to the floor. She let out another loud cry, this time one of pain. Several passengers who'd managed to get out of their seats sprang to help her while the attacker sprinted towards the cockpit door.

The struggle had now caught the attention of everyone onboard, including the attendant about to serve the meals to the pilots. She was frozen in place, exactly what the man wanted. He lunged at her, grabbing her as she stood defenceless with a tray in each hand.

Her cry of fear and alarm drowned out the drone of the engines and filled the cabin as he shoved her effortlessly aside, sending the food trays flying, and leapt through the door, pulling it shut before anyone could react.

Michael wondered if the pilots would be able to fend him off before remembering that at least one of them was strapped helplessly into his seat, just like most of the passengers were. And the hijacker, the word shocked him even as he thought it, had the element of surprise. They were expecting a meal only to be met by...by what? Was the man armed? He hadn't noticed a weapon, but maybe he had one concealed? These thoughts raced through his head almost faster than he could answer his own questions. Only seconds had passed but he had already come to the one conclusion: this can't really be happening!

Several of the first class passengers had recovered enough that they were now helping the second attendant to her feet. She didn't appear as badly hurt as the first one had been, and once they were sure she had no serious injuries, two male passengers helped her into the rear-facing seat she had occupied during the takeoff.

What had started out as shock and indignation on the part of the passengers quickly turned into a fear that filled the cabin. Every one of them began thinking about the same September morning that had changed the world. The whole plane was engulfed in a uneasy silence.

What had happened took a while to sink in for the attendant who'd been about to enter the cockpit. When it did she sprang to her feet and grabbed the door handle only to find it securely locked. She pulled at it frantically, then grabbed for the phone hanging beside the door. There was no answer from the other side, but she kept trying.

Watching her trying to do something served as a cue for everyone else. They all began talking at once. Many started sobbing. Parents rushed to comfort children, husbands hugged their wives, and people travelling alone looked around helplessly, desperately seeking someone to talk to. In the midst of all the confusion the cabin crew's training took over. They began attempting to restore order and get everyone seated and quieted down, with no success at all.

Everyone who had a cell phone pulled it out and turned on the send-and-receive function, despite what the air regulations demanded. Frantic calls were attempted to family and friends all over the globe. Without exception everyone was wishing that they had booked the trip with a different airline.

It seemed wrong, somehow, that the aircraft was continuing to fly on and on as if nothing had happened. The engines droned steadily, it was flying straight and level, there was no change whatsoever in altitude or heading.

Around the cabin small groups of passengers began forming. Michael joined the nearest discussion because, just like everyone else, he had the overpowering need to talk with someone. The need to do something was also overwhelming, but there was nothing to do but talk. The talk, at first, was speculative.

"He's a terrorist! He's going to fly us into something," raved one man with a German accent. His voice sounded abnormally high with fear and panic becoming stronger with each word.

"Nope." Replied a man with an accent from somewhere in the American south. "He's a Russian. A Commie, not an Arab," he pronounced the word Arab with a long "A". His slow drawl was having a calming effect on some of the other nearby passengers. "I'll bet when he gets a suitcase full of good old American currency, he lets us all go."

"I hope you're right," responded his seat-mate dubiously.

Just then a man from another group of passengers walked over and the discussion was no longer speculative.

"We've been talking over there," he pointed back to a group of four other men who were looking at them with nervous but determined expressions on their faces. "We think we should try to take him out. Unless he knows how to fly one of these things the pilots must still be alive. If we can break down that door we've got enough guys to overpower him. Plus we can get some knives from the stewardess. They've got a ton of them on those trays." Most airlines had returned to the practice of entrusting their passengers with real cutlery rather than the plastic kind. They weren't exactly sharp, but they would likely do in an emergency. And this was definitely an emergency as far as the passengers were concerned.

"I don't know," said Michael, speaking for the first time. "That's been tried a couple of times before. Neither of those ended well." He was thinking of footage he'd seen of a hijacked airliner crashing into the ocean off the coast of Africa. The pilot and a hijacker had been fighting for control of the plane as it attempted a forced landing along the shoreline. And everyone aboard knew what had happened in Pennsylvania: it had been the subject of numerous books and movies. Those passengers had been heroes, no doubt about that, but they had known what their fate was and the risk had been worth it. No one on this flight knew what was happening. Yet.

"He's right," another voice with an accent unfamiliar to Michael agreed, "Besides, those doors are locked, and reinforced with Kevlar or something. We'd never be able to break in there."

Michael nodded in agreement. "The only reason that guy got in there was someone opened the door from the inside."

"So we're going to sit here and do nothing? Just wait here at the mercy of some terrorist and let him kill us all without a fight?" The passengers were quickly dividing into two opposing groups.

"And what if you end up getting us all killed trying to play hero while some negotiator on the ground is already settling everything?" The new voice came from yet another passenger who up to this point had been sitting and listening to the conversation. "You might come out a hero if it works, but if it doesn't at least you'll still make the news."

A loud, confused babble broke out with loud arguments for and against taking action. Everyone was speaking at once until one voice rose over all the others. "What are you all waiting for?" he shouted angrily, "If we end up in diving into the Vatican, or the Med, it'll be too late to figure out a better plan. Anything is better than giving up without a fight!"

Without warning the plane banked suddenly to the left. Everyone froze and all conversation stopped. All eyes were fixed on the door to the cockpit as if somehow, by looking at it hard enough, they could figure out what was happening up there. Then a soft chime announced that the PA system had been activated and the silence became even deeper as they waited for the coming announcement.

The captain began speaking, using the low growl that all airline pilots used in making announcements to their passengers. That voice had to be a prerequisite for the left front seat of an airliner, Michael had often thought. The voice was carefully cultivated to instill confidence and trust in the minds of the passengers, always sounding in control, as if the speaker were bored by the simple act of flying an airliner seven miles above the ground at five hundred miles an hour. Despite the terror lurking in everyone's heart, this captain's voice was no exception. Hearing something, anything, from up front, quickly calmed the atmosphere in the cabin.

"Ah, ladies and gentleman this is your captain speaking. I know you are all aware of the," there was a short pause as he searched for the right words. "The, ah, the incident that just occurred. I want to let you know that everything is fine up here on the flight deck. We've been asked to make a slight change in the route of our flight this morning. I've advised Air Traffic Control and we've been assigned a routing to our new destination." Michael thought back to all those documentaries he'd watched on Discovery Channel where the pilot figured that an onboard fire meant they had a "slight problem on board." He also noted that there was no mention of what the new destination was. "I've been asked to assure you that no harm will come to the aircraft, or to any of the crew or passengers, and to advise you not to try anything as the man up here with us is not acting alone." There was a long pause during which the passengers glanced around nervously, wondering if there really was a second hijacker among them. "I'll provide you with more information when, ah, when I'm able to do so. Please take your seats and follow the instructions of the cabin crew."

The cabin remained quiet after the captain's announcement, the passengers looking around uncertainly, wanting to believe that what they'd heard was true, that they really were going to come out of this unharmed. The flight attendants took full advantage of the change in atmosphere and began directing everyone back to their seats, reminding them to keep their seatbelts fastened. The five men who had been ready to storm the flight deck still looked like they wanted to do something, but the reassuring voice of the captain and his instructions seemed to have taken most of the wind from their sails. Supposedly he was still in some kind of control, so they too returned to their seats.

"Where do you think we're going?" asked the man beside him.

Michael looked at the man and his wife and shrugged his shoulders. They were headed east he figured, or close to it. He tried to remember the geography of Europe. How far south had they flown already? Where were they headed? Hungary? Serbia? He reached for the in-flight magazine. There was always a map in the back, wasn't there? His trembling fingers desperately flipped through the pages of the magazine for the maps, but he couldn't find them. Desperate for an answer he looked around for someone close by who might know.

Across the aisle from him sat a man that looked very out of place somehow. He'd been the late arrival, the last one to board the flight. There was no surprise or uncertainty in his expression. He seemed to be the only calm person on the whole flight. Michael had been too engrossed in what was happening, and concentrating too hard on the discussions around him to notice something unusual about the man. He was the only person who'd remained both seated and silent throughout the entire ordeal.

"What country is east of us?" he asked, thinking that somehow this man looked vaguely European and that he must know the geography of this part of the world.

The man turned slowly to face Michael, his expression calm, but his face ashen. He looked Michael square in the eye and said one word in a thick accent, the same accent the hijacker had spoken with, "Ukraine." He turned to face straight ahead again and repeated the word, but this time his voice was tinged with fear, or was it with resignation? It came out as a mere breath. "Ukraine."

The tone of his voice sent a fresh chill through Michael's heart. It wasn't resignation or fear he was hearing, and the look on his face wasn't calm, Michael now realized, there was no expression on it at all. The tone of his voice was beyond resignation, it was total despair, perfectly matching what he saw in the man's eyes. It was hard to look at that face, yet he couldn't look away either. He was looking at a dead man, someone who had no expectation of surviving. This man knew something about what was happening and had given up all hope. That frightened Michael more than anything else that had yet happened. Were they going to share the same fate?

CHAPTER 2

Arrival

The phone in Danic's pocket was ringing again. "Yes?"

Yuri was watching him sharply, "Is it Vasili?" Danic nodded, trying to listen to what was being said on the phone, but Yuri was motioning impatiently so he passed the phone to him while Vasili still thought he was speaking with Danic.

"What has happened? Is it on its way?"

Vasili paused, realizing who he was talking to and quickly changing the tone of his voice. Danic was, after all, many rungs below him while Yuri ranked much higher.

"Yes, sir! My source has confirmed that the plane is now flying eastward and has requested permission to land here, just as I had planned." He didn't explain that his 'source' was an air traffic controller who had been slipped a few American dollars to phone him should a flight out of Frankfurt suddenly turn east and request a new clearance. A 'source' sounded much more official and permanent. It might even be worth a bonus when this was all over.

"Is everything in place at the airport?" Yuri's voice sounded anxious and excited now, rather than impatient.

"Yes, everything is prepared." He didn't add that it had all been ready for over a day. Didn't Yuri Stepanovich trust him to carry out the operation? Well, he admitted as he thought about it, recent events had proven that they couldn't trust anyone.

"How long before they arrive?"

Vasili glanced at his watch, trying to remember exactly what the controller had told him, and when. "They should be on the ground in less than three hours. I don't know how long before the authorities will let the passengers off the plane. It may take several hours before our friends can make the necessary arrangements."

"What?" Yuri shouted into the phone. "You were supposed to look after all that! You used a lot of my money to make sure the right people were compensated!"

"We did, Yuri Stepanovich, we did. But this will cause an international incident. We cannot keep something this big a secret." He'd worked for Yuri for many years and was getting very good at remaining calm and patient while explaining things that should have been very obvious to anyone with a gram of patience. While Yuri must have been very intelligent to get to where he was, he no longer took part in real operations. People like that tended to micro-manage tiny details while forgetting some of the larger ones.

"The right people have been compensated, and they will ensure that everything runs smoothly. But it will take time, Yuri Stepanovich."

"Call me when you have him." This time he didn't even push the end button before tossing it in a perfect arc towards Danic. His assistant caught it with a silent sigh of relief, ended the call, and shoved it back into his jacket pocket.

* * *

The plane continued on its new flight path, banking gently to one side or the other as it passed navigational checkpoints and made small course corrections. Michael was wishing that the captain would give them another update, or at least say something. It was agonizing to drone along through the skies not knowing where he was or where he was going. The man across the aisle had not said another word in over an hour and, despite Michael's many glances and long looks, he had not so much as acknowledged Michael's presence since their brief conversation. He had seemed very certain about their destination and Michael wanted to know why.

He looked over at the man again. There was something in his dress and bearing that Michael could not quite put his finger on. Something had made him certain that the man was European even before he had heard him speak. Even sitting down, he could tell the man was quite a bit taller than he was. He had dark hair, but a fair complexion. While he was not heavy he did look powerfully built, like he worked out and took it very seriously. The proverbial 'guy you didn't want to meet in a dark alley', but whom you wouldn't mind having on your side if you were in a dark alley. He also looked like he had not shaved in a day or two. At that thought, Michael rubbed his own chin, realizing that after a day and a half of travelling he probably looked the same way.

He wasn't purposely being ignored, he knew. The man was staring straight ahead with the same expression as before. Had there been any acknowledgement at all of his presence he would have asked the man why he was so certain of their destination. It would be a lot more awkward to ask why he was so afraid. What was he thinking? Was he planning something? Or preparing for something? Michael felt the same chill he'd felt when they had spoken, and reached for the inflight magazine to try and take his mind off things.

Now that he wasn't so frantic he easily found the page with the map of Europe on it. Kiev looked to be roughly the same distance from Frankfurt as Athens was, give or take a few miles. And it was the only airport in the country of Ukraine that showed flights going into it. Of course there was no guarantee that they were landing at an airport that normally had passenger service. Surely there were other airports in the country, or at least air force bases. Although, as he considered that thought further, if he were hijacking an airplane, the last place he'd have it land would be at an airport with a full contingent of armed soldiers.

Using his fingers to measure, and guessing at where they had made the turn to the east based on the elapsed time since taking off, he was trying to estimate when they would reach Kiev. He also eyeballed routes to several other major cities in that direction. That hijacker did have a Russian accent, didn't he? But did they talk that way in the other former Soviet republics as well? There was no one he could ask at the moment, and like everyone else on the plane he found not knowing the worst part. It was even worse than the fear. At least if you knew what to be afraid of you could try to prepare yourself.

As he continued his amateur attempts at navigation, the drink cart was making its way through the cabin again. Perhaps the flight attendants were trying to keep everyone calm, or maybe they just needed something to do too. He grabbed a Coke and offered the attendant a smile. She smiled back, but it was a very distant, distracted smile that came more from training and force of habit than from anything else. He looked around the cabin again. Almost no one was talking, not even the men who had wanted to storm the cockpit. But no one was as sullen and withdrawn as the man seated across the aisle. Maybe, he thought to himself, he's right and we are going to the Ukraine. A glance at the map told him that they were likely over that country now. That is, if they were going the direction he assumed. They were going roughly east but that was as much as he could tell. It might be north-east, south-east, or anywhere in between. The sun was on the right-hand side of the plane and it was just after noon local time. Frankfurt time, he corrected himself. Just where was local right now?

The need to do something was still overpowering, but there was nothing to do. He glanced across the aisle yet again and noticed that the man's eyes were narrow slits. They had been ever since his brief and decisive declaration of their destination. This man had an advantage over the rest of them; he knew what was happening. He was dealing with a real fear. He was planning something.

Michael's mind was racing now, but it could still only go in circles. He knew that it was useless to ask him what was happening. Likely he'd caught the man off-guard when he'd asked what country was to the east. That opportunity might not come again. Was it a good thing or a bad thing that he was seated so close to one of the two men on the flight that knew what was happening? Why did he have to book his trip on this flight? Why was he next to this man? Why didn't they give passengers parachutes so they could leave whenever they wanted?

His thoughts were broken when the engines throttled back and the nose of the plane dipped slightly. They were descending. Everyone strained to look out the nearest window but they were still over a solid cloud deck. Once again there was a soft steady buzz of conversation throughout the plane. Michael looked over at the man once more. This time, much to his surprise, the man looked back. For a brief moment there was a self-satisfied look on his face, as if to say, "I told you so." But almost before he recognized the look it was gone again. Reality once more took over the man's thoughts. What was that reality? If only he knew what this man knew, there was a possibility that he could plan for it as well. He could either help this man with whatever he was planning, or at least do something to protect himself and maybe some of the other passengers. The look on the man's face, however, told him that no more information was forthcoming.

Michael sensed movement behind him and looked back to see

that the flight attendants were moving through the cabin picking up all the drinking cups and other assorted garbage that always seemed to multiply during a flight. Except for the look in their eyes, which could only be seen if you looked closely, they seemed to be treating this like any other arrival. As they were making their way up the aisle the seatbelt sign flashed on. Despite their imminent arrival, there had been no further announcement from the cockpit since the one brief message shortly after the plane had been taken.

His anger began to rise towards the captain, hadn't he promised more news when he was able to give it. Surely he knew where they were landing, wasn't he flying the plane after all? But even as he felt the anger rising, he knew it was pointless. The captain might be flying the plane, but he was certainly not in control. It wasn't his fault if the hijacker wouldn't let him talk.

Maybe the pilot was dead. The thought flashed through his mind with a jolt that was almost physical. Maybe the hijacker was in control and was going to fly the plane into some important target. And it was all out of Michael's control. And beyond the control of anyone who had the slightest care for the well-being of the plane and its passengers. He forced himself to take a deep breath and tried to think. Ok, he told himself, the plane isn't diving from the sky. It's in a slow, controlled descent, just like the other three arrivals he'd made in the past day. Too bad he hadn't missed one of those connecting flights.

He took another deep breath. So, if we're not screaming out of the sky, we're probably landing not crashing. The pilot is still up there at the controls. That means, hopefully, this is just a normal hijacking. Given the circumstances that last thought didn't seem strange to him at all. So this hijacker is after what? Money maybe? A political statement? Surely there had to be some motive. But was it totally random? Was this flight just a target of opportunity? Any flight with the range to reach New York or Washington would have worked on September eleventh. As he considered the probability that this flight was specifically targeted he couldn't help but glance across the aisle again. Was that man someone important, someone worth hijacking a plane over?

"Hey! I can see something down there!"

"There's land down there!"

Voices from window seats rang out all over the plane and a chorus of loud clicks rang through the cabin as seatbelts were flipped open to allow the occupants to stand up and look out the windows.

They were still up quite high, but the clouds were thinning and glimpses could be caught of wide open farmland. Fields stretched out in every direction and small clusters of buildings forming tiny villages could be seen dotting the landscape. They looked nothing like the towns back home. He knew that even from cruising altitude vehicles were easily visible on the highways, but he could see almost no traffic at all.

He searched desperately for something, some landmark that would tell him where he was, knowing even as he did the futility of trying. This was the first time in his life he'd been on this side of the Atlantic and everything looked strange and foreign. He realized how ignorant he really was about the geography of this part of the world. Then he noticed the railroad tracks. Several could be made out running off in different directions. All the lines looked like they were double-tracked and were framed by rows of trees on either side. While back home railroads were not an uncommon sight, trains were often few and far between. But these tracks appeared to be quite busy and he noticed through one gap in the clouds multiple trains on the track that was running roughly parallel with their flight path. A glance up at the sun, and another at his watch, told him that it was early afternoon. So if the sun was there, he looked slightly to the right, then just a bit to the left of it should be more or less south. They were definitely flying east.

Even the flight attendants were ignoring the seatbelt signs and trying to look out the windows. If anyone besides the pilot knew where they were, Michael figured it would be them. Maybe one of them had flown into wherever this was before. Everyone was looking, except the man across the aisle. Michael couldn't keep thinking of him as 'the man' so he decided to call him Ivan. He sat motionless in his seat staring straight ahead.

Only now, for the first time, Ivan seemed to be forcing himself to look straight ahead. As if he wanted to look, but that seeing something out the window might prove to him that he was right, and he wanted desperately to believe that he was wrong.

Michael had had enough with the silence. He reached across the aisle and tapped him on the shoulder. "Hey, is this the Ukraine," he asked?

The man looked at him in surprise, but not anger. He was genuinely shocked at being spoken to. He looked at Michael for several seconds as if trying to understand the question, then slowly, as if forcing himself to look at something he really didn't want to see, he turned and rose slightly, peering past the couple seated between himself and the window. Ivan looked out the window so long that Michael decided he must have forgotten the question. He was just debating asking again when Ivan looked back at him. He must have seen something to make him certain, or perhaps it took him that long to gather the energy to speak.

"Is it the Ukraine?" Michael asked again, growing impatient for a reply.

"Da," the man answered, and then switched to English. "Yes, is Ukraine. Not 'the Ukraine.' Just Ukraine."

The grammar lesson was lost on Michael, but he decided against asking how the man knew. The certainty in Ivan's voice left no doubt in Michael's mind that he was right. Michael once again had the feeling that this man knew more about what was going on than anyone besides the hijacker. Or, maybe, he knew just as much as they did. Even as he watched the man's face he saw a change in his eyes. He had reached a decision, but what had he decided? Nothing changed in the man's posture, or even his facial expression, but there was something in those eyes now besides resignation.

He'd have to make a decision too, and possibly very soon. But he didn't have the same knowledge about what was going on that Ivan did, so how could he make the right one? He was convinced that this hijacking had something to do with the man beside him. Whatever negotiations might be taking place between the cockpit and the ground, the real object of interest was seated beside him. He was certain of that. This man had a plan based on his knowledge. So should he get as far from Ivan as possible, or should he stick close to him?

This part of the world was not known for suicide bombers, at least not as far as he knew. So it wasn't likely that the plane would blow up with the hijacker still on board. But would the hijacker slip off the plane once they were on the ground and blow up a plane load of passengers just to get Ivan? It was possible. But if that was the case what could he do about it? Or what could Ivan do about it? If Ivan had a plan then for whatever reason he must feel that he would be able to get off the plane. Or that something could be done from inside the plane. He shook his head in confusion and frustration. There was simply not enough real information for him to make what might be the most important decision of his life. Or might it possibly be the last decision of his life?

He looked past the man and woman beside him and out the window. They were much lower now, but there was still no word from the cockpit. He glanced at his watch again, which now seemed to be standing still. On the last few flights he'd been on, the descent had begun about thirty minutes or so before the landing, but he couldn't remember how long it had been since the engines had throttled back. The plane was manoeuvring now, small changes in heading and power settings as the pilot guided the plane towards its destination. Every small bank caused the passengers who weren't seated at window seats to try to see past those who were. Many had their view blocked because those at the windows had their faces glued to the double-paned ports.

"Cabin crew, prepare for arrival," came the clipped voice of the captain. He must have steeled himself to make the earlier announcement, because for the first time in his limited travel experience, Michael could hear tension in the voice of the captain. It made him wonder just what was going on up in the cockpit, and the uncertainty brought back the fear more powerfully than ever. If the captain sounded like that, it must be bad.

"Hey, there's a city down there," several voices cried out. Despite the admonitions of the cabin crew, seatbelts snapped open and necks craned to see what was beneath them. Between the heads crowded to the windows, Michael could see a sprawling city stretched out below him. They were passing over a wide river and still descending to the east. He could make out rows and rows of what appeared to be almost identical apartment buildings stretching out in every direction. It was nothing like the cities back home, or like those he'd seen from the air in Western Europe while flying into Frankfurt. He couldn't see a downtown core, at least not from the view he had, and his eyes scanned frantically as he tried to find something familiar in what he saw below him. If it was the Ukraine, or Ukraine as Ivan had insisted, was this Kiev, or some other large city? Were there any other large cities? The only other place in the country he knew of was Chernobyl and surely they weren't landing there.

"Ladies and gentleman, please take your seats now to prepare for landing, and fasten your seatbelts," the head attendant shouted into the handset, and then repeated the command in two other languages. Most of the passengers complied, some reluctantly, some in embarrassment at having to be told. But here and there a few disregarded her completely and remained on their feet staring out the window. She and her colleagues made a last attempt to get everyone in their seats, finally giving up on a remaining few, and strapped themselves in for the landing. They glared collectively at those still standing until they took the hint and finally, if for no other reason than self-preservation, took their seats as well.

The aircraft slowed noticeably as the flaps were fully deployed; the plane banked sharply to the left, and after a minute or so came the thud of the landing gear falling into place. He could hear the wind whistling past the extended gear and knew the landing was just a few moments away, but not another word had come from the cockpit. Even from his aisle seat Michael could now see the ground rushing past and rising to meet them. He felt the nose of the plane rise and then a gentle bump as the landing gear met the pavement of the runway. Somewhere in the back a few passengers clapped, but it was subdued and didn't last long, dying out as if they were embarrassed for celebrating the arrival. This flight might be over, but there might be a long way to go yet on the journey.

There was a sudden roar from the engines as reverse thrust was engaged, throwing everyone forward against their belts as the plane slowed to taxi speed and turned off the runway to the left. Almost the moment they cleared the runway, the plane came to an abrupt stop, engines idle.

Five minutes passed, then ten, and still they sat there. A soft but uneasy bustle filled the cabin as passengers shifted in their seats. Their wandering gazes alternated between the view outside and the door to the cockpit. Outside all they could see was grass, asphalt, and a few unfamiliar looking planes parked in the distance. The cockpit door remained closed, but might it open at any moment bringing this all to an end? Was that something to hope for, or something to fear?

As the passengers grew more and more restless, the chief attendant picked up the handset for the PA system. "Ladies and gentlemen, please remain seated until the captain turns off the seatbelt sign." It seemed a rather hollow order, given the fact that even she didn't have any idea when that might happen, but it did serve to keep everyone seated. Maybe because they were afraid of what might happen if the hijacker suddenly emerged from the cockpit.

A sudden exclamation from someone in first class focused everyone's attention back outside. A white van had driven up on the right-hand side of the plane. At first Michael strained to make sense of the lettering, which he recognized as Russian, or Ukrainian, which was slightly different as he was to learn later. Then his eyes found the English lettering. "Boryspil Airport," he read out loud as several other passengers repeated it at almost the same time. He glanced over at Ivan, his eyes speaking a silent question. Ivan met his gaze and nodded, confirming that this was indeed Ukraine.

The look on his face was different now that he had made his decision, whatever it was, and now that they were where he had expected to be.

"Where is Boryspil?" asked Michael quietly. He would have been afraid to speak, except that all around him people were breaking into quiet conversations.

"Is few kilometres east of Kiev, capital of Ukraine," came the subdued reply from Ivan. Michael still wasn't about to ask him his real name.

"So we're in Kiev?" Michael ventured a second question.

This time he got a mere nod in response.

"So what's going on?" He asked as casually as he could, trying to not let his suspicions show.

This time he got a mere shrug of the shoulders and realized he had pushed his luck a little too far. Once again Ivan was shutting down the conversation.

Needing someone to talk to he turned to the couple beside him. "Have you ever been here before?" He knew even as he asked what a stupid question it was.

But they needed someone to talk to as well. "No," replied the woman, "We heard that man say we are near Kiev," she nodded towards Ivan. "Why are we here? What's he going to do with us?"

All Michael could do was give them the same reply that Ivan had given him, shrugging his shoulders and turning the palms of his hands outwards to emphasize his ignorance. But they weren't really expecting an answer, just as Michael hadn't been.

The PA system came to life again and the voice of the captain came on. Most of the stress was now gone from his voice, or maybe he just had it under control again. "Ladies and gentleman, as you can see we have landed, however, I'm going to have to ask you to remain in your seats for a bit longer." Was that a typical pilot understatement Michael wondered? "We, uh, don't have a gate here, or landing rights, and we are in, ah, negotiations with the local authorities while we sort out just what is going to happen. I've been reassured that once…" There was a long pause. "That once demands have been met you will all be allowed to deplane. I'm going to shut the engines down now so please just be patient with us as we get everything sorted out. Please remain seated with your seatbelts fastened." He had hardly stopped speaking when the engines were throttled back and the cabin grew completely silent.

The sudden silence seemed to punctuate the final instruction to remain in their seats. At that moment almost everyone aboard had the same thought, that they could quite easily open all the emergency exits and make a break for it. But even as they glanced towards the exits two men stood up. One at the back of the cabin and one just forward of the wing exits. They said nothing, but the way they glared at the passengers, as if daring them to try to escape, conveyed more than any words could. The flight attendants didn't even consider asking them to sit down.

Michael sucked in a deep breath. Ok, he thought to himself, we've made it this far, so no one do anything stupid and we might just all get out of this with nothing more than an exciting story to tell our friends back home. The thought was still forming in his mind when he glanced across the aisle to Ivan. But there was no indication, nothing in his expression at all, to suggest he was going to try anything just yet.

Outside, through the insulated walls of the fuselage, came the muted roar of a jet as it passed behind them on its take-off roll. The sound only emphasized the silence in the cabin as everyone on board, with three exceptions, wished they were on that plane. It would take off, fly a routine, planned flight path, and land safely somewhere. Its passengers would be brought safely to family and friends, to somewhere they wished to be. Of the thousands of flights crossing the entire world that day, why, they asked themselves for the hundredth time, why did this have to happen to them?

As the minutes passed a steady stream of arriving vehicles formed a growing barrier around them. Some of them were simply marked 'Boryspil Airport', while the others were a mixture of police cars and assorted airport support vehicles, which together formed a display of flashing lights of every possible colour. Michael figured that somewhere there must be a lot of talking and furious activity going on as police, air traffic controllers, and hijackers worked to sort this out. The problem was that each of them had their own agenda which may or may not include the safety of those onboard. If this were a movie, they might change the scene and he could listen in on the negotiations, perhaps gaining some insight into why this was happening. As it was, all he could do was sit, wait, worry, and imagine.

All conversation had ceased once those two men stood up. He wanted to give them names too, but the only other Russian names he could think of were Boris and Natasha. Neither of them looked much like a Natasha. They were still there, not saying a word, simply glaring at the passengers. The two of them did a better job of keeping the plane under control than the cabin crew had.

What was going on, Michael wondered? Were they negotiating for money? Or was it for the release of some prisoners? Why were they being kept at the mercy of these men? Michael shook his head, looking around the plane without trying to be too obvious, as if somehow the answer was there to be seen if he just looked in the right place. His gaze rested on Ivan for a moment, wondering if it really did have something to do with him.

Outside he could see that the overcast had finally burned off and that the sun was shining brightly. Somehow the brightness made it feel that much darker in the plane despite the fact that the temperature was steadily rising as the minutes slowly ticked by. Before long the humidity was becoming as uncomfortable as the heat; the windows fogged over, no one spoke. The only movement was the flashing lights from the vehicles outside racing along the cabin walls and flickering strobe-like through the windows, but even that was somewhat obscured by the fog forming on the windows. From the flight deck came nothing but silence.

* * *

This time when the phone rang Danic the checked call display. He had received several calls since Vasili had last made contact that he had deemed important enough to put through, but attempting to do so had earned him verbal assaults unlike anything he'd experienced before. He wanted to be able to warn his boss beforehand if it were anything other than the call he was waiting for. Yuri was glaring at him as he delayed answering till he knew for sure who it was. Seeing it was indeed Vasili this time, he passed the phone directly to Yuri without answering it himself.

"Yes, Vasili?"

"The plane is on the ground now, but no one is sure who is in charge." Vasili laughed softly for a few seconds, unknowingly infuriating Yuri. "They may not know who is in charge, but we do. Do not worry, Yuri Stepanovich, the wait is almost over. We will have him by tonight at the latest. He may know where he is and why, but there is nothing he can do. He cannot get away from us this time."

CHAPTER 3

Detour

By Michael's watch a little over two hours had passed since the engines had been shut down. He stirred uncomfortably in the seat and wished he had a change of clothes as he now felt like he was bathing in his own sweat. Like everyone else, he had loosened the collar of his shirt, loosened his seatbelt, and tried to sleep to pass the time. But the cabin of the airplane felt like a sauna. What had begun as a three hour and ten minute flight had turned into about four hours of flying and two hours of sitting in a steam bath. The monotony had been broken only by the sound of the occasional plane landing or taking off on the runway behind them. There had been no further news from the captain, and the vehicles out there were doing nothing but flashing their beacons.

He twisted a bit in his seat hoping to get more comfortable, but with his clothes pasted to his body, it only made things worse as they bunched up and pinched him with each movement. He kept his eyes closed only because it made it worse to look around when absolutely nothing was happening. As far as he knew Boris and Natasha were still standing watch. Served them right to have to stand in this heat. His stomach growled.

An hour or so earlier the head flight attendant had asked Natasha if it would be possible to serve the passengers some snacks and drinks, but the request was met only by stony silence and a curt gesture to sit back down. A few muted complaints had been all that had come of the incident, and the looks on the faces of the two men had quickly silenced even those weak protests.

A soft chime sounded, dramatically breaking the silence, and the flight attendant in first class, the one who'd been attempting to serve the meals to the pilots, turned to look at the handset hanging on the bulkhead. She started to reach for it, and then quickly brought her hand back down, looking nervously at the hijacker closest to where she sat. He was leaning against the divider that separated the main cabin from first class, and nodded, granting her permission to pick it up. The cabin was completely silent and Michael could hear her as she spoke.

"Yes?" Her voice was anxious, but held a glimmer of hope. There was a short pause during which her face fell. Obviously she had not heard what she had hoped to hear, and her disappointment spread rapidly to everyone who could see her expression.

She held out the handset to the closest hijacker. "He wants to speak to you." There was a note of contempt in her voice as she spoke the words 'he' and "you", but if the hijacker noticed he chose to ignore it.

He took the handset from her, turned to keep an eye on the cabin, raised it to his mouth and spoke a single word. "Da?" That one word used up half of Michael's Russian vocabulary. He knew "da" and "nyet" for yes and no, but nothing else. Even if he'd been fluent it would have done him no good because the man cupped his hand over the mouthpiece and dropped his voice. The intercom system had been designed to allow clear communication even with the engines at full power and a cabin full of noisy passengers. In the complete quiet of the cabin, he did not need to speak loudly at all. Continuing to look suspiciously around the cabin he spoke to the hijacker in the cockpit for several minutes, occasionally nodding his head. Without being able to see the man's mouth it was hard to read his emotions, but he didn't seem to be getting upset. Maybe the negotiations were going well. Was that good for the passengers or not?

Finally he hung up, looked back at the other hijacker, and then his face broke into a grin. He raised his arm and pumped his fist, announcing to the whole plane that they'd won whatever it was they'd been seeking. He shouted out something Michael could not understand, and the other hijacker gave a sudden whoop of victory startling the passengers in the back of the plane who could not see what was going on. All over the plane passengers looked at each other, some terrified, some hopeful, and some not knowing what to feel. The two men continued their vigil, but all the tension was gone from their faces. It was as if they knew that nothing could go wrong with their plans now. Something had been decided. And whatever it was had been decided in their favour.

Boris and Natasha's change in mood was contagious, the passengers relaxing along with them. They still didn't have any idea what was happening, and many of them still didn't know for sure where they were, but at least their guards didn't look ready to tear someone's arms off anymore. For the first time in five or six hours they no longer felt in any immediate danger.

A sudden noise that was felt as well as heard startled everyone, including the hijackers. They looked nervously around the cabin and out the windows afraid that they needed to react to a new, unseen threat. It had come from the front of the plane. After a few anxious heartbeats the more seasoned travellers realized that a mule, the vehicle that was used to push an aircraft back from the terminal gate, was being hooked to the front landing gear. They were going somewhere.

The gentle jolt as they were hooked up and began moving rocked everyone in their seats while Boris and Natasha were forced to make a grab for the nearest seats to steady themselves. The plane began to move forward. Those with window seats used their hands, and the sleeves of their shirts, to clear off the condensation, hoping to learn something about where they were going. A gaggle of airport vehicles, lights still flashing, accompanied them on both sides.

Almost as an afterthought Michael glanced across at Ivan. His attention had been diverted, first by the phone call, then by the fact that they were moving again, and he had neglected to watch for Ivan's reactions. But if there had been any reaction in the man's face or eyes he had missed both it, and the chance of learning something from it. Ivan was sitting back in his chair with his eyes closed, as if trying to sleep. Or as if he was conserving his energy. Was he waiting for some opportunity?

The plane bumped along over the uneven joints of the taxiway surface, lightly jostling them twice each time as first the nose gear, then the main gear, traversed the joints. From time to time they caught glimpses of other aircraft parked on various tarmacs, and of the myriad buildings that were inevitably scattered across and around most airports. A sudden chorus of voices announced the sighting of the terminal buildings, but they weren't headed there. Instead they were towed onto a deserted area of the tarmac, several hundred yards from the nearest terminal and far from any other parked aircraft. The cars and vans escorting them suddenly peeled off, and many of them left the area completely. The remaining few took up station at the far reaches of the apron they had stopped on. Another soft thump from up front told them that the mule had been disconnected, and moments later it could be seen driving back towards the terminal building. They were once more all alone.

Glances were again exchanged and Michael briefly wondered if they had simply been moved out of the way. They had parked just off the runway and maybe they had been blocking a needed taxiway. But then he remembered the reaction of the hijackers and knew something was happening.

Without any announcement the door to the cockpit opened and the two pilots came out, looking tired and haggard. First came the captain, followed immediately by the first officer. The hijacker came out last, leaving the door open behind him. The hijacker already in the first class section yanked two first class passengers from their seats and shoved them roughly towards the back. Without a protest they slinked down the aisle to find empty seats somewhere among the peasants occupying economy class. The two pilots were shoved into the vacated seats and only when they had fastened their seatbelts did the hijackers look at each other. They broke into grins, speaking words Michael could not hope to understand, but they were obviously congratulating each other on a successful outcome.

One of them pulled out a cell phone, punched in a number and then stepped back into the cockpit as he jabbered away with someone, nodding and smiling as he gave his report. He finished the call and slipped the phone back into his pocket, then picked up a clipboard and bent over to speak to the captain. He must have been asking how to use the PA system because he picked up the handset, hesitantly pushed a couple of buttons, and began speaking.

"We have what we need." The words came in heavily-accented but passable English. Not a man used to diplomacy or public speaking, he just got straight to the point. "When buses come you will be allowed to leave airplane. We have…" His voice trailed off as he looked at the clipboard. "We have man-ee-fest. List of names." He looked up again, directing his gaze at people randomly around the aircraft. "When you talk to police, you will say nothing." That message came across clearly to everyone aboard. "We know who you are and if you say anything, we will find you." Everyone squirmed nervously, most knowing that they were obliged to tell the authorities everything they could possibly remember, but also knowing that the threat would hang over them as they did so.

The hijacker paused as if he was uncertain what else to say, and then finished his announcement. "Sit down until buses come."

He exchanged satisfied looks with his cohorts while the passengers and crew hoped it really was over. Michael could think of more than one hijacking where the plane had been flown to multiple airports over a span of several days. Were they really being set free? If they were, he needed to find out if there were direct flights to Athens from Kiev, how long the police would need to keep him, and how soon he could resume the trip. Was he going to have to stay here? Would these guys get caught and go to trial? Would they bring all the passengers back to testify? Fear turned to anger as he started to realize just how complicated his life could get because of the act of a few men who thought risking his life was a reasonable price to pay to get what they wanted.

Right now his wants were simple and basic: a meal, a shower, and a ticket to Athens. The meal was definitely at the top of the list. It didn't even have to be a good meal, just something to eat. He wiped some sweat from his brow, and added a jug of ice-cold water to his wish list.

"Hey! They're bringing some stairs," came an excited voice from someone in a window seat on the left side of the plane. "And buses too!"

All over the plane came bursts of applause and cheers, and none of the hijackers seemed to mind. They were likely glad to get out of the airplane too. Whatever it is they were after, Michael was sure that they did not enjoy being cooped up in the heat any more than the rest of them did.

The truck with the portable stairs pulled into place and several buses lined up alongside the aircraft. The anxiety level in the cabin was rising; everyone hoping that this really was the end of the ordeal, that there never had been any real danger. All they hoped to get out of the whole experience now was an exciting story to tell their friends back home. One of the hijackers had resumed station at the back of the cabin, presumably to make sure no one made a dash for it out the rear door. They gave no instructions, or any indication of what was happening, but Michael was sure there were still several missing pieces to the puzzle. Surely these guys were not going to just board a bus and ride off? Were they going to release the passengers and keep the plane and crew and fly off somewhere else? Would they be receiving a suitcase full of money? How did they plan to get away with this?

He knew he should just be thankful that he was being let go, if that was indeed what was about to happen, but somehow he still felt that Ivan had something to do with all of this. Was he involved somehow with the hijackers? Had all that nervousness been because he'd been worried about their plan being successful? He shook his head to clear his thoughts. No, that had not been nervousness, there had been raw fear in his face and voice when he'd realized where they were heading.

Michael, like everyone else aboard, wanted to know why they'd been dragged into this whole mess, but the important thing was to get safely off the plane and then hope to solve the mystery by listening to the six o'clock news. He made up his mind that if, no, make that when, they were allowed off the plane, he'd get as far from Ivan as possible. The mystery could wait. He wanted off the plane and out of this country, and the sooner the better.

A thumping sound on the outside of the door signalled that they were ready to de-plane the passengers. The hijacker who'd been in the cockpit motioned to the pilot and co-pilot to get back into the cockpit and ordered all the flight attendants, except one, to the back of the plane. Then he had the remaining attendant open the hatch. It was a hot humid afternoon in Kiev, but after being stuck in the equivalent of a tin can for so long, the relatively fresh air felt wonderful as it blew in the door.

"Leave luggage," the head hijacker ordered, standing beside the cockpit door, "All passengers get off now!"

The sound of clicking seatbelts rippled through the cabin and people began standing up and filing down the aisles. A few ladies grabbed their handbags as they stood up, but no one tried opening any of the overhead bins to retrieve anything else. There were, no doubt, a lot of valuables stashed up there, but they could be retrieved later. No one was going to turn down the chance to get off the plane for anything as minor as that.

Because they had both been in aisle seats, Michael ended up just ahead of Ivan as they made their way down the aisle and past the hijacker. They turned left to step outside onto the air stairs. The hot, humid wind was the most refreshing thing he'd ever felt, possibly because with it came the feeling of freedom. He walked down the stairs and was directed, by a very serious-looking man wearing some sort of official uniform, towards the first bus. There was a bit of a delay at the door, but everyone filed into the bus in an orderly fashion. Inside a police officer was ushering each passenger into the first available seat, filling up the bus from the front to the back. Michael was directed into a window seat on the driver's side of the bus, but was barely seated when he realized that Ivan was standing in the aisle looking at him.

"May I sit by window?" he asked, though the tone of voice made it clear he was not making a request.

Michael hesitated for a second until the irritated voice of the policeman barked out what sounded like a command. "Seet down!" he repeated in English. Startled into action Michael nodded at Ivan, slipped into the aisle seat, and let Ivan squeeze past him into the one by the window.

A little unsettled by the harsh command, he was a victim here, not the hijacker after all, he settled back into his new seat. If anything, it was even more uncomfortable than the seat on the plane, which had felt like an overstuffed armchair in comparison. But then he realized there was air conditioning and opened up the vent above him, revelling in the blast of cold air. He noticed Ivan taking a good, long look around the bus, but not out of curiosity. It was obvious he was giving it a thorough looking over. The phrase "casing the joint" came to mind.

It grew even cooler onboard when the last of the seats were filled, another policeman entered the bus, and the door was closed. It almost felt like being back on the plane with an armed guard standing in both the front and back of the bus. He wondered for a moment why they were even being guarded until he realized that no one on the ground knew for sure which of them were hijackers and which were innocent passengers. Was that how the hijackers planned to get away, to hide themselves among the passengers and sneak away? But then what would they have gained by hijacking the plane? They paid for the flight to Athens so why not just buy a ticket to Kiev if that is where they wanted to go? Why hijack a planeload of passengers and then just turn them loose? There was something else going on here, but he was almost too tired to think anymore. He closed his eyes and tried to will the whole thing to be over.

Behind them a second, and then a third bus, swallowed up the line of passengers marching down the stairs and onto the tarmac. When the final bus was filled, a police car swung in front of the lead bus and with lights flashing, began to lead them across the tarmac towards the terminal building. Somehow that seemed to be a signal to everyone that it was safe to talk now and the excited passengers began expressing opinions and asking questions of each other.

The drive to the terminal building was not a long one, but rather than pulling up behind another bus that was already disgorging a group of passengers from another flight, their bus continued on past the terminal. The police escort was still leading the way and at first they all assumed they were being taken to another building, possibly for a debriefing from the authorities, but then a man watching out the back window yelled out, "The other buses are stopping back there!"

The policeman in the back grabbed him, spun him back around, and gave him a glaring look that not only made the man shut up, but sent a fresh wave of fear through everyone onboard. For some reason, their bus was being given special treatment. The driver didn't react to either the man's outburst or his treatment by the guard. He slowed the bus, turned right between a couple of large, propeller-driven cargo planes, wove around several other vehicles, and sped through an access gate that put them onto a road leading through a parking lot. When a few passengers began protesting and questioning what was going on, the policeman in the front gave them the same treatment that the man at the back window had received. The police car that had been escorting them pulled aside in front of a building labeled "Terminal B". The bus made a left turn and accelerated down a street lined with trees, all with the bottom few feet of the trunks painted in a dull, faded white. They flashed past a hotel, and a few other buildings still under construction, before picking up speed.

In another couple of minutes the driver guided the bus onto an overpass and merged onto a busy highway crowded with small compact cars and large, awkward-looking trucks. By now everyone on the bus was in just as much shock as when they had first been hijacked. No, not everyone, Michael saw: Ivan was watching with a detached look. He alone had suspected something from the moment they boarded the bus, or maybe even before that, and that was why he wanted a window seat for such a short trip.

Michael was now more convinced than ever that the man seated beside him was the reason for the hijacking of the plane. He was also the reason this bus was speeding off to some unknown location while almost every other passenger on the plane was now safely in the terminal building. He'd been on the wrong plane, and now he was on the wrong bus. What had this man done, and why was Michael paying for it?

CHAPTER 4

Exit

The bus didn't remain on the main road for long. The driver soon took an exit to the right and then turned back and forth onto a series of roads that soon had his passengers completely lost. They finally settled onto a narrow, winding, tree-lined highway. There was not a lot of traffic, though Michael was surprised to see several carts being pulled by horses. He even caught a brief glance of a farm wagon that looked for all the world like it was being pulled along by something resembling a roto-tiller, with just wheels and no tines on the front end. The bus sped by too fast for him to get a good look at it.

Exhaustion, both mental and physical, began to take its toll, and he was finding it hard to keep his eyes open. He'd given up trying to figure out how many time zones he had gone through and how many hours it had been since he'd last slept, but every time he closed his eyes the bus hit a pothole or a rough patch and he was jolted back awake. After one hard jolt caused him to bite his tongue, and likely loosened the suspension of the bus, he gave up trying to sleep and just sat there watching the endless line of trees slide past. They passed numerous small towns and villages but he could not even recognize the letters, let alone read the names of the towns. He had no clue where they were going.

The rough ride had caused even the two policemen to sit down. Suddenly, it occurred to him that they might not even be policemen. Without a direct threat of someone watching them, many of the passengers were breaking into quiet conversations throughout the bus. The noise of the diesel engine added to the road noise made it impossible to hear much of anything unless you were right next to the speaker. He looked over at Ivan and shrugged to himself; why not go for it? He'd survived two hijackings already today, maybe his luck was about to change.

As his gaze fixed on Ivan there was no reaction at first, but he kept looking until finally they made eye contact. He stuck out his hand. "Michael, Michael Barrett." There was no response from the man at all.

"Hey, after all we've been through together today, don't you think we should at least introduce ourselves?"

The man looked at him in stony silence for a long time, the look gradually turning to one of suspicion. Then his eyes softened just a bit and he raised his own hand.

"Dmitri," Was all he said.

"Nice to meet you, Dmitri." It sounded dumb even as he spoke the words. He might just as well have said, 'Glad we got hijacked together.' All he got in response was a grunt.

"Do you have any idea what these guys are after? And why those other buses stayed at the airport while we get a free tour of Ukraine?"

Ivan, or Dmitri rather, didn't even bat an eyelash. He just stuck out his bottom lip a bit, shook his head, and muttered a single word. "No."

Michael knew the man was lying, but he would not have wanted to play poker with the guy. If he hadn't been watching him earlier on the plane, he'd have thought him just as clueless as the rest of the passengers.

"I wonder what they're going to do with us," Michael ventured. It wasn't spoken as a question, just a statement of his confusion. He was hoping Dmitri might offer to fill in a few blanks.

Dmitri paused for a long time, presumably so he could ponder the options, but Michael felt he was considering just how much to give away.

"I would be ready for anything," was what he finally said.

Michael nodded in agreement. So, *Dmitri*, he asked silently, *is that your way of warning me of something?*

"But what can we do on the bus? Those guys have guns," he nodded towards the uniformed man sitting in the seat behind the driver. As long as he had him talking he wanted to keep the conversation going, and maybe learn something useful. Maybe even something that would save his life.

This time he caught the guilty look in Dmitri's eyes. It wasn't there long, but there was something unnatural in the pause before he spoke. He wasn't trying to formulate a plan or weigh options, he was trying to decide what to say, and what not to say, about a plan he had already decided to carry out.

Finally he just shrugged. "You watch and you wait for right opportunity. Maybe it comes. Maybe it doesn't." He shrugged again and turned to face the window.

Michael gave himself a mental kick. He'd pushed too hard and too soon and lost the chance. Or maybe Ivan, Dmitri rather, was suspicious of him. But why? Obviously the bad guys knew who he was and what flight he was going to be on. They'd gone to a lot of trouble to arrange the welcoming committee. What could he possibly learn from Dmitri by sitting beside him on the plane and the bus that these guys didn't already know? Guess he's just looking out for number one, he thought bitterly. You got us into this mess; why not give the rest of us a fair chance? Or at least a fighting chance? Don't we deserve to live too?

Michael looked around, sizing up the situation. They had the guards outnumbered at least twenty to one. Even if you added up all the bullets in both guns, there was no way they could take out everyone. Were enough of the passengers prepared to be heroes to make an attempt? The driver would have to be looked after too, though he couldn't do anything while navigating these roads. But how do we plan it without alerting them? He briefly considered waiting until they got wherever they were headed, then realized there might be twenty more men there with any number of weapons.

He was beginning to think that maybe the man on the plane was right. They should have tried something while they had the chance. Maybe it was already too late.

The sun had been setting as he'd introduced himself to Dmitri, and now, as he pondered his options, it had grown completely dark. He'd never seen such complete darkness. There were no lights from farmhouses, and even when they passed villages, there were no lighted signs. Few lights were visible from the windows of the houses and there weren't even any streetlights. It gave the whole countryside a deserted feeling and made the atmosphere in the bus all the more gloomy. He fought the urge to give up hope and resign himself to whatever fate these men had in store for him. He glared at Dmitri, unnoticed in the darkness, and wondered if he threw the guy off the bus if the rest of them would be let go. Whatever this was all about he was central to it. Michael was certain of that now. If the bad guys were after him, he reasoned, and he was one of the good guys, shouldn't he be working to save their lives as well as his own? What was this all about?

Well, he decided finally, if Dmitri isn't going to help, maybe it's time he did something himself. After all, it was his life. If nothing else, maybe it would provoke a reaction from Dmitri. He leaned forward, speaking just loud enough for the man seated ahead of him to hear.

"I don't like this. Once we get wherever we're going, there's no telling what these guys are going to do. I think maybe we should make a move now."

The man leaned back without turning his head as he replied. "I was just talking to my friend here about that." The voice came back in a very prim and proper British accent, he gave an almost imperceptible nod towards the man seated beside him, "I don't think this is going to end well at all. When these chaps didn't let us go at the airport, I knew something was up. If we split into two groups some of us can handle the front bloke while the rest handle that chap in the rear."

Michael nodded, "I was thinking the same thing. They might shoot some of us, or we might end up driving off the road, but if we stay here till the end of the line, we might all be dead anyway."

"Quite right," the tone of his voice suggested that they might be talking about the weather, or the latest cricket scores. "I think we need to do something very soon. Fortune favours the bold, eh?"

"This guy beside me seems to know the country," Michael added, speaking a little louder so that Dmitri was sure to hear, "I'm sure he can help us if we can just get off this thing. How many others have you talked to? We need more guys than they have bullets." There was something completely unreal about the whole conversation, and yet at the same time Michael had a strong feeling that they had to do something, and soon, because there was nothing unreal at all about the situation. He glanced at Dmitri, but there was no reaction at all. "What do you think, Dmitri?"

The man's face turned suddenly towards him and if the flash of his eyes had borne any physical force at all Michael, would have been tossed across the aisle. Was he mad because I spoke his name, or because I'm dragging him into this? Or have I done something to ruin his plan?

Dmitri forced himself to calm down before speaking, but the words still carried a lot of anger. "I think if you want to play heroes and get yourselves killed, then do it. Or be smart and wait for right opportunity. But please, do not let me stop you from trying. Maybe some of us will be left alive."

Despite the anger and sarcasm in Dmitri's words, Michael knew he had a plan of some sort. Just what he planned to do and when he planned to do it were anything but clear, but he'd had hours to plan something, and Michael and the Englishman were making it up as they went.

"He's right, we need to wait for the right time," Michael said, leaning forward once more.

"Don't wait too long, or we may not have the opportunity to act. Are you with us or not?"

"I'll get back to you. Soon. Very soon."

The Englishman nodded, accepting his answer for the time being, and then leaned forward to resume his discussion with his seatmate.

"Watch out!" Michael grabbed the seat in front of him as the tires of the bus shrieked in protest at a sudden turn of the wheel. The sound of the tires matched almost perfectly those of the passengers. The driver must have pushed the brake pedal right to the floor, throwing everyone violently forward. Almost at the same time he had cranked the wheel to the left so hard that Michael had to hold on to the seat in front of him to avoid being thrown into the aisle. Out of the corner of his eye, he caught the shadowy shape of an unlit farm wagon flash past just inches to the right of the bus. The tires screeched again when the driver swung just as sharply back into his own lane to avoid an oncoming car, throwing Michael against Dmitri who cracked his head against the window. The bus rumbled over an extra rough patch of pavement and then almost before anyone could realize how close they'd come to a catastrophe, the road ahead was clear again. The driver fed in the gas, revving the diesel engine to what sounded like its redline. Whoever was driving this thing seemed completely oblivious to the fact that there might be more wagons out there somewhere in the darkness ahead.

"This guy's going to kill us before those guys with the guns do," Michael blurted out angrily. He was looking directly at Dmitri and there was no way the man could avoid the cold daggers he was shooting at him with his eyes. Michael lowered his voice, which made him sound even angrier. He spat out the words, venting his full rage at Dmitri. "I don't know what's happening here, but you do! This is all because of you." He jabbed his finger towards him to emphasize the last word.

Dmitri met his gaze, giving away nothing with his expression, or by way of words, so Michael continued. "Whatever it was you did is your business, fine, I get that. But now you've endangered the life of everyone on the plane, and everyone on this bus." He struggled to keep his voice low, and managed to succeed, but all the pent-up anger of the day, combined with his lack of sleep, was bursting out now.

"All I had to do was sit at the back of the plane, or pick another flight and I'd be safe right now. I think we all deserve to know what's happening."

Dmitri pursed his lips thoughtfully and nodded in agreement, which had the effect of calming Michael slightly.

"You are right. Bus has microphone; maybe I use it to make announcement and explain situation to everybody. Good idea, yes?"

"No." admitted Michael, a tone of defeat in his voice as he lost the momentum of the conversation. "But, come on, give me something here. What do you have planned and when?"

Dmitri studied him carefully, debating what might be the motive behind the question. "I do not know. But I will know if opportunity comes." Michael kept looking at him, but had nothing else to say. Something in the man's tone of voice told him that he was being given the truth, or at least part of it. "But we have few more hours before we arrive." With that he sat back in his seat and turned to face the window again. Once more he'd succeeded in ending a conversation before Michael could get all the information he was hoping for. Well, he thought, at least Dmitri had more or less admitted that he was somehow to blame for all of this.

The bus slowed down slightly and Michael glanced out to see they were passing through another small village. A sign proclaimed what he assumed to be the name of the place, but it was about 20 letters long and Michael didn't know any of them. A few pedestrians and parked vehicles narrowed the road somewhat and the bus driver, perhaps having learned his lesson from earlier, was exercising extreme caution by almost slowing down to the posted speed limit. Once they had cleared the town limits he downshifted aggressively and quickly brought the bus back up to normal cruising speed.

The droning of the engine and the sound of the tires on the pavement would normally have put everyone to sleep, but the ride was far too rough to allow that. Even if the road had been smooth, most of them were too keyed-up to sleep. The fact that no one had said anything to them since they had boarded the bus made it almost worse than the hijacking. They knew now that they were in Ukraine, but where in Ukraine were they going? At least on the plane someone had admitted to them that they were being forced to go somewhere against their will.

Those facts, coupled with their earlier near-miss with the horse and wagon, likely explained why those in the first couple of rows were watching the road intently. And that is why all of them shouted out a warning at the same instant.

Michael looked up sharply, wondering if something was happening with their kidnappers, and barely had time to brace himself as the driver again shoved the brake pedal all the way to the floor. He was thrown forward, smashing his chin painfully against the seat ahead of him, though it was a long time before he realized he was bleeding. The bus veered sharply to the left, then back to the right, then left again. The driver's first instinct had been to veer around the wagon that had appeared in the beams of his headlights, until he realized that there was a string of cars coming at him from the other direction. The first two oncoming cars took the ditch causing the driver to swing left again. With the tires screaming he managed to bring the bus to a stop in the wrong lane while the next two oncoming cars cut to their left and barely missed the horse and wagon.

Just as they'd begun to realize that they'd narrowly averted another accident they heard the blaring of a horn coupled with a loud screech behind them. They just had time to brace themselves again when there was a sharp jolt as the driver of an American-made SUV plowed into the back of the bus.

Dmitri leaned over and whispered something in Michael's ear, his voice coming to Michael through a haze of confusion, panic and pain. "Opportunity is here."

As Michael turned towards Dmitri he saw the Ukrainian reaching for the latch that activated the emergency exit. Even before he fully realized what the red handle was, the bus window fell to the ground with a loud crash. Dmitri grabbed Michael's shoulder tight-ly and yanked him to his feet, pulling him through the window with him. As they jumped, Michael could feel a growing press of bodies behind him as others seized the same opportunity.

CHAPTER 5

Scenic Route

Michael landed, or rather half-landed, on a car that had stopped beside them. The bus had come to rest at an angle across the narrow highway, effectively blocking traffic in both directions. He bumped painfully off the vehicle and came down hard on one knee, coming to rest amongst the loose stones littering the highway. Angry shouts that he couldn't understand were coming from every direction, some no doubt from their captors, but most of them from other drivers. Horns were blaring and more windows were crashing from the bus as other passengers followed Dmitri's lead. The whole scene was one of noise and confusion and he was slightly dazed from pain, the darkness of the night, and the blinding blaze of the headlights shining on him.

He gripped the bumper of the car he had landed on and tried to pull himself to his feet, knowing more by instinct than by conscious thought that he needed to get away. Even as he tried to do so three more people landed on top of him and it took several attempts to stagger back to his feet. As he tried to decide which way to turn, someone grabbed his shoulder and barked out an order, "This way!"

He was half-dragged back up the highway in the direction they'd just come from. For a few anxious moments he thought he'd been recaptured until he recognized Dmitri's form pulling him roughly along. The Ukrainian was glancing into the driver's seat of each empty vehicle they passed until they came to one that was still running. Without warning or instruction he was stuffed head first into the car through the driver's door. Another shove from behind pushed him towards the passenger's seat, causing him to bash his injured knee into the park brake handle, and then the gear shift in the process. Trying to climb past them he smashed his head against the window as Dmitri shoved him once more. He was still twisted sideways in the seat when he heard the door slam shut behind him.

Dmitri shoved the gearshift into first, popped the clutch, and spun the car around. Weaving through the maze of cars parked at odd angles along the road, he accelerated as fast as the tiny engine would allow, pushing it well beyond its redline before each shift. Working against the swaying vehicle, and the jolts and bumps, Michael finally managed to twist into a sitting position and, in a futile attempt at self-preservation, started fumbling for a seatbelt. There wasn't one.

"Where are we going?" He tried to demand. But the words came out weakly, with no breath to support them.

"That way." Dmitri replied, raising his head to point up the road with his chin.

"What's that way?" He tried again, this time his anger coming through.

"Road with no bus blocking it. Maybe you like it better back there, Mikhail? I take you back?" Dmitri had the car floored in top gear now, despite the roughness of the road, leaving Michael convinced that they were spending as much time airborne as they were on the ground.

Michael only grunted in response, not wanting to admit that he hadn't had a plan at all, and trying not to feel resentful. After all he was getting his wish now, benefiting from all of Dmitri's planning. He glanced over at the speedometer and saw that it was pegged firmly on zero. Well, at least the engine was working, he acknowledged, as they bounced over yet another pothole.

Or was he benefiting from it? If he had just been left beside the bus, those goons would have left him alone and gone after Dmitri. Once the police showed up, they'd have taken him back to Kiev and put him on a plane for Athens. Now the hijackers were still after him.

"Anyone following us?"

"Da. They are following."

Michael turned around in panic, but saw nothing behind them. "Where?"

Dmitri shrugged. "I don't see them, but they follow us, Mikhail."

"Then drop me off here. I'll...I'll tell them you went a different way if they see me."

Dmitri had his eyes fixed on the road, doing his best to dodge the worst of the potholes with the help of the weak beam of the car's headlights. "No. I cannot do this."

"Why not?"

Dmitri suddenly slapped the gearshift down into third and Michael tried to brace himself on the dashboard as the sudden deceleration threw him forward. They'd reached the small town they'd passed earlier on the bus, and he was using the engine to slow the car down, cranking the wheel hard to the right as he turned up one of the town's streets.

"We talk later, okay?"

"Yeah," Michael responded, bouncing and lurching in his seat as the car tore down the unlighted dirt street. His right foot was frantically reaching for a brake pedal that wasn't there. Dogs and pedestrians jumped out of their way as they tore through town. Row after row of small houses lay partially hidden behind an unbroken line of fences. Each yard seemed to have its own unique fence style and he could see in the glare of the headlights that some of the gates looked very ornate. He also caught glimpses, at irregular intervals, of wells. The same kinds he'd seen pictures of as a kid, each with a crank and a bucket.

The road was bare dirt, though there may have been gravel on it at one time, and was filled with long, deep ruts worn by years of traffic and a complete lack of maintenance. The car twisted and turned, taking side roads randomly until Michael was completely confused as to which way they were going or had come from. After what seemed like countless turns, Dmitri slowed down to a more sensible speed and stopped at the next corner they came to.

Michael could not make out the buildings and houses very well in the dark. There were no streetlights at all, and even if there had been, the fences all rose well above eye height. Dmitri looked both directions and then turned to the left, proceeding at a very slow pace, which almost made the ride comfortable in comparison with the last few frantic minutes. He continued driving straight ahead, suddenly turning off the headlights and gliding to a stop beside a few other cars parked near an intersection. He left the car in gear with engine running and his foot on the clutch.

Michael realized after a few seconds that it was a highway they'd stopped at. "Is this the same highway we came in on?"

"Da. Yes." Dmitri was still concentrating on escape and didn't want to waste time answering, let alone explaining whatever his plan was.

They sat in silence for a few minutes before two pairs of headlights appeared racing up the highway from the direction of the bus. The cars slowed and one pulled up alongside the other when they reached the intersection that Dmitri and Michael had first turned at. The occupants of the car must have been deciding which of them would search which direction. One turned onto the same road they had taken, while the other continued straight ahead. Without being told Michael slouched down in his seat as much as possible so that the outline of his head wouldn't appear as the car passed. Fortunately the driver of the other car was assuming that they were still fleeing down the highway and sped past them without so much as a glance at the row of parked cars.

The moment they were out of sight Dmitri let out the clutch and, still with the lights out, pulled across the highway and up a side road. As soon as he thought it was safe he turned the lights back on and picked up speed. Again he took several random turns until Michael, and perhaps Dmitri himself, had lost track of where they were going. They continued on at a fast, but not excessive, rate of speed. They were barely going faster than the road conditions seemed to warrant. This road was not in as good a shape as the highway had been, but they both felt a little more relaxed knowing that their pursuers had split up and had both been going the wrong way when they'd last seen them.

Still, Michael kept leaning forward to use the side view mirror and felt his heart skip a beat when he spotted a pair of headlights behind them.

"Lights!"

"I see them," Replied Dmitri, downshifting to third and rapidly picking up speed, sending the car bouncing over ruts and potholes.

"Is it them?" Michael asked, the tone of his voice revealing his fear.

"Not good idea to think is someone else."

They were both searching frantically for a side road, but for what seemed an eternity the road continued straight as an arrow. Michael saw the line of trees first, Dmitri's attention being focused primarily on avoiding the worst sections of the road.

"There! To the left!"

"Hang on," Dmitri ordered, turning off the headlights and downshifting from fourth to second, skipping third altogether, and sending the car fishtailing over the loose, scattered stones. He reached for the park brake lever and yanked it back to help slow the car further, wondering if the park brake would activate the taillights and hoping that it wouldn't, because he was going too fast to make the corner without using it.

The car tires bounced and skipped sideways, reluctant to alter course as he cranked the wheel hard to the left as fast as he dared, waiting till the last possible second to take the corner, desperately hoping they'd slowed down enough.

They made the corner, barely. He released the park brake handle and remained in second as he accelerated hard up the road, quickly backing off the gas when a huge pothole appeared. This wasn't a highway, or even a secondary road. It was just a dirt trail through a field, likely used by tractors and farm machinery, but it was too late to turn back now unless the vehicle behind them was not one of their pursuers. That was a chance they could not take; this road was the best option they had now.

The car bounced and jolted violently over ruts and fist-sized rocks heaped along the trail. Someone had thoughtfully placed them there to fill in the soft spots in the road, but it made it impossible for them to drive in anything above second gear. At times even that was more than the car could take.

"Look for another road!" Dmitri yelled, for the first time a hint of fear was in his voice.

"I am!" Michael yelled back, angry both at Dmitri for telling him to do what he was already doing, and at the fact that he couldn't see one.

Suddenly the road smoothed out a bit giving both of them a

chance to look behind them. There were no lights to be seen any-where. Dmitri fed in more gas and brought the car up into third gear. They were practically gliding over the smooth stretch of the road as it made a broad curve to the right and then back to the left. The road narrowed as they cut through a copse of trees and then widened out again, but it remained smooth, completely free of bumps and holes.

They both relaxed just a bit, at least their hearts no longer felt like they had just sprinted a mile, but both kept a constant, wary eye on the mirrors. Dmitri's fear was stronger than Michael's, as he understood that ultimately his life depended on getting somewhere safe as quickly as possible. Michael's fear was less concrete, a vague dread of falling back into the hands of his former captors.

While Dmitri concentrated mostly on the road, Michael spent more time looking backwards than forwards. But as they rounded a corner and some trees blocked his vision, he glanced forward, catching sight of it before Dmitri did, and without knowing quite what it was yelled out a warning.

Dmitri saw it a split second later, but too late to slow down enough. With a sickening thud the car hit a slab of concrete that had been laid across a small creek to serve as a bridge. It almost stopped them completely, but there was just enough momentum for the car to drag its frame across the edge and onto the bridge itself. There were no guardrails or anything else to warn of its location to anyone unfamiliar with the road, and years of rain and traffic had worn deep ruts into the approach to the bridge, leaving the sharp corner of the slab to catch unwary drivers.

They bumped off the other end of the bridge before Dmitri tried accelerating tentatively, hoping that the car was still driveable. It wasn't so much that he cared about damaging the car, but at the moment it was his only hope of safety. First, second, and even third gears worked fine, but he had to shift back down into second as they started up a steep hill where the road was flanked by thick trees on either side. Just as they decided that they had survived with just a few dents, the engine sputtered. With Michael staring at him, silently and frantically urging him to nurse the car back to health, Dmitri popped it back into first and fed in more gas. The engine surged back to life briefly, sputtered again, and then died completely.

For a moment they sat there in complete silence, Dmitri staring at the dashboard in disbelief, as if the car had betrayed him by stalling. He snapped out of his shock, pounded the wheel in silent rage, and then set the park brake. They both stepped out to survey the damage. They began by popping the hood, but without tools or even a flashlight they knew the chances of getting it running again were remote. Then they both smelled it at the same time. It was the unmistakeable odour of gasoline.

Michael reached the back end of the car first, feeling the dampness of the earth as he knelt. It was too dark under the trees for even the moon to provide any help in seeing what had happened, so he reached beneath the car and then made a face as he looked up at Dmitri.

"There's a hole in the gas tank, I can almost get my fist inside it." He wiggled one edge of the gash and felt the rusty metal crumble in his fingers. The tank was completely empty.

Dmitri pounded the trunk lid with his fist and looked around in a mixture of frustration and desperation. He'd have to be a lot further from the bus to feel even remotely safe, but there was nothing around them except fields and trees. The road was used by farmers to get to and from the fields. No one had occasion to be using it right now, and even if a vehicle had come along, their first instinct would be to hide, not hitchhike. "We have to hide car. If they find it too soon, they will catch us before we have time to steal another one."

With a stab of guilt Michael realized for the first time that he'd made a get-away in a stolen car. That feeling turned briefly to rage at Dmitri for getting him even deeper into this twisted mess. He took a deep breath.

"But there were only two of them, and they both went the wrong way," He began to say.

"No, by now there are many more than that. We must work fast. We will put it in bushes at bottom of hill, Mikhail. You stand in front," he pointed to the front of the car. "Help me back down hill and we will push it into bushes and cover it."

As the adrenaline rush of their flight began to fade Michael became aware of the throbbing pain in his knee. He reached down to rub it and discovered that his pant leg had been ripped open. There was a lumpy scab just under his kneecap. He hobbled around to the front of the car as Dmitri slipped back behind the wheel, rolling the window down so that he could hear Michael's instructions. He put the gearshift into neutral and the car began rolling back down the hill.

Michael's knee was throbbing and each step became more painful, but by using hand signals as well as his voice, he slowly guided the car to the base of the hill. There was a gradual bend to the left as they descended and with the trees so close on each side Dmitri had to ride the brake hard to keep it under control. Not even Michael cared as tree trunks and branches on either side of the narrow trail left long scratches in the faded paint of the car.

* * *

Vasili answered his phone on the first ring, knowing it had to be Sasha and that the most difficult part of the job had now been completed. They'd known since the plane had departed Frankfurt that Dmitri would be boarding the first bus, but it had not been easy to make sure they'd paid off or blackmailed everyone that might prevent the bus from leaving the airport. For as fast as the job had to be put together, it had gone off remarkably well, and now the fun would begin. They had him back and he would talk. Oh yes, he would tell them everything. But hopefully not too quickly; there wouldn't be much fun in that.

"Da, Sasha?"

He listened to Sasha's report, feeling his chest tighten, not only in anger and frustration, but also with the knowledge that calling in the report to Yuri was his responsibility. Actually the whole job was ultimately his responsibility. Sasha and the rest of the team were doing the fieldwork, but he was supposed to be planning and overseeing everything.

"Find him!" he barked into the phone, ending the call, his rage a façade for the much stronger feeling of fear. He took a few deep breaths and punched in Yuri's number.

* * *

If Danic had thought for even a moment that he might get away with leaving the room, he would have chanced it. Yuri had been yelling into the phone for several minutes now, and when the call was over, it would be his turn to take the brunt of the anger. He was being ignored for now, but that wouldn't last too much longer. The details of just what exactly had happened were still a mystery to him, but somehow the plan had failed and Dmitri had escaped. That much was abundantly obvious from what Yuri was yelling.

"So you have lost him because you hired a driver who does not know how to drive?" Every vein in his neck was standing out and his face was turning redder by the moment.

Yuri gave him a few seconds to explain before continuing his tirade. "Find him or you will repay his debt! I want him tonight! Do you understand me?"

Danic could not hear the words being spoken on the other end of the line as Yuri paused to regain his breath to make possible a fresh volley of threats and insults. But whatever they were, it was very obvious that Vasili understood perfectly, and it made further verbal assaults almost unnecessary.

"All right then. You will have him at the house by morning, and you will find out what he has done with it. I want it back tomorrow! If not, I will find someone who has no trouble handling a single, unarmed man being held on a bus with two armed guards. When I do, I will have no further need of your services." Danic blinked hard when he heard the last phrase. It would not be the first case of an employee taking an early, unplanned retirement. Working for Yuri Stepanovich had many perks, but also some very serious drawbacks.

Yuri paused again, enjoying Vasili's panicked assurances that his orders would be carried out by morning, and then he ended the call without another word. He didn't bother to listen to Vasili go on about how seriously he took the assignment. This time he tossed the phone onto the corner of his desk and turned to face out the window. The lights in the room prevented him from seeing anything in the darkness, but then Yuri was not looking at anything that could be seen. He was cursing Dmitri, Vasili, Sasha, and his team. He was also cursing himself for trusting Dmitri in the first place. That one had been allowed to rise too far and too fast. He should have been put in his place long before it had ever come to this.

"I am going to bed," he announced, and left the room without another word. Danic pocketed the phone wondering if he had been spared from the wrath of Yuri Stepanovich, or if it had simply been deferred until the next morning when it might be much stronger.

* * *

Dmitri was fuming at himself as he rode the brake pedal while backing the car down the hill. It was obvious by now that no one had been following them, that the accident at the bridge, even being on this road, had been totally unnecessary. The car should still be running and they should be many kilometers further down the road right now. If anyone was back there, they'd have caught up to them by now, but to leave the car blocking a road, even this road, would be to advertise to everyone that they were on foot and somewhere nearby.

They finally reached the bottom of the hill and looked around in the faint light offered by the moon. There was a large stand of thick bush to the right of the trail and a closer look convinced them that they could push the car far enough into it to hide it from view. Dmitri leaned in through the open window, pushing on the doorframe and steering as Michael took up station at the rear of the car. Working together they managed to push it well into the cover of the thick branches.

It was cool now, but very humid, and the exertion had left both of them covered in sweat. As Michael paused to wipe the beads of perspiration from his face, he felt the trail of dried blood on his chin and wondered where it had come from until he remembered their sudden stop on the bus and how he'd smashed into the seat ahead of him. That made him pause to wonder what had become of the other passengers. There had been two armed policemen on the bus, and two cars chasing them, most likely driven by those same two guards. Somehow Dmitri felt sure that there were more of them involved in the chase by now but surely the bus driver could not have handled all the passengers by himself. Michael sat down on the rear bumper with a heavy sigh. So two thirds of the hostages were safe at the Kiev airport. The rest were likely being picked up by the police or friendly passers-by at the scene of the accident. And that left the two of them. How had he managed to be so lucky? If he'd demanded a window seat on the plane, he might be safe in some comfortable hotel room by now, watching TV or taking a shower after enjoying a big meal. At worst he would be giving the authorities his version of what had happened.

"No rest yet," Dmitri said, his voice sounding as tired as Michael felt.

"No rest? I haven't slept in forty-eight hours, and I can't remember when I last ate. I've been hijacked, kidnapped, and bounced to death in this old crate. He punched the trunk lid to emphasize his point. And now you want to take a relaxing ten-mile hike to the nearest police station? Give me half a break at least!"

His outburst caused Dmitri to chuckle softly. "No hike, Mikhail. But we must hide car, then we rest. Or maybe we let them find us and then we have very nice long rest."

With a grumble Michael stood back up and began helping Dmitri break off branches from another nearby grove to throw over the back end and roof of the car. It was hard work snapping off green branches, he found he had to bend and twist them in every direction until they finally tore apart. But after another twenty minutes they were satisfied that the car was invisible to anyone that might pass by. At least it would be for a few days until the broken branches started to die off, but they both hoped to be far away from this spot by then.

This time Michael just plopped down on the grass, too tired to worry about keeping out of sight of the road. They hadn't seen a single vehicle since turning onto this road and he figured he could hear anything that approached in enough time to crawl safely into cover.

"Ok, I want an explanation," he demanded, glaring at Dmitri who was crouching a few feet away. "Who are you, who are the guys chasing us, and why can't you just drop me off somewhere?"

Dmitri studied him as closely as he could in the moonlight, considering what to say. Michael was just about to repeat the questions when he finally answered. "If you are who I think you are, then you already know answers to all those questions. If you're not, then you don't need to know." He shrugged indicating that his logic was flawless and that he owed Michael nothing further by way of explanation.

"Maybe it is I who should ask questions," he continued suddenly, " Who are you? Who sent you? How did you know where I was?" The way the volume of the man's voice was rising he knew they were not idle questions. They were almost threats.

"What is it you think I am? I'm a Canadian. I've never set foot in Europe until this morning! I have no idea who you are, or what's going on. I just want to get something to eat and go..." he paused in frustration, not knowing where he wanted to go. Home sounded pretty good right now. "I want to be anywhere but here."

Dmitri grunted as Michael's tirade fizzled out. "So you say."

Michael patted his pockets, but they were mostly empty, he didn't like carrying more than he had to through airport security. Finally he pulled out his wallet. Everything else, traveller's checks, passport, everything he'd left home with, was still in his bags on the plane. At least he hoped it was, maybe someone else had claimed it by now. He dug through its contents finally pulling out his driver's licence. "See," he said triumphantly, "I'm not even from this continent!"

Dmitri turned it over a few times, examining it in the light of the moon, finally shrugging and passing it back. "I have never seen Canadian licence. Maybe it is forgery."

If he'd had more strength, he might have tried to choke Dmitri out of sheer frustration. "What do you want from me? How can I prove I'm just an innocent bystander in all this?"

Now Dmitri's look and tone took on a more sinister edge. He pointed at Michael accusingly, his accent growing stronger as he became angrier. "How you know they were after me on plane and bus? Why you talk so much to me? You know because they send you! And now you lead them to me! If I let you go, you will tell them where I am!"

"Do I look like one of them? Do I talk like one of them? I have no idea who you are or who they are," Michael blurted back. He took a deep breath to control his anger, fearing what Dmitri might do to him if he pushed too hard. But then, what would happen to him if he didn't prove his point? "You were the only one on the plane besides the hijackers who knew where we were going. You told me as soon as we turned east. I saw the look in your eyes. I could tell you had a plan, you practically told me that on the bus!"

Dmitri paused, considering Michael's words, realizing there might be some truth in them, but not yet prepared to take the risk of trusting him. Then he began speaking, in Ukrainian. Michael tried in vain to recognize something, anything. But the only other language he knew was a smattering of his high school French. Dmitri continued to speak, looking intently into his eyes the whole time.

"What did you just say?"

"I just told you my story, how I got here."

"Well, tell it again, in English this time."

"You don't need to know."

"Didn't I just prove that I don't speak your language? How could I possibly be one of them?"

All that got him was another shrug from Dmitri. "It proves you do not speak Ukrainian, or that you can pretend you do not. I risk too much if I tell you. I am sorry." He didn't look or sound at all sorry to Michael.

"What about the risk to me? If those guys find us, do you think they are just going to send me home before they take care of you?" Michael's voice sputtered, searching for words that might convince Dmitri that he had nothing to fear from him. "Fine, you don't want to tell me your story. I can accept that. So just let me go. I won't say a word to anyone. Just drop me off at the next town and I'll leave this country and you'll never hear from me again."

"But you will talk to police."

"Of course I'll talk to the police. I've been hijacked, bus-jacked, and kidnapped. They're not going to let me out of this country unless I do. But I won't have to talk to those guys chasing you. I'll just tell my story to the police and get on the next flight home."

"Mikhail, you do not understand, you must be foreigner." Dmitri shook his head, searching for the words to explain. "In my country are two kinds of police. Some are honest, but some work with men chasing me. When you talk to police, wrong ones will know where they found you, and that I am nearby, and they know where to look for me. Those men on bus were real police. So were police at airport, they were paid to make sure our bus did not stop, that it takes me to where they want me to go."

He paused to make sure Michael understood what he had just said. "You will be in danger too, Mikhail. If wrong police find you, they will not believe what you say. They will find ways to make sure you tell them everything."

Michael had no answer to that. He had no desire to be where he was, but he was here anyway, and if Dmitri was telling him the truth, then it sure sounded like it was safer to stay with him, at least for the time being. The next problem was that Dmitri might be safer without him. The only solution to that problem, from Dmitri's point of view, might be to get rid of him permanently. They were stuck with each other for now, but neither one of them needed or wanted the other.

"What if I can find an honest cop?"

Dmitri laughed at the thought. "If you do, then they will know you were with me and they will want to arrest me. And then my friends will get me back. So you see, Mikhail, I cannot let you go. Not now."

"What about later?"

Dmitri answered with a nod, but did not say anything. Then he leaned over and patted Michael on the shoulder in a patronizing way. "We sleep now. You sleep in car, I sleep here." Michael started to protest that the car was too small and that he'd sleep outside too. "No," he replied sternly, "You sleep in car!" His voice softened a bit. "In morning, we find food."

Michael crawled into the car reluctantly, realizing that Dmitri wanted him in the car so he had a better chance of hearing him if he tried to sneak off in the middle of the night. But he had neither the energy nor the inclination to try anything that night. Maybe he needed to wait for an opportunity like Dmitri had. But, he admitted reluctantly to himself, not knowing the language or where to go made him dependent on Dmitri. For now. He was so exhausted that despite the cramped quarters of the passenger seat, he fell into a deep sleep almost immediately.

CHAPTER 6

Local Hospitality

It wasn't the daylight that woke Michael the next morning, or the fact that he was well-rested. It was the heat. Even in the shade of the branches the warm, moist air filled the car, making it almost unbearable. He stretched as he came slowly to full wakefulness, becoming conscious of the pain in his knee as his senses became more alert, and realized that yesterday's events had not been a bad dream after all.

"Dmitri, you there?" he asked as he cracked the door open.

"Da," came a tired reply from behind the car.

Michael felt a heavy weight in his stomach when Dmitri replied. He'd been hoping that he wouldn't be there, that he'd continued his escape in the middle of the night. But he hadn't wanted to startle Dmitri into doing anything rash so he'd asked more to announce his presence than anything else.

Climbing stiffly from the car, he looked around at his surroundings, somewhat disappointed that in the daylight it looked almost like any wooded area would have looked back in Canada. He had somehow been expecting something more foreign-looking, more exotic. Around them were several fields of different crops. Not being a farm boy, he wasn't sure what any of them were, except for a field of sunflowers growing to the left of the trail as it wound up the hill. Then his stomach growled and he remembered that he had not eaten since the snack they'd served yesterday on the plane.

Dmitri was slowly and groggily rising to his feet, also looking around, partially to size up the area but also to make sure they were not being watched. The faint buzz of insects was the only noise they could hear; everything looked and sounded just like a deserted country road should.

"So do you know where we are?"

"Da," was as much as he got in the way of a response.

"Do you know where we can get something to eat?"

"Not yet. Do you have any money?"

Michael pulled out his wallet and looked into it. "You're the host here, Dmitri, shouldn't you be paying for everything?" He pulled out all the bills he had. "Okay, I have fifty bucks Canadian, some Euro, and a wad of traveller's checks somewhere in Kiev. Unless someone made off with them after I left them in my carry-on."

"Okay, we can use Euro, I can change them to Greeven." Michael assumed that to be the local currency. "I too have some Euro, but no Greeven. Give me all your Euro."

"What is this, a hold-up?" Michael hesitated, holding the bills uncertainly in his hand.

"You are going to change money yourself, ok, then keep it." Michael could hear the exasperation in Dmitri's voice and handed over the small wad of bills without further protest, knowing full well he couldn't change them himself.

Dmitri took the bills and jammed them into his pocket. "If you told me truth, Mikhail, I will help you get to Canada again." He pronounced the name of the country with a heavy accent on the second syllable.

"What if I didn't tell the truth?" He hated to even ask the question.

In response he received a pat on the shoulder. "Then you will stay in Ukraine."

Michael was well aware that there were at least two ways to interpret that answer, but managed a weak smile in response. "Then I guess I'm going home again."

* * *

Yuri had spent the morning making phone calls and attending to matters completely unrelated to the extensive search Vasili had underway. He was aware that more of his men had been called into the search overnight, and that Vasili was widening the search area, but they had not talked since his threatening call the previous night. Both of them knew that it was Yuri's manner to make such threats and that it would not be carried out simply because the night had passed with no results. But Yuri also knew that Vasili was well aware of the fact that those threats could not be ignored indefinitely. Results would have to come soon. There was too much at stake to wait too much longer. Yuri knew that Dmitri's initial disappearance last week could be blamed on Dmitri alone. But if he were not returned, along with everything he had taken, someone would be found to pay the price. His threats to Vasili aside, he himself would have to bear the brunt of it if the search came up empty, something he was not willing to do.

Danic had long ago lost count of how many times his boss had looked at him that morning. Each time the gaze seemed to blame him for the fact that there had been no further calls.

"Shall I call him, Yuri Stepanovich?" he asked, as Yuri looked at him yet again. Inwardly he prayed that he would not be asked to make the call, but he had to do something to show that he was not the guilty one in the matter, as Yuri's withering looks seemed to imply.

Yuri gave a disgusted grunt in reply. "No. Do not call him yet. He will call when he has something to report. Which better be soon."

Danic was far too young and inexperienced to have even the slightest idea that Yuri himself was afraid. The idea that his boss had others to report and give account to had never crossed his mind. As far as he was concerned, there was no one to be feared more than Yuri Stepanovich.

* * *

"Well, Mikhail, if you are to go home, and I am to get out of country again, we need to move." He slapped Michael on the shoulder, and rose to his feet.

Michael rose stiffly to his feet as well, rubbing his knee and peeling back the loose flap in his khaki pants to examine the scab formed over the gash. Meanwhile, Dmitri was looking back and forth along the dirt trail. The bridge that had so abruptly ended their escape last night was plainly visible to the left, while to the right the trail disappeared up the hill. He pointed up the hill and muttered, "Sooda."

"What?" Michael looked up at him.

"Sorry, this way. We go this way."

They set off up the hill, with Michael limping slightly, but as he walked he found the stiffness begin to disappear a bit. "So is breakfast this way? I haven't eaten in, well, I'm not sure how long, but it's been a while."

"Yes, I think we find breakfast this way. We also find some clothes for you," he pointed to the rip in Michael's pants. Then he suddenly turned off the trail to the left and pushed his way through the low brush between the road and the field of sunflowers. He examined a few of the flowers and then broke off two of them. Returning to the trail he handed one to Michael and said, "Breakfast."

"Thanks," said Michael, looking dubiously at the flower. He'd never eaten sunflower seeds from anything other than a bag, and even then he preferred them shelled and salted. But he followed Dmitri's example and began picking the seeds from the centre of the flower. The big Ukrainian held each one up to his front teeth and seemed to be able to pop them open and suck out the seed with one swift motion. He was eating them almost as fast as he could bring his hand from the flower to his mouth.

Michael was hungry enough to eat something a whole lot worse than raw sunflower seeds, but after a few attempts to mimic Dmitri's technique, he gave up and started cracking them open with his teeth, spitting out the shell. It was a slow process but at least his stomach was getting something. Dmitri watched him in obvious amusement, but said nothing as they trudged up the hill, fighting their way through a mass of spider webs strung across the trail between the bushes and trees.

After fifteen minutes they reached the top of the hill, made their way around a large mud puddle, and found themselves back on pavement. It was a narrow road with no shoulders and more potholes than Michael would have thought possible. It was a promising sign that there might be a town or village somewhere nearby, but at the same time they knew they might be spotted by someone who might want to give them a ride to somewhere they did not want to go. For a long time they just stood there, watching and listening, but there was no sound other than the incessant buzz of flies.

Finally Dmitri turned to the left, making the choice more by instinct than by knowledge.

"Sooda, right?" Michael asked. Was it only yesterday he had been considering learning Greek? Well, he thought, might as well learn some Ukrainian.

"Yes, Mikhail, soon you will speak good Ukrainian." He looked at Michael suspiciously, but Michael was not sure if it was in jest or not.

"Well, you know what they say. When in Rome, do as

the Romans."

"In Rome?" Michael almost had to laugh, the Ukrainian looked completely perplexed.

"It's just a figure of speech, Dmitri. It means go with the flow." He could see from the look on his companion's face that his explanation hadn't helped any. "It means do what the locals do." Dmitri nodded vaguely, his mind already on other matters, but he seemed to understand at last.

It was still early in the morning, but it was already hot enough that both men were wishing that the trees alongside the road offered more shade. Neither had had anything to drink since the last beverage service on the plane the day before, so when they came to a creek that ran under the road, they both knelt down and drank greedily, then poured handfuls of water over themselves to help cool down.

They were still enjoying the cool water when they heard a car approaching from behind them, and judging from the noise it made, it was travelling very fast for a country road. They both dived into the nearby treeline and knelt down, holding their breath.

It was a late-model Mercedes, black and shiny with tinted windows. It shot past them without slowing down and they started breathing again. They had no idea if the occupants were looking for them or not, but each silently promised himself that he'd be more careful to listen for approaching cars next time. They took a final, long drink before continuing down the road, keeping an ear out for approaching cars. For the most part, they were within a few steps of the tree line, but now and then the trees thinned out and they found themselves hurrying along those stretches, craving the security offered by the trees.

An hour or so later, and after hiding from a few more cars that looked much too old to be driven by the men chasing them, they heard behind them the distinctive sounds of horse hooves on the pavement. They continued walking, but Dmitri turned just as the wagon was about to reach them and held up his hand as if trying to flag down a ride. Michael stood there self-consciously as Dmitri spoke with the old man holding the reins. Unsure as to whether he should look at the two men as they spoke, or at the scenery, he finally decided to examine his shoes. The conversation seemed to be progressing pleasantly enough, so he decided to risk looking up at Dmitri.

"Spaciba," Dmitri said to the man and then turned and said something to Michael that he didn't understand at all. But Dmitri managed to translate the phrase without speaking English by tugging on his arm, guiding him towards the rear of the wagon. Following the Ukrainian's lead he climbed into the back and settled into the load of hay that filled the wagon.

As the wagon started up again, Dmitri spoke softly to Michael, hoping that his words would be drowned out by the clop of the hooves and the creaking of the wagon. "I told him we are on our way to visit family and that we needed a ride to the next village."

"Did you ask him if he was going as far as the border?"

Dmitri actually laughed at that. "No, Mikhail, I did not think to ask him that. But at this rate it will take many days to get there. Maybe we should look for another way, yes?" Michael gave a wry smile and settled back into the soft, dusty hay. The warm sun, combined with a serious case of jet-lag, overcame his hunger and within a few minutes, he'd drifted off to sleep.

He awoke to a gentle shaking of his shoulder and a hand clamped firmly over his mouth. For a second he panicked, thinking he'd been caught, but then his vision cleared and he saw the amusement in

Dmitri's eyes. He quickly realized that Dmitri was just making sure that he didn't blurt out something in English as he woke up, but he didn't see the humour in it the way Dmitri obviously did.

"We are almost there, Mikhail. I will thank driver, you just smile and nod, ok?" Michael nodded and the hand was withdrawn from his mouth.

He sat up and looked around. Ahead of them he could see a cluster of buildings. The ones he could see, on the edge of the town, were widely separated with a scattering of outbuildings surrounding the houses. They appeared to be small farms with a number of cows and other assorted livestock dotting the fields. Most of the animals were fastened to stakes by long chains about their necks, making the lack of fencing of no consequence.

Beside the road was a small concrete structure. At one time it had been brightly painted and covered by coloured tiles, but was now faded by years of sun and snow, and many of the tiles were missing. "What's that?" he asked, pointing at it.

"That is how we get to next town, Mikhail. Is bus stop." Dmitri then turned to face the driver and called out a few words. The driver reined in the horses, who seemed relieved to have another break, and the two men slid off the back of the wagon.

"Spaciba." Dmitri called out with a wave towards the man who was already urging the horses back into motion.

"Pajoulsta." He called back without bothering to turn around, which was just fine with both of them.

They stood together, surveying the cluster of buildings that made up the village. During the ride the stiffness had returned to Michael's knee and he flexed and stretched it, trying to work out the kinks. Most of the houses were very old, though many of them had been kept up well. The ones they could see on the outskirts of the town didn't have high fences like those in the village last night, and here and there he could see people working in the small fields and gardens spotted around the landscape.

"So where's the nearest store?" Michael whispered to Dmitri. Even though no one was in earshot, he still felt speaking in English made him stand out, which was not something he wanted to do right now.

Dmitri shook his head. "No store here, I think. But it does not matter because we have no money yet."

"So where do we eat?" If he sounded like a little kid whining for food, he didn't care. The sunflower seeds had not done much to take the edge off the ache in his stomach.

"We eat where no one is."

Michael was still trying to figure out what that meant when Dmitri turned and headed for a house just to the left of the main road. He ran a few steps to catch up. "What are you going to do?"

"I don't know yet, Mikhail."

A few minutes of walking brought them to the steps of the house. As he raised his hand to knock on the door he whispered to Michael. "Say nothing, and do nothing." Since Michael had no intention of saying or doing anything anyway, he just shoved his hands in his pockets and waited to see what would happen.

A woman answered the door, opening it just a crack. She was older, wearing a scarf over her hair and a long, tattered dress. She looked suspiciously at the both of them, so Michael tried out his most innocent smile on her as Dmitri began talking. A bit of her suspicion seemed to wear off as she and Dmitri traded words, but she made no move to open the door any wider. Michael figured that living in a small village she likely did not get too many people showing up at her door that she didn't already know.

Dmitri reached into his pocket as he spoke and pulled out a few of the Euro notes. The woman curled up her lips and the suspicion that had begun to fade returned in full force. "Nyet!" she said firmly and closed the door. The two men turned and walked back to the road.

"Guess that didn't go too well, huh?"

Dmitri almost managed to hide his smile. "I was hoping that no one would be home. When she answered door, I told her we had worked for farmer and he paid us with Euro. I offer her very good exchange rate. She did not like my offer."

"But if no one was home, how could you get the money changed?" He could not quite figure out Dmitri`s logic; it may have been jet lag, or more likely the fact that he simply did not think the way Dmitri did. No answer came from the Ukrainian as he let Michael try to figure it out for himself.

Michael's eyes suddenly opened wide in understanding. "You were going to rob the place if no one was home?" The words came out in an accusing tone that crossed the language barrier between the two men.

Dmitri stopped walking and turned, glaring at him as he spoke. "Mikhail. There are men following us who will do anything to catch us. I want to get out of country. To do that we must do certain things. If you have better idea, tell me now." His anger was rising, or perhaps his frustration at their predicament. "If you have money or car we can use to get to border, you show me now. If you have better idea, tell me now. If not, we do what we must to stay alive and get out of Ukraine. What is your better idea?"

Michael didn't like what was happening, but he didn't have a better idea and Dmitri knew it. "How `bout we try another house?" His words came out weakly, mingled with a touch of fear.

Exactly the reaction Dmitri had been hoping for. He laughed and half snorted. "Now you understand."

"So who are these guys chasing you anyway? Are they KGB or something?" It would be nice to have some idea why he was about to become an accessory to a crime.

Dmitri gave a rueful laugh, and dropped his guard enough that he almost answered the question. "No. They are worse. Much worse."

* * *

Vasili had not eaten in almost as long as Michael and Dmitri, and hadn't slept at all last night either. At first he had been searching himself, chasing taillights back and forth over country roads and through villages. But as morning broke he realized that his efforts might be better spent co-ordinating the search. All he had to do was drop the name of Yuri Stepanovich and all the resources he needed were his for the asking.

The panic that had seized him when Dmitri had first fled had been replaced by careful thought. Thanks to the marvel of smart phone technology, everyone in their organization could now recognize Dmitri on sight. A vague description of the man with him was also included, though he`d had no idea who the man was until the Ukrainian media thoughtfully broadcast a story on the hijacking. A Canadian named Michael Barrett was one of only two passengers unaccounted for. The Canadian embassy in Kiev would be releasing copies of his photograph shortly, asking anyone that spotted him to offer assistance and report his presence to the local authorities.

He sat, sipping coffee, taking reports, and giving orders over his cell phone. A nearby road map was now well marked with the areas that had been searched, as well as which towns already had spotters in place. Within a few hours he hoped to have informants watching bus terminals and train stations from here to the western borders of the country. His phone also made it possible to call up train schedules to be better able to predict which routes Dmitri might try to take. Some of the spotters were his own people, but many were men, even teenagers and children, recruited by the promise of a substantial reward should either of the men be sighted.

* * *

At the next house they tried the door was opened by a teenaged boy who was wearing a t-shirt with English writing on it. Michael had to force himself to stay quiet; he almost laughed out loud as he read the misspelled words on the shirt. Even with the correct spelling, the words would have made no sense at all placed together the way they were. Unlike the woman at the first house, he was eager to make a quick profit on the favourable exchange rate that Dmitri offered him. If he suspected anything was wrong with the deal, he sure wasn't going to let that stop him from turning the quick profit a trip to a bank would make for him. So a few of the Euro notes were peeled off and a fistful of Ukrainian notes of various colours and sizes were received in exchange. Just what that cash would buy, or how far it would take them, Michael had no idea.

Dmitri walked past several more houses without trying the doors before Michael picked up on his pattern; he was selecting houses with doors not easily visible from other homes. They were circling the village and were about half way around it now. The results at each house varied from the suspicion of the first lady, to the willingness of the teenaged boy. They had used up about half of the Euros and Michael was beginning to wonder if Dmitri would have to cook up a new story when they finally reached a small, well-kept house where there was no answer after three or four knocks.

Dmitri nodded towards the road. "Stand out there. If anyone

approaches house, cough as loud as you can."

"Cough? It would be louder if I called your name. I could pretend I was calling you, you know, I could look around, shout your name out like I was looking for you."

"That will not work."

"Why not?"

"Because when you say my name, you say it with American accent. There are not many Americans here."

Michael looked vaguely insulted at the idea he had an accent. He tried saying "Dmitri" several times out loud, and could hear no difference between how he said it and how Dmitri did.

"See," Dmitri said, "You have American accent."

"It's not American, it's Canadian," he mumbled back, "Besides, you can't even say 'Michael'. " But almost before he could finish Dmitri had turned the handle and slipped into the house, leaving the door slightly ajar to better hear what was happening outside.

Michael wandered as casually as he could back to the edge of the road and leaned against a tree in the ditch. He nervously scanned the road in both directions; his heart beating wildly as he silently urged Dmitri to hurry up before someone tried to talk to him.

A few villagers passed by, giving the stranger curious, sidelong looks, but thankfully no one tried to speak to him. At any rate, he found that by the time they were close enough to speak with, most of them had broken eye contact and would not look at him. He glanced down at his watch and was surprised to see that Dmitri had only been in the house a few minutes. It already felt like hours.

A car went by, and then a motorcycle with a sidecar on it, something that Michael had never seen except in old movies and TV shows. It left a plume of blue smoke behind it that caused him to cough a few times, but he managed to stifle the noise so as not to needlessly alert Dmitri.

Finally he heard the creak of the door as Dmitri slipped out, shutting it behind him. The door made enough noise, it seemed to Michael, to attract the attention of the entire village. He managed not to look, but waited until Dmitri was standing beside him, carrying a couple of plastic shopping bags and wearing a hat. Wordlessly he handed one of the bags to Michael and they began walking back up the road in the direction they'd come from.

When they once again reached the spot where they had been dropped off earlier, Dmitri led him into a stand of trees that hid them from the view of the village. They sat down and Dmitri opened the bag he'd been carrying. Inside were two small loaves of bread, a block of cheese, and a length of sausage. Next he produced a two litre bottle of water, two glass teacups, and a small knife with which he began to divide up the spoils of his raid.

The bread was dark, heavy, and very filling. Topped with slices of cheese and sausage it was the most delicious thing Michael could ever remember eating, even if the sausage was very heavily spiced. They ate in silence, pausing only to brush away the flies that buzzed around the food, and found they were full before they had finished the bread and sausage. Dmitri wrapped the remains up in the bag for later. Neither of them got quite enough to drink, but with full bellies for the first time in over a day, they were no longer going to complain.

Michael leaned back against a tree and savoured the feeling of a full stomach and the cool of the shade. He had managed to forget how they had acquired their meal, but now that hunger was no longer a concern, other things began weighing on his mind. He had no idea where he was, where to go, or how to get there from here. He was completely at Dmitri's mercy. Then Dmitri's earlier comment came back, the one he hadn't finished when he'd stated these guys were worse than the KGB.

"Dmitri, why are these guys, whoever they are, looking for us?"

The Ukrainian finished tearing apart the long blade of grass he'd been toying with since finishing the meal and tossed the pieces aside. "Because I have something they want."

He was wise enough not to ask what it was, but thought he'd try a different angle. "So why not give it to them? Everyone's happy and we walk away."

"Is not that simple. Once they have it back, they will have no more use for me. We are safe as long as they do not have it." Dmitri studied Michael's face, seeing the unasked questions in his eyes. "You want to know what I have and where it is, you think maybe you can buy your own freedom with information?"

"No! I wasn't thinking that! But I would like to know what this is all about. I mean, my life's at stake here too. Don't I deserve to know that much?"

"Is better if you do not know." His eyes narrowed as he spoke, and Michael felt a chill pass through him as he saw once again a side of Dmitri that frightened him.

Better for you, or better for me? He wondered, but didn't dare ask just now.

Dmitri rose to his feet and stretched, then pointed at the other bag lying in the grass beside him. "For you. Put them on."

Michael had forgotten the second bag until it had been pointed out to him. Opening it he found a pair of faded black pants that looked to be about his size, a hat, and an old pair of shoes. The shoes looked much too long for him, but as he was about to say so he looked at Dmitri's shoes and noticed they too were long and pointy. Must be the local fashion trend, he figured.

Modesty demanded he step behind a nearby bush to change. He found that the pants, though a bit baggy, would do the job. He put his own shoes back in the bag and tucked them under his arm. They were a new pair he'd bought for all the walking tours he had been hoping to take. Sizing up the rip in the knee of his own pants he realized they were beyond repair and shoved them under a bush.

"Ok, Dmitri, I'm dressed like a Ukrainian. Now what?"

"Now we do what Ukrainians do, we ride bus."

CHAPTER 7

Sighting

Vasili drained his coffee cup and gave the map another long, critical look. There had still been no sign of the two fugitives, but they were somewhere on this map, he knew it. It might take time to find them, but that didn't stop him from hoping for a quick sighting. He was trying to think like Dmitri would. He doubted very much that they were still in the same car. No one had managed to get a plate number, or even the make of the car, but Dmitri had no way of knowing that and had likely ditched it even before Sasha had called to let him know about the escape. It would be difficult to get a stolen car across the border, so either they had stolen another, which wouldn't help them in the long run, or they were travelling by bus or train.

What other options did Dmitri have, he asked the network of roads and rail lines on the map? He knew for a fact that the man had no living relatives, any friends he had were part of Yuri's organization and they would think twice before trying to help him. He had dated one of Yuri's secretaries, but he'd heard she wanted to be first in line to shoot him for running off on her. No one would dare help Dmitri unless they had a death wish, because Yuri was almost certain to find out if they did. As he thought about Yuri he winced inwardly and realized that he had been keeping himself busy to avoid having to make the call which was now hours overdue. With a sigh of resignation, and a sinking feeling in the pit of his stomach, he picked up his phone and scrolled through his contacts until he found Yuri. He took a few moments to steel his nerves before pushing the button to make the call.

"Yes, Vasili, what can you tell me?" Yuri's voice was icily calm, not a good sign. The weight in Vasili's stomach got even heavier, and that weight could not be blamed on the coffee. He had also answered the call himself. That was another very bad sign. If Danic was no longer running interference for him on this line, then he was likely not taking any calls unless they had to do with Dmitri. That, in turn, meant that all of his attention and wrath could be directed at Vasili.

"Yuri Stepanovich, we believe that they have now abandoned the car and might be attempting to travel by train or bus." Well, he did believe that, didn't he? "I have men placed at bus terminals and train stations in many of the larger towns and cities watching for them. I have a name and a picture of the man who is with him so our men are watching for both of them. Even if we only find this Canadian…Michael," Vasili tried to pronounce it in English as opposed to calling him Mikhail, and almost succeeded, "I am sure we can persuade him to talk."

"I'm sure we can," Yuri agreed, subtly reminding him who was ultimately in charge. "Where do you think he is heading?"

"He will head for the West again, most likely Romania or Poland. I think it will be Romania, but we will watch both."

"What if he heads to Moldova, or south to Turkey, or even to Moscow?" Vasili grimaced at the added possibilities; he had considered them as well but didn't have enough men to cover every possibility. Besides, he was fairly confident that Dmitri would head west again. If he went that way the first time, then he must have had a reason, and what they were looking for was likely there as well.

"I had thought of that as well, Yuri Stepanovich. But Romania is closest to where we, uh, to where we lost track of him last time. It is part of the European Union so if he makes it there, it will be easier for him to get wherever else he wants to go in Europe." Even as he spoke he knew he was making things worse on himself. In trying to explain Dmitri's thinking he was talking about the possibility of another successful escape. If Dmitri made it across the border again they'd be right back where they started from. "Also, you do not have enough men to cover every possible route. I am sure that is the way he will go."

"If, Vasili Petrovich, we had a bus driver who knew how to keep his eyes on the road, and guards who could keep track of one man on one bus, then all these men you have searching for Dmitri could be doing something productive right now." Yuri's voice was still calm, but anyone who knew him well could tell when he was on the verge of losing control, and Vasili had been on the receiving end of enough of his tantrums to know that this was one of those times. "I have lost enough already. I want it back! I should have had it yesterday!

"Yes, Yuri Stepanovich," Vasili said, before realizing that he was speaking to dead air. Setting the phone back down, he reached for his coffee cup, raising it to his lips before discovering that it was empty. His hand was trembling as he set it back down and he chided himself for his fear. Usually he was the one causing fear in others, but he knew he had really messed things up this time. Or rather, circumstances and the incompetence of others had prevented him from accomplishing his goal. If he didn't get some concrete results soon there would be a lot more than empty threats and sarcasm to worry about. But even the realization of the ultimate price of his failure gave him no sense of empathy for all the others he had threatened or worse, in the past. In his whole life Vasili had never felt sorry for anyone but himself.

* * *

The two men sat silently in the scant shade offered by the concrete shelter of the bus stop. They had talked a bit at first, but when an elderly woman carrying a string of dried fish had joined them they had stopped talking. Perhaps they were being paranoid, but there was no sense in advertising the fact that there was a foreigner in the area, especially if the news might get back to the wrong people. Michael pulled the brim of his hat a little lower over his eyes.

It would be so easy back home he thought, not for the first time. Just dial 911 and his problems would be over. He didn't know what Dmitri's plan was, likely he wouldn't tell him even if he asked. Well, he'd got out of the country once before so surely he could do it again. Maybe if he could convince Dmitri that he wasn't part of the plot to catch him, he could be dropped off in Kiev and make his way to the Canadian Consulate. Did Dmitri still have his own passport? Michael hoped his was still safely with his luggage in Kiev.

A young couple joined them, glanced at the two men a bit suspiciously, nodded to the older lady, and exchanged a few words which Michael figured was some sort of greeting. Dmitri then spoke a few words to the young man who looked at his watch before giving his reply. Obviously he had been asked when the bus would come, but there was no way Dmitri could pass the answer on to him. Or so he thought. The young couple were making eyes at each other, the older lady looking on scornfully, and Dmitri used the distraction to flash all five fingers of his left hand at him, twice. Ok, he thought, ten minutes.

He leaned against the faded, worn wall of the shelter and did his best to look bored. Inwardly he was anything but, and the waiting only made his anxiety worse. He was worried about how the trip on the bus would go. He wouldn't be able to talk to Dmitri so he planned to just try to sleep, or at least pretend to sleep. If the ride were anywhere near as rough as the one the previous night that might not be too easy to pull off. He adjusted his hat again. He wasn't used to wearing one.

When three more elderly people shuffled up to the shelter, he figured it couldn't be too much longer. By his watch it was close to twenty minutes, before a rolling, grey cloud of dust announced the arrival of the bus. It arrived from a gravel-covered side road, rather than coming down the highway as he'd assumed. He had been expecting a vehicle like the one they'd boarded at the airport, which had been very much like a Greyhound bus. Instead it was a smaller white vehicle that didn't look a whole lot bigger than a full-size van.

As its brakes brought it to a smooth, if somewhat noisy, stop, Michael had unconsciously expected everyone to line up in an orderly fashion. Instead there was a bit of a scramble as they all tried to force their way through the tiny door at the same time from every direction. He stuck close to Dmitri and managed to squeeze in ahead of the fish lady, feeling somewhat guilty as he did, in order to stay right behind his companion. Dmitri spoke a few words to the driver as he handed over a couple of the bills and they filed towards the back of the bus.

Every seat was occupied so they forced themselves as far back as they could to make room for those behind them, grabbing for the overhead hand rail as the bus lurched back into motion. The heat and humidity on the bus were almost unbearable and Michael found himself standing armpit to armpit with both Dmitri and the lady ahead of him. Doing so he realized that he didn't need to worry about not having showered in two days, or was it three? He was losing track. The windows of the bus were covered with thick, purple curtains that blocked any view he might have had of the countryside. Not that he cared too much, because they were actually heading back the direction they had come from. Peering over the head of the lady ahead of him he was able to catch occasional glimpses of the road ahead, but the view was never quite good enough to allow him to prepare for the bumps and jolts the road threw at them.

After twenty minutes or so they came to a stop sign, which the driver neither completely ignored nor obeyed. The bus turned right after almost stopping, picking up more speed. Fortunately, the new road was quite a bit smoother and wider than the one they had been on. Though Michael had never suffered from motion sickness in the past he was feeling a bit uneasy now. Between the heat, the lack of sleep, the rough ride, and the inability to see out the window, he was beginning to feel a few pangs of queasiness. Not enough to panic over, but enough to make him feel very uncomfortable and wish for the end of the ride. He had no idea how long it would be.

* * *

Vasili grabbed for the phone on the first ring, but didn't answer it until he had checked his call display. When he saw it was not Yuri, he relaxed a bit.

"Yes, Sasha?" He wanted to ask if they had been found yet, but decided to show some self-control in front of his men.

"Still no sign of them, but we are talking to all the bus drivers and conductors we can. We have also shown their pictures to the cashiers at the train stations. No luck yet."

Vasili recognized that Sasha was trying to show how thorough he was being, perhaps hoping for a word of praise for his diligence. Forgetting that not that many years ago he had been doing the same thing, he barked back into the phone, "Don't call me to tell me about your failures, call me when you have some real news!" He punched the button to end the call, surprised by his own anger. Really he should be angriest at Dmitri. How could he be so foolish as to think he could get away with this ridiculous plan? As far as he knew, no one had ever succeeded at what this fool had tried. Now the burden of making sure Dmitri wouldn't be the first was squarely on his shoulders. The penalty for failing was not something he wanted to consider. But what would be the reward for succeeding? Like most men hungry for power, he didn't stop to consider that he was only doing a job where success might mean nothing more than being allowed to keep it.

* * *

Though it had seemed much longer, it was only about forty-five minutes before the bus pulled into what was obviously a much larger town than Michael had seen since leaving Kiev. He still could not see much out the front window, as several more passengers had been picked up along the way. The bus wove through the bumpy streets of the city until finally coming to a stop in front of a bus terminal where it was just one of many mismatched buses loading and unloading passengers.

Getting off was similar to getting on, but worse. Everyone seemed to think they had the right to be the first off the bus, and those lucky enough to have seats did their best to shove their way into the line of passengers already standing in the aisles. It was made worse by the fact that most of them were carrying shopping bags or suitcases.

Somehow Michael made it off the bus in one piece, grateful to breathe in a lungful of fresh air. It was still hot and muggy, but after the confines of the bus, even the faint breeze was a welcome relief.

His next concern was to make sure he didn't lose Dmitri in the crowd of passengers as several buses were loading and unloading around them. As it turned out, he didn't need to worry about that, Dmitri was more determined to keep tabs on him than the other way around. Dmitri led him across the street to a bench in front of a large, brick church with golden spires reaching up into a clear, blue sky.

Settling himself onto the bench he finally had time to look around him. If the countryside had disappointed him somewhat by not looking foreign enough, this city certainly didn't. The first thing he noticed was the number of people. They filled the sidewalks and scurried across the streets between speeding cars which seemed determined to mow them down rather than to swerve around them.

He couldn't recall ever seeing streets crowded with so many people. Most of the men were dressed more or less as they might have been back home in Canada, except for the shoes. While some wore western type sneakers, most wore long, pointy-toed shoes similar to those he had on.

The ladies, on the other hand, looked like they were vying for spots on the covers of fashion magazines. The term 'latest European fashions' came to his mind, and he couldn't help but laugh at himself when he realized this was Europe. Most of them were wearing skirts and high-heeled shoes, and even the ones that weren't had on stylish dress pants instead of jeans or sweat pants. It was almost like watching a fashion show.

Then he looked at the buildings. Some of them were smaller shops, like he might have seen in the older parts of town almost anywhere. But they were overshadowed by large apartment and commercial buildings. Most of them looked like they'd been constructed from the same set of blueprints. He had once seen a documentary on Moscow and realized that he was now seeing first-hand what he'd seen in the film. If the buildings had looked drab and imposing on TV, they were even more so in real life. He couldn't quite put his finger on why, but they looked old and somehow tired. It was as if they had lasted longer than they should have. In contrast, there were much older buildings that looked…what was the word he was searching for? They looked fresher, as if they had many more years of service left in them. A few of the communist-era buildings had broken from the mould a bit and someone had tried to add some artistic touches here and there. Somehow, rather than improving them, those little flares only served to emphasize the drabness of the rest of the building.

His eyes searched back and forth. There was so much to look at that it took him a few minutes to realize that he could not read any of the signs. They were all in Ukrainian. It was not just a matter of not recognizing the words, he couldn't even make sense of the alphabet and had no idea what was sold in most of the shops and stores. He'd already experienced a bit of that in Kiev, and on the road the previous evening, but now he was immersed in it. Everywhere people were walking around reading and understanding those signs without even thinking about it. He couldn't tell a drug store from a clothing store. This was definitely more than foreign and exotic enough for him. He felt more alone than he'd ever felt in his life.

"We should find something to drink, Mikhail." Dmitri's words, spoken barely above a whisper, broke his thoughts and he realized he was parched. "You wait here, I will be right back."

Dmitri walked over to a small kiosk a few steps away and returned with several bottles. He was startled to recognize, and be able to read, the bottle of Coke. He took it and quickly drained the entire contents of the cold, sweet liquid. He could never remember it tasting so good. In fact, it seemed to taste better than it did back home.

Next, he was handed a two litre bottle of water. It was ice cold and he quickly cracked the lid and began gulping it down. "I didn't know if you like gas or no gas, most Americans seem to like no gas."

Michael didn't bother to correct him this time, but stopped drinking to look at him with a puzzled expression. "Gas?" he asked. Dmitri held up his own bottle, which was bubbling slightly. "Oh, you mean carbonated water. Never tried it. I like it without gas, thanks."

They rested a few more minutes on the bench, sipping at their water bottles until Dmitri screwed the cap back on his bottle, and Michael did likewise. "We see if we can find train. This way."

Before Michael had a chance to ask where they were heading Dmitri rose, turned to his left, and began making his way along the crowed sidewalk with Michael in tow. He didn't dare strike up a conversation with so many people walking alongside them, so he fumed silently to himself hoping for a chance to ask what Dmitri's plan was.

As they rounded a corner, Michael spotted a long, low building that was much older than most of the others he'd already seen. It was so ornate that his pace slowed as he looked it over, his eyes sweeping over the turrets and cornice work. He'd never seen such an ornate building, except in pictures. It might not be a piece of ancient Greek architecture, but it had once been a beautiful building. Even today, faded and slightly run down, it was impressive. It was the city's train station, and hopefully a quick way to the nearest border.

In Ukraine, almost everyone seems to have a cell phone, or a mobile phone, as Europeans call them. At least half the people they passed seemed to be either talking or texting. So it was no wonder that in that crowd of people and phones they did not notice a young man carefully look them over as they passed by. When he fell into step behind them he was just one more person in the crowd, and even if they had turned to look at him he was just one more person talking into a mobile phone.

* * *

With a sigh, Vasili answered the incoming call. No doubt it was another useless report from someone wanting to earn a few points by appearing as if they were accomplishing something special by merely obeying their orders. He recognized the number when it came up on call display. "Da, Vadim?"

"We have found them!"

He sat bolt upright, knocking over his coffee cup, hardly daring to trust his ears after the night's frantic but fruitless search. "What? You are sure?"

"Yes, someone we hired to watch a train station saw them going inside. He has their pictures on his phone. They are buying tickets as we speak."

"Do you have more men in place, or just the one?"

"Just the one, we are spread pretty thin. I can have more men there in less than thirty minutes. If they get on the train before that, he will either get on with them, or let us know which train they are on."

"Good." He punched the end button without even a thank you and began mopping up the spilled coffee. Should he call Yuri now or when they had him, he wondered? Best to wait, he decided, if they did get on the train they might not get them for a few stops down the line, which might take a few hours. No sense in making the man even more impatient than he already was. He would call when he could say that he had them both.

* * *

Michael kept one eye on Dmitri, following him through the crowds inside the station so as not to lose him. Was there anywhere in this country that wasn't crowded, he wondered? At the same time he tried to take in the faded glory of the station. The high ceiling, combined with the thick stone walls, kept the temperature relatively cool despite the number of people crowded into it. The hardwood floor was a work of art, even though it was worn from years of hard use. The woodwork around the cashier's wickets, and even the wooden benches and seats themselves, were of a quality of craftsmanship that simply couldn't be found anymore. Back home this place might have been turned into a museum, but here it was still in daily use.

Among the dozen or so wickets, Dmitri singled out the one he needed and joined the throng of people clustered around it. Rather than forming a line, people simply crowded around the counter, turning the process of buying a ticket into a competition. At least it seemed that way to Michael. How the cashier knew who to serve next, or if she did know, he couldn't tell. Eventually Dmitri managed to gain the girl's attention and purchased two tickets. They worked their way back through the crowd and outside, having to search for a while till they found a place far enough from the crowd to talk without being overheard.

"Where are we going?" Michael demanded, before Dmitri could say anything.

"I bought ticket on train heading the right way, but we will not stay on it very long."

"What? Why are you buying tickets to somewhere we aren't going?"

"Because from here all trains across border go to big cities. Is more likely we will be spotted. We will take train to get away from this region, then get off, then find another train to town near Romanian border."

"Can't we get a train all the way to Romania?"

"Of course we can, and when border guards ask for your passport you say sorry you lost it. But they let you go into country because they like you so much, yes?"

"Or you let me go back to Kiev, I go to the Canadian embassy, and they give me back my passport, or get me a new one. Then I fly home."

"I told you, I cannot do that, is too much risk." Dmitri shook his head to emphasize his point, and this time almost seemed genuinely sorry. "Many people will be watching for us, both of us. And if wrong people find you, you will tell them where I am. You are my, how you say? You are my insurance."

"Dmitri, I won't tell them, I promise."

"You will tell them, Mikhail. They will make sure you do." Dmitri looked him straight in the eye, and Michael could see that Dmitri didn't have a doubt in the world that Michael would tell them everything he knew. Despite the warm sunshine on his back he felt a sudden chill and an involuntary shiver ran up his spine.

"Ok. So I'll stay with you. But what is your plan?"

"I think maybe is best for us to go to Romania. It is member of European Union. Once there is easy to cross other borders. Problem is to get out of Ukraine."

"And how do we do that? If those guys chasing you have the police in their pockets, then what about the border guards?"

"Border guards have our pictures. Most likely when we try to leave Ukraine they will invite us inside for tea. And before we finish tea, my friends will come to visit us too."

"So how do we cross the border then?"

"During communist times many soldiers patrolled the border all the time."

"Why?" Michael interrupted, "I thought Romania was communist too, wasn't it?"

"But it was not part of Soviet Union," Dmitri explained, "So they patrol border to make sure no one could escape to Romania, and then go to Europe. Today, there is still fence there, but is not guarded so closely. If we can get to border, is easy to get to Romania without worrying about border guards. In Bucharest they have Canadian embassy, or maybe American. You talk to them, they send you home."

"Ok, so all we have to do is take a couple of train rides past all these guys looking for you. Then we cross the border illegally without getting caught, make our way to Bucharest and we're free?" There was a heavy note of sarcasm in his voice, but if Dmitri recognized it he didn't acknowledge it.

"Yes, easy." He waved the tickets at Michael. "Our train arrives in few minutes, we should go."

Michael could see nine or ten sets of tracks behind the station, but had no idea how to get to the platforms until Dmitri led him down a flight of steps and into a tunnel. Scores of passengers, arriving and departing, were jostling back and forth in the dark, damp tunnel under the tracks. The walls were lined with vendors, many of them older ladies selling almost anything a traveller could want. Their wares included magazines, ice-cream, bottled drinks, and even dried fish which made him glad they still had some bread and sausage. The odour of the fish seemed to overpower everything else and he almost had to hold his breath as they made their way through the tunnel entrance. Why did the one cool place in this town have to smell so bad?

Regularly spaced staircases ran up and to their right, each one labelled with a track number. At least they use the same numbers we do, thought Michael. At track number five Dmitri turned and headed up the stairs. They were made of poured concrete and were well worn by the hundreds of thousands of passengers who had gone this way before them. They were not quite evenly spaced and despite his best efforts, half way up he missed a step, tumbling forward and almost knocking Dmitri over.

"Sorry!" He blurted out, from force of habit. Dmitri turned and shot him a look that scared him back into silence. A few of the nearby passengers looked curiously at him upon hearing his English and he heard several voices use the word 'Angleeskee.' For a few gut-wrenching moments he thought he had blown their cover, but no one stopped or tried to question him. All he'd done was to raise some curiosity about why some English speaker might be in this part of Ukraine. He had no way of knowing that their cover had been blown long before he'd said anything out loud.

Rising into the bright sunshine he had to blink hard several times after the darkness of the tunnel. There was no train at their platform yet, though several tracks over a string of blue passenger cars with yellow striping was just beginning to pull away from its platform. He didn't have a clue which way their train would come from or go, so he just watched Dmitri and did his best to fade into the crowd.

Dmitri's eyes were sweeping over the crowd, hoping to pick out anyone else that might be trying to fade into it. In his mind there was no question that they were being looked for, and though Yuri's resources were vast they weren't infinite. There was no way they could cover every possible route out of the country even though Yuri most definitely knew he would be trying to get out again.

It was like some massive game of chance. Yuri's problem was that he could not watch everywhere. Dmitri's problem was that Yuri was watching a lot of places. Yuri's men had the advantage of knowing what he looked like and perhaps what Michael looked like as well. He knew some of Yuri's men, but not all of them, and if he did spot a familiar face, it would almost certainly be too late.

So he scanned the crowd constantly. So far he had not recognized anyone, but there were hundreds of faces out there, not all of them clearly visible to him. He began watching eyes. Who was looking at him? After five minutes or so he began to hope he was just being paranoid. But just when he was beginning to think he could relax, a pair of eyes turned away too quickly when he looked at them.

His gaze froze on the young man. Then he allowed his gaze to drift a few faces over to one side. Then he looked quickly back at the young man who again averted his eyes. Not a lot of eye contact was made in Ukraine between strangers, so why was this young man looking at him?

This time he kept his gaze on the man, who was now pretending to watch a pretty girl making her way through the crowd. That might be perfectly natural for a young man to do, Dmitri allowed, but something about the way he watched the girl was forced and unnatural. It was as if he were not so much looking at the girl, but rather not looking at Dmitri. Then his eyes flicked up towards Dmitri, saw the tall muscular man looking at him and immediately looked away again, this time with an uncomfortable, almost guilty look on his face.

Turning to face away from both the young man and Michael, Dmitri spoke just loud enough for Michael to hear. "We do not want to be on this train, Mikhail."

"Why not?" Michael whispered back.

"Because is too crowded. Go back to tunnel, slowly, I will be right behind you."

The two men turned and headed back into the darkness of the stairwell with Michael in the lead. Most of the passengers were already on the platform so the stairs were all but deserted.

"When you get to landing, stop, turn around, and tie your shoe."

By this time Michael suspected what was going on. He could feel his heart pounding in his chest. His first inclination was to start running, but he forced himself to slow down and as he reached the landing he turned around, putting one foot a step above the other and bent over to tie his shoelace. Dmitri stopped several steps above him, leaning against the wall to give him a clear look back up the steps.

"Young man, maybe twenty. Brown hair, blue jeans and green t-shirt. He is holding cell phone. You see him?"

Michael tried to look up the stairs without raising his head, not wanting to look like he was looking. It wouldn't have mattered anyway. Anyone looking down into the tunnel from the bright sunshine could not have made out anything more than shadows in the dimly lit stairwell. But it was a good thought for someone that usually didn't do this sort of thing.

"No, there's no one there. Yes! I see him. He started to come down the stairs but stopped. Now he's texting or making a call or something."

"Head back towards station, but walk, don't run."

Michael tried to swallow, but his mouth was too dry. His heart was pounding so hard he was sure that it could be seen hammering through his shirt, but still he forced himself to walk at a leisurely pace along the tunnel. He ignored the old ladies who were no doubt offering him the best deals in all of Ukraine. Was the man alone? Did he have a gun?

Suddenly Dmitri's hand grabbed him and pulled him into another of the stair wells. Several of the vendors looked at them curiously as they huddled against the wall to stay out of view of the man
following along behind them. But after concluding that they were
nothing but two more crazy men passing through the station that
day, and there was nothing unusual about that, they turned their
attention back to those that might be more interested in making a
purchase from them.

Behind them they could hear the soft tread of the young man's
footsteps. Unknown to them, he was in a mild state of panic himself. He'd been mentally spending the reward he'd been promised,
but had unwittingly given himself away somehow. His prey was nowhere to be seen. He quickened his pace hoping to spot them again
before they disappeared into the crowd at the station, so he was not
prepared for the hand that suddenly shot out and clipped him in the
side of the head.

He went down hard, letting out a sharp cry of pain. Dmitri
grabbed the cell phone from his hand, gave the man a kick in the
side that sent him sprawling backwards, and sprinted for the exit.
Michael was a few seconds slower, stunned by Dmitri's sudden, vi-
olent action, but not concerned enough to stay behind to check on
his victim.

They shot out of the tunnel and into the parking lot. Once again
they were in a crowd and Dmitri hesitated for a few seconds. He
didn't know the town and wasn't sure which way to go. He had no
doubt that he could handle the young man whose cell phone he
now had. He could handle him permanently, if necessary. But was
he alone, or were there others? It didn't take long for his question
to be answered.

Behind them the young man hobbled out of the tunnel, looking around desperately. He wanted to find both the men and his precious cell phone. As he searched the crowd, a black Mercedes pulled into the far end of the parking lot and four men jumped out. Everyone in the crowd, including Michael and Dmitri, turned to stare because a car like that was not exactly a common sight at the station. One of the men was punching buttons on a cell phone and a few seconds later the phone in Dmitri's hand began wailing out a loud heavy metal song.

The young man from the platform heard his phone and quickly picked out his two subjects in the crowd. He had a score to settle now, a stolen phone, a bruised cheek, and possibly a fractured rib or two. He let out a loud yell as he pointed out Michael and Dmitri.

Everyone in the crowd was staring at him, wondering what he was yelling about. Then they turned to the direction he was pointing. The men from the Mercedes finally figured out what the man was screaming about and began shoving their way roughly through the crowd. Dmitri quickly answered and hung up the phone, buying them a few precious seconds as the music ceased, making them harder to find in the flow of pedestrians. A street ran through a tunnel under the tracks and offered them the best way to get out of sight in a hurry. Michael saw Dmitri drop their bag of food and water and head for the tunnel. For just a fraction of a second he thought he should pick up the dropped bag, then thought better of it and sprinted after him. Behind them was death, or something even worse, and despite all he'd been through he found the strength and stamina to catch up with Dmitri, following him to somewhere they'd be safe. He hoped.

CHAPTER 8

Dead End

There was something completely unbelievable about the fact that he was running for his life. There was no way this could possibly be happening to him!

But it was happening.

If it were just a dream then his legs wouldn't be working, he would be trying to run and he wouldn't be able to.

But they were working.

He could feel his lungs struggling to draw in enough air, and the beginning of the burning sensation that came from running too far too fast. Five men he'd never seen before were after him and would beat him, or worse, if they caught him, though he still had no idea why.

They raced along the road and through the narrow tunnel, even though there was a sign prohibiting pedestrians from using it. Not that they were the only people in the tunnel, but it was barely wide enough for two cars so most of the foot traffic was crowded against the walls to make room for the traffic. Their mad flight through the tunnel set off a chain reaction of blaring horns and shouts of protest as both cars and people swerved to miss them.

They burst out the far end into the middle of an outdoor market. Michael had a fleeting glimpse of rows and rows of small blue booths with crowds of people wandering among them. Dmitri headed for the crowd hoping that they could get lost in it. Darting between two rows of booths he broke trail for Michael, forcing people to scatter, dropping bags and parcels as they made way for the two fleeing men.

Angry shouts from behind told them that their pursuers were still on their trail and Dmitri began weaving back and forth amongst the maze of booths, not staying in any one row long before changing directions. It didn't matter which way they went, Michael knew, as long as it was away from the men chasing them. But what if they had split up? Were they going to bump into one of them around the next corner? He hadn't had a good enough look at any of them to recognize them if he did.

After a few more twists and turns they burst out into the open. Not where they wanted to be, Michael knew, but Dmitri kept going and he had no choice but to follow. Sprinting across the street they ducked between two buildings and found themselves in a courtyard surrounded on every side by old, brick apartment buildings. In the middle was a small playground filled with aging but brightly-painted equipment. It was full of kids and moms on this hot, summer afternoon, all of whom helped to provide cover as they turned and headed through the park.

They hurdled a low fence and wove through the mass of kids, strollers, and playground equipment. There had been no shouting from behind them since they had left the market and Michael was beginning to hope they'd lost their pursuers. Just as they were about to round the corner of one of the apartments he caught a glimpse of a man sprinting through the park and knew they'd been spotted just seconds before disappearing from sight.

"There's one right behind us." He gasped breathlessly to Dmitri, who didn't bother to answer.

Somehow Michael was finding the strength to keep running, but he wasn't sure how much longer that would last. Hopefully long enough. He was glad he didn't have to decide where to go next. He was just following Dmitri's lead as he was already lost himself.

Thankfully the next corner brought them into yet another court-yard with several streets branching off in numerous directions. Dmitri chose one and they managed to get around the building and out of sight before they could see anyone behind them.

But the street Dmitri had chosen ended when it came to the next cross street, which ran uninterrupted to their left and right as far as they could see. There were no other intersecting streets close enough to hide in, no way they could get out of sight before their pursuers showed up. For a few seconds he thought Dmitri might back track, but it was already too late for that. Then the Ukrainian spotted his opportunity.

Veering across the street, he leapt across the sidewalk and launched himself into one of several dumpsters lined up along the street.

Michael was winded from their run and didn't quite have the stamina of the slightly older man. He was only a few steps behind, but as he tried to jump in behind him he caught his shin on the metal lip of the container. He managed not to shout in pain, letting out a stifled grunt instead as Dmitri grabbed him by one arm and hauled him the rest of the way in.

The smell was so strong he started to gag and tried to hold his breath, but the desire to avoid the stench finally lost out to his need for oxygen. He was sure the loud gasps he was making as he tried to draw air into his burning lungs could be heard blocks away. Dmitri glared at him with his finger to his lips, warning him to be quiet. He was already being as quiet as he could but all efforts to slow and quiet his breathing were futile.

Seconds later they could hear the noise of running feet and from across the street they could clearly make out the voices of two men. Though he could not understand their words it was obvious they were arguing about which way they should look next. Fortunately it had not occurred to the hunters that the game might have stopped running and were now hidden somewhere. When they'd last seen their prey, they'd been running flat out and they assumed they still were.

From what they could hear, it sounded like the two men finally went in opposite directions. Likely, Michael thought, their little group had divided each time they'd lost sight of them. He wasn't sure if it was better to have one group of five looking for them, or five men each looking in a different place. Although, come to think of it, Dmitri had dispatched that kid without even trying. Somehow he had little doubt he could have got rid of him permanently had he really been serious. Maybe one at a time was the best way to meet these guys after all.

"Ah!" A disgusted grunt came from Dmitri. He quickly pulled the phone from his pocket and fumbled with a few buttons before figuring out how to turn it off. They looked at each other, wide-eyed in fear as they realized that if anyone had thought to call the phone any earlier it would have given away their hiding place.

"Does that thing have GPS?" Michael asked, his breath not quite back to normal. "Can they use it to find us?"

"I don't know." Dmitri said in frustration, after studying it for a few seconds. Nothing he could see on the outside could tell him that, but he continued to study it anyway. The way he held it made it appear as if he was afraid the device would bite him.

"Better leave it off for now. I'm not sure if they can use it to find us, but we can try to figure that out later."

"It's off now!" He could hear the irritation in his voice, but wasn't sure if it was directed at him, or if Dmitri was still upset with himself for having left it turned on. "But maybe we can use it to keep track of them too."

Neither of them had anything else to say so they simply sat and waited, not daring to look out into the street until they were sure it was safe. But how long will that be, Michael wondered, and how would they know?

*   *   *

"Idiots!" Vasili roared into the phone. "You let them get away because some idiot you hired can't figure out how to watch someone without giving himself away? And then four of you can't find them? "

There was no response from the other end. He waited a few moments to let his words, and what they implied, sink in. "Find them!"

He set his phone down, but needed a further vent for his frustration, so he grabbed his empty cup and launched it across the room, finding brief satisfaction as it shattered against the wall. The only good thing about the whole mess was that he had not yet called Yuri. Maybe he could turn this to his advantage. With a grim smile he picked up the phone.

He didn't recognize the voice on the other end, but when he said who he was he was handed over to Yuri immediately.

"Yuri Stepanovich, I have some good news to report."

"It is about time," was the clipped reply.

"They have been sighted. A young man we hired to keep an eye on things in a town…"

"So you have them?" Yuri interrupted impatiently.

"No, not yet. Unfortunately he was not able to get help before he lost them in the crowd. They were near a train station but did not board a train. They headed into town. We have more men there now, and more on the way. We will continue to search for them and we have both the train station and the bus terminal under surveillance."

Not one word of which was a lie, he thought to himself with satisfaction.

"Good. Thank you for updating me. Let me know when you have them."

If he didn't know better, he'd almost have thought Yuri really did feel thankful. Maybe he was getting soft in his old age. No, not Yuri. That one would never soften.

*   *   *

It unnerved Michael to sit in the dumpster and listen to conversations that he could not understand, and the sound of the odd car driving by caused him to shrink further into the piles of garbage. What if their pursuers were patrolling the place where they'd lost track of them? His watch told him they'd been sitting there for the last forty-five minutes. Unfortunately, he had still not become used to the smell. Or perhaps it was fortunate; he hated to think he'd ever get used to a stench like this one. While there were a few garbage bags in the mix, most of what filled the bin was just loose garbage.

Without any more warning than an approaching set of footsteps, a load of fresh garbage sailed over the rim of the container and landed between them. With a start they jumped in opposite directions, both crying out in pain as Michael bashed his elbow, and Dmitri his head, against the dented metal sides.

A stream of surprised and frightened sounding words echoed their cries and the face of an older man peered over the edge. He looked back and forth at the two men and Michael understood the tone of the message if not the words. He was definitely angry and was giving them each a good tongue-lashing, no doubt fuelled by the scare they had given him.

Dmitri said a few whispered words back to him, which surprised him, Michael saw from his reaction. He stepped out of view for a moment and then peered in again. He was shaking his head as he spoke but all Michael could understand was the word "Nyet."

Looking rather sheepishly at Michael, Dmitri motioned for him to get out and they clambered over the side and back down onto the street. They received a few curious looks and smirks from the small crowd that gathered as they brushed off damp, smelly left-overs, and the other assorted bits of even less pleasant garbage clinging to them. This would be a great place to open a business selling garbage bags door-to-door, Michael thought.

Dmitri spoke to the man as they cleaned themselves off, laughing and pointing to Michael as he spoke. At first the man smiled knowingly at Michael, then began to chuckle, and finally to laugh.

Not having a clue what was being said he still knew that the joke was on him. What he didn't know was that the look on his face only made Dmitri's tale all the more believable. He glared sharply at Dmitri, trying to make him stop talking. But the old man noticed the look in his eyes and that only made him laugh harder.

With a last loud laugh he winked at Michael, patting him on the back with a look of humorous sympathy, and then turned and walked back towards his apartment. Along the way he spoke briefly to a crowd of his friends who, staring at Michael, also began to laugh.

"What was that all about?" He asked, glaring at Dmitri.

"I could not tell him we were being chased and went in there to hide," Dmitri replied looking as sincere as could be. "If I did, he might call police."

"Even if he knew we were running from bad guys? Why would he do that?"

In response he first got a shrug, then an explanation. "In communist times, if you did not report when something was wrong, then you were arrested for knowing and not telling. For many people, especially old ones, they still think that way, so they report everything."

"So what did you tell him?" Michael's eyes narrowed accusingly, knowing he was not going to like the answer.

"First I ask if he sees black Mercedes or any strange men on street." Michael continued to glare at him.

Dmitri then smiled innocently. "I tell him we go out drinking last night and not come home till this morning. Then your wife gets very mad because you come home drunk and she chases us out of house with broom. So we hide from her until it is safe for you to go home again." He gave a helpless gesture, "It was only thing I can think of."

"What about the strange men and the Mercedes?" Michael was not appreciating the humor at all.

"Your wife's brothers look for you too."

"Fine." Michael replied sharply. "But next time it is your wife with the broom!"

"Mikhail that story will not work. I do not have wife." The smirk on his face showed just how sound his logic was.

"So what do you do now?"

"We must get out of town. We cannot go by train, or by bus, they will be watching. We must find another way." He motioned for Michael to follow him and led him down the street and then through a narrow passage he discovered between two small stores. The passage brought them into an alcove behind the buildings. Dmitri fished the cell phone out of his pocket before squatting down.

After turning it on, he began going through the options on the phone menu, searching for the GPS locator function. Whoever owned the phone didn't want anyone to be able to find him as it was already turned off. Then he began searching through the files on the phone, starting with the pictures, still talking to Michael.

"Is best if we wait until after dark so there is less chance we are seen. There may be many more men here looking for us by now."

Michael's frustration, which had been simmering for some time, once more reached the boiling point. He barely managed to keep his voice down as he stood over Dmitri. "I want to know who these guys are! Why are they after you?"

Dmitri didn't look up from the phone, infuriating Michael even further. Then he turned the screen of the phone so that Michael could see it. "They are not just after me, Mikhail."

"What?" He felt as if he'd been kicked in the stomach. Snatching the phone from Dmitri's hand he looked closer, not believing what he was seeing. "How did they get this?" Here he was hiding out in some back alley in the middle of a country he couldn't have even found on a map yesterday morning, yet there on some stranger's cell phone was his own passport photo.

"They have ways of getting what they need."

"Why do they need me?" He wanted nothing more than to smash the phone to pieces on the ground, as if it would bring an end to this whole mess.

"Because you are with me," Dmitri admitted with a touch of guilt in his eyes. "Mikhail, I believe you now. They would not need your picture if you were with them."

"Well a fat lot of good that does me now!"

"I could not risk believing you yesterday." It was almost an apology, but came out as little more than an explanation.

Sensing what he wanted to do with the phone, Dmitri reached for it, gingerly removing it from his grip. "Maybe there is more information on here we can use," he said as he took it. Michael stared around the alcove in silence as Dmitri flipped through more pictures. Several were of him, not surprisingly, but the rest were meaningless to him, friends and family of the owner no doubt. He tried the email folder.

"I want some straight answers Dmitri. Who are these guys and what do they want?"

Dmitri opened his mouth to answer but the back door of the store opened and a woman wearing a uniform and a nametag stepped out with a pack of cigarettes and a lighter in her hand. She looked startled to see two strange men in her break area, but quickly recovered and began scolding them in a loud, harsh voice for being in her space. It may not have been private property, but she sure seemed to think it was.

Wordlessly Dmitri rose to his feet and the two men walked back to the street. They both felt completely exposed there, so they headed for the nearest side street. Both sides were lined with houses, all of them with tall fences made of brick or metal. They could easily have been seen from a long ways off in either direction. For a few moments Dmitri hesitated, then continued down the street, speaking softly.

"There is text message that says you are my assistant. So they think if they find you, they find me. Or they get what they want from you. Mikhail, they will not believe you if you tell them you do not know anything."

Several people were working in their yards, and even on the street. Repairs were being done to fences and gates, two ladies were sweeping the stretches of the street in front of their yards. All those people made conversation difficult and risky, and Michael was finding it hard to keep his voice under control. The words came out in a low hiss. "Who are they? What do they want?"

The tall Ukrainian looked around to make sure no one was within earshot. "They are Mafia."

"What? Mafia?" The only Mafia he'd ever heard about were the Italian variety, all the gangsters in Chicago and New York he'd watched in movies and read about in books. Those men at the bus station, and the ones on the plane sure didn't look or sound Italian. "They come here from Italy?"

That almost gave Dmitri something to smile about, but not quite. "No, Mikhail, is Ukrainian Mafia. But maybe very much like Italian Mafia."

"So why are they after you? Did you testify against them or something?"

They came to an intersection and took the road to the right. As they rounded the corner, they saw it led up a small hill, through a gate, and out of the town into a heavily wooded area. It looked like a perfect place to hide out for a few hours. Dmitri didn't speak again until they had passed through the gate. The area was so overgrown that Michael did not realize they were in a cemetery until they were sitting down in the grass.

Behind and among the uncontrolled growth of the trees and bushes were small fences surrounding graves covered by wilted and dying flowers. Most of the markers were simple metal crosses painted silver, and many of them showed patches of rust where the paint had long since chipped or peeled off. Some were made of stone and even had etchings of the person interred there. He didn't like cemeteries at the best of times, and the pictures and the unkempt look of the place made him feel even more uncomfortable. It was as if the dead were looking at him and asking him how soon he planned to join them.

He tore his gaze from them and faced his companion. "So what gives, Dmitri? Why are they after you?"

"Because I have something they want."

"Yeah, you told me that already." Then he realized just what Dmitri was saying. "Are you crazy? You stole from the Mafia?"

"Mikhail, I was Mafia."

* * *

Yuri was trying in vain to tend to the scores of irritating little duties that required his attention. In all his years of making his way up through the ranks, he'd never fully appreciated that the higher he rose the more responsibility he would carry. He had been hungry for the money and the power, and also for the respect. Now, as he was approaching his goal, he had come to realize the headaches that came with the privileges. Right now, he had a very big headache, and he could blame it all on that ungrateful traitor, Dmitri.

With a disgusted grunt he shoved his chair away from the desk and leaned back, rubbing his eyes and staring out the window into the distance. He could make up the losses Dmitri had cost him. The fact that it would cost him out of his own pocket would hurt, and it would take time to make good those losses. But the betrayal was what would really cost him.

Most dangerous would be the loss of respect of those below him. Dmitri had been one of his most trusted lieutenants. He was an up-and-comer in the organization, feared and respected by those below him and trusted by those above. Yuri had been the one to see his potential and groom him, but he'd obviously brought him too far and too fast.

Not quite so dangerous, but in the long run perhaps worse, was how it would make him look to his peers and those above him. Not everything that Dmitri had taken was Yuri's, it had simply been passing through his hands, and as a result, he now had debts to others. It was not the first time something like this had been tried, though it had never happened on this scale. Again, he could make up those losses, but it would cost him a lot of respect among his peers and his superiors. Until a few days ago he had thought that he could go higher. Much higher. Now, thanks to the actions of Dmitri that opportunity could be gone. Or at least delayed for several years. He had to find him and prove to everyone that it was not possible to treat Yuri Stepanovich like this and get away with it. He would pay back every kopek. And then he would keep paying.

The phone rang and he picked it up, seeing Vasili's number on the call display as he'd expected. He'd excused Danic from office duty for a few days. For one thing, he was needed in the search, for another, he didn't want anyone around right now.

"Yes Vasili? What excuses are you giving me now?" He smiled in satisfaction as he heard the awkward silence at the other end of the phone. If it was going to be bad news he could at least make someone else feel miserable. Vasili had originally tracked Dmitri down and organized his return to Ukraine, which admittedly had not been an easy task. Yet amazingly he'd failed in what should have been the easiest part of the whole job. He would pay as well, just how much and in what manner Yuri had not yet decided.

Vasili felt the verbal sting, tried to ignore it, but found he needed to swallow the anger he felt before he dared to speak. His plan had worked. Well, it would have worked if not for one random, unforeseeable accident.

"We are sure they have not left town. We have men watching the buses, trains and taxis. They could not have left by any of those means."

"And what if they find other means?"

"If they walk, they will not get far. We are watching other nearby towns. I will find them, Yuri Stepanovich, if it is the last thing I do I will find them."

"I hope so Vasili. I hope so."

As the line went dead, Vasili could not help but wonder: Does he hope I catch Dmitri? Or does he hope that it is the last thing I do?

*   *   *

Michael sat in silence for a long time, contemplating what Dmitri had confessed to him. It made sense. He should have figured it out himself and he supposed that on some level he had suspected it. But now it was out in the open and he had to face the fact that he had been aiding, and was being aided by, a criminal. He studied Dmitri's face as he stared off into the distance. Just what was he seeing or remembering? All the past crimes he'd committed? What had he done? The Mafia back in North America were known for a wide range of horrific and spectacular crimes, at least those were the ones that made the news and were used in TV shows and movies. How much of those sorts of things had Dmitri participated in?

More to the point, why had he left? And above all, what had he taken? It might be information, he thought, lists of names to be turned over to the police in exchange for a reward or immunity. Or something tangible perhaps, drugs? money? Whatever it was, they wanted it back badly enough to hijack a plane, and Michael's safety and perhaps even his life were at risk. Since that was the case, he decided that Dmitri owed him the truth.

"You said you were Mafia. You're not anymore?"

Dmitri shook his head, but did not look at him. He was still lost in thought.

"Why did you leave?"

He made a face as if he were disgusted with something, or someone. He was considering the question Michael could see, and as he did so he picked a small twig off the ground, studying it intently. He began slowly breaking off pieces and tossing them into the grass in front of him.

"Better question is, why did I start?" Michael could see the anguish in his face and wisely chose to let him speak in his own time.

A few more segments of the twig joined the other pieces in the grass before he spoke again. He stopped snapping off pieces, holding an end in each hand instead, twisting it back and forth as he began speaking.

"Mikhail, I grew up in small village. My father went to Moscow because there was no work here, and my mother had to go to city every day to work. So every day after school I am alone. Many children like that in my village." The twig finally broke in two. He tossed one of the pieces aside, twirling the other half in his fingers as he continued.

"Yes, many children like that in my village. But me, I did not want to be boy from village. So, I go to city after school every day."

Michael could guess what was coming next.

"But going to city takes money. So I steal it. From my mother, my teacher, from other children. Then I think, why just steal money to buy things? Why not steal things also. Some I steal and keep some for myself, some I sell to other children. Then one day, some-one sees me steal and he catches me."

"That didn't scare you enough to make you stop stealing?"

A bitter laugh was Dmitri's first answer to the question. When he began speaking again, his accent began to get heavier as he began thinking about the past rather than concentrating on his English. "No, Mikhail, it did not scare me. Man who catch me is thief too. He tells me I am good thief and he will pay me to steal things for him.

So I stop going to school because I have job. Soon I am working for Mafia, and they teach me many things about how to make money. Lots of money. I give some to my mother, but she knows I get money in bad way, that I not do right, so she say I must leave home."

Michael just sat and listened, not knowing what to say. The sun was going down behind a hill to the west and long shadows were beginning to fall across the two men. The drop in temperature, the growing darkness, and the graves hidden in the shadows of the trees all lent a sombre, sinister edge to Dmitri's story. Michael shivered.

"After that, I become member of Mafia."

Michael cleared his throat uncomfortably, sensing that there was more Dmitri wanted to say. "What did you do for them?"

"At first, just simple things. Then I become," he hesitated looking for the right word. "I become, muscle?" Michael looked puzzled for a few moments, then realized what he was being told and nodded that he understood. "I go to people and ask for money. If they not give, I make trouble for them. They pay for protection, they pay money for loans they take to keep business going."

Michael kept nodding as he listened. He'd never been involved in anything illegal, or even known anyone who was. He shivered again, painfully aware of the fact that he had to trust this man to somehow get him back to safety, wherever that might be. Could he go to jail for being associated with Dmitri, he wondered? It wasn't like he had gone willingly or known who he was, but would that matter to the police?

"So you...I mean, that's what you did?"

"For a long time, yes. Then I was put in charge of others. I was very good at what I did. I make a lot of money in many different ways." It was not something that he looked happy about at that moment.

"Why did you leave?" He was dying to ask Dmitri what it was he had taken from them, but though he had his suspicions, he couldn't quite bring himself to ask that just yet.

"Mikhail, I cannot do this anymore." Dmitri looked him in the eye for the first time since they had started speaking, and he could see that the man was remembering something very painful. "I had to leave. I cannot do these things anymore. I cannot live with myself!"

A wave of relief washed over Michael as he heard the words from Dmitri. There was obvious and real sorrow and regret in them, even if they were slightly obscured by the accent. So he was not a member of the Mafia anymore; he was trying to go straight. Somehow that made things a lot more comfortable.

Dmitri peered into the gathering darkness, as if trying to decide if it was sufficient to conceal them. Satisfied that it would offer enough cover, he rose to his feet. "Come, Mikhail. We need to find way out of country."

CHAPTER 9

Roadblocks

The sun had completely set by the time they made it back to the edge of town, and once again, Michael was struck by the lack of streetlights and the complete darkness in the streets. Only the odd light from the window of a few apartment houses disturbed the darkness. Had it not been for the light of an almost full moon rising in the East, it would have been very difficult to stay on the narrow road leading from the cemetery back into town. The two men walked together in silence, Dmitri having nothing else to say and Michael feeling too awkward to ask any more questions.

When they reached the edge of the town, Dmitri paused, looking both ways. In neither direction could they see any evidence of other roads running into the town.

"There will be others looking for us by now. Maybe is best we do not go into town. We will find another road."

They turned to their right and began making their way through the field of grass running behind the row of houses on the outskirts of the town. He had been expecting a nice, smooth, meadow-like field, but at his first step his right foot sank to the ankle in the loose soil, and then his left foot caught a small, hard pile of dirt. "Ouch!" he cried out, much too loudly, as he lost his balance.

He hit the ground with a hard thud, almost winding himself, but felt Dmitri's hand grip his arm and help him back to his feet. He dusted himself off, more from force of habit than because he could see any dirt in the dim light. Dmitri chuckled a bit, but said nothing about his outburst. "Walk more carefully, Mikhail."

Michael grunted in reply, but was more careful to feel his way across the field as they resumed their trek. It slowed their pace somewhat, but was much less painful.

Ten minutes of walking brought them to a tree line separating two fields. They found a pathway through the thicket, skirted a small pond, and emerged into another field. In the distance, through another tree line, they could just make out the headlights of the occasional vehicle flickering through the trees, and knew they had found one of the main roads out of town. With the train and bus stations no doubt under surveillance that road might be their safest route out of town. Once they made it to the highway, they could hitch a ride in the back of a truck or on another wagon. A car would be more comfortable and they could even offer the driver a little gas money to sweeten the deal. Anything would beat walking. If they didn't get out of these fields soon, Michael was sure he'd sprain an ankle.

* * *

Despite his assurances to Yuri, Vasili knew that it was very unlikely that the two men he was searching for would try to get out of town by any means of public transportation. He knew that Dmitri was too smart for that. He tried not to consider the fact that if it were anyone other than Dmitri they were looking for then it would be Dmitri himself who would be leading the search. The defection of that traitor had given him the opportunity to move one rung up on the ladder. This was his chance to prove himself to Yuri and he was not going to fail, but it meant he was tasked with finding one of the best hunters in their organization.

He leaned over the map, trying to think like Dmitri might. "How are you going to get back to the West, Dmitri Ivanovich," he asked aloud. That trains and buses were not an option seemed obvious, as Dmitri had come too close to being caught the first time to risk it again. But just as obvious was the fact that he had to watch the stations anyway. Walking would take too long and they would be spotted along the roadside even if they did try.

"So what are you going to do, Dmitri?" He sat up again, trying to figure out the how before he concerned himself with the where. Time was on his side, Vasili knew. The longer it takes for them to get to a border, the greater the chance they would be found. Watching buses and trains would work well to slow him down, but it would also force him to find another way. It was his job to figure out what that other way would be and make sure it didn't succeed.

His contacts in the police force had turned up the report of the car that had been stolen at the scene of the near miss with the farm wagon. Unconsciously, Vasili shook his head in disgust at that thought. All his hard work in planning the hijacking, the money for the bus and driver, not to mention the police at the airport; all of it wasted because of that idiot driver and a chance encounter with a form of transportation that should have been banned from the highways years ago.

The car had not been found, but the two men were less than an hour's drive from where they'd first escaped from the bus. For whatever reason, they had not gone far with it. Where it was and why they'd abandoned it were not his concern, only the fact that as of a few hours ago, they were on foot again. He'd already checked for reports of stolen cars in the town they were now in, and there were none. Unless they planned to walk hundreds of kilometers to the border they needed another form of transportation. Hitchhiking? Not the most dependable, he thought, but perhaps a safer alternative than some of their other options. It was worth pursuing.

He flipped through his notes until he found the one with the right number on it. It was for the chief of police in the town his men were now scouring. Punching in the number he picked up the map, smiling to himself as he saw that there were only a few roads leading from it.

"Vasili," he announced to the voice that answered the phone. "The men we are looking for may try to catch a ride out of town. If they were heading to the Romanian border, which routes might they take?" He studied that map as he listened to the man who'd spent a good portion of his working life on those roads, circling junctions and intersections as they were suggested.

"Very well, place men at all those locations. If they turn up, I want you to hold them until I can pick them up personally. You are not to turn them over to anyone else. Do you understand?"

A tentative objection was raised on the other end because of the number of men he would need to cover all the locations. Vasili understood that the man's resources were somewhat limited, but he also knew how much this man relied upon the ongoing compensation he received from Yuri's organization to maintain his lifestyle. So did the chief, which was why his objection was rather tentative.

Vasili's voice was low and even, but with an underlying edge of harshness as he replied, "You are being paid enough to supply the men you need for this job. If you cannot do as we request, we will find someone who can. Or perhaps you would like to discuss this personally with Yuri Stepanovich?"

A grim smile spread across his lips as the man made suitable apologies and promises. It did not occur to Vasli that he was treating this man the same way Yuri was treating him, he just knew he needed results and expected obedience from those he saw as beneath him.

As soon as his order was acknowledged, he punched the end button. This could work out well for both of them, he knew. Not only might they locate Dmitri and this Canadian, but the officers could make a little extra pocket money by collecting fines from the drivers they stopped. Most of it would never make it into the official records.

* * *

Yuri Stepanovich hung up the phone, thankful for the fact that no one else had been in the room during the call. He needed those around him looking up to him, showing him respect. If they didn't, then his control over them would be lost. Never could he show any weakness or humility around them. But he'd shown plenty of both of those traits speaking on the phone just now with his own superiors. Though he could not see it, his face was crimson from embarrassment, and not a little fear. Over and over again he had promised results in the ongoing search for Dmitri. He had tried to smooth the waters somewhat by explaining that if nothing else the traitor had been found and forced back onto Ukrainian soil, that he had been spotted, and that so far he had not managed to get very far.

Not that it had done much good. They were anxious to recoup their losses and were already calculating the interest due. He brought his fist down on his desk, the loud bang startling his secretary in the next room. His outburst had done nothing but fuel his anger. He had been required to grovel in front of these men, promising to make up their losses with his own funds. They would be repaid shortly, even if Dmitri was not found right away, he had assured them. Then whatever was recovered when Dmitri was found would be his. If there were any shortfalls, he would have to bear them himself.

He could repay them, he knew. It would not be too difficult, but it would leave him unable to complete a few other deals which could have turned some large profits. Dmitri owed him a lot more than what had been taken and it would all be repaid, he vowed, even if not all of it was in hard currency.

He picked up the phone to begin making the necessary arrangements, just in case, but then decided to make another call first. He had been disgraced in front of men he had to deal with almost daily, and someone would have to bear the brunt of his anger. He punched in Vasili's number.

*   *   *

Michael had managed to navigate the remainder of the second field without anything more serious than a few trips and stumbles over the invisible lumps and ruts the absolute darkness hid from his view. The worst had only caused him to stumble a bit, so that nothing but his feet had made contact with the ground. The tree line was narrow and easy to pass through, but they did not step out of it completely. For several minutes, they remained in its cover, the shadows of the trees helping to hide them from view.

Traffic was very light, with a few more vehicles heading into town than out of it. The first vehicle they saw coming from the town was a motorcycle, which would not do them much good. Then a couple of transport trucks rolled past, a possibility they both knew, but Michael wasn't sure if trucks here had the same rules as those back home about picking up hitchhikers. He'd just watch Dmitri and follow his lead. Right now he seemed hesitant, and Michael didn't have to ask why. Some of those vehicles might carry the very men looking for them. Their options were limited and the risks were high.

In the somewhat cooler air of the evening, sound carried further, and they could hear the noise of another vehicle approaching from out of town even before its headlights came into view from around the bend. Then, from the direction of the town, came the sound of a loud chime followed by a female voice. It had to be coming from some kind of loudspeaker and she was delivering a message in a steady, even voice which was devoid of any emotion. That much was clear, even if the words were foreign.

"What's she saying?" Michael whispered to Dmitri, wondering if perhaps there was a city-wide announcement being made to be on the lookout for two fugitives, one of them a foreigner. Did they do that kind of thing in communist countries? Was this still a communist country?

"It is announcement from train station. Train is about to depart." A few minutes later, they heard the shrill blast of the engine's horn and the low throb of the diesel as it laboured to overcome the momentum of the cars and start them on their journey.

Michael remembered a quote from somewhere about it being nice to hear the whistle of a train even if you weren't going anywhere. At this moment, he really couldn't relate to that thought. "I sure wish we were on it. I don't know where it's going, but I wish we were on it."

Dmitri nodded, the motion barely visible in the darkness of the trees. "We would be safe if we were on it," he agreed. "Problem is getting on it." He paused suddenly, as if something had occurred to him. Then he began laughing. "I am not thinking like village boy anymore, I think too much like man from city now."

"What do you mean?"

"You are from city or village, Mikhail?"

"The city, why?"

"So where do you go to get on train?"

"We don't ride trains back home. We mostly drive our cars everywhere."

Dmitri seemed genuinely surprised by that. "Then that is why you don't think of it either."

"Think of what?" He couldn't keep a bit of irritation from creeping into his voice, he was getting tired of this game. "How do we get on a train if it's not at a station? Jump on it as it rolls past?"

"No, Mikhail. In city you buy your ticket and board train at station, yes?" Michael didn't answer, waiting impatiently for Dmitri to continue. "But in some small towns and villages, they not have stations, or maybe train does not go into town. So they have places, platforms, where you can board train when it comes. No station, no one watching. If no one else is on platform, we board there!"

"Ok, I'll take your word for it. Where do we find one?"

"We follow train tracks to next small village. There should be one not far from this town."

"Ok, I'll follow you."

Ahead of them, across several more fields, they could hear the sound of the train gathering speed. Dmitri looked both ways down the highway. Hearing and seeing nothing, they stepped into the ditch, clambered up onto the road, and sprinted across to the other ditch. Wary after his stumbles in the field, Michael gingerly felt his way down the slight embankment and into the shelter of the trees.

Squinting into the darkness he found he could see nothing but the vague forms of the trees separating this field from the next, but somewhere up ahead were the train tracks. Michael was not sure just how far he could trust a member of the Mafia in most areas. Well, an ex-member of the Mafia. Dmitri had caused this whole mess, and had singled him out to get him in even deeper. But he could be certain that he didn't wish to be caught and returned to his former companions. So if he felt this was the best way to put some distance between them and their pursuers, he'd go along. But just how far could he trust the man? If he'd known from the start who and what this man was, he might have tried to escape from him sooner. Why hadn't he just minded his own business on the plane? He'd be headed back home, or maybe even to Greece by now.

His thoughts were interrupted by a sudden sound from behind them. Both men turned to see two police cars racing down the highway from the direction of the town, lights flashing and sirens wailing their strange-sounding cry. Well, it was strange sounding to him, Michael thought. Like those sirens he'd heard in the movies set in Europe. That thought made him remember just how far from home and how alone he was, and how real the danger was.

"Where are they going in such a hurry?"

"Maybe they go to bus accident. Maybe bus ran into wagon full of hay." His voice was a perfect deadpan, which only made Michael laugh harder.

Without another thought towards the police cars, which were rushing to establish roadblocks at two important junctions, they turned back to the direction from which they had heard the train. They could no longer hear it, but somewhere up ahead of them lay the tracks. Michael was starting to get the hang of walking over the uneven surface of the field; he just had to stop assuming that the ground would be smooth and even, testing with each step until he could trust his footing.

A light of some sort would have been helpful. A flashlight, even the light from the screen of the cell phone they'd acquired, would make it a lot easier to walk, but he wasn't sure how that might look to any curious town folk. He'd found his spirits raised a bit when Dmitri had first suggested a way to get onto the train but now that hope was waning a bit with the drudgery of slugging his way through the fields. He had no idea how much further it was. He was hungry and thirsty again, and even the exertion of walking could not quite warm him enough to fend off the chill of the evening.

The field eventually brought them to another road, this one obviously a secondary one with little traffic. It was easily crossed with no one observing their passage, and then it was back into another field.

It was then that they heard the noise that encouraged both of them, the whistle of an approaching train. They could almost feel the rumble of the diesel as it headed into town. A moment later they caught the flicker of the engine's light through the trees at the far end of the field. They were almost there.

Their pace was not quickened at all. They were both too tired for that, and the rough terrain would not allow it in the darkness. But their steps were a little lighter now and a few more minutes brought them through the thin belt of trees and within sight of the tracks.

There were two sets of tracks running between twin rows of trees, just like the ones he'd seen from the air. Was that really only yesterday? The train ran on an elevated berm with wide ditches on either side. The light from the moon illuminated the scene and he could make out small garden plots in the ditches.

"So where's this platform, Dmitri?"

"I don't know." His companion pointed up the track, away from the town. "It will be up there somewhere, near the next village."

"The next village? You don't know how far it is?" The disappointment was obvious in his voice. Somehow he'd thought that once they'd made it to the tracks, it would be a matter of simply waiting for the next train.

"Mikhail! They cannot have trains stopping every kilometer along the track. Some trains do not even stop at smaller villages, only big towns. We will find the next platform and wait until train stops." Not up to forming a reply Michael simply fell into step with

Dmitri, following the tracks away from the town.

Walking in the ditch was not much easier than walking in the field had been, so before long they made their way up the embankment and began walking between the rails where the going was much easier.

They walked along in silence for a while, until it felt almost awkward. Questions about Dmitri's past were spinning around in Michael's mind. There was so much he wanted to know about the man's history. Several times he almost started to ask, but he couldn't quite get up the nerve.

A steadily growing rumbling from behind warned them that a train was coming, and though it was not on the track they were walking on, they stepped off to the side. Even though trains passed each other all the time on these tracks, both of them were a bit leery of having something of that size and speed passing so close to them. Even standing in the ditch it was somewhat frightening, the noise almost deafening as the engine roared past, followed by the noise of the wheels clacking over the rail joints.

It was a freight train consisting mostly of tanker cars. They looked somewhat smaller than the ones Michael was used to seeing, though more than large enough to be frightening when seen rushing past so close. He couldn't help but wonder how often trains derailed, as the ground shook and rumbled beneath him.

When the train finally passed and they made their way back up onto the track, the night seemed even quieter than it had before. Without realizing it, Michael took in a deep breath and let it out with a long, loud sigh.

"What is it, Mikhail?" Dmitri asked, having a pretty good idea what it might be even as he asked. He still wasn't sure how much he should tell this man. He would hardly admit it, even to himself, but he did feel somewhat guilty about getting the Canadian involved in all of this. True, he had been suspicious about how much he seemed to know, and had hoped to pump him for information about what Yuri was planning. But he had not thought through how it might end, or how he'd get rid of him once he'd learned everything the man knew. He shook his head at how different things were now. A year ago, such matters would not have concerned him in the least.

The question caught Michael off-guard. "Um. Well, just wondering how much farther we have to walk. I'm kinda tired, you know?"

"I do not know this region well, but I do not think it will be too far. Villages are sometimes very close to each other. But if it is far, we do not have other choice, do we?"

"No." Michael kicked himself mentally, wondering if that had been his opportunity to ask what he really wanted to ask.

Dmitri stopped abruptly and turned to face his companion. "What is really bothering you?"

Michael let out another loud breath, sounding almost exasperated. "Look, I want to know what I'm into here. You're ex-Mafia. You left because you couldn't take being a thug, I get that, ok? But why are they chasing you?" His voice was rising and becoming more forceful as he vented not only his questions, but his frustration and fear. "What did you take from them?"

Dmitri paused for a long moment before replying. "Maybe it is safer for you if you don't know. Have you thought of that?" He had himself almost convinced of the truth of that statement, but down deep he knew it was much too late for that kind of logic.

"Why? So I can't tell them anything when they ask me?" He spat the words out bitterly. "They might not believe me and try to force it out of me. Have you considered that?"

Another rumble began coming towards them, this time from

the direction they were heading, and so they stepped down into the ditch again. They watched as a passenger train sped by them heading into the town from which they had just departed, the noise making any conversation impossible. Michael thought that its timing was very convenient for Dmitri, giving him a chance to avoid the question or change the topic, so when the train finally passed, he just stood in the ditch, refusing to move until he got his answer.

This time it was Dmitri's turn to sigh, knowing the time had come to tell him everything. Well, at least more than he had revealed so far.

"You are right, Mikhail. They would not believe you, so is best we do not get caught, yes?"

Michael nodded his silent agreement, still waiting for some answers.

"I decided a few months ago that I must leave. But I cannot just leave and find new job, it does not work that way with Mafia. I needed to leave Ukraine." He paused, a faraway expression on his face as if recalling how he'd come to the decision, and how much thought and anguish had gone into it.

Michael could sympathize in a way, even with no family to leave behind, leaving your country would not be an easy thing to do. But he couldn't give the guy a break now that he was talking, so he simply nodded in understanding and said nothing.

"I need money to start new life, yes?" He sounded like he was trying to convince himself, but Michael could understand his reasoning, knowing that what he was about to hear was what he'd come to suspect. "So I wait until I hear of large sum of money being transferred within our organization and I intercept it. I did not wish to steal from anyone else, Mikhail, but I needed money to get away. To start new life. I hired computer expert and we divert money to new account. I gave him some for his help. Now, they want it back."

"How much did you take?"

"Fifteen million dollars."

"Fifteen million dollars?" Michael just stood there in disbelief. He'd expected a few hundred thousand, maybe a million or so, but fifteen million? It was beyond anything he could even imagine.

Dmitri grinned sheepishly and shrugged. "It was all together in one place. Why leave any behind?"

Michael knew it was always wrong to steal, even from thieves, but he wasn't sure he could get that point across to Dmitri. Even if he could, hadn't he made use of a stolen car to get away from the bus crash? He searched for something to say, but in the end all he could come up with was, "Well, no wonder they want you back so bad." It wasn't until he spoke the words that it struck him that it also gave them a lot of reasons to want Dmitri's Canadian accomplice as well.

* * *

Both the roadblocks and the search of the town had so far proven fruitless, and Vasili had to finally admit to himself what he had feared since the report of the near miss at the train station. They must have found some way out of town. They had not managed to get far from the scene of their initial escape from the bus, and if they were trying to get to the West, they had so far been going in the wrong direction. But that was likely just to get on a train, and the one they had been trying to board had been going in the right direction.

The more he thought about it the more certain he was right about where they were trying to go. That had been Dmitri's initial escape route, Western Europe. He might be a very smart man but his assets, and therefore his options, were limited. He didn't likely have much in the way of cash with him. Given time and money, a more elaborate route through Moscow or Turkey might work, but he needed out of Ukraine, and he needed out fast.

Why could that fool of an informant not have stood behind them, or just avoided looking at them? They were about to board the train; there was no need to give himself away so foolishly. But, most of these men were hired because they needed money and liked to act tough. They weren't paid for sophisticated thinking. They weren't capable of it.

Being forced to sit and plan was still new to him. He was sure that given the chance, he could track them down quicker than the fools out there could. But if he was to prove himself a good lieutenant, he'd have to stay and oversee things from this office. He picked up a map of the region and studied it for the hundredth time. "Now, where are you going, Dmitri Ivanovich, and how do you plan to get there?"

He knew that his opponent was not known for making a lot of mistakes. He was not necessarily an overly-cautious man, but he took only calculated risks. That was one reason he'd risen so high in the ranks as quickly as he had. He saw and anticipated problems and obstacles before others could see them, and planned for and around them. He needed to think like Dmitri would, or he needed Dmitri to make a mistake in his desperation. Or, he needed a lucky break. He deserved one.

CHAPTER 10

Train Spotting

It had taken them several more hours of trudging along the tracks before they finally came to one of the platforms that Dmitri had been hoping to find. Heartbreakingly, at least for Michael, several passenger trains had passed them while they were walking, two of which had been travelling in the direction they wanted to go. Even after it was again explained to him that not all trains stopped at every station, that some were 'through trains' and only stopped at larger centres, he still was not very happy that they might have missed an opportunity to board one of them.

He wasn't sure exactly what he'd been expecting of the platform, but was surprised to see a simple, open platform with no seats, just standing room. It offered no protection from the elements at all, not even the wind. It was nothing more than an elevated concrete slab set at the approximate height of the train cars to make boarding as easy as possible. A set of stairs sat at one end and led to a well-worn path that ran parallel to the tracks for a while before disappearing into the trees. Presumably a village lay somewhere in the darkness behind them.

Michael and Dmitri had been leaning against the railing since mounting the stairs about half an hour earlier. While their pace had not been brisk, they'd been moving enough to keep warm. It also helped that they'd been at ground level and sheltered from the cool evening breeze by the trees. Now, standing motionless and slightly elevated, it felt much cooler. With no jacket, only the shirt that Dmitri had scavenged earlier in the village, there was not much he could do to warm up.

Dmitri turned to look at him, as Michael let out a soft grunt and slid down to sit on the concrete, his back against the guardrail. He knew better than to ask again when the next train would be along since he'd already been told several times that it would be here when it arrived. Dmitri didn't seem to put much stock in the train schedules, and didn't know them, at any rate.

"I'm bagged, Okay if I take a nap?"

"Bagged?" Dmitri asked with a puzzled tone.

"Tired. I'm tired. I'm beyond tired; more like exhausted."

The tall Ukrainian sat down beside him. "Me too. I think we both sleep for a while."

"What if the train comes and we're both sleeping? Won't they just keep going?"

"No." Dmitri let out a tired sigh as he stretched his legs out a bit. "They make all stops according to schedule. We will hear it when it comes." Too tired to reply, Michael closed his eyes and dozed off almost immediately.

"What?" He shouted loudly, arms flailing he grabbed the first thing he could find, which turned out to be Dmitri's arm. The other man jumped to his feet, knocking him off balance. The platform was shaking, and a sudden burst of wind felt like it was blowing him off the platform. It took both men a few seconds to realize that they'd been startled from deep sleep into sudden wakefulness by a passing freight train.

Michael's heart rate slowly returned to normal. He had no clue what had shattered his sleep until the train had almost passed. Dmitri scanned the darkness around them. His senses had gone into overload when he'd been startled into wakefulness, certain that Yuri's men had found them. It took him much longer to calm his nerves and find sleep again.

* * *

It was well past midnight when Vasili's phone rang. It startled him from an unplanned sleep and it took a few moments for him to realize where he was and what the noise was. He shook a few cobwebs from his head and picked up the phone, feeling a tightening in his chest as he recognized the number. At this time of night, it would not likely be Danic. In fact it seemed like ages since he'd last talked to Yuri through his aid.

He cleared his throat, steadied his nerves, and did his best to sound awake and alert. "Da?"

"I know you have not yet succeeded in finding your missing friend." A swell of anger rose in Vasili's chest at the reference to Dmitri as his friend, as if somehow Yuri himself had no association with the man at all. It was, after all, not his fault. Yuri had known Dmitri much longer than he had, and had been the one to promote him. His seething pride wanted to inform his boss that if he had been the one put into that position, instead of Dmitri, there would not have been any need of a search in the first place. As tempting as it was, it would not be a wise thing to do.

"No, we have not, Yuri Stepanovich. Not yet, but we will."

Yuri brushed aside his reassurance and confidence. "Before I go to bed I want to know what you are doing besides sending my men on useless searches all over the country."

It took all the self-control he had not to snap back. Yuri had wanted to cover more routes than Vasili thought necessary, and now he had the nerve to complain about the number of men he was using! A deep breath before he replied may have saved him from more than he realized.

"It is quite possible that they are no longer in town. I have arranged roadblocks and searches along the roads, so if they are going by car, we will find them. I have also arranged for some of the men in town to board the trains heading west. That way, if they have made it onto a train, or try to board a train somewhere else, we should spot them."

"Keep me updated. I want a call tomorrow morning at ten."

"Yes, Yuri Stepanovich." He was about to add that he hoped to be able to report that he had them by that time, but thought better of it, best to avoid potential trouble by not over-promising. The line was dead anyway.

He rubbed his eyes, stared at the ceiling and decided against another cup of coffee. He'd sleep for a while again. They were out there somewhere, with limited resources, and he had an ever-growing number of eyes searching for them. They faced the challenge of getting across the border with no passports and no one to help them, so it was only a matter of time.

* * *

Several more trains had wakened them from their sleep, including a passenger train heading their way. But none of them even slowed down as they passed by the platform, leaving Michael to wonder if any of them ever would.

When yet another rumble was heard in the distance, he didn't bother to leave his eyes open. But then the sound of squealing brakes caught his attention and he opened them again to see the lights of an engine as it approached them, quite obviously decelerating.

Dmitri was already on his feet as Michael rose unsteadily to his, using the guardrail to haul himself upright. His left foot was asleep and the rest of him wasn't too far behind it. He stretched a few times, trying to rouse his body to the point he felt he could trust himself to walk.

A self-satisfied I-told-you-so smile was on Dmitri's face.

"What about tickets?" Michael wondered belatedly.

"We can buy them from conductor." He laughed softly, "Or we can ride with no tickets."

"How do you do that? Hide in the baggage car?"

"Many people ride without tickets. Sometimes they climb in window. Sometimes you just tell conductor you do not have ticket. They cannot throw you off train while it is moving. They argue with you, tell you to buy ticket, but they cannot do much. So some people do not bother to buy them."

For someone who'd always followed the rules, and was not used to the way things were 'sometimes' done, it was not something he wanted to attempt. "But we've got money for tickets, right?"

Dmitri could tell from the tone of his voice that he was not asking a question, but that didn't stop him from laughing as he answered. "Yes, Mikhail, we have money for tickets. If we do not buy them, they will not sell us drinks or food."

The mention of food and drink helped him to wake up fully. Exhaustion was taking its toll on his body, and they'd lost the food they'd appropriated in the village earlier this morning. Make that yesterday, he corrected himself. Even if train food was like airline food, he was hungry enough to eat anything.

The train took ages to come to a complete stop, and then the doors to several cars opened up. A few bleary-eyed passengers, some carrying bags or small suitcases, stumbled off the cars and onto the platform. The cool night air seemed to waken them somewhat as they shuffled off to head for home and bed.

Michael followed Dmitri wordlessly to the door of one of the nearby cars, pausing as the Ukrainian exchanged a few words with the conductor. Or perhaps he should say the conductress, it was a young lady who didn't even look like she was out of her teens. Yet she somehow carried an air of self-importance and authority that came from the fact that she had a uniform and they didn't. She spoke a few harsh-sounding words to Dmitri and himself, which he pretended to understand, and then the two men stepped into the car.

Inside the lights were shining brightly, causing them to blink at the sudden contrast with the darkened platform. A centre aisle divided two banks of seats, most of them arranged in pairs on either side of a small table. A luggage rack ran down each side, much too high to reach while standing on the floor. Not that it mattered to them as they'd lost what little luggage they had. At either end of the train, a television blared loudly. The show appeared to be a Ukrainian sitcom, as evidenced by a laugh track that sounded just as artificial in Ukrainian as it did in English.

The car was less than half full so they had no trouble finding seats that were out of earshot of anyone else, though Michael could not help but notice that no one seemed to pay them any attention anyway. Back home, he was sure, there would be more than a few curious glances at the new passengers, but the most they seemed to get were a few sidelong glances. Maybe everyone else was just as sleepy as they were.

The seat was comfortable enough, he decided, and he found that he could even recline it a bit. That would make sleep a little easier once he'd had something to eat. The odour wasn't as bad as it had been on the bus but he was still assaulted by the aroma of unwashed bodies and fish. Fortunately he was hungry enough that it didn't force him to lose his appetite. He didn't think he'd ever get used to smells that strong, but wished somehow he could. Maybe he'd dream about fish once he fell asleep.

"Once we start moving, I will get us some tea and something to eat," Dmitri whispered quietly.

Just as he spoke, the car gave a soft lurch, quickly followed by a more solid-feeling jerk as the slack between their car and the next was taken up, and then they were accelerating smoothly along the track. Back home he'd ridden some old tourist steam trains, but rather than the rhythmic click-clack sound they had made, he heard and felt a double thunk as the wheels rolled over the joints in the track. He recalled a friend once telling him that in Russia they did not stagger the joints in the train tracks like they did in North America, that instead they were side by side. At the time he didn't really understand or appreciate what that meant, but he did now. The short rides he'd taken in the past had been rhythmic and soothing; this one was irritating, at least until the train had built up enough speed to make it less noticeable.

A few minutes later, once they'd reached top speed, the conductor approached their seats and she and Dmitri spoke at length before he reached into his pocket and pulled out a few brightly coloured bills. He peeled off a few and handed them to her before she disappeared behind them.

"She will bring us something soon. This train does not go as far as I'd hoped, but it will get us further from those men that are chasing us."

"Good," Michael replied sleepily. Now that he was relaxed and warm he was no longer sure that he could stay awake much longer. Watching the TV show helped a bit and gave him something to think about. He almost thought he had some idea of what the plot line might be. Even without being able to understand the dialogue, he could tell that it was about as predictable as anything back home.

As they waited for the conductor to return with their order, Michael divided his attention between the show and the other passengers. Some of them were sleeping, a few were talking amongst themselves, and a few were getting up and heading to what he decided was the lavatory. A few more were making their way back and forth to other cars. Dmitri was lost in thought and staring out the window into the darkness, so only Michael saw a man in his mid-thirties passing through their car from the front of the train. To him it was not odd the way the man made eye contact with him. Nor was it odd that he was holding a cell phone. Had he been Ukrainian himself, he might have recognized the brief eye contact for what it was.

* * *

The ringing phone once again startled Vasili from a restless sleep. Even after blinking several times he still could not recognize the number. In his sleep-deprived state, it did not at first occur to him that this fact likely meant good news.

"Da?" His voice was heavy with sleep.

"Vasili? This is Igor."

Vasili racked his brain but could not remember who the man was. But it did not matter anyway. Only what he had to report was important. "What is it, Igor?"

"I have found them. They are on a train only a few kilometres from where they were last seen. They just boarded the train at a village west of town."

Vasili sat bolt upright, fully awake now. "You are sure it is them?"

"I can see them from where I am sitting right now, but only the backs of their heads. I did get a good look at them when I entered the car though. Yes, it is definitely them. Dmitri and the Canadian. I have their pictures on my phone. It is them." He too was already spending the reward money in his imagination.

"Where are they going?"

"I do not know, but I will talk to the conductor and see what I can learn."

"Let me know as soon as you find out. I will see if I can get some help for you. Yuri Stepanovich will not be happy if they escape again." The implied message was that he would not be either, but Yuri's name carried more clout.

"Yes sir." He was somewhat displeased that there had not been a thank-you, or even any real acknowledgement of his accomplishment, just a rather thinly-veiled threat. No matter, he reassured himself. He had them and the only real thank-you he needed was the reward money.

He heard a noise behind him and turned to see the conductor coming up the aisle with two cups of tea. He waved to her as she approached, holding a large bill in his hand to ensure he got her full attention.

The conductor paused as she recognized the note, her demeanour becoming suddenly very polite. "Yes sir? What do you need?"

"Your cooperation," his stern look did as much to hold her attention as the money had done to catch it. He folded the bill in half and slipped it into her jacket pocket. "Say nothing to anyone, but I need to know where those two men are getting off the train."

* * *

It is often the case that the more tired you are, the harder it is to fall asleep. A hot cup of tea and a light snack had taken the edge off the discomfort in his stomach, but the sleep Michael sought would not come. The show on the TV must have been running on some kind of loop because after the second episode finished the first one started playing again. He noticed his companion was half-watching the show, but also watching the passengers around them. Once or twice he laughed along with the laugh track, and Michael wished he could ask him for a translation; more to see if he really was following the plot than because he had any interest in it.

Dmitri leaned over to him, speaking softly, just above a whisper. "I go to use toilet now." He slipped past Michael's seat and into the aisle, stretching as he rose, and using the motion as an excuse to get a good look around the car. No one seemed to pay him any attention, which was a very good thing. Then he walked to the back of the car and into the toilet.

Michael wasn't sure if he'd gone there to get a better look around the car or out of necessity, but decided that it wasn't a bad idea. He waited until the door opened and Dmitri stepped out to make his way to the back, swaying slightly with the motion of the car and having to use his hands on the backs of the seats to steady himself along the way.

"Whew!" he said out loud as he opened the door, and then looked nervously to see if anyone had noticed. Apparently they either hadn't heard, or didn't care. *When was this thing last cleaned?* he wondered as he closed and locked the door. The toilet, including the seat, was made completely of metal and was set a bit lower to the floor than he was used to. The motion of the car seemed to be amplified in the cramped confines of the room, but it was noticeably larger than the lavatories on the airliners.

After a careful examination of the toilet, he realized that there was no flush lever, just a foot pedal on the floor. He pushed it tentatively and heard a rush of air and saw the tracks flashing by beneath him. Well, that was certainly different!

The sink had him baffled for a while too. There was a small tank above the basin but no taps, only something that looked like a spigot. Finally he realized there was a plunger-like thing in the spigot and when he pushed up on it, water flowed down from the tank. He washed his hands as best he could, and then dried them on his pant legs, very thankful his mom wasn't there to see that. Even with no towels to use he would still have earned himself a stern lecture.

As he was about to leave he glanced at himself in the mirror and was mildly shocked to see just how scruffy he appeared. He hadn't shaved in several days now and wondered if even his friends would recognize him. Hopefully they wouldn't, and neither would anyone else.

He opened the door to find a man of about his age practically standing in the doorway. They passed each other without making eye contact and he made his way carefully back to his seat.

Making sure no one was within earshot he leaned over to Dmitri, "How far to where we're going?"

"I don't know how far we are going, Mikhail."

Michael looked at him in surprise.

"I don't know how safe it is to be on train," he explained.

"I thought you figured it would be safe if we got on at the platform," Michael argued.

"Safer. We were not seen on the platform, but many people see us on train." Michael had to agree with that. There were maybe twenty people in their car, plus the conductor. Then there were the people that kept travelling back and forth between cars. So far they'd been seen by maybe forty-five or fifty people.

Dmitri wasn't quite admitting to Michael that he was having second thoughts about this idea. There was no question that they were making good time. Every minute on the train brought them that much closer to the border and safety. Or, that much closer to Yuri's waiting men. He made a face, wondering to himself if he was getting too impatient, too eager to get to the border. Somehow he'd screwed up last time and almost been caught on the flight to Athens while being fully convinced he'd already made it to safety. He couldn't take that chance again.

"I don't know how long is safe to stay on train," he finally admitted. "But I think we will get off soon. Be ready."

Michael was getting used to the sinking feeling in his stomach. Ever since that ride on the bus, life with Dmitri had been pretty much one disappointment after another. Once aboard the train he thought they had all but made it, but the look on Dmitri's face convinced him it was for the best. He wanted to ask what the new plan was, but that look on his face also told him that so far there wasn't a new plan.

CHAPTER 11

Derailed

The two men continued their journey in silence. Though they had not discussed it, they had somehow wordlessly agreed to take turns looking around the car. Neither of them spotted anything unusual or out of the ordinary. The problem they both faced was that neither of them knew for sure who they were looking for. The young man at the station had given himself away by paying too much attention to them. They might not be so lucky if it were to happen again, but the longer they rode, the more uneasy they both became, until even Michael was wishing they were off the train. If he had to, he'd walk all the way to the border.

The train made its next stop at a small station; this time they were actually in the town itself rather than at a platform. A few passengers got off and several more made their way onto the train, all of them moving groggily as if too tired to be travelling at such an early hour. He looked expectantly at Dmitri, but he made no move whatsoever after glancing out the window with a bored expression. A female voice came over a loudspeaker outside announcing the departure of the train and soon they were back in motion.

He'd now lost track of how many times the same two sitcoms had played and he still didn't quite understand the whole story. With a sigh of exhaustion and frustration he reclined the seat fully and closed his eyes. This time sleep found him. It was a restless sleep, filled with vague, unseen things to fear. He awoke often but managed each time to get back to sleep, only to be confronted by yet another new threat in his dreams. Dmitri also napped off and on, but was ever alert to the passengers around them.

Michael awoke again as the train lurched gently, stopping at yet another town. A small station was bathed in the weak glow of a few widely scattered lights, revealing several small knots of passengers waiting for their trains. Several of them boarded the one they were on. It was the dead of night and with the engine shut down during the brief stop, everything felt too calm and quiet for comfort.

"Mikhail," Dmitri said softly, "Stand up when I do and step into aisle. Look towards back of car. Tell me if anyone does anything."

With a nod Michael stood up and turned around, stepping out into the aisle. Immediately a short, stocky man seated near the back of the car looked up at him, a look of surprise evident on his face, as if he was being shocked into action, though he didn't move otherwise. The look was barely there long enough for him to notice, but it had been there. Michael had been too tired earlier to recognize him as the man who had entered from another car, the one with the cell phone. Shifting his own gaze away from the man and out the window on the far side of the car he stretched and, just for fun, took a couple of steps towards the back of the car. Behind him he could sense Dmitri's eyes on him and hoped that he'd follow, thinking that maybe they could flush the guy out if he was watching them.

He caught the sound of Dmitri's footsteps behind him, smiling to himself as the stocky man also stood, looking slightly confused. Then he felt Dmitri's hand upon his shoulder and turned to face him. Pointing back towards their seats he spoke a few phrases in Ukrainian. Playing along, Michael shrugged, nodded, and returned to his seat. But his heart was pounding furiously. The satisfaction of flushing out their pursuer was replaced with the realization that they had been found. Even worse was the fact that by now he'd likely alerted many others who also knew where they were, and which way they were heading. They were heading into a trap, if indeed it hadn't already been sprung.

"Do not turn around again." The words were spoken softly, barely even coming out as a whisper.

"What are we going to do?"

"We wait for opportunity."

"Humph," was the only response Dmitri got as Michael settled back into his seat. All thoughts of rest or sleep were gone now. He stared at the TV without seeing it. Dmitri and his opportunities, he fumed to himself. Well, the last time he had waited one had come along, and that had worked out alright. But really it had worked out for Dmitri more than for Michael. Then again, how long had he waited for the opportunity to make off with fifteen million dollars? Maybe there was something to his method after all.

The train eased out of the station and back onto the main line, picking up speed as they continued the journey in silence. Dmitri looking for his opportunity, and Michael hoping one would present itself.

The first hint of daylight was barely visible in the Eastern sky when the train began slowing again. Michael shook his head, slightly confused and startled, not to mention angry, for having fallen asleep with danger so nearby. Glancing to his side he saw that Dmitri was slumped down in his seat and at first he appeared to be asleep as well. But without turning he whispered very softly, "Pretend you are still asleep, don't move or look around."

"Why?" Michael kept his voice as low as possible.

"Maybe this is opportunity."

He felt his heart beating a bit faster, recalling the excitement of the last opportunity. Was that only last night, or was it the one before that? He couldn't remember for sure. He was fully alert now, and dying to ask Dmitri what the plan was. It would be a lot easier to help in the escape if he knew what to expect. But it was too late to ask now. Whatever it was, it required him to keep still and quiet as the train continued to slow.

No one else in the car was stirring. At a few of the other stops passengers had risen and gathered their possessions in preparation to get off the train, but not at this one. So this must be a small town or another platform he concluded. Why would that be an opportunity? Wouldn't it just make it harder for them to disappear? Now he could feel beads of sweat running down his forehead. He didn't dare look at Dmitri again.

The train lurched slightly as it came to a stop and Michael could see that they were indeed at another platform, almost identical to the one they had boarded from. The conductor made her way to the door at the front of the car and opened it, stepping down onto the platform just as she had at the other stops. A young couple with a sleeping baby boarded and settled into the first available seat while the conductor stood outside waiting for the signal that the train was ready to depart. A refreshing wave of cool night air flowed slowly through the car.

Dmitri remained motionless in his feigned sleep the whole time and Michael did the same. If anyone else was awake in the car, they were too tired to put forth the effort to move.

"Get ready," Dmitri whispered beside him.

The conductor was stepping back into the train and began pulling the door shut just as the brakes released and the train started moving.

A sudden loud cry from Dmitri as he sprang from his seat startled Michael and he leapt to his feet as well. Despite the warning to be ready he was caught off-guard and thought for a few anxious heartbeats that Yuri's men were storming the car. Dmitri shoved past him and bolted towards the door yelling a stream of Ukrainian at the startled conductor. Whatever he was saying she obviously didn't like it and began yelling back at him, motioning furiously for him to return to his seat.

But he ignored her shouts, sidestepping her easily in the wide aisle, and continued towards the door. Fortunately for Michael she turned to pursue Dmitri, leaving him free to chase both of them up the aisle.

The train was still moving slowly but beginning to gather speed as Dmitri yanked open the door and threw himself from the train. It was just what Michael was afraid he'd do. He had no choice now but to follow even though the train was picking up speed. He shoved his way past the conductor and made for the door.

He froze for what seemed an eternity in the open doorway, the conductor was still yelling and Michael knew everyone on the car was now looking at him. He wondered briefly what the guy who'd been tailing them was doing, and how close behind him he was. He hesitated for what seemed like ages. What if he stayed on the train, told the conductor who he was? Maybe she could alert the proper authorities and get him to safety. But even as he grasped at that hope, his imagination was working overtime in another direction and had him convinced that a pair of hands was about to close around his neck and drag him away from the freedom offered by the open door. The fear of being captured gave him the courage he needed to launch himself into the darkness after Dmitri who, strange as it seemed, was the only person in the whole country he dared trust right now.

"Oooff!" he grunted, landing painfully on his side and rolling with the momentum the train had added to his leap. He came to rest facing the departing train. He caught a brief glimpse of the door to their car as it slammed shut just before passing the last light at the end of the platform. No one else had followed them off the train.

For what seemed a long time, he just lay there. It took a while to come fully to the realization that they had made good on their escape. As the last car disappeared into the darkness, he felt Dmitri's hands on his arm, helping him up onto his feet.

"I almost thought you were going to stay on train, Mikhail," he said lightly.

"I was going to, but then I realized how helpless you'd be without me," he countered, as he dusted himself off, and checked to make sure nothing was broken. He was still slightly winded from the fall, but everything else seemed to be intact. He nodded in the direction of the departed train. "Nice move. Guess we gave him the slip, huh? But don't you ever get out of a vehicle in a normal way? Either you jump out a window or use the door only if it's moving."

Dmitri laughed briefly, but quickly turned serious again. "For now, yes, we give them slip. But he has already told them that we were on train. He will also tell them that we got off, and where we got off. I do not know where next stop is, but he will be back here soon. With more men."

As he spoke he was patting himself down in the same way Michael had, checking to see if everything was intact. He suddenly made a face and removed the shattered remnants of a cell phone from his pocket. It was the one he'd taken from the young man at the train station. One look was all it took to see it was beyond repair, so he tossed it over the wall of the platform into the trees behind it.

"So we keep moving, right?" Michael asked.

"Yes," he replied thoughtfully, sorting out their options. "We must get away from here. They know which way we need to go to get out of Ukraine, that is fastest way out, so that is direction they will look."

Michael remained silent, recognizing that Dmitri was doing his best to make full use of their opportunity.

"We will go south," he announced finally.

"What's south of here?"

"We will go south because they will use most of their men looking further west. If we wait long enough they will be too far away to find us, then we head to Romania. Once we cross border it will be easier. Maybe we can even trust police there."

Michael tried to take some encouragement from the fact that Dmitri was talking about crossing the border as if it were only a matter of time. To him it was starting to feel as if it were more a question of 'if' they crossed the border, and he could still measure his total time in the country in terms of hours.

He followed Dmitri along the platform until they came to the stairs. Descending them they found that the trail at the bottom led to their left, which was north. Nothing was visible that direction, but that didn't mean much. As he'd seen last night, smaller villages hardly had any lights showing at night and they might be only a stone's throw from a cluster of houses.

Dmitri looked up the trail, then to their right across the tracks, in the direction they wanted to go, pondering their next move.

"If they send someone back this way, the village will be the first place they look," Michael thought out loud.

"Da." Dmitri always seemed to lapse back into Ukrainian when he was deep in thought, Michael had noticed. Not that he could blame him, it was his native language after all. It was hard to think of yourself as a foreigner, but in this country, that's what he was. To everyone here, all this was normal; he was the oddball. That was harder to fully comprehend than it should have been.

Dmitri pointed up the tracks in the direction that train had been heading. "We follow tracks again," he announced. "They will be searching villages and watching roads and trains. But they are not able to travel along tracks. So that is where we go."

"But don't the tracks go west? I thought you wanted to go south."

"Mikhail," Dmitri began, as if explaining his plan to a very small child, "We follow tracks until we come to road. Then we wait for…"

"For opportunity!" Michael interrupted, unable to resist the temptation to use his best attempt at a Ukrainian accent, causing Dmitri to laugh out loud.

"Yes, Mikhail. We wait for opportunity. I am good teacher, no?"

"A good teacher, or a creature of habit?"

"Creature of habit?"

"It means you do the same thing all the time. Like wait for opportunities."

They struck out along the tracks again, the sky to the east becoming brighter by the minute. Michael could see Dmitri's wisdom in sticking to this route. They were sheltered from view by the tall rows of trees on either side of the right of way, and only someone else on a train would be able to spot them. This was definitely their safest route during daylight.

"I do it because it works." He almost sounded defensive, Michael thought. "Many people do something because something has to be done. But they do wrong things many times. I wait until time is right and opportunity is there. It always works."

"Hmm." Michael grunted in response, thinking about Dmitri's philosophy. He had to admit that it was working. Back on the plane and the bus, a lot of them had wanted to take action. Dmitri been scared when the plane was first hijacked, there was no doubt about that. For a while it had looked as if he had given up all hope.

But he had waited and an opportunity had come along. So far they were still free. So, does fortune favor the bold, or do good things come to those who wait? Or was it a case of being bold when the opportunity came? That must be what Dmitri was doing, he decided. So far he couldn't argue with the guy. He did, after all, have fifteen million dollars from exercising his options during a previous opportunity.

"Dmitri, can I ask you a question? About when you were still in the Mafia?"

The Ukrainian shot him a sidelong glance, his mood becoming suddenly very guarded. "Yes. But I do not know if I can answer."

"Did you ever have to do what they're doing now? Look for someone, I mean? Did you ever have to hunt someone?"

"Yes, a few times."

"Did you find them?"

"Yes, every time." He had to laugh in spite of himself when he saw Michael's crestfallen look. "But do not worry, Mikhail, I am not helping them look. And I learn from mistakes of men I catch. They will not catch us."

Michael hoped he was really as confident as he sounded. "When you caught those guys, what happened to them?"

The look on Dmitri's face was suddenly one of immense pain, as if a memory he had tried to suppress was forcing its way back into his consciousness. "My job was to catch them. Once Yuri had them," he paused for several paces, "Once he had them, it depended what they had done. Yuri would decide."

His words did not convince either of them. Both of them knew that he was trying, unsuccessfully, to distance himself from the fate of those he had hunted down. Dmitri also knew of those he'd dealt with first-hand before he'd risen high enough in the ranks to be able to keep his hands clean— well, if not clean, cleaner. Yet here he was echoing the words of low ranking soldiers, crooks, and even government officials everywhere, who defended themselves with the claim that they were merely carrying out orders and doing their duty. If anyone in that long line of people who claimed no responsibility for their actions had convinced themselves, they certainly never managed to convince anyone else.

They walked in silence for several minutes. The sun was rising almost directly behind them, and casting long shadows in front of them that rippled across the ties between the tracks. Dmitri offered no further explanation, but one thing still bothered Michael.

"What if they catch us?"

"They won't."

"But what if they do? What will happen to us?"

"If they do, then they will get money back."

The words, even though spoken as light-hearted as Dmitri could make them, cast a chill over Michael that even the early morning sun could not dispel.

* * *

Back aboard the train, Igor was fuming at the conductor, as if it were her fault the two men had gotten off the train much earlier than they were supposed to. He hadn't seen her talking to them, but perhaps they had paid her as well, to let them know if anyone was asking about them. He could never admit to himself that he had tipped them off, so it must have been her fault. Given a chance he'd have asked for his money back, but causing a scene would not help him in any way. Many in the car were still laughing about the two men who'd almost slept through their stop. And then there was that third man; they were still talking about him, he knew, from the sidelong glances cast his way. He'd been so close to grabbing that foreigner; just a few more meters and he would not have made it off the train.

He knew what he had to do, he just didn't want to do it. Reluctantly he pulled out his phone and dialled Vasili's number.

"Vasili? Igor. They got off the train."

"And you still have them in sight." It was not a question.

"No. I was not able to get off the train."

Vasili's voice was calm, much too calm. "You were not able to get off the train? Why is that? You were sleeping?"

"N-no, Vasili, I was not sleeping…"

"No? Then why were you not able to get off the train? Did someone tie you to your seat perhaps?"

"No. They waited until the train began moving and then jumped off before I could catch them. If I had tried to jump after them I might have broken my leg!" He winced, realizing how weak the excuse must have sounded to Vasili, even though it made perfect sense to him.

"I would hate to see you with a broken leg, Igor," Vasili responded icily, as if hinting that such a fate was still a possibility.

It was almost a relief when his superior finally lost his temper and began yelling. "Fool! Idiot! You let them know you were following them and they outsmarted you! It was obviously not very hard for them to do that!"

Even as he spoke the words, Vasili knew that Dmitri had a lot more street-smarts than Igor did. He was experienced at this type of game and it would take someone much smarter than Igor to run down a man like Dmitri. Twice now men like him had proven useful in spotting them, but inept when it came to following them. At least they were staying close, and he and the Canadian were still a long way from the border.

"I think maybe the conductor warned them. I should not have asked for her help. If I had just waited for them to get off, this would not have happened. I'm sure she told them." He was starting to sound desperate even to himself.

"Shut up! Now, where did these two men manage to make a fool out of you?"

The vicious sweep of his pen tore a hole in the map as Vasili circled the small dot representing the town. There was the new starting point. They were either on foot or waiting for another train. If he knew Dmitri, and he did, they were not remaining in one place. Once again, the man had slipped from their grip, but not yet from their reach. It was time to make more calls and make more plans. They had a starting point, and with the resources at his disposal, that would be enough. It had to be enough. Not only for the sake of Yuri's money. The stakes for him were becoming much more personal than that. And much higher.

*   *   *

The sun was climbing higher into a cloudless sky and beginning to swing in a slow wide arc over their left shoulders. They'd been hiking down the tracks for some time now and all they'd seen, besides an unbroken line of trees on both sides of the tracks, was a few freight trains heading in either direction. Both of them were thankful that they weren't passenger trains. The chances they'd be spotted if there were any of Yuri's men on board weren't that great, but the fewer people who saw them the better.

Michael glanced behind them, squinting into the sun before turning his gaze forward again. There was nothing to see ahead but the straight lines of trees and tracks disappearing into the horizon. The sound of birds and insects, and the rhythmic crunch of the ballast under their feet, made everything seem calm and peaceful.

He wiped the sweat from his brow and knew it was going to be an uncomfortably warm day. Already the heat and humidity were becoming unbearable. "No offence, Dmitri, but next time I take a tour of your country, it's not going to be a walking tour."

The Ukrainian looked at him as they took several more paces before finally cracking a smile. "Ah, you make joke! Yes, next time we hire big limousine to drive us around."

"Just make sure there's something to drink in it." He knew that Dmitri had bought them some bottled water, yesterday was it? He thought so, but everything seemed to be a blur. He couldn't even remember where they'd lost it, only that he'd never had a chance to drink it. Dmitri gave a grunt of agreement in reply.

"I don't think we can risk going into village to buy more water. But maybe we will find well. We will need something to drink soon."

The rumble of an approaching train broke off their conversation. It wasn't in view yet but they both dashed into the trees at the side of the tracks. If anyone onboard was looking for them, they didn't want to be seen. A few steps into the thick brush offered enough cover to conceal them fully, so they knelt down and remained as motionless as possible. The roar of the diesel and the clatter of the wheels bouncing over the rail joints drowned out all noise, but still they remained as motionless as possible as the passenger train sped by. They remained still for another minute even after it passed, partially in relief, partly in fear that they'd been spotted. Finally they rose tentatively from their concealment and resumed the trek to wherever they were heading. To safety; that is where they were heading. The problem was neither of them knew where that might be. Or which way it lay.

As the sun rose higher in the sky, the heat intensified, amplifying the humidity. In a few more hours there might be some shade from the trees on the south side of the tracks, but for now it was still almost directly behind them, and there was no relief to be found.

"Can we take a break? Just sit in the shade for a bit? We've been walking for hours." Dmitri looked over at him, then longingly at the inviting shade offered by the trees. They were far too thick to walk through, otherwise they'd have abandoned the tracks when the sun rose. The Ukrainian's face was red and wet with sweat, just as he was sure his own was.

"Da, we take short rest. But we must keep moving. They know where we got off train and will be watching for us."

"Ok, just a short one," Michael agreed reluctantly. They turned to the left, and sank gratefully into the relative coolness of the shade. A breeze would have been nice, but the air was dead calm, not even enough to move the leaves of the trees and bushes that sheltered them from the sun.

"What's the plan, Dmitri?" Michael asked after a few minutes. "Besides waiting for an opportunity to come our way." Dmitri did not respond, not even a grunt or a shrug. He simply stared off into the distance. It was the same look he had worn on the airplane. He'd come up with a plan then, so, Michael thought to himself, it might be best to just let him think.

There were many times in the past two days that he'd been so intent on running and hiding that he occasionally forgot that he was in a foreign country. Now that he could sit and think he remembered it, and it made him feel even more afraid than when Yuri's men were chasing them. It reminded him of just how far out of his element he was. He didn't know the language or the culture, or even exactly where he was. His only knowledge of the country was the map he'd looked at on the airplane, and that hadn't shown much. He looked at Dmitri, whose mind was still occupied with plans and opportunities. He was totally dependent upon this man, and he'd known him a very brief time. All he really knew was that he was ex-Mafia, and that knowledge made him almost sick with fear at times. But there was no other choice. Anyone else he met might be Mafia, or someone willing to turn him over to them.

"We need to find somewhere to stay for a few days." Michael started as Dmitri spoke unexpectedly. His fear was getting the best of him.

"Okay, why? I thought we needed to keep moving."

"The longer they do not see us, the farther they will think we have gone. They will be spread far apart to find us. It will be easier for us to move that way."

Michael gave a tired nod. "So we escape by not moving for a while."

"Da." Dmitri responded, still obviously lost in thought.

Michael waited a while for Dmitri's thoughts to return to the present, but eventually gave up waiting. "Where are we going to hide?"

Dmitri snapped out of the trance he was in, smiled at Michael and gave him a punch on the shoulder. "We wait for opportunity!"

"How did I know you were going to say that," Michael replied, a touch of resentment in his voice. He was used to making and having plans, and making it up as he went was not something he liked to do. Not even on his holidays. He thought of his travel guide, maps, and notebook. Hopefully they were stored safely in some locker in Kiev. He still wanted to get to Greece, but that might have to wait until next year. If there was a next year.

CHAPTER 12

Hitching a Ride

Vasili let out a long, tired sigh as he sat back in his chair, rubbing his eyes. He knew he needed sleep, but his mind would not let him get the rest his body needed. He stopped rubbing his eyes and let them come back into focus, scanning his list of names and locations. Would someone on the list find them? If not, what was he missing? He was almost certain they would not risk getting on another train for fear of being spotted again, and knowing Dmitri, he would not attempt it. So what were their plans?

Rising from his chair he crossed the room to the coffee pot. Tea was a much more common drink in his country, but the long hours he kept had fostered first a use for the extra caffeine, then a craving. Now it had become a need. His stomach was tied in knots and he knew he really needed food, not the strong, acidic beverage in the pot he was reaching for. But still he filled his cup and returned to the notes and maps scattered over his desk.

Once again he began pouring over the plans for the search. One map showed their route since their escape from the bus, or at least the spots at which they'd been sighted. West. They were definitely working their way in that direction. He had been right in his initial assumption. That gave him a slight advantage in being the hunter. Well, perhaps not an advantage, he admitted to himself, but at least he didn't have to spread his assets even more thinly than they were already. At some point, if they made it that far, they had to cross the border. At an official border crossing? Not likely, but possible. At an official crossing point they would have to get past the Ukrainian guards first, and he had the resources to buy many of them off before they got there. That might not even be necessary, since nei-ther of them had their passports. It would likely have to be an illegal crossing.

He sat up, took a sip of coffee and felt his enthusiasm returning as he pondered this new line of thought. Either they would have to bribe their way past Ukrainian passport control, or they had to sneak across the border. They didn't have the money to offer a bribe, at least as far as he knew. And even if they did, there was still the matter of getting into Romania. A bribe might not work there. So they were going to have to sneak across.

That would not be as hard as it had once been. Many sections of the border were patrolled only once a day, if at all. But if they could keep tabs on them as they headed that way then he could nar-row down the likely crossing points, concentrate his forces along a smaller section of the border. Yes, that might work. Not that he'd stop looking for them between now and the border, but he wanted to be ready if they made it that far.

He was just beginning to mark up the map with likely spots when the phone rang. For a brief moment he thought it might be a call that they'd been sighted, or even caught, but then he saw the name on the call display.

"Da, Yuri Stepanovich."

"You alone are to report to Me, Vasili, so that I do not have to deal with everyone in the field."

He knew what was coming, but he played dumb in a futile at-tempt to deflect some of the anger. "Of course, sir. You do not have the time to trouble yourself with all the details," he replied as calm-ly as he could. But he had to pull the phone back from his ear as Yuri continued.

"Then why have you not called me? What is happening? Have

you sent them all off on vacation?"

"No, Yuri Stepanovich. As I have told you we have sighted them several times. There is a definite pattern to these sightings, in fact, they are moving just as I predicted they would." He forced himself to sound more confident than he felt, knowing that would take some of the force from Yuri's words. "I've identified several possible points that they are heading towards," that was true enough based upon a couple of circles on a map. "We will concentrate our men in those areas."

There was hesitation on the other end of the phone, so he pressed forward. "In fact, I am just about to head out myself. I can direct the men from out there by phone, and I want to be there to see the look on Dmitri's face when we get him. I will bring him to you personally. Though, perhaps I will, how should I say…discuss…, a few things with him along the way?"

Yuri actually chuckled at that. It was a very sinister chuckle that made Vasili glad to know that the brunt of his wrath would fall on someone else, eventually. "I will call you when I have set things up, though out there I may not always have good reception."

'That ought to keep him off my back for a bit,' Vasili hoped. Life would be a lot easier without Yuri to deal with. He stopped for a moment, realizing that that thought could be carried far beyond the current situation. It would not be the first time a change in power had occurred that way, and it wouldn't be the last. But it was something that could not be rushed into, it had to be planned and thought through. It was something worth considering once Dmitri was dealt with, and the more he had to do with his capture the easier it might be to convince others that he deserved a higher position.

"I will call you when I can, Yuri Stepanovich." He pushed the end button and then realized that for the first time ever, he had cut

Yuri off, instead of vice versa. It felt good. But there was no time to savour the moment, thumbing through his contacts he found the number he was looking for and pressed it.

"Bring the car, and make sure the tank is full of gas." Gathering up his collection of notes and maps he stuffed them into a bag, and headed for the door.

*   *   *

Michael used his hand to wipe the sweat from his brow once more. Even in the shade, the heat and humidity were becoming unbearable. He wished with all his heart for a breeze, but the air remained perfectly calm. A breeze would help with the bugs too, he thought, swatting at something buzzing around his left ear. The thought of venturing back out into the sun again was almost beyond what he could endure. His body was craving sleep and the heat amplified it. Dmitri was still sitting silently, lost in thought, but Michael thought he was starting to be able to read the look in his eyes, and it looked very much like he was reaching a conclusion.

Sure enough, less than a minute later, Dmitri moved his head slightly, a determined look crossing his face. "Enough rest, Mikhail, it is time to go."

"Go where? What are we doing?"

"We go to find place to stay."

"Where will we stay?"

Dmitri looked at him as if to ask if he understood English, which was after all Michael's native tongue, not Dmitri's. His voice changed and became rather condescending. "Mikhail, I said we go to find place, not we go to place. We will not know till we find it." Michael gave a deep sigh at the thought of stepping out once more with no plan. When he'd planned his trip to Greece, he'd booked his hotels six months ahead of time.

Dmitri, somewhat to Michael's surprise, turned away from the tracks, working his way deeper into the stand of trees. It was not very deep and they soon broke clear of it at the edge of a field. There were no roads in sight, and they were effectively shielded from the view of anyone on a passing train, which suited both of them. The only problem was that they were on the south side of the trees and the sun had a steady bead on them. Michael rubbed his neck, feeling the heat of the deep sunburn already there.

They walked in silence along the trees, the only sound was the rumbling and clacking of the occasional passing train. Ahead of them, Michael could see another tree line angling in to intersect the one they were following. He doubted that Dmitri would consent to another break, but at least there would be a minute or two of shade. It looked further away than he felt like walking just now, but he kept putting one foot in front of the other, trying not to think that right now he should be on the shores of the Mediterranean sea, enjoying the hospitality of a resort that most likely had umbrellas to shield their guests from the very same sun that was currently sapping his energy.

This thought was only making things worse, so instead he tried reminding himself that as slow as the trip was, every step he took brought him closer to their destination, even if he didn't know just where that was. All he knew was that it would be somewhere safe. An unbidden thought suddenly turned him cold despite the heat. Was there anywhere safe? If they had his passport, they knew where he lived. And they knew where his family lived, he'd listed his parents as his emergency contacts. What if this Yuri guy was already trying to get to him through them?

"Dmitri? Does, uh, does Yuri ever go after the families of the people he's, uh, mad at?"

"Yes, Mikhail, he has done that before." Turning to look at Michael as he spoke, he saw the fear, or maybe it was even panic, in his eyes. "Do not worry, though. It is me they want; they can gain nothing from you other than access to me. They will not go after your family." Even as he spoke the words, he was not really sure of their truth. They had no idea who this Canadian was. For all Yuri knew, he was Dmitri's accomplice, the contact in the West who had aided him in his plan. He gave Michael his best reassuring smile, but found he had to work a lot harder at it than he'd had to in the past.

In the past, his job, and even at times his life, had depended upon the ability to smile at someone while lying through his teeth. It had always been so easy to do. The consequences to others had meant nothing to him just so long as there was something in it for him. But he felt a stab of almost physical pain as he realized that his actions might somehow cause someone innocent to suffer. He'd wanted out of this wretched business, but now all he'd done was draw someone else into it along with him. Michael smiled weakly at him, which was cold comfort to the pain he felt. He feared that this man did not believe him any more than he believed himself.

"Mikhail, I am doing all I can to get us out of this." His words were meant to encourage, but they came out as more of a feeble attempt at an apology. It was true he had been suspicious of Michael's questions and comments on the plane and on the bus. It was also true that he was trying to save his own life and escape from his past. But all that had happened to him had fallen out as a result of his own choices. He was not a victim of circumstances, or even of the Mafia; it was all his own fault. That realization came to him like a physical blow. He'd never admitted that to anyone, not even to himself. Sure, he took credit for his successes, but for the failures and consequences? Never. But Michael's smile had become more genuine as he had spoken the words.

"I know you are, Dmitri. Besides, what other choice do I have but to follow you?"

He trusts me! That was another shock to Dmitri's system. Few had trusted him in the past; most had regretted it in the end; even Yuri had come to that point. Would Mikhail regret it as well? Dmitri didn't, couldn't, reply to what Michael had just said, and was relieved to see that they had reached the tree line, as it gave him the opportunity to change the subject.

"We will cross through trees and then turn that way." He motioned to the left and Michael realized with some relief that that would put them into some shade, at least for a while.

"That way to opportunity, huh?" Michael managed a short but genuine laugh.

Dmitri laughed as well, but to himself he admitted that all he could do was hope an opportunity did indeed lie in that direction; there were no guarantees. For the first time in as long as he could remember, he was worried about someone else.

* * *

"We will stop here," Vasili informed the driver. They had arrived at the village closest to the platform from which Dmitri and the Canadian had managed to escape from the train. The road leading to the next village did not even come close to following the rail line, which was not that uncommon, so this is where he would start from. They wouldn't have had time to walk to that village yet. He had men stationed there, though he knew already that they would not be heading that way. Dmitri was too smart for that. "Get us as close to the platform as possible."

"Yes, sir," the man replied, rolling down his window to ask one of the passing locals where they could catch the train. Upon receiving directions he nodded a curt thank-you, put the car into gear, and made a left turn down a side street. A few more minutes brought them to the end of the rough dirt road. A well-worn footpath continued past the end of the road and disappeared into a gap in the trees.

Vasili opened the door of the car, stepped out, stretched, and looked around. Had they found some place to hide here in the village? It should be easy enough to ask around and find that out. The promise of a little bit of money usually managed to find its way to those willing to loosen their tongues. The nice thing about a small village is everyone soon knew everything, and several of them would be more than willing to talk about it. But first he needed to do something. It would accomplish nothing, but he had to see where they'd last been sighted.

His driver remained in the car while he followed the path down to the trees. Two older ladies carrying bags heavily laden with groceries were coming back the other way and had to step aside to let him pass. It did not even occur to Vasili that it should have been him that stepped aside to let the ladies pass.

The side of the trail was littered with broken bottles that had once contained beer and vodka, which he passed without really noticing. The trail was not long and he soon reached the clearing through which the tracks passed. There it was; the platform where Igor had lost them. It would have been all but impossible to do anything on the train, and he had to admit that from the account Igor gave, Dmitri had planned and timed his escape well. But it was still frustrating.

He tried to imagine it as he approached the platform and put his foot on the first step. They had been here just a few hours ago. They had descended these steps and touched this handrail; it was as if they had left something almost tangible behind. Touching the rail himself made them feel closer, more within his grasp. If only someone had been here then. But that event, that intersection of paths, was still in the future. Very soon one of his men would meet them again, he could feel it.

He continued up the steps, standing on the platform and surveying the area. There were footprints everywhere in the dusty soil around the platform, making trying to track two specific people impossible. But they had to be somewhere nearby. He'd start by having the man who'd driven him here ask around the village. Someone who acted official and asked about strangers was often answered without question. That was one advantage of all those years of communism. Waving some money around wouldn't hurt either.

Not that he would call off the wider search, but if he had to be out here getting his hands and his suit dirty, this is where he'd do his own searching. Because somewhere near here is where they would be captured.

* * *

Michael found that the tree line now provided just enough relief from the sun to make the walking bearable. Dmitri was fairly confident that they would come to a road or village soon, and that they could begin looking for their opportunity. There was neither a road, nor even a trail, but they were able to pick their way easily along the edge of the trees. The problem was that now that he was no longer worried about the sun and heat; he found the rumbles in his stomach growing more and more noticeable. He also realized there was no point in complaining to Dmitri about it, because there was nothing he could do. If they found a village, hopefully they'd be able to buy or scrounge something.

"Mikhail, stop!"

Michael instantly froze. The sudden, sharp outburst from Dmitri caused his heart to race and he felt a sudden sweat break out on his brow that had nothing to do with the heat. He scanned in every direction searching out the possible threat, trying not to make any sudden moves that might draw unwanted attention, all the while wondering which way they should run.

"What is it?" he whispered hoarsely to Dmitri, not even looking at him yet, still scanning for the unseen threat. When finally he did turn to him, he was surprised to see a big smile on his face. He was pointing towards a cluster of trees and shrubs.

"I do not know word, but that is good to eat."

Michael looked closer, still not seeing what Dmitri was pointing out, then followed him a few steps before realizing what it was he was supposed to be seeing. "Raspberries!"

"Yes, razz-berries," Dmitri repeated as they began plucking the berries and popping them into their mouths as fast as they could. They were a much darker colour than Michael was used to, but they were juicy and sweet and tasted right. It might take a lot of them to satisfy their hunger but they were in no rush to move on at the moment anyway. Both men kept glancing around as they ate, but they couldn't see or hear anything in any direction. Even the noise of the passing trains had begun to fade into the background. It was as if they were the only people in the whole country.

Dmitri was busy chewing a mouthful of raspberries and therefore couldn't speak, but he pointed to another tree a little further down, swallowing his mouthful with some effort. "Apples," he said nodding towards the tree.

Michael looked at the apples rather dubiously. They were small and very green. "Are they ready to eat?" he asked after swallowing his own mouthful, already gathering more with both hands, ignoring the thorns in his eagerness for more.

"They are, how you say, not very sweet? But you can eat them. I get some." He picked his way past a few shrubs and through some taller grass to the apple tree as Michael continued to pick raspberries. A few of them weren't quite ripe but he didn't let that stop him. Dmitri plucked a couple of handfuls of the small, green apples and made his way back to Michael, dropping several into his outstretched hand.

After looking dubiously at them for a few moments, he bit into one. It was rather tart, especially after the sweetness of the berries, but it also felt more substantial in his mouth. He quickly finished them off and then went back to plucking berries.

"So, if we come to a village, we're going to look for an empty place again, like we did last time?"

"Yes, we could do that," Dmitri agreed, "We will have to see." He sounded very non-committal.

Fair enough, Michael thought to himself. "What if we come to a road?"

"Then we wait until right person comes. We will know when it happens."

They ate for a while longer in silence, pausing now and then from the work of picking berries to gather more apples. First Michael, and then Dmitri, ate his fill and sat down in the shade of a particularly bushy shrub. A gentle breeze was beginning to make itself felt. It was just enough to offer some relief from the heat.

"I was wondering," Michael began, Dmitri didn't acknowledge his words in any way, but he knew the Ukrainian was listening. "I was wondering, what if you gave them their money back? Would they let us go? Are you sure it wouldn't work?"

Dmitri felt a flash of anger at the suggestion. Giving back the money had never been an option, or even a consideration in his mind. Even as he thought about it, he knew he would never do that. It would do no good, but even if it would, he could not bring himself to do it. The thoughts took just a few seconds to process before he replied.

"It would not work, Mikhail. Like I told you before, with these men you cannot say, 'sorry, here is money, I didn't mean to take it.' If I paid back every dollar with interest they would still need to make an example of me to others." He thought of Yuri and of what he was likely doing and thinking right now. "I embarrassed Yuri personally and made him look bad in eyes of others. He needs to punish me or someone else may try to do what I did." He'd known this somewhere in the back of his mind when he'd taken the funds, but he'd been so sure at that time that his escape would work that he had not given it any serious thought. Would he have done it if he'd thought it through more carefully? Yes, he decided after a few moments of thought, besides, there was no turning back now.

"Yeah," was Michael's disappointed response. "I figured that was the case, but if it would have worked it would have been worth it."

"It would not be worth it to me!" Dmitri shot back with more anger and force than he had intended.

"Yeah, well, you're getting a ton of money out of this." Michael replied bitterly. "All I'm getting is a holiday in Ukraine instead of Greece. Why couldn't you have taken a different plane?"

"I booked five different flights from Germany," Dmitri shouted. "I watched all the gates, I was the last one on the plane when I saw no one I recognized on it. It should have worked. I had it planned!" He sounded as if he were angrier at himself than anyone else.

They both knew they were angrier than they should have been and dropped the discussion there. What Dmitri had said about the position Yuri had been put in was true, even Michael could see that so it was pointless to argue the matter. Michael knew he needed Dmitri, and Dmitri felt an obligation to help Michael. Each of them had made decisions that had brought them to this point, so regardless of how they had arrived here there was nothing to do but go on together.

"Let's go," Dmitri said, still sounding rather gruff as he rose to his feet. Without a word Michael rose and followed a few steps behind him, snatching one more handful of berries for the road.

Another half hour of walking brought them past several more fields of various crops, including another field of brilliant yellow sunflowers.

Then they heard it in the distance, almost unconsciously at first before it fully registered in their minds what they were hearing. It was the unmistakable sound of a car speeding down a road from somewhere up ahead. Unconsciously Michael drew even with Dmitri and they both quickened their pace; the heat and humidity were suddenly forgotten.

The argument was too fresh in their minds to allow any small talk as they crossed the remainder of the field and then came to a stop rather than passing through the trees to the road beyond. All was quiet on the road, no vehicles were anywhere nearby at the moment. They looked at each other, both knowing that catching a ride of any sort was the fastest way to make progress, but it was also a risk. Any of the passing vehicles might contain Yuri's men. The chances that they would be searching this stretch of road at the same time that Michael and Dmitri were passing by were admittedly small, but with their lives on the line, the chance was not worth it.

"We wait for something besides a car, right?"

Dmitri nodded before replying, "Yes, Mikhail, you are learning.

It is only way we can be safe, or safer."

"So we need not just an opportunity, but the right opportunity." Dmitri nodded again. "I'm thinking maybe another farm wagon, or a truck?"

"You are thinking like Mafia guy now."

"Yeah, Mafia guy on the run." He got a grim smile in return. "Well, I'm going to get comfortable while we wait." He sank into the tall grass and leaned back against a tree. The breeze had vanished, but somehow having a plan helped him to relax a bit. This stage of the journey might be drawing to a close, and that brought a glimmer of hope. His eyes began to feel heavy and though he tried to fight it at first, he quickly drifted off to sleep.

The roar of a speeding car snapped him immediately back to wakefulness, disoriented at first his initial reaction was to leap up and run, but he caught himself half way to his feet, remembering where he was. Judging from the startled look on Dmitri's face he had also fallen asleep.

"Is okay, Mikhail. Anything that is safe for us to take will be much slower than car. We will have time when we hear it." He stretched out lazily and closed his eyes.

Michael settled back down, getting as comfortable as was possible on the lumpy ground, but couldn't quite bring himself to allow sleep to come over him again, even after his heart beat returned to normal.

Time seemed to slow down, as if the buzzing insects and the bright sunshine were determined to make the beautiful summer day last forever. A few more cars came speeding by, out of sight behind the thick trees. The only other sound was the constant buzz of insects and the odd bird singing in the tree tops. Eventually, faintly in the distance, he heard the low, growling sound of an engine. It sounded like it was working as hard as it could, yet it was approaching very slowly.

The noise was still too faint to rouse Dmitri from his nap, so he reached over and gave his leg a hesitant shake. His companion woke instantly, but with a confused, almost dazed look on his face. "Shto?"

"Something slow is coming this way. A tractor maybe?"

It took a few seconds for Dmitri's sleepy senses to pick up the sound. He listened carefully and then nodded in agreement. "We make sure nothing else is coming first, but this might be opportunity."

Time continued to a crawl as they waited for the vehicle to get close enough to risk a look. Thankfully there was still no other traffic in sight by the time the noise from the tractor became loud enough to be irritating. Both men rose and pushed their way through the lower brush and into the ditch on the side of the road.

It was a tractor, as they'd suspected. It was blue and white and blowing far more black smoke out the exhaust stack than it should have been. The engine seemed to be growling in protest at having to pull a wagon that appeared several times too big for it. Piled on the wagon was an odd assortment of rough cut lumber and logs. Dmitri waved frantically at the driver who seemed surprised to see two scruffy looking men appear at the side of the road. The thing in their favour was that the driver looked almost as scruffy as they did, and as they'd hoped he brought the tractor to a halt. From the look on the driver's face, he'd stopped more from surprise than from a desire to help them.

Dmitri climbed up onto the back of the tractor and the two men began yelling at each other over the sound of the engine, which didn't seem much quieter at idle than it had at full throttle. By now

Michael was almost used to not understanding a word of what was being said, but it appeared to be going well. Finally the driver of the tractor nodded and jerked his thumb towards the wagon.

That needed no translation, and Michael was heading for the wagon by the time Dmitri had jumped back down to the road. They clambered up onto the wagon and managed to find a spot to sit among the piles of wood that partially concealed them from the view of any passing motorists. With a slight increase in volume, and a hard lurch, the tractor fought its way back into motion, the wagon following rather reluctantly.

"We will have to pay for ride when we reach his house," Dmitri bellowed above the din of the motor."

"How much?" Michael was aware that their supply of cash was rather limited and hoped that the fare would be reasonable.

Dmitri threw back his head and laughed. "Is very expensive ride, Mikhail. When we arrive, we must unload wood." Michael joined in his laughter.

CHAPTER 13

Home Away from Home

As far as the villagers were concerned, there were only two possibilities: the men that had invaded their otherwise quiet village were either Mafia or police. They were asking questions about strangers passing through and not being at all polite about it. There had been no spoken threats, but even with the offer of a reward, it was obvious that if anyone had information and was less than forthcoming with it, there would be dire consequences. Many of the locals had satellite dishes and televisions and had seen enough of the news to know that they were looking for the same men missing from the plane that had been hijacked. Though somewhat intimidated by this invasion, they still found it rather exciting that the search had come to their village, especially since one of the missing men was a foreigner. There were no hard facts, just a variety of rumours as to why they were missing and who they were.

Vasili didn't care who the villagers thought he was, Mafia or police; both assumptions were enough to bring about full cooperation. He was happy with the cooperation, but frustrated that there were no solid leads to follow. He'd considered setting up his headquarters somewhere else, but all the nearby villages were being combed and questioned by his men and he still felt confident they were somewhere nearby. Besides, not only had he easily coerced a villager into giving him the use of his kitchen as a headquarters, he was also pretending to be out of cell phone range from Yuri. That fact alone was helping him think more clearly. He was able not only to keep the searches going in the nearby villages, but he was also getting patrols organized along the border. Officials at the crossing points had been bribed and promised a sizeable reward if they were detained while trying to cross the border. The villages that had been searched already were under instructions to call various numbers if the two men should appear or pass through.

He sipped his coffee slowly while looking out through a window that had rippled slightly with age and was stained inside and out with layers of grease and dust. He knew he was drinking way too much coffee, a lot more than usual, but with the stress of the search he seemed to need it for more than just the caffeine boost. He would cut back when he found Dmitri, he promised himself again. He was sure things were as well organized as they could be and was actually contemplating taking a nap. Setting the coffee mug back down, he leaned back and stretched out his arms and legs. Yes, a nap would feel good and the rest would help him to think even more clearly. He deserved it. Pocketing his phone he rose and crossed the room to a bed against the back wall, stretched out and drifted into a pleasant sleep. His sleep was full of dreams of catching Dmitri and the Canadian. Had anyone been watching, they might have been surprised to see the tension melt from his face and be replaced by a twisted smile.

* * *

They were approaching a village that appeared very similar to the first one they'd stopped at, the one where they had "acquired" their clothing. The tractor made a right turn off the main road and pulled into the yard of what back home Michael would have taken to be a small acreage. There was a tiny white house as well as a few outbuildings. The largest of the buildings, the barn, was just a bit bigger than the house. Several other similar farms were dotted around the perimeter of the village, while a stone's throw to the west sat the main cluster of houses making up the village.

The wagon rolled forward slowly and then jerked to a halt against the tractor signalling that the trip had ended. Michael hung back as Dmitri asked where to unload the wood. Michael could understand his gestures and he began pulling pieces of lumber from the wagon even before Dmitri returned. Then he caught sight of the well. He didn't dare speak, but waited till he could catch Dmitri's attention and gestured towards it. The farmer caught his gesture and nodded while motioning towards the well.

He approached it a bit uncertainly. It looked just like an old well from the pictures in the books he'd read as a kid. He lowered the bucket to the water, which wasn't as far below ground level as he'd expected, and raised it back up with the crank. A quick look around didn't reveal anything else to drink from, so he took a long pull straight from the bucket. It was ice cold and had a very hard taste, but water had never tasted so good to him.

He drank his fill before he became conscious of Dmitri waiting impatiently beside him, so he passed the bucket across to the Ukrainian who also took several long pulls of the cold water. Forgetting himself in the satisfaction of the moment, he set the bucket down and turned to face Michael, speaking in English. "Is good water, Mikhail, yes?"

The farmer gave a start and looked at them in surprise. Michael tried to cover things over by nodding and replying, "Da!" But he knew even before he had said it that he was fooling no one. Even if he got the accent right, the English had already been spoken and heard. It took Dmitri a few seconds to understand the look on Michael's face and what he'd done. By the time he looked guiltily at their host, the man had already studiously directed his attention elsewhere, having sensed their embarrassment. Without another word they returned to the wagon and began unloading it.

They toiled for over an hour under the broiling sun, sorting the wood into the various piles the farmer had pointed out to them. The work and its related instructions were so simple that Michael did not need a translation, so for the most part they worked without speaking, and even then it was mostly Dmitri giving instructions in Ukrainian, while giving enough gestures to make translation unnecessary. Anything else was spoken barely above a whisper, and only when the farmer was busy enough elsewhere so that there was no chance of anything being overheard.

But it was all a sham and all three of them knew it. Though he had said nothing to them, the whole time they laboured, he kept stealing quick, curious glances at them that he thought they were not noticing. Then, with the wood about three quarters unloaded, he disappeared into the house. The next time Michael returned to the wagon, he noticed motion in one of the windows; the curtain was being drawn back and the face of a woman could be seen, her gaze following them.

He turned away on purpose, leaning against the wagon and wiping his brow to give himself a reason to wait for Dmitri to return from his latest load. They both gathered an armload of wood and as they walked towards the growing pile beside the barn, he whispered, "We have an audience."

"Yes, I see."

"Do we make a break for it?" Dmitri gave him a puzzled look. "Do we get out of here?" he tried again.

Dmitri had obviously given that some thought, as he quickly gave his head just enough of a shake for Michael to notice. "They are already watching us. I promise him we unload wood. If we leave, it looks worse. They can look, but as long as they do not tell neighbours, we are okay." He paused as they dropped their loads.

"We finish job and then we go. If we leave now, is bigger chance he will tell someone."

"Okay, if you're sure." Every instinct of Michael's was telling him to drop everything and run for the nearest cover, but Dmitri was the expert, supposedly, and so despite the heat and his fatigue, he increased his pace and tried to carry more wood with each trip. As far as he was concerned, he needed to put this place and these people as far behind him as he could, and as soon as possible.

They completed the job in silence, and then returned to the well for another long drink, desperately wishing there was a way they could take some with them and keep it this cold. It would sure make the long trek a lot more bearable. This time, Dmitri drank first and when Michael took his turn he spoke quietly, his back to the window, "I thank him for ride now and then we go."

Michael didn't bother to ask which way; it didn't matter. They just needed to get away from anyone that knew that there was an English-speaking man in the area. For the first time, he began to fully appreciate Dmitri's attitude in looking for opportunities. It was cold consolation to know that it had been Dmitri, not him, who had slipped up. He remained by the well as Dmitri approached the door to make their farewells.

Before he even reached the steps, the door swung open and the woman they'd seen at the window stepped out. Dmitri bobbed his head politely and began speaking to her, asking her to thank her husband for giving them the ride and explaining that they had to be on their way now. She brushed off his words, stepped around him and walked towards Michael. Michael's heart began pounding and a cold sweat broke out on his brow which had nothing to do with the heat or the work he'd just done. Despite Dmitri's nearby presence, he suddenly felt all alone in an unknown country, and this woman was putting him to the ultimate test. There was no way he could understand or reply. He was so scared that he didn't notice her pleasant smile.

"Good afternoon," she said.

Michael was so frightened, and so busy bracing himself for the worst, that it took his brain a few seconds to realize that he was being spoken to in a language he knew. He shook his head thinking he must be hearing things.

"Good afternoon," she repeated, her brow furrowing, "I said that properly, did I not?" She spoke with a definite accent, but it was much, much lighter than Dmitri's and the English words seem to flow effortlessly.

"Yes, yes, you said it properly." He looked nervously at Dmitri who just gave a helpless shrug; there was no point in trying to pretend anymore. "You speak English very well." He forced what he hoped was a reassuring smile.

The woman's smile broadened, so he must have succeeded. "Thank you. I am an English teacher in the village school, but I do not often have a chance to talk to a real English speaker." She actually blushed slightly. "Maybe I do not speak it as well as my students think."

"No, you speak it very well." He didn't add that her grammar might even be better than his.

She now motioned towards the door. "Please come in, I have prepared some food." Her invitation and the conversation had left both men confused, especially the offer of food. The deal they'd made was only for a ride into town.

They exchanged another look before he reluctantly responded, "Thank you, but we need to be going, and we have to go..." Michael had just realized he'd talked himself into a corner. Where was he going to say they had to go? To somewhere safe from the Mafia, or where they could cross the border unseen? That would make it much less awkward, wouldn't it?

Her smile faded and her voice became much more serious, as if her words were supposed to mean more than he understood. "Please, you must come inside." She looked at both of them, and then lowered her voice as she continued, "My husband and I know who you are. You are the Canadian that the authorities are looking for."

They were too stunned now to refuse the invitation and so followed her obediently into the house. As the shock wore off, they realized that it was not all that surprising that they had been recognized. Their pictures had been in newspapers and on television, they were a nation-wide story. Dmitri's slip in using English would have been the first clue. After that error, their host's curiosity would have been aroused to the point that even several days' worth of stubble on their faces and the tattered clothing wouldn't be able to hide the identities of two men who were constantly making the nightly news.

The inside of the house was dark and cool, in stark contrast to the glaring sun outside. It took Michael's eyes a few seconds to grow accustomed to the dark, and in that time he became aware of the musty aroma in the house, mixed with the lingering scents of many, many meals cooked over a tiny gas stove. He coughed slightly and managed to catch his breath.

After blinking a few times he saw a small table set in the midst of the room, piled high with small dishes overflowing with an assortment of food, some of which he couldn't recognize. The farmer was motioning for him to take a seat so he and Dmitri sat themselves down while the woman carried a few more plates of food to the table. He waited until both his hosts took their seats, already having decided he was going to sample everything on the table. It had been so long since he'd eaten properly he didn't really care what it was or how it tasted; he just wanted food. As hungry as he was, he could not help but find it hard to believe this much food had been set out for only four people. Only the manners his parents had drilled into him prevented him from loading his plate immediately.

Somewhat to his surprise, rather than dishing up or passing around the serving plates, the man and his wife both bowed their heads and the husband spoke words that could only have been a blessing on the food. Belatedly, and self-consciously, Dmitri and Michael bowed their heads as well, waiting until the man finished his prayer. As soon as he finished, he began serving up, and his two famished visitors lost no time in filling their plates.

Michael took some boiled potatoes, and then what he took to be the local variety of devilled eggs. That was followed by cabbage rolls and perogies. At that point, it was too hard to wait any longer and he went to work with his knife and fork. The meal was eaten in almost complete silence, except for the sound of the cutlery brushing against the plates; their hosts seeming to sense how hungry their guests were and the farmer's wife smiled proudly as they devoured what she had prepared for them. Despite their near starvation, when they were both full, the serving plates on the table appeared almost as full as when they'd begun. Michael pushed back from the table slightly, knowing he'd eaten too much.

The farmer and his wife exchanged a few words before he rose from his chair and began clearing the table while she sat smiling at their two guests. Michael started to stand up as well, his mom's training kicking in once more.

"No, please sit," the woman said. "My husband will do the work so we can talk."

Michael nodded and sat back down. "Our names are Andrei," she motioned towards her husband who smiled at them as he heard his own name, "And Katya." Michael started to introduce himself, but she cut him off. "You are Michael, and your friend here is Dmitri."

Dmitri was still silent. Neither he nor Michael were particularly pleased that complete strangers knew all about them, but Michael had more practice at being polite with people.

"We know from the news that you are Canadian and Dmitri is a fellow Ukrainian. You were both on the plane that was hijacked to Kiev. We also know that the bus taking you to the Canadian embassy was in an accident and that you were missing. They said on the news you had injured your head and could not remember who you were. Anyone seeing you was asked to call in and report it."

Michael started to correct the story, but she cut him off and continued, sounding very much like the school teacher she was; used to finishing what she was saying before allowing others to speak. "Dmitri here was one of the hijackers and may have taken you as a hostage, hoping to become rich when your family pays the ransom he demanded of them."

She looked back and forth between the two men and smiled. "We knew when we heard the story that it was not true; everyone knows that. Now that we have seen you, your head appears fine and you do not seem to be a hostage."

Michael thought back on how this whole thing had started. He had been a hostage at first, but that was not completely Dmitri's fault; it was a misunderstanding at worst. "I'm not," he confirmed, "And Dmitri was not one of the hijackers, he…"

Dmitri spoke up for the first time. "I was just passenger on my way to Greece. I was offered job there."

Katya's smile hinted that she knew the truth was somewhere in between what the news reports were saying and what Dmitri had just told her.

"How did you know who we were?"

"My husband did not know who you were when he picked you up, but when your friend here spoke English to you, my husband was rather surprised. We do not get many foreigners here, at least not many dressed like you. He could tell you did not want him to know, but he told me, and when we looked at you together, we knew that we recognized you." She looked back and forth at them, an amused expression on her face. "You are not quite like the pictures they showed on the internet, but we figured it out."

There was a long, awkward silence. "Look," Michael finally said, "We need to get across the border. There's some, well, some guys after us that want to make sure he, uh, we, don't get there. So far we haven't met anyone that we could trust enough to help us." Dmitri was shooting daggers at him with his eyes, but Michael went on anyway. "Can we stay here, just for the night? We can sleep in the barn. And if there's any way you can help us find some way to get to the border, I'll pay you back somehow."

She reached across and patted Michael's hand in a motherly fashion. "You and Dmitri will sleep here tonight, and not in the barn. We have room here in the house. You are less likely to be seen if you stay here."

"Thank you," said Michael, with a sigh of relief, sinking down in the chair. He was almost afraid to believe that they had found someplace safe, even if just for one night.

"Spaciba," said Dmitri, admitting reluctantly to himself that Michael's approach seemed to have worked. These people had already had the opportunity to report them and hadn't, though he didn't find himself too happy about the situation. Maybe he was just upset because he'd expected to be the one to discover the opportunity and Michael had snatched that victory from him. Well, they still had to find a way to the border, and then a way across it. There was a long way to go yet despite the meal and the safe place to sleep for the night that Michael had arranged.

Michael, on the other hand, found himself fully relaxing for the first time since the hijacking and let out a long, tired sigh. He tried but failed to stifle a yawn. Katya seemed to understand, "You need to sleep now. Don't worry, you are safe here. Please, come this way."

She pushed herself back from the table and led them to a doorway. It was a doorway, but there was no door, just a curtain separating the two rooms. As far as he could see, it was the only other room in the house aside from the one they were eating in. Michael tried to object, but Katya would not listen. She turned and left the room, drawing the curtain shut behind her.

The room had two single beds. Well, more like cots, to Michael's way of thinking, but on the other hand, they were like plush beds in a five star hotel compared to what he'd been experiencing lately. He hadn't slept in a real bed since the night before leaving home. He plopped down and took off his shoes before stretching out. It was warm enough that he didn't need the neatly folded blanket at the end of the bed. It was not that late in the afternoon, so when he closed his eyes, he was planning on taking only a short nap, but he quickly fell into a deep, dreamless sleep.

He awoke again hours later. The room was pitch black and he knew that it was either very late at night, or very early in the morning. Dmitri was snoring lightly in the other bed, and from the other side of the curtain came the slightly louder snoring of the farmer.

What was his name again? Andrei, that was it. He stretched out, rolled onto his left side, and fell back asleep.

CHAPTER 14

Traveling Companion

Michael didn't awaken again until the next morning. It might have been the bright sunlight streaming in the window that roused him, or maybe it was that for the first time in several days his body had got almost all the rest it needed. It was almost a novelty to sleep on a bed. There had been a night on a plane, another in a wrecked car, and the previous night in a train seat, which reclined almost as far as the seat on the airplane. Rolling over, he saw that Dmitri's bed was empty, and then with a sigh he swung his feet to the floor and pulled his shoes back on. Had his companion still been asleep, he might have been tempted to roll back over, but now he felt vaguely guilty about sleeping later than Dmitri had. With his laces tied, he made his way through the curtain into the kitchen.

Dmitri and Katya were talking quietly and sipping tea over a collection of empty plates. Andrei was nowhere to be seen so Michael assumed he was out doing chores, as most farmers were at this time of day.

"Good morning," Katya said, rising from the table and walking to the stove. She had already cooked up some eggs and now she scooped them onto a plate. Setting them down in front of Michael, she also slid a basket of sliced bread towards him. Then she poured hot water from the kettle into a cup and handed it to him along with a box of assorted tea bags.

"Thanks," he replied with a grateful smile, and began devouring the food before remembering supper the previous night. With a sheepish look on his face, he set down the fork, folded his hands, and mumbled some words he remembered from his Sunday School days. He nodded another thank you to Katya, picked up the knife and fork, and quickly polished off the eggs. He didn't feel the least embarrassed when he was offered, and accepted, seconds.

It wasn't until after he had finished the second serving that he realized Dmitri had not yet spoken to him, so he turned to him, trying to sound casual and friendly. "So, what's the plan? Do we have one yet?"

Dmitri was just starting to shake his head when Katya answered for him. "My husband has gone to see some friends of ours. We are hoping that they can help us get you to the border."

Michael blinked at the words, and swallowed hard. That must be why Dmitri was so sullen. He wasn't all that thrilled with the idea either. It wasn't that the couple weren't trying to help; he was sure they had good intentions. But the more people that knew about them, the greater was the risk that news of their whereabouts would get back to Yuri and his men.

"Don't worry; my friends can all be trusted." She could tell the men were uncomfortable with the idea. "We are all Believers."

"Believers?" Michael wasn't sure what she meant.

"We are Christians," she explained, "One of the men my husband is meeting with is our pastor. Andrei cannot drive you to the border on his tractor," she and Michael shared a forced laugh at that thought, but Dmitri remained stone-faced. "We are trying to find someone with a car. Someone we can trust and who would be willing to drive you there."

"We have some money so we could pay for the gas, and for their time," Michael offered.

"That can all be worked out later," she responded, patting his hand is if it were not even worth talking about. But now that his stomach was full, he was beginning to feel a bit guilty about accepting free help from these people. One look around their house and property was all it took to see that they didn't have much. He decided then and there that if he ever got back home, he'd have to repay them somehow, but he also knew this was not the time to discuss it.

"Well, maybe while we're waiting we could at least help out around here? There must be something we can do."

"We will find something to do," Dmitri said gruffly. "Let's go, Mikhail."

The two men rose from the table, thanking their hostess once more before making their way outside. Dmitri walked briskly towards the barn and Michael had to almost run to keep up with him. "What's wrong with you, man? These people are trying to help us. You wanted a place to stay, and they've fed us, and they're trying to get us to the border."

Dmitri's reply was not verbal. Without even turning towards him he grabbed a couple of pitchforks and thrust one towards Michael. He took it awkwardly, wondering how much self-control it took for Dmitri not to stab him with it.

"What's your problem?"

Dmitri spun and glared at him. "My problem is two hundred men out there looking for me," he swung his arm around, pointing in every direction to emphasize his point. "Until now, only you and I know where we are. Now whole village will know!"

"He's only talking to a couple of people," Michael began to object.

"And who will those people talk to? Who is one that will turn us in? They might trust these other people, but I do not. And neither should you."

Michael realized that Dmitri's anger was not necessarily directed towards him, and perhaps not even towards their hosts. It was the result of the fact that he'd lost control of the situation. He did have a point, Michael had to concede. "Well, it's done now. We can run again or we can get a ride all the way to the border. I say we stick it out and give them a chance to help us."

"Maybe you stay and I go."

Michael was shocked at the outburst. A day or so ago he would have jumped at that opportunity, but now Dmitri had become… become what? A friend? Maybe, but more than that; he was the one person he knew in the whole country he felt he could fully trust. He was willing to trust Andrei and Katya enough to accept their help, but he realized he trusted Dmitri with his life. Maybe because both their lives were at stake, and only they could really understand the situation they were in.

"Okay, Dmitri. If you want to go, I'll go with you. We can leave right now." The words were spoken calmly and without sarcasm; he set his pitchfork down to emphasize his point.

The words came as almost a physical blow to Dmitri. All his life he'd done what he wanted, or obeyed orders to get what he'd wanted. He'd bullied and even beaten people into giving him his way. He felt guilty about getting Michael into this mess, and feeling that way was a first for him. Michael's willingness to pass up this opportunity and stay with him was another first, and it knocked the anger right out of him.

"Okay, Mikhail," he tried to sound reluctant as he spoke, "We will give them chance and hear their plan. But if I don't like it, we leave."

"Fair enough," Michael said, smiling in relief. "But even if you like it, and I don't, then we still leave!" He got a surprised look in return.

In the heat of their argument neither of the men paid any attention to the people passing by on the road. The barn was set back too far back from the road to allow anyone to notice that they were speaking in English, but they drew a few curious looks as all of the passers-by were locals and they weren't. Though several wondered about them, asking about someone else's business was not something generally done in this part of the country, not even in a friendly, conversational way. Everyone knew Andrei and Katya, and most of their family. These two men were a complete mystery.

Most of them forgot about the two strangers as soon as they'd passed the yard, but not the man driving the horse-drawn wagon. He was returning with a load of hay he'd picked up in the neighbouring village. Two men in an old blue Mercedes had been stopping everyone that entered or left the village he'd just come from with the promise of a reward for information about two men who were thought to be in the area. He had no idea who the men in the Mercedes were, or for that matter why they were looking for the two men, though he did recognize them from the news reports. None of it mattered to him at all, but the reward money would ease the burden of trying to scratch out a living on his small farm.

He hadn't really thought too much about it at the time. He rarely saw any strangers in the short distance he travelled from his home, but he'd taken the piece of paper with the pictures and the number to call if they were seen. Since his horse knew the way home he reached into his pocket and drew out the paper. He could no longer see the men, and even if he could, the pictures were taken in a much different setting than Andrei's farmyard. It might or might not be them, but there was no harm in calling, was there? It might turn into some easy and much needed money.

It took a long time for his old phone to turn on and allow him to punch in the number on the paper. When the call finally went through, it was answered on the second ring. "This is Ivan Petrovich. You gave me a paper describing two men you are looking for. I think I just saw them."

* * *

Vasili did not recognize the number on his call display, and he didn't recognize the man's name when he identified himself. It was, after all, just another call among the dozens he was receiving every day. But as the man spoke, he sat bolt upright.

"What? Say that again!"

"We have been passing out the flyers and received a call from a man who says he may have seen them just a few minutes ago."

Vasili grabbed the map and a pen, making notes as the man spoke. He knew that nothing was confirmed yet, but it was the first good lead since that leap they'd made from the train. He'd even admitted to himself that it had been a good move on Dmitri's part, but the man was going to slip up sooner or later. He'd done it in trying to get to Athens, and he may just have done it again.

"No, don't do anything," he instructed the man on the other end of the phone. "I will come there personally and check it out for myself. Call this man back and have him find some reason to pass by again for another look." He reconsidered that almost as he spoke the words, that had been his impatience talking, it would be a very bad idea to have the man return. "No, don't even do that. The fool will sit there and watch them. Don't do anything until I get there. Nothing at all!"

The village was a little over 40 kilometres from where he was sitting and he could feel his excitement rising. Despite the lack of confirmation, he had a feeling that this was it. He contemplated calling Yuri, but then thought better of it. No sense in giving the pompous fool any reason to get mad at him if things did not work out. He'd call him if, make that when, he had them.

"Get the car," he shouted to the man sleeping on the couch, "We are going now."

He gathered up his map, cell phone, and notebook, already heading out the door by the time the exhausted driver had managed to get his feet on the floor.

* * *

There is no end to the work that needs doing on a farm, especially when the workload includes an assortment of cows, pigs, and chickens, so the two men were able to keep themselves occupied with a variety of chores. Having grown up in a village, Dmitri was well versed in what needed doing. It helped the time pass quickly, and it was a welcome change from being on the run and constantly having to look over their shoulders. They were still working when Andrei returned with another man in tow.

He was much older than Dmitri, even older than Andrei, and smiled pleasantly at them, offering his hand to each in turn. He spoke a few words to Michael which he did not understand, but they came across as a friendly greeting, so he offered an embarrassed, "Hello, nice to meet you," in response. He and Dmitri exchanged a few pleasantries before Andrei ushered them towards the house.

Inside Katya had prepared tea for them all, and had a few plates of cakes and cookies waiting for them on the table.

"This is Pastor Nicolai," she said by way of introduction. The man smiled at him as he recognized his own name. "I think he has some good news for you."

She switched to Ukrainian without missing a beat and spoke briefly to Pastor Nicolai. He nodded and answered her, speaking at some length before Katya interrupted him. "He speaks so much I will forget half of it before I can translate it," she laughed.

Dmitri broke in, "You do not need to translate all of it. Just enough that Mikhail understands what is to happen. I can give him details later."

Katya was obviously disappointed that she could not practice her English skills, but she deferred to Dmitri's surly mood. "Pastor has arranged for a man to drive you to the border two days from now when he has a day off from his job. Slavic is his name. You will leave in the evening and he can have you there in several hours. But he cannot cross the border himself; he has no passport."

Dmitri cut her off, speaking first in Ukrainian, then catching himself and switching to English. "He will not need to cross border, and we do not wish to go to official crossing point. We will be seen and caught."

Katya and the pastor exchanged a volley of words and Katya turned to Michael again. "You can discuss that with Slavic later today. We will take you to his house after dinner and you can tell him what you would like him to do."

Michael let out a relieved sigh. They were going to make it! He might even have a chance to get to Greece after all. Surely the airline and the hotels would understand his predicament and make some kind of allowance to help him salvage what was left of the trip. Still, he couldn't help shaking his head at the fact that no one there thought that it was at all strange that they would be making an illegal border crossing. If things weren't so tense, he might even have laughed out loud at the thought. Then again, he'd never entered the country legally in the first place, so why worry about formalities now?

"Tell him thanks very much. I will repay him, I promise. I just don't have much with me right now."

"He is doing it to be a blessing and a help to you, that is all. He does not expect to be repaid."

"I know, but still, if he helps us like that it is the least I can do."

She turned and spoke with the pastor, who answered with a few words and a shrug.

"He says you can speak about that when you meet him tonight."

* * *

An hour and a half after their evening plans had been finalized, a shiny, late model car pulled up in front of another farm house on the opposite side of the village. The passengers had drawn a few envious and resentful looks from the handful of locals who'd seen them, but no one bothered to find out who they were or why they were here. The house they'd pulled up to didn't exactly belong to the best-liked resident of the village, so it pleased them, in a perverse way, to have one more reason to resent him.

Vasili waited a few moments after the car shut down. No one seemed to be paying any particular attention to him now that the initial stares from the villagers had ended. He made a mental note to pick up a much older car somewhere for the occasions when less attention would be better. He walked as casually as he could to the door of the house, which took a lot of self-control. After all this time they were finally, he hoped, within his reach. Knocking once on the door to announce his presence, he opened it and walked in before anyone else could see him. His driver remained with the car.

Ivan and his wife had heard the car pull up to their house and were prepared for his arrival. They introduced themselves and offered him a cup of tea, which he accepted without acknowledgement.

"Who else have you talked to about this?" he demanded sharply of both of them. Slightly taken aback at his abruptness, they hesitated for a few seconds. Ivan in particular had expected a thank you, and possibly some mention of a reward.

"We…we have told no one, just as we were instructed by your man." They looked at each other uncertainly, wondering for the first time just who they were dealing with. But neither of them dared to ask now.

"Good," Vasili said. It was only one word, a word acknowledging that they had done right. But it struck fear into their hearts because it seemed to imply that had they not followed the instructions, there might have been serious consequences. He could see the fear in their eyes and knew they were telling the truth. It was exactly what he wanted them to feel, because it put him in complete control.

He reached into the inside pocket of his coat and pulled out the photographs he carried of Dmitri and the Canadian. "These are the men you think you saw?"

The man took the photos, relieved to have something to look at besides Vasili's eyes; something in them made his blood run cold. His wife looked at them intently for the same reason.

Ivan looked at them longer than he needed to. He had not got a close look, but he was almost certain it was them. Somehow he had the impression it would not be completely wise to come across as certain with this man, though. There was a small chance he was wrong and it might be best to be wrong from the start.

"I told the man who answered the phone when I first called that I thought it was them. I did not get a good look from the road and I thought it would be best not to go back for another look." Vasili nodded condescendingly as the man spoke, as if he were saying something too obvious to really need stating.

"Where is the house they are staying at? What do you know about the people who are harbouring them?"

Ivan swallowed hard and clasped his hands together so that the slight tremble in his fingers would not be so noticeable. There was certainly no love lost between himself and Andrei, but he'd never wished for anything really bad to happen to him. All he'd wanted was the reward for finding the two men who'd disappeared so mysteriously after the hijacking. "They live on the other side of the village. You cannot see their house from here." That seemed to please Vasili so he continued. "There is not much to say about them. They have lived in this village their whole lives."

"You do not think they know Dmitri, then?"

"I do not think so. He is not from this village and they do not travel far. No one here does. We do not even have a train nearby." He felt an overwhelming urge to defend Andrei. "Maybe they do not know who these men are. They are Believers; they often help other people." He didn't understand that concept himself, but he'd noticed it in them over the years. "Maybe someone from their church asked them to look after these men."

Vasili ended his train of thought with a dismissive wave of his hand. "It does not matter. I need you to show me where they are so that I can get a look at them myself."

"And then?" Ivan asked with a faint glimmer of hope.

"If it is them, then I will do what is necessary to take them into custody." The answer to that question seemed obvious to Vasili, until he caught the hesitant look in Ivan's eyes and understood what he was really asking. "And you will receive your reward." Even though Vasili rarely did anything that he did not expect to benefit from personally, it seldom occurred to him that others might operate the same way, or that they deserved any credit for his success. As far as he would ever be concerned, it was his hard work and planning that had tracked down Dmitri and the Canadian.

"Is there somewhere we can watch the house from without being seen? I need to be absolutely sure it is them as soon as possible."

Ivan had to think for a few moments, drawing a mental map of the land around Andrei's house. "No," he replied with a shake of his head. "Not unless we hide in his barn. There isn't anywhere close enough to the house where we could see them without being seen ourselves."

Vasili mulled over Ivan's answer for a few minutes and then came to a conclusion. "Then we will wait until after dark. I must borrow some of your clothes so that I will look like one of you. You will take me as close as you can to this house and stay with me. That way, if we are seen, we will be two friends walking together."

"Of course," Ivan replied, eager for an opportunity to leave the room even for a few minutes. "I will go and find you some clothes while my wife gets you some tea. After supper I will take you there. It is not far." He rose from the table and left to find some clothes that he hoped would fit his guest.

* * *

Michael pushed his chair back from the table. The meal had been simple but bountiful, and he knew that he had eaten too much again. It was the unfortunate result, no doubt, of going several days with little or nothing to eat. He had to refuse Katya's offers of more food several times before she began clearing the table. It looked to him once more as if there was more food left over than all four of them had eaten.

Andrei spoke a few words and then looked to his wife awaiting her translation. "Andrei says that we should go now. Pastor and Slavic are expecting us."

"Okay," Michael replied with a nod. He felt a tightening in his chest. Dmitri's concern must have been contagious. As much as he wanted to get to the border and leave Ukraine and Yuri behind him, he was very nervous about putting his life in the hands of a stranger, now that the time had come.

Andrei and Katya led them to the door and stepped out into the darkness. To the two locals, it was simply a visit with good friends, though the nature of the visit made it somewhat more exciting than usual. They led their two guests to the road which, like most villages in their region, had no streetlights.

They followed the gravel road to an intersection only a few yards away and made a right turn. Two dark figures appeared out of the darkness. They were standing on the far side of the road talking softly in the shadows. Andrei must have recognized them because he spoke a brief, pleasant greeting which was returned rather curtly by one of the men before he quickly turned away to resume his conversation. Even without a translation, the man's response struck Michael as very rude.

Only Dmitri paid them much attention. Something worried him in a vague way, but it was too dark to make out either of them and he quickly lost sight of them as they continued down the street. He shrugged off the icy shiver he'd felt in his spine. Andrei knew them, so it must be okay; he'd been on alert for so long that everything was bothering him. He forced himself to calm down and keep walking.

Michael decided that there was no direct route to wherever they were headed as they had to twist back and forth along various streets. As they made their way further into the village, the gravel road gave way to a deeply rutted dirt street and they began to meet even more people going about whatever business occupied them at this hour. Some ignored them, others greeted, or were greeted by, their guides. Even if they had turned around they likely would not have realized that the two men from the intersection were following them at the extreme range of visibility.

As far as Michael was concerned, this was a carbon copy of the village they had driven through on that first night when they'd been frantically fleeing the scene of the bus crash. Tall fences in various states of repair marked the property lines and effectively blocked the view of the yards and houses. Most of the windows were covered by thick curtains and with no visible light many of the houses appeared abandoned.

Andrei turned to his right without any warning and reached for an unseen latch to open a metal gate. Michael could see nothing to differentiate this yard from any other, but Andrei obviously knew this was where they were going. He stepped through and held the gate open for the others. By the time he had closed and latched the gate Katya was knocking on the door. Without waiting for an answer she opened it and walked in.

Despite the single, dim bulb inside the porch, Michael had to blink several times to allow his eyes to adjust from the complete darkness outside. A young man greeted them with warm smiles and handshakes before leading them through a door to their left. The door looked as if it had received a dozen coats of paint over a stretch of years that easily exceeded the lifespan of its owner. It led them into a large, high-ceilinged living room, filled with a collection of mismatched furniture. A cot that served double duty as both bed and chesterfield occupied the wall along the front window, while a collection of chairs stretched around the other walls. It looked as if it often served as a meeting place for a larger group of people than the room was designed for and, in fact, it served as the meeting place for Pastor Nicolai's small church. The Pastor was already seated in one of the chairs as they entered and he motioned for Michael to take a seat beside him as the rest of the group settled down around the room. Katya sat in the chair next to him to act as translator.

The pastor looked over the small gathering and spoke a few words. "Pastor would like to pray before we begin," Katya announced for Michael's benefit, and he bowed his head along with the rest of them as the man prayed. There was no doubt in his mind what the man was praying for, and he desperately hoped that it would be answered.

They all looked at each other nervously, waiting to see who would start the conversation. Michael had assumed Dmitri would take the lead, but when he just sat back waiting to see what would transpire, Michael looked at Slavic and decided to start things off.

"Thank you for taking us to the border, I would like to repay you, but I do not have much money. I will send it to you as soon as I can."

Slavic smiled with embarrassment as the words were translated, and then made his reply through Katya. "He says that it will not be necessary. He is happy to be able to help you."

Michael began to respond, but at that point Dmitri decided it was time to wade in and start making some real plans. He spoke rapidly with Slavic. Katya, unable to translate quickly enough, provided Michael with an abbreviated version of their discussion as best she could.

"Dmitri wants to know if you can leave any earlier than two days from now, but Slavic cannot do that because of his job." She didn't need to wait for his reply, she already knew that it wouldn't be possible.

As impressed as Michael was with her ability to listen and speak at the same time, he didn't have time to compliment her. It took all his concentration just to follow the conversation and figure out who was saying what.

"What time will we leave?"

"We will leave as soon as I am off work, we can bring some food with us and eat it while we drive."

"No, we should wait until after dark, I do not wish to be seen or recognized by anyone."

"Yes, we can do that."

She paused for breath, looking to Michael to make sure he was following. He nodded and she rushed to catch up with the conversation.

"I cannot cross the border with you, I do not have an international passport, but I can drop you off near the checkpoint, many people walk across the border."

"No, we do not want to cross at a checkpoint; the men looking for us may have bribed the guards to report us or detain us."

"What would you like to do then?"

"We will find a road near the border and you can drop us off there, we will make it across ourselves, it is the only way that we can be sure we will make it."

"I understand, but I do not know the region well, do you have a place in mind, it will be best if we decide where before we leave."

As obvious as that point may have been, it did relieve Dmitri somewhat to see that the young man could not only understand their need, but had a bit of foresight as well.

"Do you have a map of the border region?"

"Yes, Pastor phoned me and had me pick one up today before I came back home."

Slavic produced a map from a bookshelf beside him, opened it up, and began studying it with Dmitri. Since there was no further need of translation, Michael felt he could best leave the planning to the two Ukrainians, and Katya excused herself to make some tea for everyone. Andrei joined in the discussion as well, but the map meant nothing to Michael, so he just sat there in awkward silence and waited for his tea.

*   *   *

Across the street and two doors down from Slavic's house, a lone figure sat hunched against a gate that had once been painted bright green. He had sent Ivan back home shortly after the group of four had entered the house. It had not taken him long to find an empty bottle to complete his disguise, and he did his best to slouch against the gate as if in a drunken stupor. Alone, with his face almost between his knees, and seated in the opposite direction than they would be heading when they left, he was certain that even Dmitri would not recognize him. Not in the dark while he was dressed like this.

It seemed to him that they had been inside for hours. He had no idea what was being discussed in there, but it didn't matter. After all the days and sleepless nights he was now only a few metres from his prey. One good look would confirm what he was already certain of. He knew who he needed to call and what assets he needed in place. Just one look from close enough to confirm it was all he was waiting for. He didn't feel the cool humidity that had arrived with the setting of the sun. He barely noticed the mosquitos buzzing around him, or the smell of the smouldering garbage in the next yard. He fixed his eyes on the door of the house and forced himself to be patient.

Without any warning at all the door opened and a shaft of light shot out into the yard, but fortunately for Vasili the high fence prevented it from illuminating the apparently inebriated man all but passed out in the street. The sound of voices saying farewell and goodnight was carried to his ears by the cool night air. It was all he could do not to look up when he caught one of them speaking English. His heart began racing. Then he heard a voice that was very familiar, the voice of a man that had once been a friend. The voice of someone who'd worked with him for years. He didn't need to see the face now. He knew he had them.

He was purposely looking the other way when the gate opened, so he didn't see the sympathetic look that was cast his way by two pairs of eyes. But in the dark, out of sight, he was smiling. If Yuri had only wanted them dead, his job would now be complete. But a dead Dmitri could not return the money. They needed him alive.

He waited until the party was out of sight, then rose to his feet and began making his way back to Ivan's house. He didn't want to risk making phone calls out in the open where he might be overheard, but he already knew who to call and what instructions to give.

CHAPTER 15

Intersection

The first call Vasili made once he arrived back at Ivan's house was to Yuri. Even though there was still much to do, and Dmitri was not yet in their custody, he felt the need to let Yuri know that things were progressing. Not that he'd ever admit it, but it gave him an excuse to lift himself up and gloat a little. His call was answered on the first ring. Not after the first ring, but during the first ring.

"Yuri Stepanovich, it is Vasili." He cut the man off before he could say much more than hello, speaking rapidly as though he didn't have much time. "I saw them, both of them, not ten minutes ago." He kept talking to prevent a string of irritating questions from his boss. "They did not see me, and I must now call in some more men. I am not going to rush into this and let them get away like those other fools did, but I will have them by tomorrow. I'll call you when I know more."

Punching the button to end the call was almost as satisfying as finding Dmitri had been. All Yuri had managed was a few words interspersed between the sentences of Vasili's rapid-fire report of the day's events. With that out of the way, he could get down to the real work. He needed the right mix of muscle and brains. He could afford no more of the idiots that might let Dmitri slip away once again, but he also needed enough muscle to overpower both men. The Canadian looked like he'd be no trouble at all, but Dmitri had once made his living by beating people into submission, so one-to-one odds would not cut it with him.

It would have been so much easier if he didn't need to both capture Dmitri and keep him alive. Well, he'd have to instruct the men that no harm could come to Dmitri, at least not anything immediately fatal. The Canadian might make a good insurance policy, especially if Dmitri had revealed anything to him. It was curious that Dmitri still had him along. Why had he not lost him, or done away with him? That had been a passing thought up until now, but perhaps it bore closer examination. It was quite possible that this, what was his name? Michael? Maybe this Michael was his contact in the West. Maybe he'd met Dmitri in Frankfurt to give him access to the funds, or to divide them up between the two of them. That would explain why they were on the plane together, and why they'd escaped together from the bus. And he might prove to be a lot easier to break than Dmitri!

All things that he could look into later, he chided himself. Make the calls, and get the men in place. He could have them here by morning and set the trap. The moment they ventured outside, he'd spring it. Then it would be time to persuade the two of them to start talking.

* * *

Back at the house Michael and Dmitri were both ready for bed, but Katya insisted on serving them tea and cake before they retired for the evening. Michael was Canadian enough that he could not bring himself to refuse the offer. The conversation lagged, as they'd spent the last few hours discussing all the details of the planned escape route. Nothing else seemed worth talking about, but he did notice that Dmitri was the most relaxed he'd been since their arrival in the village.

Michael finished the last crumb of his cake. Even with the icing it wasn't as sweet as what he was used to back home, but it was good. The tea was too hot to drink in one gulp, but he finished it as quickly as possible and then unconsciously glanced at the doorway to the bedroom.

"You must be tired after all that has happened today," Katya exclaimed, noticing the glance. Michael was embarrassed, and tried to deny it, but she stood her ground firmly, saying she'd clean up and that they were to go to bed. Maybe it was the school teacher coming out in her, but both men headed obediently to their room.

They kicked off their shoes and rolled onto their beds. Barely any light was coming through the window so the room was filled with an inky blackness that left them almost completely blind. "So are you okay with these plans? Do you think it will work?" Michael asked.

There was a long pause before Dmitri answered. "Yes, I think it will work. Slavic seems to understand what we need to do and why." There was another long, thoughtful silence. "I've never met people like this. They don't know much about us, but they still want to help us."

"I guess they just know we need help and that's enough. So it will work?" He wanted Dmitri to say it would work, not that he thought it would work. Because if Dmitri said it would work, then surely it would, and that was something for him to cling to and give him hope.

"Yes, Mikhail, it should work. If we can get to border then crossing it will not be problem. There are very few patrols there now. You can go to Canadian embassy. Tell them you were kidnapped by crazy Ukrainian guy and they will help you even without passport."

"What about you? What will you do?" As he asked the question, he realized for the first time that once they were safe, they'd go their separate ways and likely never see each other again. A few days ago that would have been a welcome prospect, but now, well, they weren't exactly best friends, but he'd kind of got used to having

Dmitri around. While he'd never admit it to the man, he did have a kind of grudging respect for him. He really was trying to change his ways, as evidenced by the help he'd given Michael. After getting him into this mess in the first place, that is.

"I have something waiting for me. I will be all right."

"But Yuri tracked you down last time. If he knows you're going to Greece, won't that make it easier for him to follow you next time?"

The question was met with a scornful laugh. "I do not need to go to Greece. That was just part of route I was using. I was too impatient last time. I thought if I was out of Ukraine, I was safe. I know better now, and this time I will be more careful. And more patient. I will be fine, Mikhail."

Michael yawned while trying to respond. "Okay, that's good, Dmitri. I'm sure you'll make it. Good night."

"Good night, Mikhail."

Even the excitement and anxiety of knowing they'd soon make their final run to the border could not keep either of them awake any longer. Their bodies had still not recovered fully from all the stress and those nights without proper sleep. They were both snoring loudly by the time Katya had cleaned up the kitchen.

* * *

Vasili made the last of his calls and turned his phone to vibrate. He would have turned it off completely, but he knew there was always a chance that something might come up overnight. His driver was keeping a watch on the farmhouse for the night, and the rest of his team had been instructed to enter the village separately and from different directions. All dressed as local villagers of course, not the suits and flashy clothes they usually wore.

For a few minutes his mind raced, trying to find some detail he'd missed or some fatal flaw in his plan. But he'd been over it a hundred times already and so tonight he would sleep. He closed his eyes, settled further down into the bed, and drifted off into a dreamless sleep with a crooked smile on his lips.

*   *   *

After two nights of uninterrupted sleep, Michael awoke feeling almost refreshed. Dmitri was still snoring fitfully, and he could hear Katya trying to prepare breakfast as quietly as possible. She and Andrei were speaking in hushed tones. He contemplated trying to go back to sleep for a while, but was too awake for that. He rolled out of the bed, pulled on his shoes, and slipped out of the room without waking Dmitri.

Andrei smiled warmly, beckoning him to take a seat while Katya turned from the stove, bringing a boiling kettle with her for the tea. As far as he could tell, no one in this whole country ever seemed to get enough tea to drink. As a committed coffee drinker, he was finding it a bit hard to make the switch.

He made small talk with his hosts over breakfast until Dmitri joined them. He was in a better mood than Michael had ever seen him in, and he wondered if the Ukrainian was as impatient for tomorrow night as he was. Andrei and Katya were excellent hosts, but that was about the only thing he'd enjoyed during this whole trip. It might not be a bad place to visit again someday, if Yuri and the Ukrainian Mafia were no longer looking for him. There had to be a lot of history and culture to learn about.

They finished their breakfast. As the men lingered over their second, and even third, cup of tea, Katya began to clear the table. Michael gathered up his dishes and cutlery and rose to carry them to the sink. "Please, please, sit down," she motioned towards the table with a free hand. But Michael, instead, returned to the table for a second load.

"Sorry," he said with his trademark grin; the one he'd hardly had cause to use since the hijacking. "I have to clear the table. That's how my mom raised me."

Katya looked at him and laughed, "Then I guess you had better obey your mother." Everyone was in a good mood this morning, he noticed. Katya didn't even object when he helped with the dishes while Andrei and Dmitri chatted in Ukrainian at the table.

As he hung the dishrag over the counter, he wondered how to pass the rest of the day, and the next one. There was no TV in the house, and though there were a couple of shelves full of books, they were all no doubt in Ukrainian. The time would pass a lot faster if there was something to do besides sit around and wait.

"Dmitri, can you ask Andrei if there's anything else he needs done around here? It would sure help pass the time if we had something to do."

Dmitri smiled a knowing smile, "We have already talked about that. The barn needs some repairs, that is what wood we unloaded is for."

"Sounds good to me," he replied with a nod. "Let's get to work."

* * *

Vasili had arranged for his men to take turns watching the house before the sun had even risen. While it would have been a simple matter to walk into the house and grab them, it would have left loose ends that would need to be looked after. The quieter they could keep things the better. While many people already knew he was looking for these men, he'd rather not have anyone actually see him take them. Anyone anywhere in the country that had seen the news knew these men had disappeared and were being looked for, especially the foreigner. But if anyone were to see the fight they were sure to put up, then the illusion that he was acting in some sort of official capacity and 'rescuing' the missing victims of the hijacking, would be shattered. If that were the case, then the witnesses would have to be dealt with in one way or another before they could report what had happened to the real authorities. Even that could be dealt with, but it would take time and money that would only make Yuri angrier. It would be best to keep everything as quiet as possible.

Currently, two men walking in opposite directions had met on the road and were engaged in a lengthy conversation that might have been about life and events in the village. Before they had been there long enough to arouse much suspicion, and unless they had anything to report, they would move on and Vadim would then develop car trouble just close enough to the house to see what was happening in the yard. It was not an elaborate plan, but he was sure it would work. They would just wait for the right opportunity. He had to laugh at that thought. Dmitri was always talking about opportunities, wasn't he? He wouldn't like this one very much.

Through the modern miracle of the cell phone Vasili had been kept up to date on what was happening. So in the meantime, there was nothing to do but enjoy his morning tea.

* * *

The three men left the house and made the short walk to the barn. A short way away, Andrei noticed two other men talking, but they were too far away to recognize. Since they seemed to be wrapped up in a conversation, he didn't bother to greet them. Leading his two visitors to the barn, he explained to Dmitri what needed to be done, knowing he would explain it to the Canadian in English. He was facing the wrong way and didn't see that one of the men on the road was now talking on his cell phone. Even if he had seen it, there would have been nothing odd enough about it to attract further attention.

* * *

Vasili grabbed his phone and answered it almost before the first ring ended. "Da?"

"Vasili, we see them. They are here!" The man could hardly contain his excitement and he hoped that they weren't drawing any attention to themselves.

"Calm down! Are they leaving? Where are they going?"

There was a pause that might have given Vasili a heart attack if he were much older. He briefly considered calling Yuri and giving him the same message in the same way. "No, it looks like the farmer is making them work on his barn."

Dmitri doing manual labour? That was unusual to say the least, but not something to worry about now.

"Keep an eye on them. Try to stay out of sight and let me know if anything changes. I don't want to do anything until we can somehow get them alone. It would be best to do this with no witnesses."

* * *

There was no rush to finish the job, and even if there had been, neither of the two men were particularly skilled at this kind of work. So they worked slowly but steadily as they removed some rotting boards and replaced them with the newer lumber they'd stacked the day before. Andrei was busy with various other chores and projects and didn't seem at all concerned with their slow pace.

The two men who'd been talking on the road wandered off without being given anything more than passing notice by any of the three men. After all, it was anything but uncommon to see small groups of people wandering about a village in Ukraine. Andrei, and even Dmitri, would have thought something was wrong if the streets were empty. Michael, on the other hand, watched all the interaction between the villagers and wondered how many years it had been since it was like that in Canada.

*   *   *

Vasili now had the rest of his team moving into position around the house. Since they were all in contact with each other and working as a team, he had only to talk to one of them to confirm that they were all moving into place. They couldn't look like they were surrounding the house, but they had to cover enough of it that they could move in from any direction and cover every possible exit path. A few found cover behind buildings or trees. They weren't close enough to pounce quickly. They were too far away for that, but they were covering all possible avenues that way. Others were hiding in plain sight by moving back and forth, talking to each other, and generally mixing in with the usual foot traffic of the village.

The woman was inside the house and would likely stay there. All they had to do now was to get rid of the farmer, temporarily of course, unless he caused too much of a problem. They'd be the only ones to actually know first-hand what had happened to their guests, and while he'd like to do it even more quietly, with no loose ends at all, Vasili was willing to accept the current conditions. If the couple disappeared as well there would be too many questions for the rest of the village and the local police to ignore. If the farmer would just go into the house, they just might have enough time to grab the two men and force them into a car. If they had to do it in front of the farmer, well, he was from a village, wasn't he? The promise of some quick cash to keep quiet would be a hard offer to refuse.

Pushing back from the table Vasili turned to his host. What was his name again? It wasn't important. "I need your car, they might recognize mine." It was a statement, not a request.

"I do not have a car!"

Vasili looked at the man as if he were speaking a foreign language. "Then your neighbour's car. I need an older car." His tone of voice made it unnecessary for him to add that he needed it immediately.

"I will go and get you one. I will be right back!"

By Vasili's watch, it was just a little over twelve minutes before Ivan returned with the keys to an ancient Lada that belonged to a family who lived a few doors down. A feigned family emergency was enough to convince the owners to part with it for a few hours. Come to think if it, without the car, there may well have been a real family emergency, Ivan thought. He'd tried very hard to convince himself that the man he'd phoned had been acting in some kind of official capacity, but he knew better now.

Vasili took the keys without speaking a word and motioning for his driver to follow him, walked out the door. The driver took the keys and climbed into his seat. He started the car with some difficulty, and then nursed the engine until he felt it was safe to put it into gear.

With only a slight rattle and a brief grinding sound from the transmission, he managed to get the gearshift into first before easing out the clutch. The car bumped slowly along the deeply-rutted twin dirt trails that led past Ivan's house and towards the centre of the village. They drew curious looks from a few of the locals who recognized the car but not the occupants, but Vasili paid no attention to them, focusing instead on the task before him.

There was a growing feeling of anxiety in his stomach as they rounded the last curve and approached the house. There, he could see them. He didn't look for the rest of his men, he trusted them to be where they needed to be. Now all he needed was a small distraction, and his driver was about to create that for him.

Glancing at Vasili and seeing him nod, he pressed the clutch pedal in and switched off the ignition. The car glided to a slow stop near the approach to Andrei's yard. Vasili remained in the car while the driver climbed out and raised the hood, reaching in to wiggle a few wires and hoses for effect. His charade managed to catch the attention of the three men working near the barn.

* * *

Michael heard Andrei speak a few words to Dmitri in Ukrainian as the man from the stalled car poked under the hood. Dmitri nodded and said something back in response. Apparently Andrei was going to see if the man needed some help. Michael went back to work, figuring it was best if he kept as silent and as invisible as possible.

As Andrei approached the car, he suddenly stopped short. He'd told Dmitri that he'd recognized the car, but now he didn't recognize the driver. Not a suspicious man by nature, he shook off his curiosity.

"Do you need some help?" he asked.

"Yes, please. I borrowed the car from my uncle, but it just stalled on me for no reason."

That explains it, Andrei thought to himself, a relative has borrowed it. "There is always a reason. Let me see if I can help you." The man stepped aside and positioned himself between Andrei and the house, which did not seem odd at all, since he was simply making room for Andrei to have a look under the hood. Andrei sensed, rather than saw, that there was someone else in the car, but he was thinking about what he knew to be the usual problems with this kind of car and didn't really give the passenger any thought.

The passenger climbed out of the car, standing almost out of sight behind the raised hood. "Can you see what is wrong with it?

We are in a hurry today." He sounded anxious, but polite.

"Not yet, but there are a few tricks to keeping these things running." Andrei didn't even look up as he wiggled a few brittle wires. He didn't see anything yet but decided to pull off the air cleaner. "I want to try something. Can you try starting it while I work the throttle from here?"

The driver began walking towards the house. That caught Andrei by surprise. Did he need a drink, or to use the toilet? He started to back away from the car to ask what the man wanted, still more concerned with the man's needs than with the safety of his guests.

"Stay right where you are! Do not move!" The passenger's voice was quiet, but menacing. Too late, the hair on the back of his neck stood up. He had no idea who these men were, but he had no doubt what they wanted. Dmitri and the Canadian were his guests, his friends, and they were under his protection. He wasn't going to give them up just because someone threatened him.

Michael had caught the movement of the driver out of the corner of his eye and was already tensing as the man began walking towards them. At first it was just a fear that the man might try to talk with him. But then he sensed that there was something more going on. Dmitri was keeping an eye on the car too. Unlike Andrei, he was suspicious by nature, and he realized a split second before Michael did that something was terribly wrong.

Andrei was shouting, no, screaming something. Michael caught his own name, and Dmitri's, and though he couldn't understand the rest, one look at Dmitri's face was all he needed by way of translation.

"Run, Mikhail!" The big Ukrainian yelled, grabbing his shoulder and almost pulling him off balance as he spun him around.

Subconsciously, even before understanding the danger, Dmitri had decided that the best place to hide would be in the village itself. The fields were too open and offered no cover. Their best bet lay among the maze of streets and abandoned buildings of the village.

A few seconds more was all they had needed! In a burst of rage, Vasili grabbed Andrei by the neck and threw him against the car. With a loud thud, Andrei bounced of the fender and rolled to the ground. He curled up, shielding himself in anticipation of the next blow, but it never came. When he looked up his attacker was already sprinting across the yard in pursuit of Michael and Dmitri. He rose to follow, but was much too old to catch up.

Dmitri had half a step on Michael as they raced across Andrei's garden, stumbling a bit in the loose soil, but picking up speed as they found more solid footing in the hay field behind it. Neither of them dared look back for fear of tripping but they'd outrun their pursuers once already and they knew they could do it again. They had to, they couldn't even think about the alternative.

They both caught motion ahead of them and saw two villagers rushing to their aid, and then realized that the look on their faces was wrong. They weren't coming to their aid at all. Michael veered with Dmitri, trying to deny the two men the angle to catch them, but he could see it wasn't going to work. Dmitri may never have seen North American football being played, but he lowered his shoulder and caught the first man square in the chest, knocking the wind out of him and throwing him to the ground. One down.

The second man hesitated as he saw his companion go down and lost his momentum. Dmitri straight-armed him in the neck and he went down without a sound.

Their brief victory had come with a cost though, it had slowed them down. Now they had to look. How much of a lead did they have?

"No!" Michael screamed in fear and frustration. There weren't two men behind them, there were four. No, there were six! Two more had appeared from somewhere. How many more were there that he hadn't seen yet? They were closing fast.

"Run! Head for village!" Dmitri barked at him, shocking him back into top gear.

They ran desperately, their legs pumping as hard as they could. Dmitri had the longer legs and was more physically active, but Michael's youth and fear helped him to keep up. Something in Dmitri's voice told him that the man had a plan. He just had to keep up. He just needed to stay far enough ahead of his pursuers for long enough and he'd be safe.

Dmitri did have a plan, he just didn't know where to pull it off yet. They needed to be out of sight just long enough to get into a yard. Any village was full of out buildings, chicken coops, root cellars, all sorts of hiding places. The men would split up to look for them, and that would give them the advantage. He was confident he could handle any one of them, but not all at once. He'd made his living handling men like this.

Vasili didn't have the time to have a temper tantrum, but he knew that his hope of a quick, silent capture was evaporating before his eyes. All he could do now was join in the pursuit. He tried in vain to catch the attention of his men, get them organized, but they were all locked onto the two men who were only a few meters from the first road that wound itself into the labyrinth of the village streets. If they lost sight of their prey now, it could get a whole lot more complicated.

Dmitri didn't waste the breath to urge Michael to keep up; he knew he didn't have to. Both of them could feel their lungs burning as they rounded a corner to the right and bolted up a side street.

The only consolation was the knowledge that their pursuers were having to run just as hard to keep up, and even harder to close the distance. A quick look up the road told Dmitri he'd lucked out, just as he hoped there was another street to the left.

Gauging the distance to the intersection he thought they just might make it. If they could get around it before Vasili's men made the first corner, the instant of hesitation might buy them the time they needed to find somewhere to hide. "Turn left," he panted as they approached the corner. He could hear no shouts behind them. This just might work, he hoped. He was so intent on making it to the corner that he didn't realize he'd reverted to speaking Ukrainian.

Michael heard, but didn't understand the words, so he interpreted them himself. Dmitri was urging him to go faster. His lungs felt like they were on fire and his legs had run further than they had in years, but he called on his last reserves of strength and actually managed to close the distance between himself and Dmitri. But why was he gaining so quickly? Dmitri was turning!

Dmitri made the cut to the left and Michael tried to follow. But he was going too fast and when he planted his right foot to try to turn it landed in a pothole full of broken rocks. He felt a wave of searing pain as his ankle turned and buckled beneath him. He'd never felt such intense pain. He literally saw stars before his eyes and for a moment had no idea what had happened. His awareness returned as suddenly as it had fled, but by then he was rolling and skidding down the rough road, bleeding from cuts to his head and hands.

He tried in vain to stand up and keep going, sobbing in pain and fear, but his body wouldn't answer his demands. He collapsed back onto the road as he tried to use his ankle, harsh shouts ringing in his ears. His last instinct was to crawl, but then something struck him in the back. It was someone's boot. He rolled away instinctively, but then the same boot kicked him in his stomach, knocking the breath from his lungs. Someone rolled him back onto his stomach and his arms were jerked painfully behind his back as he was pinned to the ground, his face forced down into the gravel and dirt. Someone's loud panting was drowning out the sound of his own gasps, and he could hear the sound of several sets of pounding footsteps retreating rapidly into the distance.

CHAPTER 16

Alternate Plans

Dmitri didn't see or hear Michael go down, and still didn't know he'd lost him. Immediately after making the turn he'd spotted a lane between two houses and shot through it. To his right he spotted a yard with several houses in it, one was still inhabited while the two older ones were run down and likely used to store whatever didn't belong inside the house. He turned to point it out to Michael, but he wasn't there.

For a moment panic seized him and his mind froze even though his feet kept moving. Going back was out of the question. Even if he were to try he stood no chance against that many men. He hesitated another moment, then vaulted over the fence and made for the shacks. A quick look showed him that one had been converted into a root cellar. He slipped inside, pulling the door quietly closed behind him and descended the steps into the darkness.

He felt his way along one wall, going slowly so as not to bump or move anything that might make a noise. The sound might not carry far but his heart was pounding as he imagined one, or several, of his pursuers searching the yard just outside the door. There was almost no light, so there was nothing to help his eyes get used to the dark. The cellar had the damp, musty smell of a hundred years' worth of produce, but as it was mid-summer and not much had yet been harvested, it was mostly just shelving and empty sacks from what he could feel. He didn't know the English expression 'any port in a storm,' but he decided to make the best of it. He gathered up an armful of the rough sacks, curled up in a corner, and covered himself up.

By now his breathing and heart rate had returned to near normal and he thought back through what had happened. Somehow they'd gotten separated at one of the corners. Had Michael managed to get away, or had he been caught? Going to look for him was out of the question right now. If he was safe it would be difficult to find him. If he'd been caught there was nothing he could do. He was fairly confident that he was safe himself, for the moment. He'd last been seen at a dead run and Vasili's men would assume, at least at first, that he was still running. They'd spread out to look for him but they could hardly search the whole village. For one thing, they didn't have enough men. For another, they would create too much of a fuss if they tried.

Vasili could be thorough and ruthless when he was free to intimidate people, but even he would not be crazy enough to try to intimidate a whole village. Even with a few policemen in his pocket, he would never get away with that. It would become too public and that would never do.

If they did have Michael, they would try to use that to their advantage. They'd gladly use the Canadian to get to him, which brought an unfamiliar twinge of guilt. And the more Dmitri thought about it, the more afraid he was that Vasili now had Michael. They'd do whatever it took to get whatever information they could from him. Not that they could get much, just Slavic's name and a departure time, not even a description of the car as neither of them had seen it.

His next thought was that he had fifteen million reasons to head for the border right now. He could force Slavic to leave tonight, or steal another car and drive himself.

Escape would be much easier without Michael. There was no doubt about that. He sat in the dark, weighing his options. The original plan was to get out of the country, then access enough of the money to get somewhere safe, somewhere as far from here as possible. And to do it alone. At least at first. There were too many complications to taking someone with him, and now he was free of that burden. To ease his conscience, he could call someone; the Canadian Embassy perhaps, let them know who had Michael and even give them several possible locations where they could find him. One of them was sure to be right. He could even give them Yuri's address, which would cause his former boss no end of trouble since the police were likely already watching his house and looking for an excuse to search it.

That`s what he`d do, he decided. He would head for the border tonight. That way he stood a better chance of escape, and a squad of policemen stood a much better chance of rescuing Michael than he would on his own.

But there was one reason not to do any of that. Michael.

Dmitri didn't even have the strength to argue with himself anymore. He had to stay and help the Canadian. He'd wait in the cellar until dark, and then find some way to contact Andrei. It wouldn't be safe to go back to his house, he knew that. But he'd find a way. There had to be a way. Word would get out in the village, whatever may have happened, and it would get back to Andrei.

* * *

Michael was pulled roughly to his feet and cried out in pain as they made him stand on his twisted ankle. He tried to hop on one foot as they dragged him to the side of the road, but they were pulling him too quickly and roughly. If they understood the pain he was in, they didn't seem to care. A few villagers peered out from their yards to see what the commotion had been, but the warning looks from his two captors quickly convinced them to go back about their business.

A few minutes later, a dark car with tinted windows pulled up to them in a spray of gravel and dust. He wasn't even sure the vehicle came to a full stop as he was shoved roughly into the back seat of the car, finding himself sitting in between two large men. Two more men already occupied the front seats, but apparently none of them knew or understood English. If they did, they didn't let on or try to speak to him. The man in the front seat barked a command to the men in the back, softened his voice slightly as he spoke a few words to the driver, and then his lips curled up in a self-satisfied smile as he took a good look at Michael. The driver slammed the car into gear and began threading his way through the narrow, rough streets and back to the main road.

The man in the front passenger seat pulled out a cell phone, tapped the screen a few times, and then waited for his call to be answered. If Michael had any doubts at all about who had him, they vanished as soon as the man began speaking. He couldn't understand anything other than the first two words, "Yuri Stepanovich."

* * *

"Yuri Stepanovich," Vasili began, a triumphant ring in his voice, "We have the Canadian. He is with me now in the car."

"And you have Dmitri as well." It did not come out as a question.

There was no need to give him the full report, and Vasili had already formed a carefully worded response to the expected question. "He and the Canadian became separated, and so we took the opportunity to get the Canadian when we could. Dmitri is still in the village, and we expect to have him very soon as well. I have the rest of the men keeping track of him. In the meantime, I thought I would try to see what information I can get from the Canadian. We think he may have been Dmitri's contact in the West. He may know where the money is, and may even have access to it."

"Do you have someone there that can speak English?"

"Not with me, no. I thought I would take him to see Anton."

Yuri considered that for a moment. Anton, one of his men, looked after operations in a city only a few hours from where Vasili was now. He knew all about what was going on, and was almost fluent in English. "Good idea. In fact, I think I might meet you there. It will take me a while to make arrangements to get there. Hopefully by the time I arrive, you will have Dmitri too. I want the money, but I must have Dmitri also."

Vasili was pretty sure there was a not-so-thinly veiled threat in the man's last words, and this time Yuri beat him to the punch in ending the call. "Very good. I will see you soon and hope to have more to report to you then," he said into the dead phone for the benefit of the other occupants of the car. He turned for another look at Michael, as if to reassure himself that he actually had the man. Michael looked as if all the blood had drained from his face, and that was a good thing, Vasili knew. If Michael could have seen himself in a mirror, he'd have been struck by just how much he looked like Dmitri had when the plane had altered course for Kiev.

*　*　*

Dmitri had stumbled upon an excellent hiding place, and he was left undisturbed for the rest of the morning and afternoon. The one drawback was that he could not see what was going on outside. He could see neither the sun, nor the shadows that moved slowly across the yard with the passing of the day. He didn't dare take a nap even though there was nothing else to do to pass the time, or even gauge it. All he could do was to sit and think. Mikhail had surely been captured; the chances of him getting away were very small. He could not speak the language and therefore could not ask for help or even explain his presence in a yard or a barn. Andrei and Katya were the only people in the village he really knew and that was the one place to which he could not go. Slavic would be at work and neither of them knew where Pastor Nicolai lived.

It felt like it should be the next day already, but he knew that was just his impatience. He did appreciate how important it was to wait for the right opportunity, but that did not mean he enjoyed doing nothing. The growling in his stomach told him it was well beyond lunch time now, and a little groping around in the dark was rewarded with a few assorted containers of vegetables. He brushed them off on his pant legs and chewed on a cucumber as he pondered his options.

After dark it would be easier to move about the village without being seen, but where would he go? Andrei could likely tell him what had become of Michael, or at least if he'd been captured or not. But it would not be safe to go there. He'd have to find someone with a phone so he could call. There was still Slavic's car if he could figure out where they had taken Michael. Or was there? Vasili had known where they were. How long had they been watched? He had to assume it was long enough to know about Slavic; it was the only safe thing to do.

His mind went in circles for a while before he decided to try a different approach. What would Vasili and Yuri do with Michael, besides the obvious? They had to take him to someone that could speak English so they could question him. There was no real point to torturing someone if you could not understand what they said. Michael had two problems. First, there was really nothing he could give Yuri that he did not already know. The second was that Yuri would never believe that.

Where would they take him? By now most of the people in the

organization would know what Dmitri had done, and that a massive search was underway. They had used too many resources to track him down, get him back to the country, and then hunt him down. Even if someone had not been part of the search, too many people had been involved to keep it a secret, they would talk to each other. Everyone must know.

"Yes! Everyone knows!" He spoke out loud in his excitement, and then looked about nervously as if someone might have heard the words. That might be the solution to his problem. It would be very awkward, but it was the only thing he could think of. There was no time now to wait for another opportunity.

* * *

Michael was not sure which was worse; the car ride or the fear of what might happen when it was over. The back seat was not really big enough for him and the two large men keeping guard by either door. Neither of them appeared to have taken a shower recently. Then again, neither had he.

The trip continued in silence. They passed through a dozen villages whose names would forever remain a mystery to Michael, due to the unintelligible signs that marked them. Judging by the sun, he figured they were driving roughly north-east, which was exactly opposite to the way he wanted to go.

He was exhausted after the physical and mental strain of the brief chase through the village, and still in a lot of pain, but there was no way he was going to fall asleep in the car. He just sat there bouncing and swaying as the driver avoided the worst of the potholes.

Eventually they drew near to a larger town, and Michael felt a growing fear in the pit of his stomach. He wasn't enjoying the company of the men in the car, but at least they had not tried to harm him in any way. After what had seemed like an eternity of driving in silence, the passenger was giving instructions to the driver, and so Michael figured that they must be getting close to their destination. It was mid-afternoon as they pulled into a private driveway blocked by a large imposing gate. They must not have trusted Michael with only one guard, and the passenger must have been above doing anything menial, because it was the driver that got out of the car and swung the gate open.

He climbed back into the car and exchanged a few words with the passenger in the front seat as he pulled into the yard. For a few seconds, Michael was almost in so much shock that he almost forgot his fear. The house and yard were immaculate, and would have fit perfectly into a very upscale neighbourhood back home. The driveway was paved, the yard and garden well-manicured, and the house itself was a mansion compared to what he'd seen over the past few days. He might not have been in such awe of it back in Canada, but it stood in such marked contrast to everything else that it was like being transported instantly to another world.

The driveway ended at a three-car garage, in addition to which two cars, both high-end sedans, and an expensive motorcycle were parked outside. Apparently crime did pay. The driver switched off the engine and the fear came rushing back: a cold, dead weight in the pit of Michael's stomach. The driver and the passenger got out and stretched while the two guards eyed him suspiciously, as if he might suddenly take both of them out with one blow and make a break for it.

Finally the guard on the passenger side got out and motioned gruffly for him to get out as well. He slid over to the door, and tentatively tested his ankle. Then using the doorframe he carefully raised himself to his feet. He managed to hobble along with his escorts as they led him around to the back of the house. It was built into the side of a small hill and a door at the rear led into the basement.

Despite its outward appearance, the house, or at least the base-ment, had a dank musty smell. The room they stepped into had a wooden floor, but they ushered him towards another door that led into a storage room. Shelves full of odd assortments of boxes lined three of the walls, but the centre of the room was clear except for a single chair. Obviously they were expecting him. He hesitated for a moment, but a rough push on his shoulder forced him towards the chair. A few guff but unintelligible words sounded like some sort of command, so he took a seat, thankful to get the weight off his an-kle. But his heart was pounding at the thought of what might come next, and he found he could not quite catch his breath.

He'd half expected to be tied to the chair, but the guards simply took up station on either side of him. He had hardly taken his seat when the door opened again and a man in his early forties walked in. He had a lean yet muscular build that made the well-tailored suit he wore look even better, and the slightly greying hair at his temples added to the distinguished air he bore. Something about his presence left no doubt that he was in charge here. The man who had ridden in the passenger seat followed him in, looking tired and rumpled in comparison, though he also had an air of authority about him. Was the man in the suit Yuri?

"Michael Barrett from Canada," the man said, looking him square in the eye. His accent was much lighter than Dmitri's, but still evident. He still placed the accent in 'Canada' heavily on the second, rather than the first, syllable, just like Dmitri did.

Michael nodded, acknowledging they had the right man. No sense in trying to hide it. His picture had, after all, made the news. Besides, how many Canadians were there wandering about in An-drei's village?

"Vasili here has put a lot of effort into finding you and your friend Dmitri." Michael was half tempted to make a smart-aleck retort, but immediately thought better of it and remained silent. "You two have something that does not belong to you. We want it back!"

"I don't have anything of yours." The words came out almost before the man finished speaking.

His interrogator nodded, but not to Michael, it was a signal to one of the men beside him. Without warning, a large heavy hand dealt him a glancing blow to the side of his head. "Ow!" He cried out, more in surprise than pain. He knew that there was potentially a lot more force behind that hand. The first blow was a warning.

"I don't have it!" he repeated. "And neither does Dmitri. I think he sent it out of the country ahead of him."

"I hardly thought that you had it in your wallet, Michael," the voice was harsh and dripped with sarcasm, "Where is it? If you return it to us, we will let you go."

Michael blinked hard and looked at the man. 'This can't be happening,' he tried to tell himself, but he'd thought the same thing about the hijacking, hadn't he? What will they do when they finally realize that I can't help them? Come to think of it, there was no reason for them to let him go, even if he could tell them anything. He was already missing. They could dump his body somewhere and no one would ever know what had become of him.

Anton, his interrogator, saw the look of panic in his eyes and it confirmed his suspicion, that he'd be able to break the man easily. "Where is it?" he shouted, and for added effect, the other guard smacked him across the cheek, another warning, but harder than the first one.

"I don't know! Dmitri told me he took the money, but I don't know where it is."

"Lies!" Anton cut him off sharply. "You met him in Frankfurt to help him escape and take him to the money. You were on a flight to Athens. Is the money there, or were you connecting to another flight?"

"I never met him before I saw him on the plane," Michael spat out the words in protest. "How can I tell you what I don't know?"

Anton sneered at him as he spoke, "That is my job. To help you tell me everything you know. If you did not know him, why did you leave the bus with him? Why have you two been travelling together? It is so you can get to the money!" He bent over and stuck his nose in Michael's face. "You helped him plan all this. You were his contact in the West and you will tell us everything! The only question is how much time it will take, and how much pain it will cost you."

"I wasn't travelling with him!" 'What was wrong with this guy,' Michael asked himself, 'why won't he believe what I'm saying?' "He thought you guys, Yuri somebody, had sent me. He thought I was one of you so he kidnapped me when he escaped the bus."

Anton laughed at that, a genuine laugh. "He thought you were one of us?" To himself he admitted that this was a possibility, but Yuri Stepanovich was not paying him to come up with possibilities, only to get answers.

"Yuri will be here in a few hours; I will ask him if he sent you. Until then my friends here would like to discuss things further with you." He turned to leave the room, sharing a laugh with Vasili as the two men disappeared thought the doorway. Michael knew full well that neither of the guards spoke a word of English. One of the men grabbed him by the shoulders, pulling him deeper into the chair, while his friend stepped in front of Michael and flashed him a twisted smile. The discussion began with a heavy blow to his stomach.

* * *

Dmitri had enough of waiting. Mikhail needed him, and he needed to get out of Ukraine. With a disgusted snarl he threw aside the sacks he'd buried himself in and felt his way to the bottom of the steps, pausing to listen. He could hear no noise, not even the barking of the village dogs who usually announced the presence of anyone passing by on the street. He made his way up the uneven steps and cracked open the door. It was twilight, almost dark. He hesitated a few more moments, wondering if he should wait for full darkness. It all seemed quiet and safe, but despite his impatience, he wasn't sure he could take the chance yet.

As he sat on the top step peering through the door, the decision was made for him. The owner of the property, a man a few years older than himself stepped around the corner of the house. He didn't notice Dmitri in the dark as he was making his way to the outhouse, but Dmitri called out to him softly. The man pulled up sharply in surprise, looking for the source of the voice calling to him.

"Over here," Dmitri hissed, his voice as soft as he could make it.

"Who is that?" The man asked sharply, wondering if one of the village boys was trying to play some sort of trick on him.

"My name is Dmitri. I am one of the men who was being chased earlier." It was best to tell the truth he decided, besides, he couldn't come up with a convincing lie as to why he was hiding out in the man's yard.

The man looked around carefully. Seeing no one else around he walked to the cellar door and crouched down. "Andrei called earlier. He must have talked to almost everyone in the village, asking us to help you if we found you," he spoke in a whisper. "There are still men looking for you, but there is no one around here right now. They caught your friend and took him away. Who are they?"

"They are Mafia," Dmitri replied dismissively, wanting to change the subject, and feeling his heart sink as his fears about Mikhail's capture were confirmed. "You know Andrei?" The man nodded. "I need to speak to him, now. I need to use your phone."

"Okay," he replied, "But first come inside. There is less chance you will be seen." Forgetting his reason for venturing outside, he led Dmitri around to the door, checking ahead to make sure no one was in sight. He ushered him inside the house, which was empty except for the two of them, and had him sit at the table. Then he dialled Andrei's number and passed the phone to Dmitri.

"Andrei, it's Dmitri," he kept his voice low, despite the fact that he was inside a house and could not be heard from outside. "I'm okay, but what has happened to Mikhail?"

"I'm so glad to hear that. We feared the worst!" Dmitri could hear him passing the news on to Katya. "They took Mikhail away in a car. I did not see it happen, but others did, and you know the way news travels in a village."

"Does anyone know where they took him?"

"No, I'm sorry. We only know that they left town heading east. Slavic says he can still drive you to the border, but Katya and I thought you would want to help Mikhail somehow. We will be praying for him, but is there anything we can do to help?" It was tempting, Dmitri had to admit, to jump in the car and head for safety. He began to rehash some of the thoughts he'd had earlier in the day. But his escape plan might be compromised, he reminded himself, and even if it wasn't, he knew he could not leave Mikhail, as tempting as it sounded.

As touching as Andrei's offer was, he didn't think there was much the old farmer could do. While extra muscle might come in handy he worked best alone. Besides, he didn't want to involve anyone else. His original foolproof plan had harmed enough people as it was, and he still had one more to involve if he was to rescue Michael.

"I have a plan to get him out. I thank you for your help, but I don't think there is anything else you can do right now." His voice trailed off awkwardly. "Thank you," he repeated then hung up the phone. What he'd told Andrei was half true. He had a plan to find out where Michael was, though what he'd do from there was still a mystery.

"I need to make another call, may I?"

"Of course," his host replied.

Dmitri hesitated a moment, "It is a private call," he explained. With a nod of understanding, the man stepped back outside. Dmitri entered the number from memory but his hand hovered over the send button uncertainly before finally pushing it. He just couldn't think of anything else to do, or anyone else to call.

* * *

The mood in Yuri's office was always a lot more relaxed when he was gone. Unfortunately for his staff, that did not happen as often as it used to. As he'd aged and amassed more wealth, he'd grown more careful and spent more and more time in his home, which was where the office was located. There weren't a lot of them, but any boss, especially one with an aversion to working, needed a small staff at his constant beck and call. There were the bodyguards, of course. Then there was Danic, the office gopher who had dreams of making it big in the organization someday. A few others rounded out the regular staff that performed the myriad tasks necessary to keep things going smoothly. Of course a secretary was a necessary part of any office, and Yuri had a very good one whose name, to a Western ear, would be pronounced Youlya.

Most young women in Ukraine did their best to dress fashionably, spending money they did not have to stay up to date on the latest fashions, as Michael had observed at the bus station. But Youlya was one of the fortunate ones, as her job allowed her the money she needed to stay in fashion without worrying about having enough money to live on. Yuri was a demanding boss, but he paid well. Though she had never thought about it from his standpoint, the high wage was in some ways a necessary insurance policy. After all, an underpaid criminal might just be subject to a bribe from the authorities. As far as she was concerned, she had likely landed the best job she could have, at least when it came to the paycheques.

She hadn't set out in life with the goal of working for a crime boss, but had needed money to look after her grandmother. After graduating as a fully-trained secretary, she found it impossible to find a job, and had finally taken the job with Yuri after a friend had recommended her for the position. It was several months before her suspicions about the exact nature of the work were confirmed, but by then it was too late to quit. One simply did not leave a job like that. Even after her grandmother had passed away, she'd remained at the job, afraid of the consequences of leaving.

Though the pay was very good compared to most secretarial positions, the hours were long. Yuri's various business interests produced income twenty-four hours a day, which meant that someone had to be available at all times. All the office staff were careful to keep personal phones shut off whenever Yuri was around, as he strongly discouraged personal calls. As soon as he'd driven out the front gate, however, they had all turned on their phones as usual. Youlya had just used her phone to call a friend and had left it on. When it rang, she first assumed it was her friend calling her back. She picked up the phone and looked at it curiously, not recognizing the name or the number.

"Hello?" She expected it to be a wrong number and almost dropped the phone when she heard the voice on the other end.

"Youlya, it's Dmitri. Can you talk?"

A flood of conflicting emotions raced through her heart, and she didn't know which to heed. Resentment? Relief? Anger? But she had the presence of mind to pause before answering, as pleasantly as she could, though her smile was very tense and forced. "Not really right now, but I was wondering what had become of you." There was a definite iciness in her voice as she spoke the last phrase. "Can I call you back in a few minutes?" She glanced around the room but no one seemed to be paying any undue attention to her call.

"When can you call? I need your help."

"I'm sure you do," came the cool reply. "Give me a few minutes, I have the number." She ended the call and slumped into her chair, emotionally drained from the brief call. She'd been both looking forward to and dreading that call. She'd been expecting it since hearing that Vasili had the Canadian, but the fact that it took his capture to bring about the call hurt her deeply. For a few minutes she pretended to be working while gathering her thoughts. There were a lot of them. When she'd finally calmed down enough she stood up, announced she was going to take a break, and walked outside where she was sure she would not be overheard. She glanced at the list of recent calls and selected the unfamiliar number Dmitri had used. She punched the screen rather viciously.

* * *

The occupant of the house had returned while Dmitri was waiting for the call, and he began preparing tea. But before the water had boiled, the phone rang, Dmitri excused himself and walked into the next room.

"Hello?" he answered uncertainly. The fact she was calling back was good, wasn't it? The initial call had not gone as well as he'd hoped, but neither had it gone as badly as he'd feared.

"Are you crazy, Dmitri? What were you thinking stealing from Yuri?" She practically spat out the words, and Dmitri was too taken aback by her anger to realize it was masking her concern. "If he finds you, he will torture you until you give him back every kopek, and then have you killed!" He hesitated, unable to form a response, so she continued. "What is happening? I know they caught the Canadian but not you. What do you want?"

"I need to know where they have taken him. Is there any way you can find out?"

"They are taking him to Anton's; he might even be there by now. Yuri is on his way to question him personally."

Dmitri was silent for a few moments while he assessed this new information, his mind racing with ideas and schemes. He knew Anton, and where he lived. He'd even been in the house which might give him an advantage in carrying out his plan, when he came up with one. He didn't have much in the way of resources, but his first concern had been to find Michael and that part of the puzzle was now solved.

"Youlya, I need to get to Anton's as soon as possible. Mikhail might be in great danger, and I need to get him out."

"You are in great danger, Dmitri," her anger was returning. "And not just from Yuri and Vasili. You have a lot of explaining to do to me!"

"Can we talk about this later? They are still looking for me here, and they know where I've been staying and who is trying to help me. I need to get to Anton's!"

She hesitated long enough to make Dmitri more than a little

anxious. She might be about to do something she'd regret for the rest of her life, and if Yuri even suspected what she was considering right now, then the rest of her life might not be all that long. Finally she answered him. "Tell me where to meet you. I will be there as soon as possible. But we have a lot to talk about, Dmitri."

"Okay, we will talk about it, I promise, but come quickly. And bring your passport."

She was momentarily left speechless by his instruction.

"Okay," she said uncertainly, "I'll bring it. Where do I meet you?"

CHAPTER 17

Backtracking

Michael became aware of the pain even before he was fully conscious. The two men who'd had the 'discussion' with him had not worked him over as hard as he'd feared, but it was bad enough. He shook his head to clear the cobwebs and raised his arm to his ribcage, wincing as he took a breath that was a little too deep. He knew that they'd been holding back, trying to loosen his tongue a bit. The thought of what might come next was enough to scare him into telling them everything; the problem was that he already had. Did he dare to start making up stories? All that would accomplish would be to buy him time to recover before the next beating.

He pressed tentatively on his chest and abdomen in a few places. They'd concentrated their blows mainly to his body, and they'd been used more as a threat of what was to come than anything else. His head had received only a few glancing blows and cuffs. He didn't think any ribs were broken or cracked, but a couple were bruised. Despite the pain, he took in a slow deep breath, and let it out quickly with a wince and a painful grunt. Why was it that when you knew something would really hurt, you just couldn't keep yourself from trying it?

They hadn't tied him to the chair when they'd left, but he'd been too sore, and too afraid to move from it anyway. That door might open any moment and when it did, he wanted to be in the chair for some reason he couldn't even explain to himself. He'd managed to fall asleep with the room lights still on, the exhaustion and strain of the day overcoming his fear and pain. But how long he'd slept was a mystery to him. He didn't know if it was day or night. The room had no windows, and no sound from outside or upstairs penetrated the concrete walls to offer him any clues.

So he sat and waited. Part of him wanted to believe Dmitri would do something, that he was looking for one of his infamous opportunities. But acknowledging the facts brought him back down to earth. Dmitri could not possibly know where they had him. He didn't even know where he was himself, except that it was not Yuri's headquarters. Besides, what could one unarmed man do? There certainly had to be more than these two men as guards, and Yuri was likely to bring reinforcements when he came. From what he knew of Dmitri's past, he had always looked out for number one, so he was probably heading for the border even now, if he hadn't already crossed it.

Despite all that had happened and what might happen, he hoped deep down that Dmitri would make it. There had been a lot of suspicion on both sides at first, but he had to give Dmitri credit for trying to help him. It wasn't that Michael had despaired of life, but the uncertainty was gnawing inside him. He considered his options. He could keep repeating his story, which was the truth, and be beaten senseless. Or he could lie, but that might make things worse in the long run.

The idea of trying to overpower his guards and escape was not even worth considering. He started to sigh but stopped as the pain shot through his ribs, barely managing to stifle another moan of agony. The truth, he decided, was his only option. He didn't know what lie he could possibly tell that would help, and the truth couldn't hurt Dmitri. He had no idea where the man was or where he was heading. Suddenly his heart skipped a beat and he could feel the blood draining from his face. The door was opening.

Anton entered first. For a split second Michael felt a sense of relief, until the two guards entered right behind him. They took their usual stations on either side of his chair, each of them laying a hand on his shoulders as if he needed a reminder of their presence. His inquisitor didn't speak a word until two more men entered behind him. The first was Vasili, which was no surprise, but he had not seen the second man before. He was heavy-set with graying hair. Without being told, he knew he was looking at Yuri Stepanovich.

* * *

"I hope you got some rest, we have a lot to talk about, Michael," Anton began, the tone of his voice calm and reasonable. "First, I should introduce you to Yuri Stepanovich. It is his money you stole and, understandably, he would like it back."

"If I had it now, I'd give it to him, honest. But I don't have it and I don't know where it is. I told you, I got stuck in the middle of this whole thing when you guys hijacked that plane. There's nothing else I can tell you!"

The panic and the fear in Michael's eyes almost convinced Anton that he was telling the truth as he translated the outburst for Yuri.

Yuri could see the fear also, and from the talk he'd already had with Anton, he was fairly sure of what Michael was saying, even before the translation came. He scowled and shrugged his shoulders as if to say, 'Maybe you are telling the truth, maybe you aren't.'

Michael had a moment of panic as Yuri reached into an inner jacket pocket, but he merely took out a package of cigarettes, pulled one out, and placed it in his mouth. As he reached into another pocket for a lighter, he walked slowly back and forth in front of Michael, not looking at him. He paused his slow pacing as he lit the cigarette, taking a long pull on it as he replaced the lighter, as if he had all the time in the world. Finally he turned to Anton and spoke, his words slow and deliberate.

Anton listened and nodded to Yuri before turning to Michael with the translation. "He says that he understands that Dmitri is a very good…how do you say? He is a good con man. He promised you much but will not keep those promises. We have known him for a long time. This is the kind of man that he is. If you co-operate with Yuri, he will make it worth your while."

For just a split second, Yuri reminded him of a sleazy salesman trying to soft soap a gullible customer. "If there was anything else I could tell you I would!" His eyes were wide with panic now, and both men thought that he might just be telling the truth after all, and there really was nothing further to learn from him. That really was a pity, in more than just one way.

"Maybe he really doesn't know anything, but then why did Dmitri take him when he escaped the bus?" Yuri pondered the possibilities.

"He certainly does look like he's telling the truth. He did not talk at all when Dennis and Pavel tried to throw a scare into him. I don't think he was being strong. He does not have the stomach for this kind of thing."

Yuri snorted in contempt at Anton's observation. "If that is the case, then we must get rid of him. He's of no further use to us. But maybe we should try one more time."

"I think that would be a good idea. We may have Dmitri soon. I do not see how he can get out of the village without us knowing," Vasili spoke for the first time. "But the Canadian may know something that he doesn't know he knows. Have Dennis and Pavel work him over again, harder this time, and we will try again."

Yuri nodded in agreement, and Anton was about to give the order when Yuri's phone rang. He decided to wait until the call was over. It would not do to have the sounds of a beating in the background during the call.

Yuri looked at the phone quizzically. Why would she be calling, he wondered? She knew better than to disturb him with something trivial when he was busy. It must be something important. "Hello, Youlya?"

"Yuri Stepanovich, I know where he is!"

* * *

Waiting for Youlya to arrive after spending most of the day in the cellar was almost more than Dmitri could bear. He needed to get to Mikhail as quickly as possible, before it was too late. He paced back and forth, but avoided looking out the window in case someone might be looking back. He had drunk several pots of tea, and even tried to take a nap. It had taken over six hours, but he finally heard the muted sound of a car engine as it pulled up in front of the house, and the soft sound of gravel crunching beneath its tires. His host, Anatoly, cracked the door open before she'd even stepped out of the car and motioned to her to come inside. He immediately offered her a cup of tea, which she declined politely.

When she turned to face Dmitri, the politeness quickly evaporated. "We need to talk." Dmitri turned a light shade of red and nodded. He was embarrassed, and also on the defensive, never a good combination with his temper. He had not intended to just disappear, at least not from Youlya, but neither had he expected to face her like this. He forced himself to take a deep breath to try to calm down.

Anatoly had been expecting some kind of joyous reunion between two friends, or possibly lovers, so the obvious tension between the two of them made him suddenly very uncomfortable. He excused himself and took his cup of tea outside.

As soon as the door closed Dmitri turned to face Youlya and

asked, "What do we need to talk about?" It didn't take long for him to realize that this had been the wrong question to ask.

"What do we need to talk about?" She was repeating Dmitri's question, but she wasn't asking anything as the words exploded from her lips. "What do you mean 'what do we need to talk about?' You run off with a fortune without a word to anyone, not even to me! You could not even tell me? What am I supposed to think? That everything you ever said to me was a lie? Who are you meeting when you run off to wherever you are going?"

Dmitri did not dare to interrupt her by trying to answer. He was bright enough to know that she wasn't really asking questions. He might not know a lot about women, but he could understand that much.

"You let me think you are interested in me and then you run off without a word. You could have got yourself killed! You still might! Do you have any idea what Yuri will do to you?"

"Yes, I know what he will do, the same thing he is already doing to Mikhail," he shot back angrily, regretting it immediately. He held his hand up to try to stop her verbal assault, one which he knew he deserved, but it would have to wait.

"I'm sorry," the words came out a bit harshly, but with enough sincerity in them that she calmed down enough to give him a chance to explain.

"I know what he will do to me. That is why I must get to Anton's. I have to try to help Mikhail."

She wouldn't stand for that idea. "No. How could you help him? You will die and so will he, whether Yuri gets his stinking money or not, he will kill both of you." He could see she was struggling with emotions she wasn't sure what to do with. "Please, let me drive you to the border. If you don't want me, fine, but run, get out of here before they find you. You don't have to take me, you don't want to anyway, but get out yourself. There is no sense in throwing your life away."

Dmitri finally realized there was more than anger in her words, and it touched him. But he knew he had to do something about Mikhail as quickly as possible. "I can't leave. He is there because of me, and I have to do something."

"Sacrificing yourself to Yuri is not doing something," her frustration was returning. "Come! Now! I can have you to the border in a few hours. Just leave and don't ever come back. He is not the first innocent person Yuri has murdered, and he will not be the last. You know that. Go, get out while you still can. He will never know I saw you, I promise that. I will not tell him anything. I may mean nothing to you, but I will not let you die on some worthless mission to save some foreigner."

Dmitri forced himself to remain calm, something which was very foreign to him. He was almost in a panic over Michael, but he needed to let Youlya know what he had done and why.

"I will explain everything that's happened. Later. But I will tell you that I did not plan to leave without letting you know…"

"So it just slipped your mind the morning you left?" Her words were harsh and sarcastic. "If Vasili had not found you in Frankfurt, you would be safely in Greece and I would not even be a memory!"

"That is not true!" Now it was his turn to be angry. As much as he could understand how she might believe what she'd just said, it simply wasn't true. They were talking in circles now and he didn't have time for that. "I wanted to tell you, but I knew you would be in danger if you knew anything. What would Yuri have done if he had found out you knew I was leaving, even if I had not taken the money?" Her understanding was evident in the shocked look on her face and her sudden silence, so he pressed on. "I needed to leave. I could not stand who I was becoming. I don't want to be that person anymore."

He was getting angry again, but Youlya could see he was angry with himself, and with his life, not with her. "I needed a new life and it could not be in Ukraine, Yuri would never have let me do that. It is not a job you retire from. Do you know how many men in the Mafia die of old age?" It was a question that men in their line of work did not want to think about, but none of them could help dwelling on it at some time or other. As rhetorical as the question was, he answered it anyway. "Almost none of them!" "That is not how I wanted my life to end. I was dead anyway, leaving was my only chance to live. I needed money to leave, more than I had, so I took what Yuri stole from others to start my new life."

"You needed fifteen million dollars to leave?"

"No, but it was all there in one place and it was just as easy to take all of it as it was to take none of it. And I made a lot of that money for Yuri." That last line was to justify to himself what he had done. He wasn't so sure it was working. "I wanted to tell you, but I did not want to put you at risk until I was safe. As long as you knew nothing, you were safe."

"You could not have left me a note or an email?"

"What if someone else found it? You would have been dead by now, or worse." She blinked and shuddered in acknowledgment of what he was saying. "When I was safe, I was going to let you know, and give you the chance to join me if…" he paused uncertainly, "If you wanted to." His voice grew soft, almost weak, as he finally told her what his plan had been all along. The money and even the freedom would have meant nothing to him without Youlya to share it with him. But he'd needed to keep her safe until, well, until the right opportunity had come along. Mikhail's capture had forced his hand, however.

"Dmitri, I would have come with you despite the risk, and of course I'd want to join you later. I'd have come with you when you left the first time."

"I know and that is exactly why I did not tell you. Two people would be easier to find than one, and if you knew I was going to have you join me later, you might have acted suspiciously around Yuri. If you were mad at me for leaving, you would have been safer. You were safer."

His honesty took away most, if not all, of her anger. "I understand what you were trying to do, but you should have trusted me, Dmitri."

"I know that now." That might have been a lie, but it was a white one, he rationalized. They could talk more about that later. Right now he had something that was, at least temporarily, more urgent. She cocked her head to one side in puzzlement as she saw a new look on his face, one of concern for someone else. She could not recall ever seeing that before.

"Youlya, Mikhail is in danger because of me. I want a new life but I cannot start it by sacrificing someone else. I put him there and I cannot live knowing that I did nothing to try and help him. Can you understand that?"

"Yes, I can." Secretly she was proud of him, she'd always sensed that this person was inside him somewhere, and now he'd proved it to her. She still wished they could just drive to the border and disappear, but she understood this newly revealed facet of Dmitri.

"Good," he smiled at her, and then mentally shifted gears. "I need you to take me to Anton's but we need a plan. I need to get as many men out of the house as possible, and I need to make sure they do not hurt Mikhail." He knew it was likely too late to avoid that completely, but he needed to put a stop to it immediately. He thought for a moment. "You need to call Yuri and tell him I called you."

"What?"

"And you must tell him where I am."

"Have you lost your mind, Dmitri? He will send everyone he has to make sure you don't get out of this village." She was going to add the word 'alive' to the end of the sentence, until she remembered that Yuri would not dare kill him until he had every dollar back.

"That's exactly what I hope will happen, because I won't be here when they arrive." He began explaining exactly what he wanted her to say.

* * *

"Yuri Stepanovich, I know where he is!"

"Where who is?" Yuri demanded sharply, hardly daring to hope that he knew the answer already. When he'd realized it was Youlya calling, he knew it was important. She would never bother him with something that wasn't. But this was beyond anything he had expected.

"Dmitri!" The single word shocked him into silence as the words gushed from her mouth. "Yuri, I don't know what to do. He is asking me to help him. What should I tell him?" Her voice had just the right edge of panic and confusion to sound convincing. Despite the intentional deception, those feelings were real.

Yuri thought quickly, ignoring the questioning looks from Vasili and Anton. "What kind of help does he want?"

"He has asked me to drive him to the border. He says he will give me a share of the money if I will help him escape."

It was more perfect than he could have hoped for, and it would put Vasili back in his place as well. "Tell him you will help him, tell him that you will leave right away." He calculated the times and distances. "Tell him to stay right where he is until you arrive. We can be there several hours before you can, so he will not expect anything until it is too late. Call him and tell him that, then call me back to let me know what he says."

Yuri could not help giving Vasili a smug smile. "Well, it seems as if my office staff has succeeded where you and all your men have failed, Vasili Petrovich. My secretary has located Dmitri and will make sure he remains where he is until we can pick him up."

Vasili had already gathered as much from listening in on Yuri's end of the conversation. He fumed silently while trying not to let his emotions show. It would be futile at this point to mention that without his intervention, Dmitri could now be half a world away, or that he had thwarted Dmitri's second attempt to get out of the country. Then there was their captive, the Canadian. Wasn't that also the result of his hard work? If not for all he'd done, Dmitri would never have called Youlya. Someday this arrogant, ungrateful fool will pay for this, he promised himself.

The silence as they awaited the next phone call confused Michael. After bracing himself for the worst, suddenly everyone seemed to have forgotten about him. Whether that was a good thing or not, he couldn't even guess.

"Da, Youlya?" Yuri answered with a broad smile on his face. "Where is he?"

"He is still in the same village where you caught the Canadian; he was hiding out in a cellar."

"What did you tell him?"

"I told him what you told me to say, that I would be there as soon as I could, and I asked where I was to meet him."

"Where will he be?" Yuri asked impatiently.

"He wants me to pick him up at the bus stop. It is on the main road just as you enter the village."

"Excellent! I can have Vasili and his men there long before he expects you to arrive. We will be waiting for him." He looked directly at Vasili as he spoke his next words. "Good work, Youlya, I will see that you are suitably rewarded for this. Perhaps you should phone him every hour or so, just to let him know you are coming. I don't want him deciding to try and run again."

Sliding the phone back into his pocket he turned to Vasili, "I will give you a chance to redeem yourself, Vasili. I know your men are still in the village, but I want you to go there personally to see to his capture. Take Anton with you in case you need extra help. And take the drivers too, they will be of more use there than here." Vasili fumed silently at the put-down, but outwardly showed no emotion. "Don't disappoint me again. I will remain here, along with these two," he motioned to the two guards, and then studied Michael for a moment. "Keep him here for now; he may still be of some use to us. When we have Dmitri, we may be able to use the two of them against each other, if necessary."

As Yuri studied him, Michael felt certain that his execution was being ordered. Anton, seeing the look in his eyes, began to laugh. He was enjoying it enough that he waited until Yuri and Vasili left the room before speaking.

"Are you sure you have nothing else you'd like to tell me?" he asked, half in fun, and half hoping that he might learn something."

"I've already told you, I know nothing." Michael sounded broken, desperate, and frustrated. Anton was now almost fully convinced that he really didn't know anything. Well, it didn't really matter anymore, did it? They had Dmitri so the money would certainly be returned soon. Then Dmitri and this Canadian would simply never be found after disappearing from the scene of that bus accident.

Anton paced back and forth a few times as if considering what Michael had told him. "Maybe you do and maybe you don't. It doesn't matter. We have found your friend, Dmitri, and he will soon be joining you here. Then it will only be a matter of time before we have the money back." He shrugged dismissively, "Then we will have no further use for you."

Michael's heart sank at the news of Dmitri's capture. His last fleeting hope of rescue had been that Dmitri would try and rescue him rather than running for the border. It had never been a real hope, but it had been something to cling to. They'd escaped the hijacking, the bus, the pursuits, even the train ride. But now their luck had finally run out.

Anton spoke a few words to the guards and then the three of them left the room, leaving Michael alone with his despair. This time as they left they turned out the light, from the outside of the room. He sat there in the dark, going over the trip from the moment Dmitri had boarded the plane. When it was hijacked he had been wishing he'd been on another flight, now he was wishing he'd just been in another seat. How had the holiday he'd spent so long planning gone so wrong?

* * *

"Well?" Dmitri asked impatiently as Youlya ended her call to Yuri.

"He is sending Vasili here to pick you up, and he has offered me a reward for finding you."

"Are you considering that offer?"

She looked at him in shock before noticing the teasing glint in his eyes. "No, I am not considering it," she said in mock indignation before turning serious again. "They are on their way. What do we do now?"

"We go to where they are before they get to where we are."

The owner of the house had not returned, so they left without being able to thank him for his help and made their way to Youlya's car. They saw no sign of anyone looking for them, but to be on the safe side, Dmitri climbed into the back seat and lay down on the floor. Youlya started the car and made her way slowly along the rough streets until reaching the main road. Not until they'd left the village well behind them, and not another car was in sight, did he climb into the front passenger seat. Speeding along the highway they began discussing plans for their assault on Anton's house.

CHAPTER 18

Admit One

"No! Absolutely not!" Dmitri replied emphatically. He'd lost track of how many times he'd already spoken the words, but he had no intention of changing his mind.

They had been debating their options for gaining entrance to Anton's house once they reached it. One of the biggest problems was that they did not know for sure what they would be facing when they got there. Dmitri had been there a few times, and had a pretty good idea of the layout of the house, but he didn't know for sure where they would be keeping Michael, what shape he would be in, or how many men were in the house.

And they had precious little time to figure it all out. It would take them roughly the same amount of time to travel there as it would take for Vasili and whoever he brought with him to reach the village. It would be several hours after that before Youlya was supposed to meet him because she supposedly had further to go, but no doubt he already had the men he'd left behind staking out the bus stop. Hopefully they had at least as long as it would take for Vasili to reach the village, and he wouldn't get suspicious before then. There was no way to be sure how long it would take him to realize he'd been tricked, but if he were to call Yuri and warn him before they could get Michael out, the job would become a lot more complicated. If he did phone Yuri with an alarm, or if he called in additional reinforcements from somewhere else, their opportunity might even disappear.

All the unknowns meant that despite the time constraints Dmitri wanted a chance to look things over before committing to a plan.

Youlya, on the other hand, was pushing for a more direct approach.

"But we may not have time to wait for one of your magical opportunities," she countered yet again. "If we are not half-way to the border before Vasili returns we will not be leaving at all. We need to get into the house as soon as possible so we can get back out."

"No, we do not need to get into the house. I need to get into the house. Not 'we' and absolutely not 'you.'"

"We do not have time to argue about this."

"I know we don't, so stop arguing," Dmitri shot back, more in frustration than anger. "I will not allow you to go in alone, it is too dangerous."

"I put myself in danger as soon as I called Yuri and lied to him. The sooner we finish this and get out of Ukraine, the safer I am. This is the fastest plan and so it is the safest."

Dmitri knew she was right about already being in danger, but why could she not see that this was needlessly adding to that danger? He was still looking for the right words when she began again.

"Dmitri, I can explain my presence there, you cannot. It will give me a chance to see who is inside and where they are holding him."

At that moment he used the worst possible argument he could have chosen. "I cannot let a woman put herself at risk like that. Look out!" The car swerved violently back into its own lane as she returned her attention, briefly, to her driving before responding.

"If it were not for a woman," she spat the last two words out through clenched teeth, "You would still be sitting in a village house drinking tea while they tortured your friend. Or maybe you would have found a horse to ride to Anton's house? Would you like me to drop you off so you can find one?"

Dmitri raised his hands, either in surrender or appeasement, he wasn't sure which. "Okay. I will consider it once I have had a chance to look things over. Is that good enough for now?"

Youlya wasn't satisfied with his compromise, and was not yet ready to give up her anger. But she also knew Dmitri well enough to know that it was the best she could expect from him for the time being. She let a stream of opposite-direction traffic pass before responding. "Consider it, then look over the house, and you will see that it is the only option we have right now."

Dmitri let out a non-committal grunt before settling back into his seat, staring out the window into the darkness. There was nothing to see out there, but his mind was racing, trying to come up with another option that would make Youlya's scouting trip unnecessary.

"I promise that if I go in first I will not take them all out by myself. I will leave that to the big strong man." There was an edge of sarcasm to her voice, but the statement was also her way of agreeing to let him have a look once they got there. This time she kept her attention on the road, giving ample room to the oncoming traffic.

* * *

Neither Youlya nor Anton was aware of the fact that they had just passed each other on the road. To each the other was simply one more set of headlights in an intermittent but unending stream. They sped past each other, each racing to a different destination, and each hoping for a different outcome to the night's events.

In contrast to the tempestuous debate that had raged for almost half the trip in Youlya's car, Vasili and Anton had spent most of the trip in silence. Knowing that they, and the two men following them in Yuri's car, would arrive well before the time Youlya had given Dmitri, they took time to fuel the car and pick up some bread and sausage to snack on.

Vasili had made a few calls to the men he'd left in the village, ordering them to take up station around the bus stop well in advance of his arrival. Knowing that his orders would be carried out without question, he didn't care if they grumbled about them or not, he'd settled into the passenger seat as best he could and tried to rest. Having driven this stretch of road once already that day, and having had precious little sleep since Dmitri had first run off, he napped fitfully as Anton avoided the worst of the potholes. He wasn't avoiding them to make Vasili comfortable, he was just worried about the suspension on his new car. Vasili awoke about the same time that Youlya and Dmitri passed them, glanced at his watch and sat up. "A few more hours to go. The trip is much longer the second time."

Anton didn't bother responding to the comment, but he did glance at the clock on the dashboard, and found himself in agreement with Vasili's estimation. He considered the events that had led up to this trip and smiled as the car made its way through the night. Dmitri running off with the cash did not really reflect directly on him. Yuri was the one that looked bad because of that, and he was also the one on the hook if the money was not recovered. Then there was Vasili who was in the unfortunate position of having let his prey slip through his fingers a number of times. That would be remembered far longer than the fact that he had been the one to track Dmitri down and get him back on Ukrainian soil in the first place. But if Anton was able to be in on the capture, it would be a definite feather in his own cap. It would be at his house that the location of the missing millions would be disclosed, and if there was one thing he'd learned in his years with the organization, it was how to milk an opportunity like this for all it was worth.

There was no arguing the fact that Vasili had done a good job. Not many men could have followed the almost invisible trail that Dmitri had left on his initial departure. His skill, and a little luck, had been overshadowed by the failure of some of the men under his command; and some of that failure had been purely and simply bad luck. But Anton had not risen as far as he had by showing sympathy to others, and he was definitely not above taking advantage of the situation. A few well-chosen words to the right people about his part could pay huge dividends. He knew both which words to use, and who to speak them to.

Anton looked over at Vasili as his companion tossed fitfully in the passenger seat, trying to force himself to get some sleep. He was a good man, smart and ambitious, but he didn't know how to play the political game well and therefore was not likely to rise much higher than he already had. He would be a definite asset to his team when he was able to take over from Yuri. Given recent events, and assuming he could put the proper spin on Dmitri's capture, he hoped that might take place very soon.

* * *

Back at Anton's house, Dennis had agreed to stay up and keep an eye on Michael overnight. To be on the safe side they'd tied him to the chair after letting him use the toilet. It wasn't really worth their time to do that, Michael thought, as there was no way he would have even attempted to overpower even one of them. Assuming he'd felt up to the challenge and was successful, he'd be totally helpless once he was out of the house. He didn't try to explain those facts, however, as there was no one left in the house that could speak English.

Since Dennis was doing the night shift Pavel was selected, by default, to prepare a late evening meal before retiring to an extra room for some sleep. Yuri had lingered at the table, sipping an extra cup of tea after the meal, and snacking on some cookies he'd found in one of the cupboards.

Reaching into his pocket he fished out the bottle of pills his doctor had ordered him to take, the ones his wife was always nagging him to remember with each meal. He shook one into his hand and swallowed it with a sip of his tea. Lately, and especially since Dmitri had tried to make good his escape, he'd not had to be reminded to take them. The pain in his chest and shortness of breath had succeeded where his wife had often failed. It was more of an irritation than a worry, a reminder that he'd not been looking after himself the way he should have been. Once this whole mess was cleaned up, and the money was returned, he'd start eating better, drinking less, and try to get some exercise. It was the same promise that men of his age made to themselves all over the world. But very few ever kept it.

He stared into his teacup, swirling the contents slowly. He'd trusted Dmitri, hoped for great things from him. Until very recently, he'd delivered on those hopes, so in addition to the fact that he was now indebted to his superiors because of the theft, there was also the deep, surprising wound of the betrayal. Added to that was the inability of Vasili, another man he'd trusted, to perform a simple task. If only he were younger and able to do this kind of work himself the money would have been recovered days ago.

If it had not been for Youlya's call he would have almost given up hope. He certainly hoped that Vasili would not fail again this time, not after having Dmitri practically handed to him. Perhaps he'd made the same mistake in trusting Vasili that he had in trusting Dmitri. Clearly he was not prepared to handle a job this important. Hopefully Anton's presence would help keep him on track. He'd have to rethink that man's position in the morning, when this was all over. There were at least a dozen good men that were all vying for Vasili's position, and maybe they were hungry enough for it to do a better job. Yuri nodded to himself as he considered this;

Vasili had grown complacent and lazy and it was time to replace him. Permanently.

He shifted his gaze from the teacup to the window. It was pitch black outside, but he could see the lights of some apartment buildings down in the valley behind the house, which was perched on top of a hill. The lights of the town flickered as a gentle breeze caused the leaves and branches of the birch trees in the back-yard to sway back and forth.

He raised his cup and finished the tea with a few loud sips. It was growing late and he was ready for bed. A look at the clock told him that Vasili and Anton should be approaching the village soon. Well, hopefully they would do nothing foolish or rash. All they really had to do now was let Dmitri come to them.

He lifted his heavy frame slowly from the chair, not paying any heed to how much effort it took, or how laboured his breathing became as he started up the stairs. He could hear Pavel, already snoring loudly in a room just off the front hall, and was glad that he would be on the top floor and out of earshot of that racket. Climbing the stairs with heavy, tired footsteps he found an empty room to the left of the stairs and claimed it for the night.

*   *   *

About the time that Yuri was settling into his bed, Youlya and Dmitri were approaching the outskirts of town.

"Which way is Anton's house?" She was stopped at a red light and there was no through road; she'd have to turn left or right. There was no other traffic at this hour of the night, but she chose to obey the light if for no other reason than to get a brief break from driving in order to gather her thoughts. Now that they were only minutes from their destination, she was no longer feeling quite as brave as she had been a few hours ago.

Dmitri looked around, his thoughts elsewhere, as he recalled the layout of the town. "Turn right, and after you cross the tracks, turn right again. Then just follow the road through town. I'll tell you when to make the next turn."

"Do we drive up to the house, or do you want to park out of sight?"

"I'll have you park just out of sight of the house, then we can decide from there."

"What is it you expect to learn from outside?"

"I don't know yet," Dmitri was getting a bit agitated with her questions. "We will have a look first, and then I will decide."

"You mean *we* will decide." The light changed and she made the turn, making her way along the deserted street while keeping an eye out for the train tracks. Something in her tone of voice told Dmitri not to even try arguing the point.

There was a little more traffic as they approached the town centre, where knots of people milled around outside some of the bars and the local pizzeria. The largest crowd was a group of young people standing outside an internet café. Once past the town centre, the traffic thinned out again and Dmitri guided her up a narrow, winding road that made its way past rows of small, dark houses and crumbling apartment buildings.

"Stop right there."

Youlya pulled the car into a spot where the road widened slightly to make room for a bus stop. They climbed out of the car, pausing to stretch for a moment in the cool night air.

"The house is just up ahead, around the bend," Dmitri said pointing up the road.

"Then let's go," Youlya said impatiently. "We don't know how much time we have."

Without waiting for a response she began walking up the road. Like many other towns in Ukraine, the street was lined by fences that came almost to the road, leaving very little room for pedestrians. Even though they walked so close to the edge of the road that their shoulders almost brushed the fences, they still had to pause and wait when a car passed by to ensure that they weren't in danger of being hit. As they rounded the corner, the houses suddenly became larger and the fences more ornate and in better repair. It was an upscale neighbourhood that would have been out of place in most villages, and in fact, was out of place in comparison to the rest of this town, but that didn't mean there wasn't money to be made here for Anton. If he'd stopped to think about it, Dmitri would have realized that many of the residents in this neighbourhood likely made their money in ways that were not quite legal.

"That's it, right there," Dmitri pointed to a house much larger than those surrounding it. Most of the houses along the road were dark, hardly a single window had a light showing, and Anton's was no exception. That is a good thing, Dmitri thought to himself. No doubt there was someone awake in there, but the darkness meant it was unlikely that they had a large contingent of guards on duty. As far as they were concerned, they didn't need to guard Michael, they needed to find Dmitri. He began to feel a bit better about their chances.

"Where do you think they have him?" Youlya whispered beside him in the darkness.

Dmitri thought back to his visits to the house. "I don't know for sure. There are bedrooms on both the upper levels, and a storage room in the basement. I would have him locked up in the storage room. It has no windows and only one door. But without a look inside I can't be sure."

"Then I will go in and have a look. I can come up with a reason to go in there."

"Yes, but can you come up with a way to get back out?"

"I will look for an opportunity," she retorted, using Dmitri's famous line, since she didn't know what else to say.

Dmitri allowed himself a short laugh at that, recognizing the humour, but also finding some comfort in the fact that she had not quite thought this all the way through. There was still time to change her mind from that foolish idea of going in alone.

"Let's look around back if we can. I think there is a basement door."

The imposing fence at the front was common everywhere in Ukraine, but often that was just for show and some privacy from the street traffic. The back-yard was not always as secure.

They made their way further up the street and just as Dmitri had remembered, a side street wrapped around behind the houses and headed down the hill and back into town. Once they rounded the corner, the darkness was almost absolute and they had to feel their way along the narrow road, which did not quite qualify as a street. It was more of a trail that a car could use if it was really necessary.

As Dmitri had hoped, there was only a four-strand wire fence marking the back side of the properties. Counting the silhouettes of the houses, they continued down the trail until they were standing behind Anton's house. All was still, dark, and quiet.

"You stay here," he instructed Youlya. "I need a closer look."

"How do I explain what I am doing here if someone comes by? I'm coming with you."

"Fine! But be quiet then." He was tempted to add 'if you can,' but managed to bite his tongue before he said it. He didn't really mean it, he just wished she'd let him have the last word for once. He wasn't quite ready to admit that he was glad she was there, and not just because of the ride.

They squeezed between the wires of the fence, crept though the tall grass, and made their way to the stand of birch trees where they could clearly see the outline of the house. All the windows were dark on the backside of the house too, leading Dmitri to think that Michael was most likely in the basement after all. There was no way they would leave him unguarded at night, and whoever was standing watch would have some lights on.

"I think he's in the basement," he spoke softly to Youlya, not bothering to explain how he'd come to that conclusion. "And if he is, the easiest way back out is through that door." He was pointing at the left side of the exposed basement wall. The door itself was not quite visible in the darkness, but a darker area along the wall marked its location.

"So we go in?" Now that they were actually standing there Youlya's doubts about her earlier boldness grew even stronger. Never having met Michael, she was now thinking that she could live quite easily with the consequences of leaving him here to his fate and making a dash for the border with Dmitri. He was just a faceless foreigner who meant nothing to her. No, she realized even as she thought it, she could not do that. All those years of working for Yuri had hardened her to what happened to the people who crossed him. What had once shocked her was now almost routine. But as hardened as she might have become, that was not who she really was. She could not abandon Michael any more than Dmitri could. Knowing what would happen to him would haunt any kind of life that awaited her after escaping from Yuri.

"No, not yet." Dmitri was still struggling to make up his mind about how exactly to handle the rescue. Once he was inside, he was committed. He didn't even have a weapon of any kind with him. He'd left everything behind when he'd boarded the plane and had not had a chance to pick one up since then. Even a knife would give him some sort of advantage, or at least a better chance.

Taking Youlya's hand in his, he led her back to the fence in silence, neither of them speaking until they were making their way back up the trail. "We will bring the car back here and park behind the house. Then I will see if the back door is open. It likely isn't, but I will try that first." His use of the pronoun 'I' was not lost on Youlya, and she was not sure if she felt relief or resentment.

They made their way quickly back to the car, closing the doors as quietly as possible, then sat looking at each other.

"Let's go," Dmitri finally said softly, and Youlya started the car. "No, turn the lights on," he instructed as she pulled forward with the lights still off. "It will look less suspicious if anyone sees us."

She pulled on the light switch and continued up the road and around the bend. They cruised slowly past Anton's gate, studying the house as if they had somehow missed something vital in their first survey, but no new ideas presented themselves. As she rounded the next corner and turned onto the trail, Dmitri spoke again.

"When you get to the top of the hill, turn off the engine and the lights. We can roll down to Anton's yard and stop there."

Youlya swallowed hard. "Okay," was as much as she could make herself say. Her heart was pounding and the steering wheel was damp beneath her palms. As the front wheels dipped over the edge of the incline, she slipped the gearshift into neutral and turned off the engine, quickly followed by the lights. She squinted into the darkness, watching the tall grass on either side of them to keep the car more or less on the trail.

"Stop here," Dmitri whispered. The brakes squealed very softly, causing both of them to wince as the car rocked to a stop. She set the park brake and shifted back into gear to help hold the car in place on the hill.

As Dmitri pondered his next move, Youlya's hands gripped the wheel so hard that they turned white. She took a deep breath and made up her mind.

"Dmitri, I am going in, I will say I have an urgent message for Yuri. They will not question that. I can get a look around without having to worry about being seen."

She didn't even wait for the objection she knew was coming, and before he could react, she was out of the car and making her way to the fence.

"Youlya!" he whispered sharply into the darkness, not daring to speak any louder but hoping the tone of his voice would stop her. But if she heard his whisper she ignored it. He didn't catch up with her until she was half-way through the birch trees.

"Stop, what do you think you're doing?"

"Saving the life of your friend. Do you have a better idea?" He hesitated, knowing anything was better than sending her in alone, but she took his silence for something else. "Then I guess I am your opportunity!" Her words sounded more confident than she felt, and Dmitri could do nothing but watch as she crossed the open space between the trees and the house, and knocked on the door.

A minute or so later he saw a sliver of light as the door was opened just a crack. There was a pause that seemed to last much too long before it suddenly opened wider. He could see the silhouette of a large man briefly blocking the doorway before he stepped aside. Youlya was plainly visible as she stepped through the door into the brightness of the basement.

The door closed and once again everything went dark.

CHAPTER 19

Turbulence

It was very early in the morning, well before dawn, when Anton saw the sign announcing that the village was only a few kilometres further down the road. He reached over and gently shook the shoulder of the sleeping Vasili, who shifted in his seat before sitting up and rubbing his eyes.

"We are there?" His words were barely understandable as he tried to speak them through a yawn.

"Almost. We will be passing the bus stop soon."

Vasili forced himself into full wakefulness and began watching the shoulder of the road. There would be no lights at the bus stop, but the beam of the headlights should be enough to let them catch at least a glimpse of it. He hoped that Anton would resist the urge to slow down as they passed it. Anyone watching them needed to see nothing more than just another passing car.

Just as he'd hoped Anton kept his speed up as they drove past it. He caught a glimpse of the small, white, tile-covered structure as it appeared out of the darkness and then disappeared again. He could just make out a few shadowy figures waiting for the next bus and his heart-beat quickened slightly as he wondered if one of them was Dmitri. Not likely, he chided himself, but he was, no doubt, somewhere nearby. Hiding in the shadows of the trees and bushes perhaps? Youlya wasn't due to arrive for a few more hours and Dmitri was too smart to allow himself to sit around in plain sight for that long.

"There's a store to the right as you come into the village," Vasili said. "You can park there and I will check in with the others."

Without bothering to respond, Anton swung the car into the dark, vacant parking lot. The store had closed hours ago, along with most of the rest of the town, and it was pitch black both inside and out. Once the engine was switched off, the night became eerily silent. The air was cool and humid, and the windows began almost immediately to fog over. Anton sat back and cracked open a bottle of kvass, a dark, bitter liquid that he preferred over other soft drinks.

He sipped at it idly as he listened to Vasili checking in with his team. Although he could only make out one side of the conversation, it seemed as if everything was well in hand with men stationed around the bus stop and ready to move in when the time was right. It had been decided to let Dmitri get to the bus stop without trying to hinder him. They would let him get into position with no idea that he was walking into a trap. His sense of security and his trust in Youlya would be his downfall. They would move in slowly, gradually tightening the noose until there was nowhere to go. Then, when the time came, Vasili would be waiting for him in the back seat of Youlya's car with his whole team positioned around it. With luck Dmitri might even get into the vehicle before he realized what was happening.

Anton nodded silent approval as he listened to the plans being made. Without anything being said, it had been silently agreed that Dmitri would be taught a few lessons about loyalty before they brought him to Yuri. That would serve several purposes. First it would let all of them vent a lot of the frustration that Dmitri had caused them. Secondly, it would soften him up before the interrogation really began in earnest. Finally, word of what had happened to him would get out and serve as a warning to anyone else who might have similar ideas.

Yes, he decided, Vasili was doing a great job, he really was very good at what he was doing. He had been unlucky lately, but he was good. The strain on his face showed how hard he'd been working, and how badly he wanted to catch Dmitri. He would be a key member of the team Anton would put together once he had filled Yuri's shoes. He screwed the lid back on his drink as Vasili finished the call.

"Everything is in place then?" he asked, already knowing the answer.

"Yes, Youlya was told to call me when she arrives and we will meet here. If someone spots him before that they will let us know. Until then we will wait. If you want to sleep, I can wake you when I hear something."

"Thank you," he replied and immediately sank into the seat, his eyes closed.

Vasili had slept off and on during the drive, but was now too keyed-up to worry about falling asleep himself. He thumbed through his phone, absent-mindedly scrolling through old messages before calling up one of the games he had downloaded. It was a mindless game that he could play without really concentrating. His mind was racing in too many other directions anyway.

He was silently fuming at the constant barrage of insults and rebukes that Yuri had been firing at him. He knew that he needed to be concentrating on the job at hand, but he was too angry at Yuri. His fingers were stabbing at the screen in silent rage, venting his frustration with the man he'd come to despise over the last few days.

With a sigh of frustration, Vasili closed the game and glanced out into the darkness. He could not see much through the fog on the windows, but then he wasn't really looking. He forced his mind back to the present. Once he had Dmitri, he'd start planning what to do about Yuri; he could not let that man get away with how he'd been treated over the past few days. Right now he needed to finish up the current job which, in a way, was the first step in ridding himself of Yuri.

He shifted his gaze back out the window. Somewhere out there in the dark was Dmitri. Or was he there? Suddenly Vasili had an uneasy feeling in the pit of his stomach. Something was wrong, but he could not figure out just what it was. Was it merely the fact that Dmitri had managed to slip through his grasp at every turn so far? Or was it something more? He'd certainly be in a very vulnerable place with Yuri if his prey escaped again.

But as he considered that possibility, he suddenly let out a laugh. Just enough that Anton opened one eye to see what had happened. If Dmitri wasn't here, then Yuri had no one to blame but himself. He had ordered the two of them here. For once it would be Yuri's fault alone. In a twisted sort of way he almost hoped it would work out that way. Not that he would ever let Dmitri go on purpose, but it would be nice if just this once, Yuri could be directly blamed for Dmitri still being at large.

He quickly shook off that thought, but not the uneasy feeling that something was not right. He'd worked too long and too hard to give up now. Dmitri had to be here, hadn't he? Anxiously, he used his hand to wipe the condensation from the window, peering intently into the darkness, willing Dmitri to appear.

* * *

Youlya raised her hand to the door, her fist brushing against it without making a sound. Then slowly, hesitantly, she raised it, her heart pounding. She was not even sure she would have enough breath to speak as she forced herself to knock on it several times. She was more than half hoping there would be no answer. But then, when nothing happened at first, she was afraid that there actually might not be an answer. Should she try the door to see if it was unlocked?

It likely didn't take as long as it felt before she heard a voice, full of suspicion, speaking loudly enough to be heard through the heavy door.

"Who is it?"

"It's Youlya. Yuri told me he needed me and I was supposed to meet him here."

There was a moment's hesitation before the door opened a crack. Trying to appear as if she had nothing to hide, she stepped into the sliver of light, allowing the man inside to see her.

"You are Yuri's secretary? The one who called about Dmitri wanting to meet you?"

"Yes, that's me," Youlya tried to make herself sound more irritated that terrified. As she'd feared, she found she barely had enough breath to speak.

"Why didn't you come to the front door?"

"I tried, but the gate is closed and locked and no one answered." She hoped he'd accept that answer, and, after considering it a moment or two, he appeared to.

"Why did Yuri ask you to come? He's sleeping right now."

"I don't know. Ask him yourself if you want to." She shrugged dismissively as she spoke, knowing there was no way he would dare risk awakening Yuri at this time of night, and whatever she and Dmitri were going to do, they'd better have finished it long before he woke up. "When Yuri gives an order you do not ask for an explanation, you obey!" That was true enough. You didn't last long around Yuri by questioning orders.

He was being swayed her way, she could see, but it was time to go on the offensive. She closed her eyes for a moment and steeled herself, trying to sound much more confident than she felt. "If you want, I will spend the night in my car. You can explain to Yuri that you did not want me to come into the house despite his orders. He has my number and he can call me when he wakes up." She swayed a bit as if to take a step back to emphasize her point.

It wasn't the first time she'd used an implied threat to get her way with some troublesome underling. The fact that she worked closely with Yuri on a daily basis gave her a reputation among the common muscle of the organization. In their minds, she had a close working relationship with Yuri and was privy to things they did not know, and her words could carry almost as much weight as his in some circumstances and circles. That wasn't entirely untrue, though there were very small limits to the amount of pull she actually had. But if they couldn't figure that out, it was not something she was above taking advantage of.

He opened the door a little wider and she stepped inside, willing her heart to slow down. She blinked rapidly against the harsh fluorescent fixtures that flooded the room with their cold light. There were two doors, the one to her right was open and through it she could see the bottom of the stairs that led to the main floor. Another, straight ahead of her was closed. If Dmitri's assumption was right, then the Canadian must be behind it.

She nodded towards the door. "Is that where you have him?"

The man grinned back at her. "Yes, he's recovering from our last conversation now." He let out a laugh that told her just how much he'd enjoyed his side of the 'conversation.'

She forced a smile of her own. It was nothing new to her that such things happened, though what had taken place beyond that door now caused her to wince inwardly. Since first discovering the nature of Yuri's business, she had been putting a mental wall between how he earned his money, and the source of her paycheques. She did administrative work only; that is what she was paid for. Now, in the next room, was one of Yuri's innocent victims, freshly beaten by the man smiling at her. The money Yuri paid her with could no longer be neatly segregated from activities like this. More and more she found herself appreciating the decision that Dmitri had made.

"Did he give you any information?" Her question should appear normal since Michael and Dmitri had been the reason for her call to Yuri, but she was still wary of arousing his suspicion.

"No, not yet, which made it much more entertaining. He looked so terrified that I was afraid he would tell us everything right away. Now, it doesn't matter. " He gave a shrug, "Soon we will have someone new to talk to." He grinned again in such obvious anticipation that it caused a shiver to run up her spine.

"Did you speak to him yourself? Do you understand English?"

He shook his head emphatically. "No, we had some lessons in school, but I was not very good at it. I don't remember much of it."

Youlya nodded in feigned understanding. She didn't necessarily disagree with the idea that English was hard to learn, but she found it hard to believe that the man had ever been to school at all. She'd studied a little English in school, and had been forced to learn more in her secretarial studies since many businesses had dealings with foreign companies and personnel. She did not consider herself fluent, but she was confident she could recall enough to give Michael some understanding of what might be about to happen. It might make things a little easier if he was somewhat prepared for Dmitri's arrival.

"I know some English," she pretended to be considering something. "Maybe I could talk to him and learn something. I do know

Dmitri, or I thought I knew him. I could use that to put the Canadi-an off-guard, and maybe trick him into saying something."

The man was suddenly uncomfortable and guarded, as if he'd been pushed a bit too far too fast. "I don't know if that would be a good idea. Yuri gave no such instructions."

She tried to turn on her best charming smile, "Oh, it will be fine. I can throw a scare into him. Why should you have all the fun? And if I learn anything, we will share the credit. I will let Yuri know you helped. If we don't learn anything, then we have lost nothing. Yuri does like it when someone takes initiative, you know." That last statement was a bit of a fabrication, but it did imply some sort of possible reward.

Not too many men, especially those known more for muscle than for brains, can long resist a request from an attractive woman. Especially when she smiles, makes it sound like harmless fun, and implies that something good will likely result in going along with her idea.

Just to make sure she sold him on the plan, she threw in one last idea. It would not be pleasant for Michael, but it would help her to get through that door. "You go in first and threaten him, in Ukrainian of course. Scare him a bit then I will come in and see what I can learn, okay?" She could tell by the crooked smile on his face that the idea appealed to him. She wasn't sure if she should be disgusted or happy that it had worked. She was certainly repulsed by his response.

"Okay," he agreed. Before opening the door, he placed his hand on the switch that controlled the lighting in the room that was serv-ing as Michael's prison. He was laughing as he rapidly flicked the light on and off several times before flinging the door open and stepping into the doorway. She caught sight of a man bound to a chair sitting in the middle of the room, a look of terror on his face.

The guard, she hadn't bothered to ask him his name, walked up to the man, grabbed his shoulders, and shook him violently enough that only the ropes binding him to the chair kept him from falling to the floor. "Someone is here to speak with you," he barked out in his toughest-sounding voice. Michael cringed at the words. He had no idea what they meant, but they certainly sounded threatening enough; and the bruises he already had made him fear more were about to come.

"You are good at this," Youlya said with a forced smile. Then she turned to face Michael while adopting her most stern expression. Michael looked at her in confusion, wondering what these people were up to now.

"You know Dmitri!" She barked out the words as an accusation. Her accent was thicker than Dmitri's, but her grammar was a bit better and he could understand her fairly easily.

"I told that other guy already, I only met him a few days ago on the plane." His voice was tired, resigned, and devoid of any hope. "I didn't have anything to do with your missing money. Ask him yourself when Vasili brings him here."

"He's already here." Michael stared up at her in open despair as she spoke the words. Not quite wanting to believe his last hope was gone. "This man does not speak English," she pointed at the guard as if to warn Michael what might happen if he did not cooperate. "Look frightened when I speak."

Michael nodded, still confused. He already looked frightened and it was no act. Surely this had to be some kind of trick to get him to talk, even though there was nothing else he could tell them. The guard figured he was being used as a threat and did his best to look menacing. From Michael's point of view, it was very effective.

"Dmitri brought me here. He is going to rescue you." She could tell Michael was not convinced, he looked dazed and frightened at best. So much the better, with the guard in the room. "He is outside right now."

Michael looked at her in obvious doubt. "What kind of trick are you trying to pull? I've told you people I don't know anything." The contempt in his voice as he spoke the words 'you people' was enough to cause her to blush in embarrassment. She'd wanted out for a long time, she realized now, but had never had the courage to act. She hadn't thought there was any way to get out. Now she knew that Dmitri was right, it was worth the risk to leave this life behind her. She knew what these men did to earn the money they had, but then 'earn' was the wrong word, wasn't it? They earned nothing, they just took it. Every kopek they'd ever paid her had come from these sorts of acts, and even this man knew it. It had been one thing to admit it to herself, quite another to have a complete stranger make the accusation. She looked at Michael, saw the bruises and dried blood on his face, and the pain and the fear in his eyes. But she also saw the contempt. That was what made her wither inside. She knew what he felt for her was well-deserved because she was just as much a part of this organization as any of the rest of them.

Dmitri was right to leave, whatever the risk or cost. Even death might be better than living the way he had. The way she had. He was also right in refusing to leave without this man.

She could no longer look him in the eye as he went on, speaking in rage and frustration. "So you tell me I am about to be rescued and what? I'm supposed to suddenly tell you where the money is because I'm going free? I don't know anything anyway, but even if I did, why would I tell you now?"

"Quiet!" She was barely able to control her voice. He was starting to get too loud and might wake the others. For all she knew there might be a small army upstairs. Out of the corner of her eye she saw the twisted smile on the face of Michael's guard. He had interpreted Michael's outburst as a sign that she was getting to him.

In her frustration and anger, Youlya grabbed Michael's face with both hands, forcing him to look at her face. "He is waiting for the right opportunity! I am going to give him one."

Michael blinked hard at the words. Was this a trick? That certainly sounded like Dmitri. Was he really here? Or did she just know the man well enough to lead him on?

For some reason he'd been shocked into silence. She stepped back, trying to figure out what to do. Her eyes flickered across the room, searching the shelves, looking for something, anything that might be the answer. Then she saw it.

Turning to the guard she smiled a knowing smile at him and switched back to her native tongue. "Throw a scare into him, but don't hurt him anymore. He has to be able to talk. They might not need Dmitri after all."

The guard stepped in front of Michael, grabbed him by the shirt collar, and pulled so hard he almost yanked the chair off the ground. With hands and feet bound to the chair, Michael was powerless to resist, so he braced himself for the blow. A blow that never came.

As soon as the guard's attention was on Michael, Youlya reached for a heavy pipe wrench she'd seen on the shelf immediately behind her. Hardly pausing to think she picked it up, whirled around, and swung it at the guard's head.

It was her sudden movement that alerted him to the fact that something was wrong. Releasing his grip on Michael he turned, raising his hand to ward off the coming blow.

He almost succeeded, but he had started out of position and was a fraction of a second late, the fraction of a second that it took him to release his grip and start to turn. Instead of the blow landing on his head it glanced off his forearm. But even that glancing blow was enough to throw him off balance as an explosion of pain caused him to instinctively tuck his arm in, gripping it in agony with his other hand.

Youlya had swung hard enough that her deflected blow continued up and over his head, the weight of the wrench then pulling her hands downwards in an arc. She was committed now, she knew if he had the chance to recover from his initial shock, that he could easily overpower her with just one good arm. Jerking the wrench back towards him she caught him squarely in the stomach, producing a loud grunt and knocking the wind out of him.

This time he collapsed backwards, tripping over Michael's chair. They both went down, Michael helplessly bound in the chair and pinned beneath his guard, who was doubled up and cradling both his arms against his stomach. The guard was gasping in vain, desperately trying to fill his lungs with oxygen.

With the little strength she had left, Youlya gave him one final knock over the head before he finally lay still and silent. She wasn't sure if he was dead or just out cold, and didn't waste any time checking. She dropped the wrench and ran for the back door.

She was blinking, trying to clear her vision, and for what seemed like an eternity, she struggled with the door. No matter how hard she tried it would not open. Then, in desperation, she tried pushing instead of pulling and it swung open with a creaking sound that seemed loud enough to wake the whole town.

She tried shouting Dmitri's name, but no words would come from her mouth. She tried again and heard nothing but the sound of her breath struggling to escape from her throat. Then she heard someone moving in the room behind her.

CHAPTER 20

Meeting Point

Dmitri was already as close to the house as he dared to be. It wasn't fear that kept him from getting closer, at least not fear for his own safety. He'd been in more dangerous situations than this often enough. But this time he also had to consider Youlya and Michael. Both of them were relatively safe at the moment. They'd done as much to Michael as they were likely to now that they thought they had him. Youlya could likely convince Yuri, and anyone else inside, that she'd come on legitimate business. At least he hoped so. But if he were to be spotted, everything was over. It wouldn't take them long to figure out that Youlya was the one that had told him where to come.

So he waited. Usually he didn't mind waiting until an opportunity arose, a chance to take decisive action with the least amount of risk. But with more than just himself to worry about he found it very difficult, despite his logical assessment of the risks they faced.

He'd hardly taken his eyes off the door since Youlya had stepped through it, and he would have given anything to know what was happening inside. His heightened senses caught a rapid thumping noise, like a door being forced opened and shut quickly. Suddenly the door flew open and he blinked hard at the sudden flash of light from inside the house.

Forcing himself to look into the opening, he caught Youlya's silhouette outlined in the doorframe. He hesitated. Was she coming out to give him a report? Would he give himself away needlessly if he came out of hiding? Why wasn't she moving? He still could not see her clearly, but she seemed to be frozen in place and he thought he could hear her making soft, desperate noises.

It was time to act. He didn't know what he was supposed to do, but he sprinted out of the shadows of the trees and into the shaft of light being projected through the open door.

His first concern was for Youlya and he was about to stop and help her, but when she saw him she immediately turned to look behind her, wordlessly warning him that something else needed his attention first.

Skidding to a stop at the doorway he looked into the room but saw no one. Looking down at Youlya he saw she was staring in fear at the doorway opposite the one in which he stood. It took him a few moments to stop using just his eyes, and it was then that he heard sounds coming from the next room. A hand appeared clutching the door frame and he tensed, ready to spring into action, but hesitating in case it was Michael. He had no idea what was happening so he was trying to prepare for anything.

Dennis recognized Dmitri almost immediately, and the shock of seeing him jolted him back to full alertness. "Pavel! Dmitri's here!" His shout echoed through the house, but in pausing to call for help, he had lost the advantage of surprise. Dmitri had no idea who this man was, but knew he had to be silenced. The two of them were about evenly matched in weight and build, but Dmitri had the advantage of momentum as he dove towards Dennis who just had time to raise his hands in self-defence before they collided.

The force of their collision drove Dennis back through the doorway and into a shelf loaded with empty glass jars. It collapsed with a thunderous crash that was sure to wake anyone in the house not already alerted by Dennis' cry. There was no time to worry about that though. Dennis was still suffering the effects of two blows from the wrench and the impact with the shelf had winded him again. He couldn't quite get enough strength to ward off the blows Dmitri was throwing at him. He sank to his knees, but still Dmitri didn't let up. All the frustration and anger of the past few days, or perhaps of the past few years, was venting itself on a man who happened to be in the wrong place at the wrong time.

Something warm and sticky was coating Dmitri's hands, as he became aware of it he paused to look at them. They were covered in blood. For a moment he thought maybe he'd cut himself on the broken glass that littered the floor, but it wasn't his blood he saw, it was flowing from Dennis' nose and mouth, and his eyes had a vacant look to them. Somehow the guard was still conscious, but barely. Dmitri pushed him aside and his body simply sank to the floor. He was breathing, but wasn't making any effort to do anything but moan.

Shaking his head to clear it, Dmitri became aware of Michael laying on his side, still bound to the chair. He was about to reach for him when Youlya's scream stopped him.

"Who are you? What is happening here?" Pavel demanded roughly of Youlya. He was standing at the bottom of the stairs and could not see into the room where Dmitri stood.

Youlya stared back it him blankly, unable to form a thought, let alone speak.

"What are you doing here?" His tone of voice warned her that if she didn't have a good answer, he was about to do something drastic.

"I am…" she was hyperventilating, trying to buy herself time, while unknowingly doing the same for Dmitri, who spotted the wrench she'd dropped and quietly bent over to pick it up. "I am Yuri's secretary. He ordered me to come here. I'm the one who told him where Dmitri was, I…"

"What happened?" Pavel demanded again. Then, recovering from the surprise of seeing Youlya, he remembered the shout and the crash that had awakened him. "Where is Dennis?"

She nodded towards the back room, and Pavel took a cautious step towards it, not sure if this strange woman was telling the truth or not. Her answers had bought Dmitri a few precious seconds, but had not allayed Pavel's suspicion. He took another step that brought him to the threshold, from which he could see Dennis, his face covered with blood and laying comatose on the floor. If only he'd looked back at Youlya to ask her what had happened. But he was too alert, too suspicious. When Dmitri swung the wrench at him, he was almost ready for it and managed to block not the wrench, but Dmitri's arm, turning the blow harmlessly aside. The wrench crashed into the doorframe and was jarred loose from Dmitri's hand.

The wrench was temptingly close, but Dmitri saw that reaching for it would be a mistake; Pavel would be all over him before he could get to it. The two men began circling, each sizing up the other and looking for an opening. Each man knew the other was experienced at being the 'muscle' in situations like this. Neither was taking the other for granted as they traded feints and continued circling, looking for an advantage that wasn't coming.

"Dmitri!" A surprised shout of rage came from behind him. Dmitri started at the yell, but didn't take his eyes from Pavel. He recognized the voice instantly without having to look. It was Yuri. He didn't bother to respond, but he was starting to worry about how many more people were in the house. He had hoped to get in and out as silently and quickly as possible.

"Youlya, what is happening here? How did Dmitri find us?" Somewhere, deep down, he knew that he'd been betrayed again, but

like other corrupt men in powerful positions, he had so thorough-
ly convinced himself that all his underlings looked up to him that
he just couldn't face the facts. She was so intent on watching the
two men that she didn't bother to answer. She wouldn't have known
what to say anyway.

Yuri was too old and out of shape to even consider mixing it up
with the two men; he hadn't done anything physical in years, perhaps decades. He watched intently, willing Pavel to make the first
move and finish Dmitri off. Things might not be working out as he'd
planned, but Dmitri was here. He had him now.

Yuri edged along the wall, trying to keep his distance from the
two men, but making his way towards Youlya. She watched him in
panic, and then looked to Dmitri, needing his help but knowing
that he could do nothing. He caught her desperate glance and nodded towards the wrench. She caught the signal and dove for it.

The sudden motion was enough to attract Pavel's attention, causing him to think she was attacking him. That split-second was all
Dmitri needed. He threw himself at Pavel, driving him back against
the wall. Not as forcefully as he'd done with Dennis, but enough to
gain the advantage as they began grappling and exchanging blows.

Yuri thought that with the two men fighting, he was free to grab
Youlya. He was wrong. She scooped up the wrench, brandishing
it towards him as she shrieked, "Stay away from me!" He froze in
place. Her voice carried more panic than authority, but the wrench,
which she held rather awkwardly, was all the authority she needed.
He wasn't going to take a chance on what might happen if she started swinging it. Yuri felt foolish at being held at bay by a secretary
wielding a wrench, but one good swing would cause a lot of pain.
He'd wait till Pavel finished with Dmitri.

At least that was his plan, until Youlya began waving the wrench threateningly at him. "Down on the floor," she ordered, "Sit down. Now!" His face flushed red in a mixture of rage and embarrassment, but he obediently slid down the wall, lowering his bulk to the floor. "Don't move," she warned, keeping one eye on him and the other on Dmitri and Pavel. At his size and weight, she'd have plenty of warning if he tried anything.

The two men were now rolling on the floor, wrestling more than anything, neither able to get a solid advantage. Dmitri did have Pavel pinned beneath him at the moment, but there were no points for a pin in this fight. Then Youlya thought of a way she might be able to give Dmitri an advantage. They both understood English, and Pavel likely didn't.

"Roll over," she cried out in English. He looked up and saw her hovering over the two of them, wrench in hand. She'd understood his silent signal to her, now he understood her words. Being on top it was a simple matter to use his weight to roll over, especially since Pavel wanted to be on top. Pavel thought for a brief moment that he had succeeded in gaining the advantage as he unexpectedly found himself right where he wanted to be. But the thought was short lived as the pipe wrench came down solidly onto the back of his neck. Youlya was not trying to kill him, but she did intend to cause enough damage to end the fight for good. There was no way to know just how seriously she'd injured him, but it was more than enough to knock him out and he slumped heavily on top of Dmitri with a loud grunt.

"Don't move!" Dmitri and Youlya both ordered Yuri at the same moment. He sat glowering where he'd first sat down, not daring to move as Youlya turned to cover him with the wrench again. Dmitri rolled Pavel's unconscious body to the side and climbed slowly to his feet. He was aching all over and couldn't remember exactly what had caused all the various injuries, but he'd worry about it later. No one else had showed up so he began to hope that everyone in the house was now accounted for.

"Watch him," he ordered Youlya, the words coming out sharper than he meant them to, but she didn't seem to mind as she continued to brandish her weapon at Yuri.

With everything that had happened in the past few minutes, they'd both all but forgotten the reason they'd come.

"Mikhail, are you all right?" Dmitri called out, running into the storage room.

"Yeah, I'm Okay," he answered, his voice strained, but relieved.

Dmitri quickly bent over him and tried to undo the knots, but his fingers were slick with blood, and trembling too much to loosen them. Dennis and Pavel had done a thorough job of securing him. Searching the room frantically he found a utility knife and sliced Michael free.

Michael pulled himself to his feet, trying to rub the numbness from his wrists while Dmitri gathered up the rope and tied Pavel's hands firmly behind his back. He wasn't concerned about causing him any discomfort. Once he was sure there was no way he'd manage to work his way out of the rope, he repeated the process on Dennis, who was stirring slightly.

After he had both men secured he turned his attention to Yuri, glaring at his former boss with all the hatred that years of working under him had forged in his heart. "We will be going now, Yuri Stepanovich." He spat out the patronymic 'Stepanovich' with enough sarcasm to leave no doubt in Yuri's mind just how much contempt he felt for him.

"No you will not!" Yuri's face was almost purple with rage and the veins in his neck were standing out as he barked out what to him sounded like an order. To Youlya and Dmitri it sounded like the ranting of a desperate, defeated man. Michael, who could not understand the words but had a vague idea of what he might be saying, wished they'd all just shut up so they could leave. He was afraid that even now hordes of Mafia hit men were preparing to storm the room.

"You will give me back the money!"

"It is not yours. It never was," Dmitri replied calmly, insinuating the taint on the funds without actually accusing him of anything.

"You stole it from me," Yuri shot back, "You are just as guilty as I am. More guilty. You owe me! I gave you everything you have. Without me you would still be nothing."

Now it was Dmitri's turn to become enraged. "I owe you nothing! You destroyed my life. You took everything that was wrong with me and made me even worse. You turned me into you."

"You would have preferred to remain a nobody? To live in the poverty you grew up in? I made you somebody. I gave you a better life. You could have had anything you wanted."

"You gave me nothing," Dmitri roared. "I paid for everything, and I paid too high a price for it. You sat in your office and ordered me to do..." he hesitated, his voice cracking as he thought of the horrific things he had done to Yuri's many victims. He no longer wanted to do those things, or be that person, even what he'd just done to the two guards sickened him; somehow he knew the memories could never be erased. "You ordered me to destroy others so you could have what they deserved. Now, I am taking from you what you took from them. Now you will know how it feels to have someone do it to you."

Dmitri had honestly never planned to take as much as he had from Yuri. It was never about the money, only the opportunity to get out of the country, to be free of what he'd become and be able to start a new life. But somehow it now felt fitting to have taken it all and he wished it had been more. Not to line his own pockets, just for the satisfaction of hurting Yuri even deeper. He would never miss those millions as much as his victims had missed the relative pittances he'd taken from them. Even as he yelled at Yuri, he realized he was saying things he'd never expressed to anyone, not even to himself. He decided at that moment that he could not keep all the money, he'd find a way to use it wisely, maybe even give some of it away. It would be impossible to give it back to its rightful owners, but he would not be wasting it all on himself as Yuri would have. His mind flashed back to Andrei and Katya, and to their friends, and their willingness to help others despite their poverty. Yuri was nothing compared to such people. For years he'd wanted to be like Yuri, but now he wanted to be like Andrei. Was there any hope of that? There had to be!

. "I will never be the person you tried to make me into. And I will never be like you."

The amount of scorn in Dmitri's voice might have made other men stop and think about their actions. But Yuri had spent too many years thinking too highly of himself and too lowly of those beneath him. In his eyes Dmitri, would now never be anything more than a well-rewarded thug. To be scorned by such a man meant nothing more to him than that Dmitri was too much of a fool to understand how the world worked. Only Dmitri's size, and the wrench in Youlya's hand, prevented him from doing to both of them what they deserved for their betrayal.

"We are going now," Dmitri said to him, with a sharp edge of determination and finality in his voice. Then he turned to Michael, briefly forgotten yet again as he had spoken his mind to a man he thought he'd already seen for the last time. He had to concentrate to form the words in English. "Come, Mikhail, we go now."

The three of them walked to the basement door, keeping a wary eye on Yuri who made no effort to move until they had closed the door behind them. Its lock was a hook fastened from the inside, so they could do no more than push it closed. Youlya led the way through the trees while Dmitri helped Michael, who was still feeling the effects of his 'discussions' with Pavel and Dennis, as well as the numbness caused by being tied for hours to the chair.

They had some difficulty getting him through the wire fence, but the realization that the car was waiting gave Michael the energy he needed to scramble though the fence, crawl into the back seat and collapse. Seatbelt laws were not strictly enforced in Ukraine, or at least Dmitri hadn't been concerned about wearing his on their first, wild escape attempt. When had that been? How many months ago? He sprawled across the seat and closed his eyes. Not quite asleep, but not awake enough to do anything but lay there.

Youlya made no objection when Dmitri claimed the driver's seat. He didn't think anyone was watching or listening, but since the car was on a steep hill leading down into the town he didn't bother starting the engine. Slipping the car out of gear and releasing the park brake, he rode the brake pedal as they coasted and bounced silently down the rough, dirt road.

"Where are we going?" Youlya asked, her voice barely a whisper.

"Romania," he hardly dared to believe they were free once more. He'd thought once before that he had made it to freedom, only to be dragged back. The quiet of the night and the lack of engine noise lent an uneasy, almost unreal, feeling to the escape. It was as if he was waiting for Vasili or Anton to jump out from behind the shadow of the trees they were gliding past.

They reached the bottom of the hill and the trail turned into a paved road. He started the engine and found comfort in its sound. He had control again and didn't need stealth. The sound of the engine was like the promise of power, and of freedom. He worked his way up the quiet street and into the town centre. From there it would be easy enough to get back to the highway.

"You have your passport?"

"Yes, I brought it, just like you told me to."

"Good, because Michael and I will not be able to cross the border with you; we will have to find another way."

* * *

Yuri waited for a few moments after the door closed and then struggled to raise himself to his feet. He found the knife that Dmitri had used to free Michael and cut loose Pavel and Dennis. Despite a few slaps to their faces, and a lot of shouting, he couldn't bring them to consciousness as fast as he knew he needed to.

Dennis looked a lot worse than Pavel, but surprisingly he was the first to be roused enough to sit up. Yuri did not concern himself with the severity of Pavel's injuries, all that mattered was to keep Dmitri from escaping. If he was too injured to be of any use then he was like any other piece of useless equipment, fit only to be discarded or repaired later, if possible. The job came first. The money came first.

"After them. They went out the back door." Dennis shook his blood-spattered head and rose unsteadily to his feet. "Find out which way they went, and call someone. We can't let them get away!" Yuri sounded frantic, even to the still groggy Dennis, who had no choice but to follow the orders despite the pain that made it almost impossible for him to move.

Staggering to the door he shoved it open and stepped out into the dark. He was thankful for the cool air, it cleared his head a bit. There was no sign of Dmitri or the others in any direction. What did that fool Yuri expect him to do? He didn't have a clue which way they'd gone, but stepping outside brought him a few minutes of reprieve from the presence of Yuri. Without the strength to search very far, he moved into the shadows and squatted down, simply listening. There was nothing but the usual sounds of the night. A few barking dogs, an almost audible announcement from the train station that was carried further than usual by the cool air, but nothing to indicate which way they had gone. Or by what means. For all he knew or cared they could be making their escape by bicycle. But he was not going to attempt to pursue them.

Dmitri had bested him, along with the help of Youlya. Whether they'd had the element of surprise or not he was in no shape to mix it up again with any one of those three. The money was Yuri's problem, not his. He was not about to further risk his life, or his dignity, by facing them again.

He waited for a few minutes to make Yuri think he really was looking, then made his way back inside. "I couldn't see them, but I'm sure they will be heading back towards the border. They won't have changed their plans."

He was speaking as he limped through the door, hoping to ward off some insults or further orders from Yuri. But the crime lord made no response; he was slumped against the wall, his face gray, his hand clutched to his chest.

* * *

Vasili and Anton had taken turns keeping watch. Not that they'd expected anything before Youlya's arrival, but they could not take any chances. The problem with keeping watch, though, was that if anything it made the time pass even slower. After all the time Vasili had spent planning and hunting, the promise of Dmitri's impending capture should have made the final hours easy, but if anything it had been even more difficult. Too many things had gone wrong already and the longer he waited, the stronger his uneasiness had grown.

He sighed as he tried to sort out his thoughts. Glancing over at Anton he saw that the other man was not sleeping, but was trying hard at least to get some rest, knowing that things could get very exciting in the next hour or so. Each knew the other was awake, but they made no effort to talk.

Vasili once again wiped the condensation from the side window and stared into the distance. He hadn't needed the extra help from Anton who now, no doubt, would share in the credit for recovering the money for no other reason than that he'd driven Vasili here in his car. Yes, it was true that Youlya's call had played an important part in the final capture, but didn't Yuri understand that if Vasili had not found them in this wretched village in the first place, that they would not have caught the Canadian, and Dmitri would not have been forced to call her?

His vision was focused on a sign fastened to the store's door, but he didn't really see it. It was his hard work, his sleepless nights, his organization and planning that had brought them to this point. He would finish the mission. He was not about to let Dmitri go; not by accident or on purpose. But when he had him, he would make sure that he got the credit. One way or another, he vowed to himself, Yuri would not take that from him. He would see that he got what he deserved. Whether that meant going above Yuri, or beneath him, there was no way the old fool would rob him of what he had coming to him.

His cell phone rang, and he knew who it was before he even drew it from his pocket. Anton watched as he picked it up and looked at the display. Sure enough, it was Yuri. He sighed with more exasperation than he should have while Anton was listening. Couldn't the old fool just let him do the job? They were all impatient, but Youlya had given Dmitri the earliest time she could possibly have arrived here and that time had not yet come. All the more reason to be done with this old fool. For the first time he actually began to think that Dmitri had the right idea. He couldn't be allowed to get away with it of course, but it was tempting.

"Da, Yuri Stepanovich," he answered, with as much feigned respect as he could force into his voice. It was Yuri's number, but it was not Yuri's voice. For a few seconds Vasili thought that Yuri had reverted to having Danic, or some other flunky, handle the phone. But it wasn't Danic either.

"What?" Anton, hearing the tone of his voice, looked at him first quizzically, then impatiently, sensing something big had happened. "Slow down, say that again," Vasili ordered the frantic-sounding Dennis. He listened in silence as Dennis recounted, in disjointed fragments, what had happened at the house. He couldn't say he was sorry, and he could always say, with a credible witness, that he was doing exactly what Yuri had ordered him to do. His mouth started to form a self-satisfied smile, but it would never do to let Anton see that. So he drew his lips into a thin line as he listened to the story and asked for clarification on the details that Dennis was leaving out. Things could not have worked out better for him, and he also drew comfort from the knowledge that all this had taken place in Anton's house. "You are sure of all this?" he asked when Dennis finally finished. "Okay, we will decide what to do here."

He knew Anton was dying to know what had happened, which was all the more reason to take his time telling the story. "I have to call the others," he explained, dialling the number of one of the men hiding near the bus stop. "You can call it off; Dmitri will not be here tonight. Let the others know they can get some sleep. We will decide what to do in the morning."

He continued to work at supressing a smile as he slowly slid the phone back into his pocket, wanting to lead Anton along a little farther, but knowing he couldn't very well justify it any more. "We can go back to your house now. Dmitri will not be coming here."

"I know, I heard you." Anton's voice was agitated, which suited Vasili just fine. "How do you know he will not be showing up, what happened?"

"Dmitri left your house just a few minutes ago. With the Canadian. Youlya helped him." The smile started to show just a bit. "She knocked out Dennis and Pavel with your wrench." He managed not to laugh at that thought, but there was more to tell; he was saving the best for last. "Yuri is dead."

"What? Dmitri killed him?"

"No, he had a heart attack. I'm afraid Dmitri has won. At least for now. They have no idea which way he went. He will be heading for the border, no doubt, but we are too far out of position now, and there are too many different ways he can get there." Vasili's first reaction had been to get his men searching for the three fugitives. But the men here were not sufficient to cover every possible route, especially now that Dmitri had access to Youlya's car and was no longer dependent upon trains and buses. And they had too much of a head start on anyone else he could call up. They could now make a direct, non-stop run to the border and that gave them the advantage. In some ways, it was almost a relief to call off the search. He'd tracked Dmitri out of the country once already, and he would do it again. He needed to make a fresh start. Without any interference from Yuri. In fact, searching on his own could be much more lucrative than doing it for Yuri.

There was silence in the car as each man digested what had happened, and what it meant for each of them. Anton surprised Vasili by being the first to break the silence.

"You know, this might not be a bad thing, Vasili."

Vasili managed to hide his surprise, pausing for a few moments before he dared to speak. "I was thinking the same thing, Anton."

Unlike Vasili, Anton was not surprised. Vasili was not as good at hiding his contempt as he thought he was. Of course so many sleepless nights would make it harder to control his emotions, Anton allowed.

"With Yuri gone," he spoke slowly, as if only now coming to this realization, repeating himself for added effect, "With Yuri gone, no one else will be expected to repay the money." Vasili nodded thoughtfully, as if he too were considering this for the first time. They would take everything Yuri had owned, leaving his family with nothing if need be, but other than that, nothing would be done to anyone else. It had been Yuri's debt and therefore his responsibility. "So if Dmitri were to be caught, the reward might be very substantial, and it might be more than just money."

"Yes, that is true," Vasili allowed thoughtfully. Neither of them was quite ready to say to the other that if Dmitri were caught quietly enough then the money might not have to be returned at all. That might come in time, when more trust had been built.

Anton started the engine, wiped the condensation from the inside of the windshield, and swung the car onto the road. "We may as well go back to my place," he said. "I think we have a lot to talk about."

CHAPTER 21

Departure

As they left the centre of the town behind them, Michael lay in the back seat watching the beams of the widely-spaced streetlights and the shadows they created chase each other along the inside of the car. He found himself getting a little dizzy as they twisted and turned along the rough, pothole-filled streets, but his head cleared somewhat when they reached the last long straight stretch of road that led out of town. He was almost too tired and sore to care about anything more than the fact that they were free again and finally heading towards safety.

Dmitri was driving well within the speed limit and obeying all the traffic laws to the letter, possibly for the first time since getting his licence. The last thing he wanted to do was to attract the attention of a policeman at this point. Michael had bruises over much of his body and could barely walk. His own hands still had blood on them, and a glance at his face in the rear view mirror clearly showed that he'd been involved in a fight. Not so long ago, he would not have worried about being stopped; a few bills pressed into the right-hand would make almost any problem disappear. But what little cash they had right now would all be needed to get them somewhere safe.

A few kilometers out of town, Dmitri spotted a gas station, long since closed for the night. He pulled the car off the highway and behind the building. There were a few older cars parked there so he pulled up to them and turned out the lights to ensure no one would notice them.

"I need your phone," he told Youlya. He opened up the maps

function and studied possible routes to the border.

Youlya saw what he was doing, and began making some suggestions. As they spoke back and forth quietly in Ukrainian Michael forced himself upright in the seat.

"What's up?" he asked in a tired, strained voice.

"We are looking for best road to border," Dmitri explained in a whisper. Even though there was no one within earshot, or even in sight, they were all anxious to avoid being noticed by anyone. Michael's nod went unnoticed, but he watched the display on the screen as they zoomed and scrolled.

"Fastest way to get there is through village we came from, but is best if we don't go that way. Vasili is there now." Michael was too tired to ask how he knew that, but then a lot of things must have happened while he was at Anton's.

The two of them continued to quietly debate the best route until Michael gave up and lay back down on the seat. When Dmitri started the engine, Michael realized he'd fallen asleep briefly; a few minutes later, the hum of tires on the pavement gradually lulled him back into a fitful sleep.

He awoke a few hours later, the sun was rising and the light shining into the car had awakened him. Sometime during the night they must have stopped somewhere, because Youlya was now driving while Dmitri tried to catch a nap. Sitting up he rubbed the sleep from his eyes and stretched as best he could. The back seat of a compact car was not the best place to sit, let alone try to sleep, and he was stiff and sore to begin with.

"Where are we?" Even as he asked the question he realized that place names would mean absolutely nothing to him, but it seemed a natural enough question to ask.

Youlya hesitated, trying to recall her English lessons. "We are about two hours from the border."

"I don't have my passport. Will they let me through with a driver's licence?"

Youlya laughed in spite of herself at his question. "No, you have to have a passport."

"What? But mine's in Kiev, or at least it was last time I saw it. How am I going to get home?" There was a barely controlled panic in his voice, and Youlya felt bad for having laughed. She hadn't meant it to come out that way.

"Is okay. Dmitri does not have one either. I will drive across the border with the car. You and Dmitri will meet me there."

"Oh, right, Dmitri told me that." He relaxed a bit, recalling Dmitri telling him about how the border was not watched as closely as it had been in the past. It seemed ages ago that they'd discussed how to cross the border, and at the time, getting there had seemed so far off that it had been only something to hope for. In the past few days, he'd stolen a car, some clothes, and played hide and seek with the Ukrainian Mafia. After all that, crossing an international border illegally wasn't that big a deal, was it?

"I will let Dmitri tell you the details later," she replied, "My English is not good. He knows it better."

"Okay," he agreed, leaning back into the seat. He sat back and watched a never-ending row of trees slide past on either side of the car. Through the trees he caught glimpses of rolling fields full of crops that looked almost ready to harvest. It was a pretty country, he had to admit. As bad as his experiences here had been, he tried to convince himself not to judge the country by what had happened to him.

A sign flashed past that informed anyone who could read Ukrainian that a town or village was seven kilometers further up the road. Dmitri must have been at least half awake and watching because he pointed to the sign and spoke something to Youlya.

When they reached the town, Youlya pulled up to the curb in front of a small store. Since she was the most presentable of the three, she was elected to do the shopping. The two men sat in silence as she entered the store to pick up some groceries. She returned shortly and they drove up a side street, still wary of staying anywhere that they might be seen.

Once they felt they were safe from the crowds of the town centre, she parked again and they opened the bags she'd brought back. As hungry as he was, Michael finished off most of the bottle of water before he started in on the open-faced sandwiches she made with some heavily spiced sausage and cheese. He could not recall eating since they'd left Andrei's house and they ran out of food before any of them were full, but at least the edge was taken off their hunger. Next, the two men made themselves as presentable as possible through the use of some baby wipes and a comb she'd acquired during her shopping spree.

"Okay," Michael asked, taking a deep breath. "What's the plan, Dmitri?"

The big Ukrainian half turned in his seat to face him. "We cannot get across border without passports, especially looking the way we do." Michael had to laugh at that comment. "Youlya will drive us to a spot on the border where we can walk across. She will drive across and meet us on other side, and then we drive to Bucharest."

That was pretty much what he'd expected, so he simply sat back into the corner of the seat and closed his eyes. He'd thought he had caught up on his sleep overnight, but found that it was hard to keep his eyes open in the heat of the back seat. He left them shut even when Youlya started the engine, turned the car around, and headed back towards the main road.

Suddenly Dmitri called out, pointing to a small hardware store on the right. Youlya squeezed the car into a parking spot Michael thought was much too small for even a compact car. Dmitri studied himself in the mirror, doing his best to make himself a little more presentable. Then he slipped into the store and returned with a pair of wire cutters, which he tossed into the back seat beside Michael.

"Sometimes we must make opportunity, yes?" All three of them laughed as they drove off, and each began to hope, if not believe, that the plan was actually going to work.

Michael tried to go back to sleep. He knew he needed rest and it would mean at least a temporary relief from the pain, but the backseat was just too uncomfortable, and the nervous expectation of their arrival at the border too powerful, to let him sleep.

About an hour after Dmitri's purchase of the wire cutters the highway led them into another village. This time, Dmitri pulled onto a side street and wove the car back and forth through a confusing series of twists and turns until finally pulling over to the side of the road. He gestured to the right of the car and Michael's gaze followed the motion of his finger. Across a field, a few hundred meters away, he could see a tall, wire fence. It didn't look like much to Michael; it was very similar to the tall fences he'd seen around farms back home where they raised deer.

"That's the border?" He'd been expecting something much more imposing and official looking. What had seemed, not that long ago, to be an unattainable goal was now within sight. The fence could very easily be crossed by anyone, he could see plainly; and that somehow took away from the sense of safety he had expected to feel once they crossed it themselves.

"Yes, is border," Dmitri replied quietly. "We will cross it tonight.

After dark."

Michael nodded, but didn't voice his growing disappointment. Up until now the border, as unattainable as it might have seemed, had represented safety, almost as if crossing it put them magically beyond the reach of Yuri and his men. Seeing it now was a big letdown. A few strands of wire would do nothing but slow the two of them down for a few minutes. But neither would it stop their pursuers. It was nothing more than a nuisance. They'd tracked Dmitri all the way to Germany across more than one international border and through airport security, and they'd almost succeeded in capturing him. Would he ever be safe anywhere?

Dmitri slipped the car back into gear, "We will find place to stay until dark, then we will go."

* * *

Anton and Vasili had made most of the drive to Anton's home in silence. They were both exhausted and too busy pursuing their own thoughts for much conversation. Upon arriving at Anton's house they learned from a rather battered looking Dennis and Pavel that Yuri's body had been quietly removed without attracting any attention from the police, at least not any of the police that might cause problems. Too exhausted to deal with anything else, they'd both gone to bed and slept through the remainder of the night and well into the next morning.

Vasili slept until the sound of the shower running in the bathroom woke him. He sat up groggily, rubbing his tired eyes and taking a few minutes to become fully awake and alert.

It took those few minutes for him to remember that Dmitri had made good on his escape, and that the frantic activity of the last few days had finally reached an end, unsatisfactory as the conclusion might be. So why was he not panicking? That took a few more moments to figure out. There was no one to give an account to; Yuri was gone. Not only that, but the full weight of the failure would fall on his dead boss, which meant a new opportunity for him. A grim smile spread across his lips as he recalled the realization he'd come to the previous night; that this might, in the long run, be the best possible outcome. At least from his point of view. While it was true that he hated to lose, he had not really lost. The hunt was still on, but the reward for success was now potentially much larger.

When he heard the water shut off he rose from the bed and got dressed, then stood looking out the window, lost in thought until he heard the bathroom door open. He waited another minute before heading to take a shower himself. The hot water seemed to wash away all the tension and stress, and by the time he finished and joined Anton in the kitchen, he felt ready for the challenge ahead of him.

"Did you sleep well?" Anton enquired, offering him a cup of tea.

"Yes, for the first time in days." He sipped the tea slowly, letting himself relax as much as possible.

They both sat in silence for a few minutes. There was no sign of Dennis or Pavel; they were likely still sleeping off their physical pain, as well as the shock of Yuri's death. This time it was Vasili who was the first to feel brave enough to speak openly.

"They will likely take everything Yuri owned as payment for the debt." Anton nodded in agreement, so he continued. "That will more than pay off what he owes them." Yuri's holdings were rather extensive between his real estate, investments, and a sizeable cash reserve.

"But that does not mean Dmitri should be allowed to keep what he has stolen," Vasili continued the thought. They were treading dangerous ground here, they both knew. If the money was ever recovered it would be expected to go to the rightful owners, whether the debt was previously satisfied or not. They looked at each other for some time, both of them searching for some sign that they could trust the other fully. Perhaps they'd spoken a little too openly last night? Maybe they should write it off to the exhaustion and shock of losing their boss?

Then it was Anton's turn to carry the thought a little further. "If the money was returned, it would certainly help to advance our positions. Or, it could be funnelled somewhere else just as useful." It didn't seem to bother either of them that they would be doing pretty much what Dmitri had done if they were to keep it for themselves.

"True," Vasili continued, saying it without committing to it. "It would give us some options." They were just two friends speaking hypothetically, weren't they?

"So, if we were to pursue this, how do you think we would start?"

"The money was transferred electronically, as you know. I was able to trace the first transfer, but not the second, because it occurred in a foreign bank. Even electronic transfers leave a trail. It is a matter of finding the person who knows the next part of the trail and persuading them to tell us, and I already know which bank to start from." Bribing someone at a foreign bank might not be as easy as it had been at home, Vasili knew, but there were other options besides bribing. Other ways that are less expensive and perhaps just as persuasive.

Anton smiled knowingly as he followed Vasili's silent train of thought. "That would make it much easier to get started, and there are many ways to persuade someone to release the information, aren't there?"

Vasili nodded in agreement. It was not necessarily going to be easy, but it could be done. It would be done. As they began discussing more concrete plans, neither stopped to consider that they might be sharing the same ultimate plan; to take Yuri's place.

* * *

All three of them were growing impatient and by the time the sun began setting, they were more than ready to put their plan into action. They'd spent the day trying to keep out of sight, which was not that easy in a small village. They'd learned the hard way the danger of being spotted by a local who might report back to Vasili, and the excitement of having the border in sight was tempered by the fear that several carloads of Vasili's men might appear at any moment. Fortunately that had not happened. Though they would never know it, they'd escaped cleanly from Anton's house.

The summer twilight seemed to be dragging on forever, but as anxious as they all were they didn't dare try anything until darkness had fallen completely. The extra hours had left them ample time to study the map and select a rendezvous point along a stretch of road on the Romanian side of the border.

"It is dark enough," Dmitri finally decided, craning his neck to look through the windshield at the evening sky. "We go now."

Youlya was driving and at Dmitri's words she turned the key and swung the car out onto the road. In a few minutes, they were out of the village and driving parallel with the border. They couldn't see it, but they knew the fence was just across the field they were driving alongside.

The traffic was fairly light and they soon left the sparse lights of the village behind them. Normally a car stopping at the side of the road would not arouse too much suspicion, but this close to the border they did not want to draw any unnecessary attention. After all they'd been through to get this close to safety, Dmitri found himself becoming more and more cautious. He'd already been much farther from Ukraine than Romania, only to have his plans go completely to pieces.

"Is there anyone behind us, Mikhail?"

Michael turned, rather awkwardly because everything felt so stiff. "I can't see anything," he replied.

"Okay, stop here," Dmitri ordered.

Youlya brought the car to a quick stop, not even bothering to pull over, and as quickly as possible Dmitri and Michael jumped out. Michael barely had the door shut before she hit the gas and was gone with a quick chirp from the tires.

"Quickly, Mikhail, get off the road!" There was an urgent tone in the Ukrainian's voice that almost frightened him, so he limped quickly after Dmitri, through the ditch and into the field.

"Feels just like old times, doesn't it, Dmitri?"

"Old times?"

"Yeah, it means this reminds me of what we used to do. It's a figure of speech."

Dmitri had to think for a minute, "Oh, yes, you make another joke." He laughed softly. "Hopefully after tonight, we do not do this anymore."

Ten minutes of walking brought them to their goal. A high, wire fence materialized out of the darkness and for some reason both men crouched down in an effort to make themselves less visible, though there was no sign of anyone anywhere nearby. They also felt the need to be as quiet as possible as Dmitri drew the wire cutters out of his pocket.

He selected a strand and pressed the cutters against it. Both men froze at the loud snapping sound the wire made as it suddenly parted. It couldn't possibly have been as loud as it sounded, Michael told himself, but he still looked about nervously.

Dmitri seemed to be doing the same thing, but the only sound was the faint hum of the tires of a passing car coming from the road behind them. Once he was satisfied that they hadn't attracted the border patrols of either country, he made a series of quick cuts and soon had a hole big enough to crawl through.

Dmitri went first, scrambling through with an agility that seemed impossible for someone his size. Michael followed, much more slowly. He grunted several times in pain as he wiggled his stiff body through the opening and tumbled to the ground, his pant leg hooked to a strand of loose wire. He felt Dmitri pulling him free and then helping him to his feet.

"Thanks," he gasped, breathing much too heavily for the amount of exertion it should have taken to climb through the fence. It was several seconds before it occurred to him that he was in Romania, and had just entered it illegally.

"We made it!" He could almost hear the smile on Dmitri's face as he made the announcement. He helped Michael aside then spent a few minutes twisting the broken strands of wire back together as best he could. There was no point in making their passage too obvious to a casual observer. "We must go, we have to find somewhere to hide until Youlya can meet us."

"Lead on, Dmitri." He hoped he could disguise the pain and discomfort in his voice as he began limping after his guide. His ankle was somewhat better after the sprain, but he was still stiff and sore all over from the beatings. It was a good thing they'd only been trying to make him talk; he hated to think what he'd feel like if they'd been actually trying to hurt him.

According to the map they'd studied earlier their rendezvous point was still a few kilometres away. "How long before she gets there?"

"I don't know. It could take several hours to cross border. We will just have to wait."

"I sure hope this is the last opportunity we have to wait for," Michael grumbled.

Dmitri laughed aloud at his words. "No more opportunities, Mikhail, just waiting. We are safe now."

Michael barked out a short, bitter laugh. "I'm ten thousand miles from home, I just crossed a border with no passport, I've got no plane ticket home unless you can get me to Athens, and I've just had a close encounter of the painful kind with a couple of Mafia thugs. And you say I'm safe now?" He still didn't have quite enough faith to believe that crossing a line on a map suddenly put them out of Yuri's reach.

Dmitri slapped him on the back, forgetting in his own happiness how painful that might be to Michael, who winced but said nothing. "Mikhail, we are safe now, even if you were not safe then." He laughed again. "Tonight we drive to Bucharest. Tomorrow you go to embassy and everything is over."

"Right, I guess I forgot to mention that the Mafia are still after us."

"We are safe now," Dmitri said, turning serious again. "They will have a harder time finding us in Romania." He shook his head emphatically, "We are safe."

They crossed the rest of the field in silence, the moon providing just enough light to see the treeline on the far side of the field. When they reached it, they turned to the left, heading towards the spot at which they had agreed to meet Youlya. Another thirty minutes brought them to the point that Dmitri decided was the right intersection, and they crawled into the trees and sat down. The shadows made them quite invisible to anyone that might pass by on the road.

Michael found himself dozing off as they sat quietly in the darkness. He tried to fight it at first, but eventually he gave in and drifted into an uneasy sleep filled with vague dreams of Yuri, Pavel, and Dennis.

He awoke to a gentle shaking of his shoulder.

"Mikhail, wake up, I think she is here."

Michael forced himself into full alertness, noting briefly that the moon had moved noticeably since he'd last seen it, several hours must have passed. Turning in the direction of Dmitri's gaze he spotted a car approaching slowly, travelling well below the speed limit. At least it was going a lot slower than the few cars that had passed by earlier.

Both men sat perfectly still, wanting to be sure it was Youlya before they moved. The car pulled through the intersection and pulled over almost right beside them. It was definitely her car and Michael was starting to stand up when Dmitri suddenly grabbed his arm and pulled him back down.

Another car was approaching from the opposite direction and the cautious thing to do was to wait till it passed. But it didn't pass. As it approached Youlya's car it slowed down and came to a stop. Even before it came to a full stop rotating lights on the roof of the car came on. It was a police car, Michael realized in panic. A few days ago he might have run to the car, told them who he was and asked them to send him home, but now he trusted no one except Dmitri and Youlya. Even if the police could help him it might cause problems for the two of them. The two men shrank back into the shadow of the trees hoping that the flashing lights wouldn't reveal their presence.

The policeman got out of his car, crossed the road, and leaned through the window of the car which Youlya had rolled down in anticipation of his arrival. Michael could make out the sound of their voices, but not the words. He looked at Dmitri, hoping he was catching what they were saying, but the look on his face told him that he couldn't understand what was happening either.

The policeman stood up and pointed back up the road in the direction from which Youlya had come. They exchanged a few more words before he returned to his car and turned the lights off. The police car sat there until she turned her engine back on, did a slow U-turn, and headed back up the road, following close behind her.

"What was that all about?" Michael demanded, knowing that Dmitri didn't know either, but it was the only way he could keep himself from saying, 'I told you so.'

"I don't know, but we wait and see."

At least he didn't say that they needed to wait for the right opportunity.

* * *

Youlya pounded the steering wheel in frustration. She hadn't seen Dmitri or Michael, which was just as well, but she was certain they'd been there. If only she'd been a few minutes earlier, or later, they'd be in the car now. A glance in the mirror showed that the policeman was still right behind her.

Not knowing what else to do when he'd approached and noticed that she was a foreigner, she'd claimed to have lost her way on unfamiliar roads in the darkness. When he'd asked where she was heading, she'd instantly answered Bucharest, which was about the only place in Romania she knew of. He'd very helpfully informed her that she needed to turn around and take a right at the second village to put her back on the correct highway.

A forced smile had convinced him that he'd been of immense help, but now she had no choice but to follow his directions. So she was driving just below the speed limit in the wrong direction, wondering just how long he'd follow her. She wasn't quite panicking, but she was coming close. She took a deep breath to help calm her nerves and slow her racing heart. An opportunity was what Dmitri would say she needed, and surely he would not follow her all the way to Bucharest.

Then, as she approached the first village she saw her opportunity, and pulled into the gas station. One other vehicle was ahead of her so she shut down the car and sat there. She made a face as the police car pulled up behind her, then took another deep breath, put her smile back on, and stepped out of the car. The policeman met her before she reached her back bumper.

"I want to make sure you don't get lost again." He spoke Russian well, which was almost the same as Ukrainian. Many Romanians could speak and understand it even though it was not their first language, and they used the Roman alphabet just like most of Western Europe did.

"Thank you, but I will be fine, really." She kept smiling, but realized he was trying to flirt with her, and wondered if it might be better to stop smiling. "I'm sure you have more important things to do. At the next village, I turn right onto the main road," Youlya repeated his instructions back to him, "See, I know where I'm going now."

Somewhat disappointed at her reply, he forced his own smile and told her that he was just doing his job, then returned to his cruiser. For the sake of appearances, even after he drove off she remained in line at the gas pump. Eventually the car ahead of her pulled away so she paid the attendant with the Euro Dmitri had given her, and waited while he filled the tank. Her fingers drummed the steering wheel impatiently as she reminded herself that the tank needed filling anyway; this might get them to Bucharest with one less stop.

But what on earth would Dmitri and Michael be thinking? Would they still be there when she got back?

CHAPTER 22

Au Revoir

Michael felt like screaming as he watched the two sets of tail-lights disappear into the night, but instead he held his peace and glared at Dmitri. It wasn't his fault, he knew, but he had to direct his frustration somewhere. Dmitri just sat there thinking.

"Mikhail, she was not in trouble with police, or they would not have let her drive herself away," he finally said. That made sense to Michael, and he calmed down a degree or two. "I think we wait. She will come back when she can."

"And if she doesn't?"

"She will," Dmitri insisted. "But if she does not, we are exactly where we would have been if we'd been driven to border. We will go to Canadian Embassy, you will go home and I will disappear."

Michael felt a strange twinge as Dmitri spoke the words. He desperately wanted to get back to the West; he would not feel safe until he was as far away from Ukraine as possible. Yet the thought of Dmitri disappearing saddened him in a way he couldn't quite express. He would be losing a friend. It was hard to believe that, given how he'd felt about Dmitri only a few days ago.

"Yeah, you're right. I guess. So we wait one last time?"

As long as the wait felt, it was actually a little less than thirty minutes before they again saw the lights of a car approaching. This time there was no other traffic as Youlya approached the intersection and pulled over. Dmitri crept through the brush until he was sure it was the right car, and then took another quick glance both ways to make sure no one else was approaching. Satisfied, he signalled Michael and they bolted from the ditch and jumped into the car.

"I'm sorry," Youlya blurted out, not even waiting for the doors to close before wrenching the wheel around in a tight U-turn and accelerating quickly in the direction she'd just come from. Her heart was still racing and she was trying to explain to them what had happened, but she was so excited that it came out in a confusing blend of English and Ukrainian. Michael tried to listen and make sense out of what she was saying but crawling through the fence and having to walk to the pick-up point were almost more than his body could take in its painful and exhausted state. He sank down into the corner of the back seat, closed his eyes, and fell immediately into a deep sleep. At this point he really didn't care whether he ever got the full story or not.

* * *

When he next awoke the sun was rising to his left, which meant, he figured, that they were heading more or less south. He sat up and noticed that Dmitri was now driving and Youlya was napping in the passenger seat.

"Good morning, Mikhail," Dmitri said with a broad smile. Michael had never seen him in such a relaxed mood, and as tired and sore as he was, it was contagious.

"Good morning. Where are we?"

"We are still north of Bucharest, but we will stop to get something to eat soon I think." He glanced over towards Youlya who was stirring slightly at the sound of their voices.

"Yes, I think we should stop and get some breakfast," she agreed sleepily.

Michael could feel his own stomach rumbling at the thought of food and as anxious as he was to leave Yuri and his men behind him, he was thankful when Dmitri pulled up to a restaurant in the next town. They got out of the car and both Dmitri and Youlya stretched, as most people do after a long car trip. Michael tried to stretch too, but winced as a sharp pain shot through his side. He hobbled slowly behind the two Ukrainians as they made their way into the restaurant.

They sipped cups of tea in silence as they waited for breakfast. Michael was too drained to make an attempt at conversation, and there wasn't much they could talk about in public at any rate. His two companions looked tired and ragged, but very relaxed. Leaving the border behind seemed to have given them a second wind, although they also were remaining quiet, saving any real conversation for the privacy of the car.

Time seemed to slow down as they sat and waited, and everything happening around him seemed muted and distant, as it does sometimes when a person is much too tired to be awake. Michael wanted to wolf down his breakfast as soon as it arrived and get back on the road, but Dmitri and Youlya lingered over their breakfast, ordering more tea after they finished eating. They definitely seemed to feel that on this side of the border they had all the time in the world. Or maybe they just needed the break, he thought. After all, they had been driving all night while he'd been sleeping.

When they finally finished their tea, Dmitri paid the bill with some of the Euro he still had. As he made his way slowly back to the car, he looked around, enjoying the feeling of freedom. Michael was so tired and confused that he had half expected it to be dark outside by the time they got back on the road, but it was still well before noon when he crawled back into the rear seat of the car. It felt even smaller and more uncomfortable than it had before they'd stopped.

With Dmitri still at the wheel they soon found themselves back on the open road. Michael alternated between watching the passing scenery and drifting off to sleep. Each time he awoke he was greeted with a new experience in pain and stiffness, no matter how he twisted or turned, there was simply no comfortable way to sit. He began wondering how he'd ever survive the flight home, and realized with a start that he was actually thinking about going home. It was no longer a question of escape and evasion; whatever Dmitri and Youlya felt he was feeling as well. He was safe!

As they approached Bucharest, the traffic began to grow heavier, with cars, trucks, and buses bunching up and slowing down the flow of traffic. Michael began to forget about his discomfort as they finally hit the outskirts of the city.

Dmitri and Youlya were talking back and forth in Ukrainian, not quite arguing, but they seemed a bit frustrated with each other. It was apparently over the problem of navigating through the city. Youlya was staring at her phone, and by slowly twisting a bit in his seat he was able to see that she had a map of the city displayed.

"What's up?" He tried to keep his voice cheerful, hoping to ease some of the tension.

"I am trying," she glared at Dmitri and started over, "I am trying to tell him how to get to the Canadian Embassy, but he seems to think he knows how to drive through a city he's never been to in his life."

"I look at map already," Dmitri protested, a bit too loudly. "You tell me long way to get there!"

Michael chuckled, thinking that some things were the same no matter where in the world you went. "Never try to give directions to a man," he said, sharing a knowing smile with Youlya while Dmitri concentrated on avoiding an unplanned contact with two motorcycles and a truck.

Youlya took his hint and held up the screen to let Michael have a better look. Dmitri was too busy using his horn to express his frustrations to notice what was going on beside him.

"Dmitri, take the second turn to the left," Michael instructed. The Ukrainian was too busy glaring at the offending drivers to wonder how Michael might know where to go. Maybe it was because he was Canadian and just knew where his embassy was? He also failed to notice that it was exactly what Youlya had told him to do.

Michael sat back with a soft chuckle, but kept on the alert, ready to intervene if his services were needed again. According to the map it wasn't much further and Dmitri managed to get there without further protests against Youlya's navigational skills.

As they rounded the last corner, Michael sat back up again, trying to spot the building. He had no idea what it looked like, but he was expecting an old, ornate building that might match some of the architecture he'd seen already in their travels. These countries were, after all, much older than Canada.

He was surprised when Dmitri pulled up in front of a square, green building that reminded him of a child's building block, or a green piece of Lego. "You sure this is it?" He sounded dubious.

"Yes," Dmitri confirmed, "Is Canadian Embassy. You are home." He paused for a moment and turned to look Michael in the eye. "Mikhail, I am sorry, very sorry, that you went through this because of me." He extended his hand to Michael, who took it. They exchanged a long, firm handshake, and if Michael hadn't known any better, he would have thought Dmitri's eyes were tearing up just a bit.

"It's okay, man. I'd never have seen your country if not for you. And you did get me out. Thank you." He turned to face Youlya as Dmitri released his grip. "And thank you, we'd never have made it without you." She smiled warmly in return, but made no reply, so

Michael opened the door and stepped out. She looked at him for a long moment, thinking to herself that, if not for him, Dmitri would not have had to call her. Nor would she have understood so completely why Dmitri had done what he did. She owed the Canadian a lot, she knew.

He looked up at the building in front of him, and could not help but think that it really looked out of place here. The windows were covered with some sort of slats, but otherwise the front of the building was the same green colour as the sides. He hesitated for a few moments wondering where to go and who to talk to, and what he was going to say. He had no passport and for the first time felt nervous about approaching representatives of his own country. He was suddenly very conscious of the old tattered clothing he was wearing, the same ones they'd stolen that first day in the village. He also hadn't shaved or showered since, well, since before he'd left Canada.

A harried looking man carrying a briefcase was about to enter the door, but noticing Michael staring at the building in obvious confusion he let it close and walked over to greet him. When he caught Michael's attention he asked him a question in a language that Michael didn't recognize. It wasn't Ukrainian. He had listened to the language long enough to know that much.

"I am sorry," Michael said slowly, carefully pronouncing each word, "I can't understand you. Do you speak English?"

The man looked surprised to hear a man dressed as Michael was speaking English so well. "Of course," he replied in perfect English. "How can I help you? Do you need some assistance from the Embassy?"

The Canadian accent shocked Michael. It sounded almost foreign to his ears after listening to Ukrainian, Russian, and a lot of heavily-accented English; but it did cause him to relax and smile.

"Yes, I really could use some help. My name is Michael Barrett and..."

That was as far as he got before the man grabbed his arm and started pumping it frantically. "Michael Barrett? Michael Barrett! There are a lot of people looking for you, young man! What happened to you? Where have you been? How did you get here? Come inside, we have a lot of people to notify!"

The questions were coming too fast for Michael to answer but as the man paused for breath, Michael tried to use his free hand to point towards Youlya's car, only to see it was gone. He felt a twinge of disappointment. He had hoped to have a chance to say a real goodbye, but then he couldn't really blame them for the quick departure. A member of the Mafia, even an ex-member, wouldn't likely want to stick around and spend time with a government official, not even to get a thank you. He wondered if he'd ever see them again, and for some strange reason found himself hoping that somehow he would. He shook his head to clear his thoughts as the man led him inside.

"It's a long story, but I made some friends who helped me to get here." He was sure that he was going to have to give someone a lot more details about his adventures before too long, but for the moment it was just too much effort and he needed some time to think about exactly what to say regarding Dmitri and Youlya. He didn't want to cause any trouble for them, and maybe it was a good thing he didn't know what their plans were from this point on. If he didn't know, he couldn't tell anyone, could he? This was all way too complicated to sort out right now, so he didn't offer any more information than that.

The man, who had still not introduced himself, pulled the door open to allow Michael to step inside. Even if it was only legally Canada, it still felt like he'd finally reached safety. "We expected you to show up in Kiev, at least we hoped you would, but you look like you've had a rough time. Is there something I can get for you, or do for you?"

"Yeah," he replied with a deep sigh as he stepped inside the building. He was so close to Greece, he thought. He remembered from Youlya's maps that Bucharest was not all that far from the Bulgarian border, and then not much farther south was Greece. He'd dreamt for so long of being there. He was so close. He turned to face his new host.

"I want to go home."

ACKNOWLEDGEMENTS

I'd like to thank my wife, Diew, my two daughters, and all the grandkids for their patience while I spent all those nights on my laptop computer, fulfilling the dream of writing a novel. I'd also like to thank various friends and family members who read the story and offered encouragement and ideas.

I want to thank Julie and Netta of Stonehouse Publishing for taking the time to consider, accept, and then help me massage the manuscript into its final form. Without them I would not have reached the goal of becoming a published author.

I'd especially like to thank my "Ukrainian family"; the people who looked after me on my many trips to Ukraine and accepted this Canadian of Scottish descent as one of their own. During my visits I fell in love with the country and its people, and each time I sat down to write it was a little bit like going home again.

ABOUT THE AUTHOR

Doug Morrison has made many trips to Ukraine, doing volunteer work with children and young adults. This book grew out of his love for the country and its people. He is a voracious reader but when the weather is good he can often be found cruising in his vintage muscle car. He lives with his family in central Alberta. This is his first book.